WOLVES AT BAY

KEEPING
THE
WOLVES
AT BAY

stories by
emerging
American writers

IIIIIIIIIIIIIIIIIIIIIIIIIIIIIIIIIIIII

EDITED BY
Sharon Dilworth

Autumn House
Press

PITTSBURGH

"Autumn House" and "Autumn House Press" are registered trademarks owned by Autumn House Press, a nonprofit corporation whose mission is the publication and promotion of poetry and other fine literature.

Autumn House Press Staff
Editor-in-Chief and Founder: Michael Simms
Executive Director: Richard St. John
Community Outreach Director: Michael Wurster
Co-Founder: Eva-Maria Simms
Fiction Editor: Sharon Dilworth
Associate Editor: Ziggy Edwards
Assistant Editors: Evan Oare, Kriscinda Meadows
Media Consultant: Jan Beatty
Publishing Consultant: Peter Oresick
Tech Crew Chief: Michael Milberger
Intern: Athena Pappas

This project was supported by the Pennsylvania Council on the Arts, a state agency, through its regional arts funding partnership, Pennsylvania Partners in the Arts (PPA). State government funding comes through an annual appropriation by Pennsylvania's General Assembly. PPA is administered in Allegheny County by Greater Pittsburgh Arts Council.

ISBN: 978-1-932870-41-1
Library of Congress: 2010929377

All Autumn House books are printed on acid-free paper and meet the international standards of permanent books intended for purchase by libraries.

INTRODUCTION

Sharon Dilworth

I decided to publish this, the first fiction anthology from Autumn House Press, in order to feature authors—some established, others newcomers—who deserve wider audiences. Despite their widely varied careers (a social worker, a caterer, a public relations professional, a speechwriter, an advertising copywriter and a university professor) each of these authors would identify themselves as a writer immediately. It is the thread that holds together the rest of their lives and propels them to complete their next story.

That's the role that books play for many of us. Hopefully this anthology will take the place of an activity that is becoming rare, stumbling into an aisle in a bookshop and discovering a new writer or a brand new book that becomes something special to us. It's the purpose of collections like these to showcase new writing and remind readers of the discoveries that can still exist serendipitously.

In a standard introduction, the editors would now proclaim that despite all this doom and gloom, the book is still alive and well. This is so far from the truth it's like holding your breath when you pass a cemetery to ward off evil spirits. I'd love to quiet my own fears—even with the promise of the re-emergence of the local bookshop. My only hope, and it is a strong belief, is that books will evolve.

Each of us discovers books differently: some of us in a classroom, some in libraries, some in bookstores or on friends' shelves. We use books for our own purposes, as well: some make an earnest study of an author or genre, reading with intent and specific purpose. Others read as a means of entertainment, to fill the down time of a day; finally, some of us read as a form of therapy or self-invention. But serious readers understand how books come to enhance our perceptions and let us know we are not alone.

Most writers I know appreciate the teachers they had—either as undergraduates or as MFA students but not so many of them acknowledge the debt they owe to writers. I remember a college course in the Modern Period. It was a class of both prose and poetry. We studied Eliot, Yeats, Stevens, Auden and so many more. And on reflection I think that these books really determined my reading, thinking, and writing for the rest of my life. I decided then that the one thing I wanted to do all the time was read and write. I taught literature and writing for many years and though I no longer teach, I still read and write every day. The books I read so many years ago continue to influence me. I am still drawn to the narrative experiments, the complexity of feeling, the remarkable use of language.—*Diane Goodman*

Maybe books aren't the most important things in the world. The Panglosses of publishing have convinced us that the digital transformation, the precipice upon which we stand, will change our relationship to texts for the better. Those of us who grew up with books are entering a period of anticipatory mourning, however, whereby a large part of our lives and certainly a tremendous amount of shelf space will be altered irrevocably.

Like distant cannon fire, some of this has already occurred, of course. I live in a city with no neighborhood bookstores left; there are a few outside the city limits but this is a city supported by its hospital and its universities. And now, even the mega-chains are consolidating. The pleasure of browsing has been replaced by a commercial world that substitutes algorithms for taste.

Weakly, Amazon.com tries to emulate this idea of browsing and stumbling when they suggest other readers' choices when you purchase a book online. But these are books that other people have determined we might like and, let's face it, there's a marketing agenda to their decisions. They're presenting books that people have bought and sometimes the links to new books seem odd or random. I recently purchased *Major Pettigrew's Last Stand*, after reading a wonderful review in *The New York Times*, then ordered *Maniac McGee* for my 9-year old daughter because our dog had actually chewed her school's copy. I pity the reader who might try *Maniac McGee* because she thinks it might contextually relate to English villages or racial politics in modern England.

What might be lost is the anarchy of surreptitious reading. Whether or not computerized readers are cheaper, more convenient, or expand my bibliography, they are not going to take the place of an adolescent reading by flashlight late at night. Books—despite our democratic commitment to the idea of a free press—are not a public good at all but the most private of intellectual pursuits. Reading is by its nature a subversive activity. It is a way of momentarily leaving the demands of society. It is always an independent activity that forces us into a dialogue between the author's story and our own sense of individuality.

If it's true, as Saul Bellow said, that writers are readers moved to emulation, then surely teachers are students moved by a similar compulsion. I shudder to think where I'd be without Charlie, or Blanche, or Nick, or Mr. Reiss, Ms. Forbath. Not a day goes by that I don't think of some teacher or another, and still I can't recall with confidence a single thing that even my best instructors taught me, except, perhaps, to be in the world.

Maybe that was the greatest service they performed. The most affecting teachers seemed to exist as models for a kind of process—the process of being an artist or scholar—that strange and beguiling process of becoming oneself. The most gifted teachers seemed models for persistence and passion, their teaching a natural extension of some devotion, their classes a means of affirmation, a way of fueling some enthusiasm as they paid the bills.

This distinction was never lost on us as students: our most engaged and engaging instructors might want to teach, but they *needed* to do their art or science or philosophy. We sniffed for this authenticity—it's what we gossiped about as students—how certain teachers stood like sources of light to us, nothing tired or stuffy about their classrooms, teaching being part of their artistic or intellectual method, each hour almost sacred to them, all of us becoming fellow travelers on this epic journey. How could one not wish to emulate such a life?—*Bill Lychack*

This winter, J. D. Salinger died and while the press debated whether or not his reclusiveness was a mental disorder, they inevitably remarked upon the mystery of his 40-year silence. But most people I know, tired of these dead-end explorations of a man who clearly did not want to share any more of his life or his literary genius, had a different reaction. Upon hearing of his death, they began to recollect the book that forever changed the way they would think about reading and writing. They talked about *The Catcher in the Rye*—where they were when they first read it, at which parts they cried, and how they related to the characters. We had lost the writer who had introduced so many generations to the power of the narrative voice in fiction. So for many it mattered not that Salinger was dead or even that he had been silent for so long—because it was always Holden Caulfield who first spoke to them. The book, you see, was the thing.

Few things permeate my system like a good piece of writing. I write because I hope to make other people experience that intense emotional moment as I've felt it when reading. But what's best is that writing doesn't have to be about striving for the Great American Novel—if I knew there were hundreds of thousands of people reading my work, I don't think that would excite as much as the email from a passing acquaintance, the call from my mom's neighbor, the reaction to a new draft from my writing group. The individual reaction is what makes writing most meaningful. —*Jennifer Bannan*

Books can't disappear but they may become somewhat of a boutique item, if they're not already that. We're going to have to accept that what so many of us grew up with and which so many of us depend on almost as our daily bread is going to change.

> I read because I like to absorb everything the author is doing and let myself go. Let the story take me places that I probably wouldn't go. I like when I read something that makes me think, "I would have never made that decision." And then I like to think about why the author did so and why I probably wouldn't have. I think you can discover a lot about yourself as a writer and as a thinker by reading great works and actually trying to discover why you react the way that you do.—*Casey Taylor*

And therefore none of us knows what's going to happen to reading. I think people, especially those who have been so heavily influenced by reading, are nervous about what's to come, and unsure of what's going to happen.

Some early indications are not very good, though. I was in Washington, D.C. last spring for a conference and went to DuPont Circle. Heaven. I hadn't been to an independent bookstore in a year, and here were two or three within walking distance of one another. I bought ten books, books I would never had known about if they were not displayed on those tables, sitting there all smart and intriguing, enticing me to pick up and put into my hands. I discovered for example, Alain de Botton's *The Art of Travel*, a book I've since given to every friend who's got wanderlust as well as every friend who because of children or jobs can only reminisce about backpacking with a laminated orange Student Eurailpass around his or her neck.

Reading is always about uncharted discovery, even when it's upon a seemingly well-worn path:

> I just reread all of Flannery O'Connor's stories because I do that every year or so. It's geeky, but true. Something about her strict attention to her own beliefs, and her sticking to her Catholic guns always inspires me. Plus she has an evil, evil sense of humor that glitters tragically. The story "Revelation," one of her last, is the main reason I started to write. I remember reading it outside a building when I had just got off my job as dishwasher at Ponderosa Steakhouse and I had not had time to do my English Lit homework. I was a freshman in college working full-time to pay for it. Anyway, I took the big thick *Norton Anthology* out and dreaded having to read some stupid short story and then from the first sentence to the last I felt this really weird connection, like this Flannery

O'Whatever is making art and music and meaning out of all the feelings I've ever had. I'm teaching a creative writing class this semester, and I really want the kids to experience that feeling. It's not something you can tell them to do of course, but there's always a desire for me to somehow help create that situation of "meeting yourself for the first time" through reading great stuff and then trying to do write great stuff.—*Keith Banner*

There is a small secret that the most avid readers share: at one point they had lives that they needed to escape. Fundamentally happy people may not need alternative narratives in order to make sense of their existence, but the rest of us do. For most of us, this is a transient condition but for those of us who become readers and writers, the necessity of reading becomes a lifeline we utilize repeatedly, no matter where we are in the world, and no matter where we are in our lives. Revisiting a story again can remind us of how incredible our journeys really have become, when the same words in the same order take on completely different meanings at each turn in our life's course. There is nothing like it in the world.

I hope you can use this anthology as a guide.

Contents

▌▌▌▌▌▌▌▌▌▌▌▌▌▌▌▌▌▌▌▌▌▌▌▌

SEXY IDA MAKES A VOW

Jennifer Bannan

It is midnight when they smell smoke. They're chatting happily about their day, conscious, as they've been lately, of their wedlock. They've lived together for four years, but have been married only three months, and are just now realizing their bond, the strength of it, the near-impossibility and shame of ever ending it: it is much bigger than they are, but anyhow they're responsible for preserving it. They check the house, to make sure whatever's burning isn't inside, and, seeing it's not, thrust their heads out the windows, their nostrils burning with the thickness of it. They hear the sirens. He sees police-car lights up Butler Street, not far at all. She sees them now too.

He's a photographer for a local paper, and, smartly, he realizes he should get out on the street to cover the fire. It could be nothing, but why risk missing such an opportunity? He's putting on his coat and asking if she'd like to come. She says no, she's tired, but she'll wait for him.

She watches from her window as he walks purposefully up Butler Street. She tells herself he'll be fine. The neighborhood isn't too bad, and there are cops right up close to where the fire is. No one would do anything so close to the cops. Still, she watches until she can't make him out any longer. The smoke is growing so thick she worries about breathing it. She blows her nose until it is raw, but still can't seem to clear it. She returns to the window. The lights seem less significant, lazily blinking. She is tired. It's been some time now.

She imagines the sadness of losing her husband, so soon after their marriage. And the strangeness of it: his disappearing into a smoke-filled night. She thinks over the last few months. They've been good ones, no doubt. They've only argued twice, and then only half-heartedly, making up a few hours later. They tell all their friends that being married has made no difference in their relationship. But maybe they're lying. There was a time when she looked out the window, waiting for him to return from work, and she'd become horrified at the prospect that he might not, that he might be dead on the street from a car wreck, his body so mangled that days might pass before she was notified. But now, an entirely different scenario is flashing before her, one that extends beyond his possible death.

She imagines herself as the strong widow, the tragic figure who's lost her husband so soon after marrying, the singular female who must push forward, despite the suffering. And she isn't minding the image nearly as much as she should. It becomes a bit of a fantasy, more interesting than the smoky reality outside on the street. She takes the fantasy to bed with her, lets it build upon itself as she snuggles into her down comforter and hears the cars rushing by. She is up on a stage, pounding a podium, imploring senators to change the tax laws that devastate widows nationwide. She is wearing a smart robin's-egg blue suit with a silk hanky in the breast pocket, pausing while the applause dies down. She is jolted suddenly, faced with a more chilling reality: how will she pay the rent? She hadn't figured a move into the equation. She re-organizes her budget so that she'll just make it, living paycheck to paycheck, but still happy in her apartment, the young widow and her cats.

She wakes in the morning alone. The street is louder now, flatbeds clacking harshly, people calling to one another on the sidewalk. She squints across the room to the digital clock and sees that it is already seven. She had forgotten to set the alarm, expecting he would do so when he finally arrived home. But—and panic washes over her (belatedly perhaps)—he never did arrive home, did he? Her first response is anger. He must have said something obnoxious to some punk on the street. Something to get himself into trouble. He's got an attitude not everyone takes to, though she thinks she understands it, even appreciates it. When they met with the rabbi for pre-nuptial counseling, he had asked them what features they most loved about one another. She had cited his straightforwardness as a quality she admired. But, many times she has thought this same quality might get her husband into trouble. She finds herself waiting for that trouble to strike, expecting it as she would expect any other rare but inevitable event, like a call to jury duty.

This must be it, she tells herself, though he could be downstairs, asleep in front of the television.

She will enshroud herself in numbness, she thinks, steel herself against the discovery of an empty house. She gets out of bed and begins looking through the closet for something to wear to work. But, she stops, would it be appropriate to go to work? There is still the question everyday, even after so many months: *How's married life?* The question bothers her at this point, though it had pleased her only days after the honeymoon. She has taken to smiling blandly, and responding, "Same as yesterday and the day before that," or "I'll keep you informed of all new occurrences." What will she answer today? If she's to tell the truth, that her husband could be dead somewhere and she has come to work anyway, her co-workers will surely be convinced of her callousness. Though they could just as easily admire her stoicism, they won't. She'll have to say nothing. She'll have to lie, or simply nod, as though nothing has changed. Or, on the other hand, she could cry out, a woman hysterical with the rage of one betrayed, "My husband—my husband did not come home last night!" Then, she imagines, later, when his body is found, they will flock to her side, console her sincerely, for the fate befallen her is far greater than that she had ever imagined.

She picks out her best suit, cut from expensive linen. She wants to look her most elegant on this day for which she'll be remembered. When she sees how nice she looks in the mirror, she feels something not unlike giddiness, and relief. I'll just start over, she thinks, begin a fresh life. Although, of course, she reminds herself, while applying one more coat of lipstick, he could be downstairs, asleep on the couch. It's possible that he opened the front door last night without waking her. She has, after all, the feeling of one who has slept very soundly. Her mind is sharp; she has the lucidity of a person at her life's crossroads. She imagines herself on the drive to work, the muscles at her cheekbones pulling the skin of her face tightly back in an expression of total control.

She comes down the stairs into the living room, and true enough, her husband is asleep on the couch, and the television on. There is a long sigh going on deep inside of her as she looks at the TV. It's a talk show, the subject today is stunt men and the dangers of their work. She wonders if the wives of these men feel themselves armed, prepared for the real possibility of a loss. She wonders if a small part of them enjoys that suspense.

Why did she marry, she wonders, if this is the way she will feel about his death? She contemplates the potentiality of her coldness. Or maybe, she thinks, she's simply being practical. There haven't been many deaths of people close to her. Something has to give soon, and she may as well be ready. But, there's more to it than that, and she feels compelled to explain it.

"I'm not used to being married," she says aloud in the small space of her car. "There's the wedding, all the working up to it. Once it's done, you have to wonder, 'what next?'" She realizes that her view of her own marriage is immature. It's a life's work, and hard work, she's been told this by countless married people. But she's a woman who prefers to thrive on events. And a life of hard, steady work is beginning to sound dull.

They could have children, like so many of her friends. Maybe those friends—like her—are on a quest for meaning in marriage. But she doesn't want to rush a family, especially when she's not sure she wants her husband living. They've been talking about becoming homeowners, but something in her suspects that, like a wedding, once set up in their house, there would be the same yearning for a new event.

At work, she's filling her coffee mug when a co-worker asks, "How's married life?" and she answers with a sly smile, "Interesting," hoping to leave him wondering if she's a swinger, since it's common knowledge he and his wife are always looking for new blood.

At three p.m. her husband calls her at work to apologize for sleeping in the living room. The fire had been arson, from what the police could deduce, and the excitement had left him too wired for sleep. He had drifted off unwittingly after hours in front of the television. She behaves properly hurt, saying she would have appreciated his coming up to at least tell her he was home safe. He wants to take her to dinner, to make up for his bad behavior, and they agree to a Chinese restaurant near her workplace.

He stands and motions to her from the booth, and kisses her shyly on the cheek when she reaches him. They sit across from each other and he pours plum wine into her glass.

"I'm a total boob. You weren't too worried, were you?"

"Just enough. I hope you got some good shots."

"Evening edition, local section. Arson for insurance money, the police think."

"It would have been a mistake to not go. I'm proud of you."

A waiter arrives with hot and spicy chicken wings. He nods and smiles, setting them on the table.

"I hope you don't mind wings. I'm starved," her husband says.

"No, no. I'm famished." She reaches hungrily for a wing, as does her husband. She contemplates the morsel and its rich, clumpy sauce for a moment, looks up to her husband, and is about to tell him of her feelings regarding his imagined death, so he might laugh it off and call her a feverish planner, when, to her amazement, she sees that he has gotten a piece of chicken caught in his throat.

"Are you alright?"

He's staring wildly at her, pounding his fist into his neck, and she thinks for a moment that he looks particularly grotesque in his fear. She's frozen, listening to the strange, beetle-like sounds coming from his mouth. His napkin is tucked under his chin, a dinner habit of his she has always despised but can never persuade him to abandon. It makes a large golden diamond of his torso, like a road-side danger sign. His arms begin to flail and suddenly she knows what she is doing is right, calling out, "Help," faintly at first, and then loudly, bravely, like a newlywed widow.

There are waiters clustered around the booth, a swirling team of black and white polyester and Chinese, when the owner (he has a pencil behind his ear and street clothes on) pulls her husband from the table and throws his arms underneath her husband's in one motion. His strength is unbelievable, he's a slight man with a purposeful expression. He gives her husband quick thrusts under his breastbone and a skinny piece of chicken is propelled from her husband's mouth and onto the wall. It sticks for a second, falls to the table, and she sees it has left a brown stain on the tastefully striped wallpaper. Such Victorian wallpaper for a Chinese restaurant, she thinks. She looks at the greasy stain, instead of her husband, who she can hear coughing. He is fine. He is fine, she knows, and realizes that she is holding her chicken wing in the precise spot of air in which she'd been holding it when he began to choke.

She forces herself to look at him. He's holding his neck, rubbing it, and she says, her voice far from her, dreamlike, "Are you alright?"

"Yes. Oh my God. Yes," he says, between gagging and coughing. He thanks the owner profusely, sitting shakily back into the booth.

"Let's go home," she says, and her stomach grumbles.

"No. I'm fine. They're cooking our food right now. I'm fine. My throat's just a little raw."

She looks around the restaurant and sees that people are turned to them from all tables. The owner is back, with water. He leans over her husband, making sure he is fine. When he finally walks off, he seems to have a satisfied grin on his face. He must be thinking he's a hero, she thinks, and she understands why that might be nice.

"Are you sure?" She'd love a bite of her wing, but holds it away from her mouth. "Let's have our dinner packed up to go."

He relents, agreeing he is shaken up quite a bit.

They go home, she's driving, and suddenly, he's overcome with a bout of hysterical laughter. His giggling is infectious. She, too, was unnerved, though less because of the danger, and more because of the guilt she feels for having wished his death the night before. She wonders if his choking was intended for her, as a lesson. When she glances at him, wiping tears from his eyes and trying to get himself together before another surge of laughter overcomes him, she starts laughing as well, so hard that she must pull over to the shoulder of the highway. The relief is exquisite; she forgets her worries. They laugh tearfully for some time, leaning across the armrest to hug each other, feeling each other's convulsive giggling, and she's relieved that he's with her, laughing with her in the car.

Two months later they go camping for three days. Time has trotted by smoothly. She's hardly noticed how adapted she's become to her routine. In the mornings she wakes, she works, she comes home, they have dinner and wine, sometimes meet with friends, talk—politics, art, sports—into the late hours, and turn in. She feels the yearning for some event only when the phone rings, and her body tenses up with the anticipation of some pressing news, which never comes.

They have a peaceful campsite a nice distance from the dirt road running through the grounds. He lights a fire and she's impressed at how quickly he gets it going. They've never tried the outdoors together, never ventured further than the park. They grill hamburgers and eat roasted marshmallows and talk about what they will do the next day. They only have the one day left, and they must leave in the afternoon, to get back for an evening meeting he'll be attending for the newspaper.

She pours herself some hot apple cider, which stays warm in a pot on the outskirts of the coals. She takes her tin cup to a boulder they have designated as the bar, and spikes the cider with rum. She has a friendly haze forming in the part of her brain directly over her eyes. The haziness makes her amorous. She feels very in love with her husband tonight.

"I'm coming over there to snuggle with you," she announces to her husband, who is stretched out in a sleeping bag on the ground, another sleeping bag rolled under his head and shoulders, propping him up. He looks away from the stars and moves over a bit in the bag, to make room for her.

She crawls in with him, props up on an elbow, and places the cider between them. She lifts a finger and traces the outline of his jawbone. "You look good," she says, watching the light from the fire flicker and change over his skin.

"Feeling good?" he asks her.

"I'm glad we did this."

"How about being married? How's that for you?"

"I think it's going pretty well, don't you?"

"I'm happy. It's not too different from when we were living together."

She wonders if he really believes that. It's what they still say, but she feels as though they tacitly understand they're lying.

"It's pretty different though, don't you think?"

He looks at her with raised eyebrows.

"I mean, we're only half a year into it. Does it ever occur to you that we'll have to work at staying together for the rest of our lives?"

"I thought about that all the time before the wedding. Didn't you?"

"I did. I guess I've been wondering what's next."

"The rest of our lives. Plenty will happen, I'm sure. But from now on, whatever happens will involve both of us."

"I'm worried that everything else will be boring. Instead of love and commitment and forever, we'll be talking about mortgages and taxes and promotions and putting away for retirement and the children's schooling and it seems boring."

"And that's life."

"I want it always to be exciting."

"We'll make it exciting," he says, and pulls her close, kisses her on the forehead.

For two months she's been free of the nagging thoughts of his death. But now, when he talks about making excitement in that boring little way—as though they'll just look up the recipe—she feels anxious, she feels a tickle inside, like a tiny piece of chicken gristle.

"You know what I would most like to do tomorrow?" he says.

"What?" She pulls away from him and sips from her tin cup. Steam from the cider warms her face, the rum glows and then dies in her belly.

"I'd like to go whitewater rafting. I did it once with my family when I was a kid, and I remember loving it."

"OK. I've never gone before. Sounds exciting." She sees his face in the sudsy water, its whirlpool closing in.

"Good. We can go down the Youghiogheny. We'll take the short trip."

"Don't abandon your raft, whatever you do," says the fellow in charge of orientation. She and her husband smile goofily at each other. They laugh at the orange barrel chests the life-preservers have given them. The instructor tells them how to float down the river with the least possible injury "when" they fall out of the raft. They scoff at this idea, but the instructor, with a witty gleam in his eye, assures them that it does happen.

They ease their raft into the water and hop in. It's a nice size for two people, it feels comfortable for them, and they nod encouragingly at each other, saying, "This is gonna be fun," when they're already facing a hearty set of rapids. They feel the larger rocks pass under the raft like huge, angry water animals as they paddle furiously, in search of the path of least resistance. Gallons of water splash up into the boat.

They get through the first set giggling wildly. "That was nuts!" he yells.

"This is going to be harder than we thought!" she screams. They use the momentary calm to bail the water out with bottomless milk carton jugs.

"I think the instructor said to stay to the right on this set," she offers, and they begin to paddle toward the right, but the rapids are coming fast, and the right doesn't look too promising, and they don't want to hit the rushing water sideways, so they straighten out, heading for the middle of the river, where they suddenly find themselves embanked on a rock, which is raised out of the water here, but drops several feet to more water in front of them. It is a cliff, of sorts, and she is looking over that cliff to the turbulence below, thinking they'll have a little time to decide how to get off the rock, when her husband yells, "The back is coming around!" and, quicker than she can jump for the middle of the raft, it has swung completely around, and her end is being pulled off the rock, into the air, and out from under her.

She's in the water. She feels it pull her at odd angles and she fights to get her head up for a gulp of air, but she gets a mouthful of water instead. She remembers the orientation, how they said to pull your feet up and point them downstream. But all the time she is being shoved around by the river, and she is thinking, "This is it. This is it," and she is expecting her life to flash before her eyes, and as it isn't happening, she thinks the flashing concept must be a death myth.

Something bumps hard into her shinbone, and she uses all her will to pull her feet up. People drown, she learned not fifteen minutes ago, because they try to stand up, but their feet get caught between rocks, and the current forces their faces down into a certain death. She hadn't believed any of it. She hadn't believed she could drown.

Then suddenly the current is behind her head, and she can see downstream. She sees the empty raft swirling several yards in front of her, and simultaneously she realizes that her husband is not on the raft and that she is still gripping her paddle, with both hands.

She sees that the current dies down not far from where she is presently being pushed and jostled, and she feels hopeful now that she will make it. There are other rafters on the river, and one group of them is trying to get hold of her raft. "How nice of them," she thinks, and wants to laugh at her own mundane thoughts. They grab a rope on the side of the raft and paddle over to the left bank of the river, where there's barely a current.

"Are you all right?" they call to her, as she's only a few yards from the raft now, and swimming with the arm that isn't holding the paddle.

She doesn't answer them, because she won't be sure if she's fine until she's safely in the raft. She throws the oar over the side and holds onto the warm, floating rubber. It is not until this moment that she realizes the coldness of the water, thirty degrees at most, she figures. Somehow she gets a leg over the side and then pulls her body after it. She falls, exhausted, into the bottom of the raft. "Where's my husband?" she gasps. She stares into the openness of the sky, and imagines these people in the familiar cluster, breaking the news of her husband's death as gently as they can.

"Here he is," they cry triumphantly. She feels the raft being tugged and jerked as he pulls himself in, and her mind is flooded with images of stumbling, plodding movie monsters who get hurt, but never die.

In the car, they listen to a tape she's never heard before. She's intensely exhausted, and since her husband's been through the same ordeal, she's worried he'll fall asleep while driving. She chatters constantly about nothing in particular. She tries to make jokes that will keep him happily awake. "Look," she cries, "Cows. Out standing in their fields!"

He laughs, but says, "I just got this tape, and I really like it. This here's Ike and Tina." He turns up the volume and she feels cut off from him, and so tired; without talking, she knows she'll doze off. Her eyelids are at their heaviest when she becomes aware of the lyrics to the song.

Don't give your love to sexy Ida,
'Cuz she's the sister of the black widow spider.

She sits up in her seat and looks out the window at the fields. Her eyes feel like two dry stones pressed into her face. She looks up at her reflection, her eyes see themselves, and she wonders how they can work now that they've turned into rocks. Sexy Ida, she thinks: not a murderer like her sister, but just as hungry for the corpse.

"Are you OK?" he asks.

"Yes, only, I've been thinking a lot about your death."

He turns to look at her three quick times. She can tell by his alarmed expression that he'd like to study her face, but he's got to keep his eyes on the road. "That's probably natural. We just got married. We keep hearing about the rest of our lives. When you're dealing with lifelong plans, you gotta think about monkey wrenches." As is often the case with him, the words he chooses don't match his face; when his face says fear or anguish, his words say common sense and understanding.

"But there's more to it. It's like I anticipate the event. It started that night when you went to check out the fire on Butler. I kept picturing myself as the strong widow, and then the next night you almost choked to death on a chicken wing, and I thought God was getting me back for my horrible thoughts, but I kept having them anyway. I thought it was just a phase, but then today, the thoughts were there again. I thought about being a widow."

"You've been anticipating my death?" His voice is shaken, wary, and she's happy to see that it matches his expression this time.

"I know. It's terrible of me."

"It seems like, with all the brushes I've been having with death, you might try being on my side."

She senses the hotness of an argument and embraces it. She decides she doesn't like his patronizing tone, his telling her how she should behave as a wife. "I can't help what thoughts pop into my head."

"No, but you could help telling me about them."

"So, if I hope to find you sprawled on the street after being hit by a bus, I should just keep it to myself?"

"Might be something to try."

"That closes down an entire arena of communication very nicely," she says bitterly, crossing her hands over her chest.

His voice loses its edge, "Look. It's like you say. They're just thoughts popping into your head, that happen to be triggered by real life occurrences." His hand reaches up absently for his forehead and rubs the growing lump he acquired when whizzing by a river rock. "I'm not going to worry about a few fleeting thoughts."

"They're not fleeting. I imagine myself after the fact. I imagine myself as a brave, strong young widow."

"Romance. Intrigue. Lofty aspirations. Well, you're not a young widow. You're a young wife. And you're in middle management. So what. That's not bad. There's nothing wrong with that. And there's nothing wrong with imagining another life as being more interesting."

"And a happy widow. I'm a happy widow."

"I'm not going to take this personally," he says, looking stiffly forward.

"What drives you? Here I am telling you that I've been wishing you dead and you call me normal? What can possess you to be fine with every damn thing?"

"There's nothing driving me. I am made of the purest laziness."

She sighs, so hard and fast that it sounds like a sneeze.

"Hey, you're lazy too," he offers.

"I am not."

"Oh, yes you are. If you had more gumption, and if you really thought you'd be much happier as a widow, then you'd find a way to kill me without getting caught."

"Then the only reason you think I don't kill you is that I'm too lazy?"

"Unless there's more to it than that." His expression has turned playful now.

"You want me to say that I love you," she laughs. "And I want you to tell me that I'm an evil monster. You want to be loved by an aspiring evil monster."

They giggle like newlyweds. She leans her elbow on the arm rest and puts her head on his shoulder. Her seat belt tries to pull her back but she's firm against it. "I could have died out there too," she tells him. "What if I died? Do you ever think of that?"

"I don't," he admits, glancing down quickly at her. She likes the way his chin wrinkles when he bends his face toward her. "It's not healthy to be so optimistic as all that," he says, and she jabs him in the stomach.

She supposes there's not much use in dreaming up the destruction of her marriage six months into it. She imagines herself embanked on the rock again, but this time she has time to consider her next step, and if she can, she'll hold off on the inevitable pull of the raft, postpone that moment when it swings out from under her. But, in the name of what? She looks up at her husband's steady eyes, directed forward, and thinks: in the name of vigilance. Events are important, she thinks, but so is everything that happens in between. She vows to be vigilant, to absorb each detail of the most boring moments of her life. It is a different take on the world from what she's used to, but it has a nice ring to it. Vigilance. She thinks there's something about vigilance in Zen Buddhism. She'll go to the library and check out some books.

She wakes in a panic. She can't breathe. Her eyes pop open and she sees her husband, smiling as he releases her nose and uncovers her mouth. Air floods her lungs.

"You're impossible to wake up," he explains.

"I couldn't breathe." She sits up in the car seat. There is a dull pain in her neck from sleeping on his shoulder.

"In this age of the sensitive man, widowers are a romantic icon, you know. I'd watch my step if I were you," he wiggles his eyebrows.

They make their way up the three flights of stairs to their apartment; they're moving slowly, sore from rafting and loaded down with camping gear. "I'm really sick of this climbing," he says to her. "Would you like to go meet with a realtor next week? Just to see what's out there?"

Suddenly she remembers her vow to be vigilant, and curses herself for not paying attention to the stairs. She imagines all the paint chips, dead insects, and strands of hair she must have overlooked. Her husband is standing at the door to their apartment, looking at her expectantly. She forces herself to notice that all of the pores on his nose are slightly different in size. What a chore this vigilance thing is going to be, she thinks. But what other road is there to take, when your life doesn't turn out to be as interesting as you'd hoped? She tells her husband she's tired of climbing too.

WINNERS NEVER SLEEP!

Keith Banner

❚❚❚❚❚❚❚❚❚❚❚❚❚❚❚❚❚❚❚❚❚❚❚❚

1

I manage the laundromat Leslie owns. Six months ago we went out to eat at Steak N Shake to celebrate my five-year anniversary there.

"I've never trusted an employee like I trust you, Rodney," Leslie said.

His old face, like E.T.'s, made me feel sad and grateful. He used to be a projectionist at a movie theater downtown before it closed. After his wife died, he spent what money they had saved to buy the laundromat. Every-once-in-a-while I wonder what he would think if he saw me when I used to do drag. Gold and orange outfits, face made up like a beautiful whore's, lips as glossy-red as spit-out cinnamon candy. Back then I was skinny as hell. He would probably just get a kick out of it and smile. He might say, "Shady past, eh?" Something like that.

The gift Leslie presented to me at the Steak N Shake was health insurance.

"Now," he said. "You go see about that stomach stapling thing you told me about." He took a big gulp of his coffee and looked me in the eye and winked.

"I wish my wife had gotten that surgery," Leslie said. His wife had been extremely overweight like yours truly (I am now at 396 pounds). She died of a stroke when she was 49. No kids or anything. Leslie is always sympathizing.

"Thank you," I said.

"Why you are very welcome, sir."

He looked around the restaurant for the waitress.

"Don't you even think about paying," he said.

2

Ten years ago I had a boyfriend named James Partlow. He had a goatee, a suntan-booth complexion and beautiful, glazed-over eyes. I met him while doing his mother's hair in my apartment (my beautician's license had expired). Irena was her name. We always had a good time—two bitches bitching it up, one with renegade hairstyling skills, the other one skinny from alcoholism and loneliness, wanting to look like Sharon Stone.

I was in shorts and a tank-top and flip-flops, not made up at all, just leisurely male-stylish. Irena was on a kitchen chair, hair wet, severe chin tucked down into a pink towel. I'd popped in a Mel Gibson movie, the one where he was bestial and blue-faced in a kilt. That was what Irena wanted. No sound from the TV, just Janet Jackson's greatest hits coming out of my kitchen boom-box.

"I had to fire my district manager," Irena said as I snipped.

"He stealing from you?"

"Yup."

"Shit," I whispered, cutting away.

It was summer. My windows were open to the big city of Dayton, Ohio, where I had a lovely downtown apartment near a little row of restaurants and bars. Suddenly there he was, standing right outside my screen-door: goatee, camouflage shorts, Birkenstock clogs, a Bob Marley t-shirt. His hair was pitch black and shaved, except for the top, which was a little wild and gelled to stay that way.

He knocked and I was thinking he was here for a drug deal I'd forgotten about.

"Come on in, James," Irena said.

"That's your little boy?"

Irena laughed. "He's my little baby."

He walked in and told his mom to shut up and she barked back a big laugh.

"He's my chauffeur today because my BMW is getting some detail work."

James looked at me. Automatically I flashed on the relationship between the drummer in Culture Club and Boy George.

He sat down and said, "What in the fuck is on the TV?"

"*Braveheart*," Irena said.

I plugged in the blow dryer.

"I hate this fucking movie!" James said really loud above the blow-dryer sound.

I smiled at him and he smiled back at me. It was the eyes that got me, glassy and sensitive and full of little tricks to play on people who didn't understand his predicament being a momma's-boy-slash-chauffeur-slash-fag-slash-whatever-else-he-decided-he-was-at-that-moment.

I finished, gave Irena an ornate handheld mirror.

"You never disappoint, Rodney." She looked over at James with a smart-ass glare. Janet was singing "The Pleasure Principle."

"Thank you, sweetie," I said. "Do you want another drink? James, would you like anything?"

"No thanks." Suddenly he was standing right near me, smelling of CK-One.

"He's trying to quit drinking," Irena whispered, standing up. She was way taller than he was.

James grinned. Irena, in a lavender summery pantsuit, ripped the check she'd just written out.

"Rodney is a female impersonator," she said. "Look at the pictures, James."

Professional and Polaroid, in frames, they were all over the walls. I thought of my apartment as my office. When club owners came over for drugging and drinking, I would do a little impromptu "thing" for them so I might be able to headline gigs, or emcee shows, have my pick.

"Pretty," he said, pointing at me in Chicago, doing "I Touch Myself" by the Divinyls in black vinyl and mesh-net and hair like a blonde Elvira.

"Just plain pretty," he said. His voice was a practiced growl and whisper. It sounded like a cross between Jesus Christ and personal-trainer-with-a-drug-problem.

"Let's go, James," Irena said, getting her purse. "You like?" she said to him about her hair.

"Rodney, you're great. She looks one-*thousand* percent better."

Irena playfully slapped at James.

Once they were gone, I saw he had left his business card on my coffee table. It was mint-green and featured a frog in top-hat and tails: "JAMES PARTLOW, CONSULTANT."

The next day I called him and it was like we had known each other for years. I invited him to my weekend show at Petting Zoo, this little club. He said he would be honored.

After my show, I went out to the bar-floor still in drag. I was in an emerald green cocktail dress, slit to the hipbone, blonde wig puffed out like a contemporary and sweetly fiendish Dale Evans, black heels, black hose. James was at a table by himself. I sat down. The place wasn't packed, just slightly crowded. I knew everybody.

"You were fantastic," he said.

Drinks came and then more drinks. Drinks, drinks, drinks.

"I mean, come on, I just loved it," he said. More and more compliments. "If you can't tell, I was mighty impressed."

I kept smiling. He leaned in close, whispering above the music.

"It is the biggest fucking turn on," he said. Then he came over to me and kissed me on the mouth.

That first night he just wouldn't stop. It was at my place, all-out stupefying lust. The next morning he went and got breakfast for us at one of the three McDonald's locations his mom owned. Pancakes, sausage, eggs, coffee all in Styrofoam. We ate at my dinette set.

"Man," he said, sipping from the cup. "I was so turned on."

"Me too."

"You performing tonight too?"

"Yeah, same place." I delicately shoveled in little bitty bites of scrambled egg, tenderly chewing and swallowing microscopic portions, eyes dewy.

"I'm there," he said and laughed.

I took all of it in like I deserved it.

Three months later, James moved in. I found out his consulting business was basically his mom paying him to do whatever she told him to do. When she fired the district manager, James had to do some district-managing until he found a replacement. When Irena had her bathroom redone, he had to sit in the house waiting for the plumber while she went to New Mexico for a few days with lady friends.

For a while it was kind of special to be caught up in his Momma's Boy Paradise: him scolding Irena for her alcoholism and cleaning up the puke in her mansion in the suburbs of Dayton, then coming to my show and getting drunk and fucking me afterwards.

The closer we got to the Las Vegas incident, though, the more I was feeling like the movie we were making was taking a turn toward inevitable conflict.

He told me he did not want me doing his mom's hair anymore.

"You'll just talk about me. Or she will," he said.

"Does she know?" I asked.

"What?"

"That we're an item?" I was making microwavable popcorn on a Tuesday night. We'd rented movies.

"No."

I laughed, pressing the buttons.

"Does she even know you're a fag, honey?"

"Yeah," he said and laughed. "She knows that."

But then he got very quiet.

We watched the movies and ate the popcorn and got drunk on whatever I had. I went into my bedroom around 11:30 and put on my face so he could be turned on. I came out naked, in a wig, face all dolled up. We did it in the living room for a while, then took it to the bedroom, and the next day he left without telling me. No note, nothing. He came back around three. I had a client, this sweet elderly lady with the wispiest hair, like cobwebs. I was struggling with what I had to do. There he was, knocking on the screen door.

"Come on in," I said.

He shook his head no. The elderly lady was half-asleep but I went out on the porch. He was afraid maybe she might know his mom.

"Mom's in rehab. I just took her." He was grinning like George Michael during the Wham! years.

"Shit. She okay?"

"Yeah, she's fine—she'll dry out and pretend she's okay and come back. But here's the sweet part. She and a friend of hers were supposed to go to Vegas tomorrow for three days. Irrevocable tickets, baby. Her friend doesn't want to go now, so it's me and you. Vegas!"

He held me and jumped up and down, then stopped.

"Pack your bags. I'll be back around six."

He sped off in his shiny Miata. I went back in and the elderly lady in the beige outfit, with that brittle hair, was smiling almost wickedly.

"Someone has a beau," she said, winking.

I packed some clothes, thinking three days in Vegas would mean jeans and t-shirts, maybe a suit and shoes. Finally around 8:30, James showed up with his eyes bugging out. He told me he was taking a lot of speed because Vegas was the city that never sleeps.

"That's New York," I said.

He laughed real loud. I didn't say anything else.

"You ready, baby? We have to be at the airport by eleven." He looked like a momma's boy with a deep dark secret. "You got any stuff?"

We did a few lines together. When he came up for air, he went over to the two suitcases I had packed, opened one up, looked in.

Said: "No, no, no. *No!*"

"What?" I got up from the couch, taking the mirror to the kitchen sink, rinsing it off.

He took one of the suitcases into the bedroom and dumped the clothes out, laughing.

"This is our vacation!" He was yelling.

"What?" I had a high pitch to my voice now, feeling dazed, my head a helicopter piloted by the Tiny Powerful Princess of Cocaine Island.

"I want you to be my baby the whole time," he said in the bedroom, opening my closet. He took out some shoes and gowns, threw them onto the bed, next to the clothes he dumped out.

"Wait a fucking minute," I said.

I never did drag to pass in broad daylight. I never wanted to be a real lady-lady: have my dick cut off, get real tits, shots and all that. I've had friends who did that sure, but that was not in *my* program, okay? It was always about being Me and living it up, pancaked and pretty in that sick big way, someone to be feared if you really got down to the nitty-gritty. At times it felt like the only power I had was up on the nightclub stage, costumed and lip-syncing, at the center of my own marvelous little universe.

"I don't do it unless I'm on stage, James," I said. "Or here, you know, with you."

"Come on. For me. We'll be other people. I'm gonna wear my sunglasses the whole time. We'll call each other different names, huh? I'll be, um, David St. Thomas. You pick a name."

He was panting a little. He came over and whispered, "Pick a name," and his hot breath slid into my ear canal like a finger. I thought about saying no again. But I got my other suitcase out of the living room instead. I unpacked it, threw in some of my outfits, shoes and makeup in zip-lock bags. He clapped his hands.

"We are gonna have fun every motherfucking night!" he said.

I think that was from a Prince song.

Glassy heat like light bulbs melting confronted me as soon as we got out of the Vegas airport. I wasn't in drag on the plane. He gave me that at least. We jumped in a cab and James told the cabby, "The Aladdin, please."

The cab smelled of cigars and pee and old-man. Outside the back windows, the mid-morning sun glittered at its meanest. Down the strip, all the neon looked ghostly from being outshined. I wanted a drink suddenly, something precious, a Cosmopolitan or Cape Cod.

Brilliant acid-blue sky turned into dark musty plush inside Aladdin's. Huge ornate statues of Aladdin's lamp and magic carpets were painted on the ceiling. James registered us in at the front desk, got us to the room, gave me my own cardkey. The room was cool and smoke-free but I lit up. I spread the curtains to see that radioactive sunshine, the tops of awnings, Caesar's Palace caddy-corner, a big billboard with Robin Williams on it.

James downed a glass of water.

"Get ready," he said, sitting on the edge of the bed, waiting for his pills to start.

Once my whole cosmetics laboratory was set up on the big marble sink, I got out of my man clothes and started doing my face. James shut the curtains, crashed on the bed, then got back up and turned on the TV. He kept itching at his eyebrows. It took me an hour of fussing. I had one wig for two days. It was blonde and not too showy, Meg Ryan-ish, perky-fluffy.

When I was through, you still knew it was me of course. James was behind me, sun-glasses and leather sports-coat, hair freshly moussed. That tanning-booth tan.

"You look great, hon."

I stood up and pressed out my mint-green skirt. I looked down at my black high heels and hose. For a second I felt the thrill of being someone else entirely, not a drag queen but a stylish lady in Las Vegas, in complete control of her life and her pleasures. I felt pulled together to the point that I thought *yes this might work*. But then James kissed me like he had never kissed me before—a mother kiss, a fake kiss—and I knew I had fallen into a trap.

Down the elevator. On one floor, a fat old man in a Hawaiian shirt and dress pants and Italian loafers looked away from me, then back, without a smile or indication of a smile, like he knew what I was trying to do here and it was just not worth going into. James and I walked out into the casino proper. James automatically sat down at a slot machine, slid fifty bucks in, and pulled the lever down.

"Sit next to me," he whispered. "Be my lucky charm. By the way, what's your name?"

He bummed a cigarette from me, and I lit it for him after I sat down. Even though there was major AC blowing, there was still a smell of awful garbagey heat and other people's cigarette coughs. I lit up, our knees touched, and he kept pulling down the lever: nothing. He told me to get closer. I told him my new name.

"Ruth." Which was my mother's name.

"Ruth?" He laughed. "That's fucking depressing. That's fucking Biblical."

He pulled the lever and yet again nothing. I told him I had to pee, and he whispered, "Don't forget to use the *ladies'* room, Ruthie."

I felt shaky when I saw myself bathed in fluorescence in the ladies' room mirror. Women left and came in, a giggle here a giggle there. I looked like a fucked-up drag queen with jet lag, about as real as Ronald McDonald. Rhonda McDonald, his desperate drag queen brother.

After I used the bathroom, I returned to the casino, telling myself that I was going to get through *just tonight* like this. Then tomorrow it was back into jeans and a nice shirt and James and I would laugh about this. I went to the slot machine he'd been at. Its screen belched out lights and honks.

But James was gone.

I looked everywhere: by the huge spiral staircase, the three or four fancy bars that lined the way to a mall with a ceiling painted like sky. During my search I completely lost the ability to pretend I was Meg Ryan. I even went outside to look for James, and the heat started to melt my makeup. I went back into the casino, to the slot machines, blackjack and roulette tables. Nothing. No sign of James.

I sat down by the front entrance and waited. Went for a walk and waited again. Put some quarters into a slot machine. But still I felt like I was slipping into a hole I never even knew was there. Being in Vegas, this drippy, lost Meg Ryan wannabe, I had the urge to scream and rip at my clothes and hit myself. All I really wanted was simple: for James to come to me and apologize and tell me he loved me, you know, like in a Meg Ryan movie. This was all I wanted in the whole wide world that moment.

I walked around some more. I knew I could just go upstairs and take everything off but somehow I wasn't able. I wound up outside a smorgasbord called The Spice Market Buffet, on the other side of the casino. A big bulletin board displayed exotic culinary delights, like Indian and Thai fare, glistening in beautiful backlit photographs.

I realized I was starving.

The buffet was down a small escalator. The host seated me all alone near a mirrored wall in an orange velour booth. The carpet was maroon wall to wall. All the smells of food merged into one, a creamy, oniony vapor. I grabbed myself a plate, dressed up like I was, and went to each little island of food, taking as much as I wanted.

I knew even then what this was: finding out how to survive by putting everything into my mouth. Spaghetti and shrimp and pesto and apple pie, bananas Foster and tacos and olives and pickles and crepes. As I ate, I remembered the feeling of putting on a dress when I was nine, the secrecy and the pleasure and the custom-made power, like I was shifting the way the world went just by doing one little goddamn personal thing.

And I realized I had stumbled onto a new way to make myself into something else.

Soon as I finished (I was there for a very long time) I got up, dizzy with all I had consumed, filled up to the top of my skull with sumptuousness. After taking care of the bill, I went back to the room.

James came in toward dawn, saying, "Where the hell did you disappear to?"

He was red-faced and fucked-up, smelling of cigarettes and booze and sex, wearing a t-shirt that said "Winners Never Sleep!"

When he got into the bed, I could not move. He kissed my cheek.

"You mad at me?" he said.

I didn't answer. I couldn't even ask him where he had disappeared to. It didn't matter anymore. I looked at his face in the TV-lit dark. The sunglasses were off, but his eyes still looked hidden. I felt like a cornucopia had been shoved into my mouth. I had a new way of life. The next morning there would be breakfast and there would be lunch after that. And dinner. And dessert. And a midnight snack.

"Should you sleep with all that shit on your face?" he whispered.

Then he just conked out.

We woke up the next day and I told him I wasn't a lady anymore. He got totally pissed. We basically wound up having separate vacations.

His mom committed accidental suicide a few months later (pills and vodka). I was going to go to her funeral, but it just didn't seem wise. Now I think James owns a car lot in Indiana somewhere.

After that trip, as I gained more weight, I began to lose what I had been. I bought new drag outfits to suit my new physique, making sure everyone I performed in front of understood that I got the joke.

"Look here at this motherfucking heifer," I'd say in between lip-syncing songs, but then even the fun of that evaporated.

I was just the fat-ass drag queen pretending to be a drag queen, which I understood, but the show offers got fewer and further between, and the men did too. One day I took everything out to the dumpster, shoes and gowns and wigs and all those pictures on the walls, just like that. It was October, almost dusk. I got into my car after I threw everything away and drove to a Kentucky Fried Chicken drive-through. I took a whole bucket of chicken, mashed potatoes and gravy, three little chocolate brownie desserts, and a two-liter of Pepsi back to my apartment and ate it all in two hours. At the end of this feast, almost breathless from stuffing myself, I contemplated what I had become. The answer was simple. I got this way by humiliating myself in a mint-green skirt outfit in Las Vegas for some idiot in sunglasses who needed me to do that so he could be what he was.

Sadly nobody was really stirred up enough to pull me from my downward spiral. Even the old ladies who once wanted me to be their own personal stylist, even they kind of picked up on the smell. I wanted out, and I was getting exactly what I wanted. They just wanted to have their hair done.

3

Leslie picks me up at six in the morning the day of my stomach bypass.

I use my cane to get to his car, and he is smiling.

"Morning, kiddo."

"Thanks, Leslie," I say. I have a little suitcase.

It's muggy. He has a large Lincoln Continental with the AC turned up high, light rock on the radio. Every once in a while, in his sad-old-man voice, Leslie talks about the weather we're having, and how I am not to worry about my recovery and coming back to my job. I smile. I feel like I am being taken to a concentration camp.

"This is gonna change your life, my friend," he tells me, parking in the garage.

"You don't have to go in."

"I don't mind. I'll go in until you get situated."

We both walk through the almost empty garage, through a corridor of yellow walls, to the reception desk at the Weight Clinic. The office is light blue with off-white chairs and gray wall-to-wall. I've been here many times, for check-ups and tests and talks. It took five months of waiting for the insurance to okay my surgery and for the preliminary tests to come through. But here it is, the day I am to be transformed, at least internally.

I look over at Leslie: white dress-shirt, sleeves with red rubber bands to keep them rolled up, those glasses, gray-green pants, sneakers. He has on a dark brown fedora as well. I want to know why Leslie is being so kind but I just don't have the courage to ask him.

I think: what if ten years ago on the plane to Vegas the stewardess had offered me a crystal ball instead of a bag of peanuts? I would have looked into it and seen this scene, not really knowing I was in it, and definitely not knowing who the hell the little Jiminy Cricket man was. I would have shaken the damn crystal ball hard and looked again and would have seen the same scene and told the flight attendant, "Ma'am, there is definitely something wrong with this thing."

It's almost like Leslie is the gift you get when you give up on people. You get this unassuming, almost invisible man who owns the laundromat where you spend your days washing other people's clothes and giving people the key to the bathroom. Leslie is the one to escort you to your next place. Of course I wonder what James is doing right at this moment.

I fill out more papers. Then we're waiting. One other morbidly obese person, who's with her thin mother, is doing the same thing I am: sitting, waiting. In little glimpses, I look at her brown hair tied back into a ponytail, her pale jowls, her sweet empty eyes.

"This is a nice place," Leslie whispers. He smiles with yellow teeth, two or three silver ones.

They don't really cut you all the way open. It's a laser-beam, a tiny fierce finger that slices through what you have done to yourself. I can feel the singe already, searing through flab and feelings, satisfying my need to be something else. But that need gets smaller and smaller as I wait, until finally it vanishes completely. All that's left is pure fear, which is somehow a comfort to me.

I get up.

I walk out as fast as I can with my cane. Once I get back to the yellow corridor, Leslie catches up. He has the suitcase I left behind.

"They're calling for you," Leslie is saying. He's confused, but he's smiling.

I lean up against the wall.

"I can't do it," I whisper.

"What?" Leslie says.

"I can't do it."

We just stand there in the corridor. Leslie whispers a few things, but I tell him again that I can't do it. I don't want to know what else might happen.

"Take me home," I say. "I just want to go home."

Leslie and I spend the rest of the day together. He rents some movies. I have brownie mix and enough energy to make brownies. It starts to rain. Leslie has the good sense not to be angered by my cowardice. Maybe he thinks I'll eventually go through with the surgery, maybe he thinks I really know what's best.

"I like the old ones," he says, shoving one of his selections from Blockbuster into the DVD player. There's the softest thunder. I'm on the couch. The brownies are cooling. I am watching the TV screen, then I look at Leslie's face.

"Can I get you anything else?" he says.

GANGLAND

Monica Bergers

After school, Cherrie Bodine, the leader, told me I needed to get my hair trimmed. "If you got your hair trimmed," she said, slipping the fingers of her good hand into a pair of brass knuckles, "you'd be something special. Then you wouldn't be *bodyguard* anymore. The boys'd chase *you*." I was bodyguard at lunch period, when Rondell got chased behind the jungle gym so the boys could touch her.

"Here's the thing," Cherrie said. "This ain't grade school anymore. It's middle school, and you got to know the diff—even if you did just get here."

Cherrie was in Rondell's homeroom on the second floor. My class was downstairs, so I didn't pass notes or find out who Cherrie or Liz or Rondell had crushes on till recess, and that was what really sucked about sixth grade. It was like missing the bus every day because you wake up late, or daydreaming too long in the cereal aisle at Kroger's and then realizing your mom's gone. Me, Cherrie, and Liz were outside Cherrie's house, because her mom told us we were too loud and we smelled like school. Liz was by the road, trying to hitch a ride. She'd rolled up her skirt to make it shorter. Her legs were thick and white. We were waiting for Rondell to finish cleaning her room so she could hang with us.

Cherrie touched my hair with the brass-knuckled hand. "I mean it," she said. "*This* is why you stick out."

"I'll take care of it," I said, chewing my cheek. "It's cool."

"Sooner the better," Cherrie said.

"It's cool," I said. "I got it."

Cherrie was the leader because she was the tallest. She wore tight stone-washed jeans and black boots and heavy metal t-shirts, and she had a good body. Like Skipper but with tits. She was almost perfect, except her hand was disfigured. Rondell told me it was because her dad was working on a car in the driveway and the jack dropped. She lost two fingers. "Don't ask her about it," Rondell warned me. I never did. You couldn't look at her hand dead-on, because she'd notice. When she was pissed she'd wave it in front of you like it was the plague. You had to be careful about staring, because she wore a big silver ring on the middle finger.

"So, are we going to kick his ass, or what?" Cherrie said. She punched the air, and I dodged and faked in an attempt to look natural. "What's it going to be?"

"I don't know," I said.

Cherrie frowned.

"I mean, yeah. Let's kill him."

"Whoa," she said. "This ain't 'Family Feud.' We kick his ass, that's it. Ain't that right, Liz?"

"Yeah!" Liz yelled.

"Right," I said. "That's what I meant."

"Okay, cool. We get Rondell to meet us at Lion's Den, then we make a plan."

"Won't we get in trouble?" I said. "If we get caught?"

"Maybe," she said, but she was already there, punching and fighting.

Liz yelled from the road, "What's for dinner, Satan?"

Cherrie flexed her hand and winced. "Do I look like a cook, asshole?"

Thing is, I got told on in homeroom. That's what happens when you make fun of people. I sat behind this kid, Chris Strawn, who cried and sulked in his desk. Every hour, our teacher stopped class so she could give him his pills. I must've snapped. I drew him on my English folder. I sucked at drawing, but there he was in black ink: glasses sitting on a scrunched up face. It was the best drawing I ever did. I didn't want him to think it was him and hurt his feelings, so I put "Crybaby" under it.

I've never been afraid of the dark—it's being alone I'm scared of. I'd think: maybe I'll always be alone; maybe everyone will forget me. My mom said it's because I don't have any 'common sense,' which meant I needed self-esteem. She asked my teacher to make sure I ate my lunch every day, right down to the sweet potatoes.

Rondell and I used to go to the same elementary school, but this was different: this was middle school and you didn't ask people if they wanted "to play" with you, because that was gross. On lunch when my class was in the cafeteria line, I got in back so I could wait for Cherrie and Rondell's class to come in. They were always late. The rule in Grade 6 is that you have to get your food and then sit at the lunch tables in exactly the order you were in line. This was so there were no problems. Except I had big problems with this system, because I was always sitting across from someone like chubby, red-headed Kami who got a wave perm so she'd look popular, and brought her lunch in plastic bags. Everything about her reeked patheticness. She wore purple Lee Press-On nails, and even that didn't help.

One day at lunch, I was carrying my tray to my seat when all of a sudden a tater tot hit me in the head. It was from Chris Strawn. I set my tray down and told him I was going to kick his snot-nosed crybaby ass, and he started crying and yelling. It took two teachers to drag him away to detention. Then he told on me. They confiscated the folder from my cubbyhole, and I was taken to homeroom and given a week of d-hall. Thing is, I kind of liked the guy.

"I need you to trim my hair," I told my mom. She had a beautician's license in two states, and a boyfriend with a perm. Once Bruce yelled at me after I let his friends in, and they saw my mom wrapping tissue and curlers in his hair like he was a doll. I had to bite my cheeks so I wouldn't laugh.

"I'll do it when I come home," my mom said. "They're inviting me to the Mayo Clinic for tests." Me and my brother were at the table eating Lucky Charms. Bruce was pouring coffee into a mug.

"What?" I said.

"I got the green light to go to the best hospital in the world. There's even a rollercoaster in the middle of the place. A rollercoaster! How in the world do they get any work done?"

My brother squealed. "I want to go, too! I want to go the best hospital in the world!"

"Better eat your cereal, son," Bruce said with his eyebrows seriously raised. He gripped the mug handle with a bear paw; the other hand on his waist.

"No, you don't want to go with Momma. You got to stay here and learn something so you'll be strong and smart like your sister."

I made a face. "What's wrong?" I said.

"They can't quite figure it out," she said. "That's why I have to go a long ways away."

"How long are you going to be gone?" I asked.

"Couple of weeks, max."

"What's B going to do? How's he going to do my hair in the morning?"

Bruce put a hand on Mom's head. She took it and put it to her face.

"No problem," Bruce said. "I'm going to learn how to do your hair. Probably be a lot of ponytails." He laughed. I remembered the time Bruce yelled at me and my brother because we threw some empty bottles onto the ground just to see them break.

Bruce had two daughters, but he never talked about them. Me and my brother got to play with their toys, and it was like somebody had died. The dolls were large enough so they looked real. Their hair was chopped off with scissors so they looked more modern. But that bothered me, because they probably looked fine before, because who had the right to do that, I thought.

"What about me, Momma?" my brother said. He stirred up his cereal so the marshmallows spun around like in a kaleidoscope.

I used to think that when I got older, I'd have a yellow leather purse, and be on a diet. That's what being a teenager seemed like. Being a teenager seemed like having a boyfriend, and watching *Superman* without having to look away when Superman and Lois Lane kiss. It was staying up late to watch *The Golden Girls* on TV and eating candy whenever you wanted. But sixth grade was the year I learned about sex—not just in dirty pictures of people—but in novels like *Windmills of the Gods*. When I asked my mom if I could read *Lace* she told me to skip the racy parts. I think she was just glad someone in our family read.

I took it to school so me and my friends could memorize the dirty parts. That was my contribution to the gang. We balanced on the cross bars while Rondell or Cherrie read about the Arabian prince who went to sex school. He learned how to put a goldfish inside a woman and suck it out. It was amazing.

Me and Rondell were waiting at the gas station for the bus. She was putting on blood red lipstick so she'd look like Lita Ford in the music video. I was trying to perfect a one-hand cartwheel, but I screwed up and hit the Coke machine. Rondell burst out laughing.

"Next year, when we go to junior high," she said, "we should get our lockers together."

"Yeah, and we'll decorate them with glitter and stuff," I said, clapping my hands. My homework spilled out of my backpack, and I had to run to catch the papers from the wind. "Do they make locker posters—like for Skid Row?"

"Maybe," she said. Then she yelled, "I *love* Sebastian Bach!" and the old lady at the register glared at us through the window.

"No, *I* love Sebastian Bach!" I yelled.

"We should spray paint it on the side of the store!"

I liked Rondell more than Cherrie or Liz or Kami together. She didn't tell anyone I made the honor roll. She had straight brown hair and dark eyelashes that didn't need mascara, except she liked to experiment with a makeup kit her mom gave her the Christmas before.

Some days at recess, it was like something was in the air: the boys got to talking, sizing up the situation, figuring the score. Then, me and Rondell started running. When she ran, nobody could touch her. She outsmarted them a lot, turning quick, doubling back. Sometimes I stopped just to watch. Her long hair flicked around her back, and her skirt whipped up by her knees; she was the prettiest girl I'd ever seen. She wore Asics with rainbows on the sides, and it's like they were her magic shoes and made her run faster. Since first grade at Sourdeen Elementary, me and her had been friends, and for as long as we'd been friends, I'd been her bodyguard. But the jungle gym was my turf. If anybody touched her, I stepped in and yelled, "Get outta here, slick!" That's when I got to push the cutest boys in class.

"See you at recess," Rondell told me when we got off at school.

"See you," I said.

I don't know why I didn't tell her about my mom. Maybe I forgot, maybe I didn't think it was a big deal. By the time we got on the bus, I felt like I betrayed my mom by not saying anything. Like she could disappear and no one would mind.

Sometimes I look at a clock and I just don't get it. Like I can't figure out what the numbers mean, even if I tried, like saying *beard* over and over till you don't recognize it anymore. There's no connection. Mom said if you daydream too long, you get lost. I guess that's my worst fear. I was the biggest dreamer. I was desperate to be noticed, but if the boys *had* chased me, instead of Rondell, I would've felt like that girl in the "Thriller" video. She's on a date with a guy, and everything is fine, until he turns into a werewolf, and dead people come out of the ground. They chase her to an old house, and then she's the most alone person in the world. If the boys chased me, I'd run like a horse in the woods, like it was my last chance.

I tried not to get annoyed when I couldn't find the gang on the playground. There were lots of classes playing kickball and basketball, and I avoided them in case I'd have to catch the ball and throw it back. Chessica and Ellen were jumping rope. Other people were standing around in little groups, looking at each other. There was a lot of noise—whistles and people yelling. When I found Cherrie and Liz, they were talking brass knuckles and pocket knives. Cherrie said hi to me.

"What are you guys talking about?" I said, resting a hand in my pocket. My lips felt chapped when I licked them.

"Lion's Den," Liz said, all showy, like she's suddenly tired of talking about it. She held her hair in a ponytail and squinted toward the soccer field.

Cherrie stared at me. "Didn't I tell you to get your hair trimmed?" she said.

"I did," I said. "Like a week ago."

"Oh yeah, I meant *thinned*. You should get your hair thinned."

"Great," I said. I wanted to kill her.

Then Liz broke in. "Jayce gave Rondell a necklace at break. It has a crystal on it that says *R*."

"What. Ever," Cherrie said. "Jayce is such a cheapskate. Like how much did it cost—$10?"

"Did he even pick it out? It was wrapped."

Liz and Cherrie smirked. This meant he probably had his mom do it, which was a cop-out. When you get found out like that, it's like walking around with your pants unzipped. They loved that kind of thing.

"He's so mature," I smirked, reminded of the time he saved me from square-dancing with Charlie Isaac by asking me to be his partner. "But you like buck teeth, don't you?" he'd said, and it was the funniest thing. He had a stuttering kind of laughter that I liked. We'd do-si-doed around the cafeteria till second recess, and then went our separate ways.

Cherrie turned toward me with a queer grin on her face. "Have you ever really talked to him?" she said.

"He sat next to me in Art."

"And he copied your drawing," Liz said. "It was pathetic."

"So?" I said. Really, it'd been the best day of my life. I'd immediately started teaching myself to French kiss with a can of Sprite. Just in case.

While Mom was gone, I pretended to be sick so I could stay home from school, which meant I got to ride with Bruce in his truck. He put signs on the truck doors— Jamison Remodeling: We Now Do Plumbing!—they were magnets. At night, and at the bar, he took them off; in the morning they went on again.

I liked him when he was working. He wasn't stressed out or talking about bills. Everywhere we went, everybody said "Hey, Deuce!" like they were in a good mood, too, and I was the almost daughter of a real popular dad. Even breakfast at Mr. K's was full of old men who knew him. They came up and shook his hand. They looked at me like they'd never seen me before. The waitress had a crush on him.

"Whatcha want, pie-face," she said to him. He had biscuits and gravy, and he let me have French toast and Sprite.

"Don't tell your mom," he said.

We went all over town, from one construction site to another, and sometimes I sat in the truck with a book named *Cally*, and sometimes I didn't. Once he gave me his hand, and we walked in together. It was warm, smooth, and I felt grown up. He squeezed and I squeezed back. We walked over some flat wood, and I watched a man pour the driveway. Everyone was busy. Inside the house, there weren't any walls, but they had the doorways set up. There were yellow and white wires hanging down, and even though they had no walls, the stairs were already made.

"It's big," I said.

Bruce shrugged. On the second floor, he let go of my hand. "I need to talk to Richard. Stand here and be good," he said.

I wanted to pretend I lived there so I could open and shut the doors like I had company or was looking for something. After I watched *Mary Poppins*, I always went to my room and pretended to be the nanny, picking up my old-fashioned phone over and over again, wondering where the children had gone to.

"I'm Mary Poppins," I'd say angrily into the phone. Maybe I was talking to the cops. Maybe they weren't cooperating. I'd hang up the phone, dial another number and watch the dial spin.

It was boring waiting there. I chewed my cheek and played with my hair, twirling it around my fingers. My butt itched. Someone turned up a radio, and "Sugar, Sugar" came on. Mom used to play that when we came home from gymnastics, and she'd sing her heart out. I loved that song.

I looked around and thought if this was my house, I'd play cars or Barbies right there. The top stair would be a grocery parking lot, and the cars would drive in and park, careful of the cliff. Then I'd tie a rope around Barbie's waist and throw her off the cliff so Ken could save her. Rondell would've been so jealous. She loves that kind of thing. In recess, if nobody was chasing her, she'd stand around with us and make up stories about who she wanted to marry and how her hair would be. We heard somebody had a crimping iron, and sure enough, Lacy Jones showed up at school with perfect zig-zag to her hair. Rondell wanted the gang to shake her down, get that iron from her.

I wondered if they missed me at school. They were probably in third period math or social studies, writing notes with purple ink. I was glad I wasn't there. I sat down next to a board with nails sticking out of it, wrote my name in the sawdust. Regular way, and in cursive. Him and Richard were talking a long time, and I wished I'd brought my book. I thought about going to the truck to get it.

Finally, him and the boss were done talking. When they got back to me, I heard him say he had a whole box of tapes the boss could watch. They laughed, so I did, too. That seemed funny to them, and they laughed some more.

"Ready, kid?" he said, smiling.

I nodded.

"Then let's make like a tree and leave."

"You stuck with this kid?" the boss said.

Bruce clamped me on the shoulder. "The whole day," he said. "Babysitter's over to the Walmart, working. Kid says she don't feel well."

"My ear aches," I explained.

With a smile on his face, the boss said, "Long as you keep up, s'okay with me."

"I rectum," Bruce said.

We walked back through the yard, and since I was feeling confident, I waved at the men working in cutoffs. They loved to see me there with my almost-dad.

"Hey, pumpkin!" they said, or "What's shakin'? You skipping school?" Something funny or nice to make me smile. I grabbed Bruce's hand.

In the truck, he said, "Thanks for nothing, Richard. Rick Dick. Duh-duh-duh-dickhead!"

I loved it when he played Porky Pig. Dickhead was his favorite word—it always made me laugh.

"This is what real life is like," he told me, lighting a cigarette. "Real life is breaking your back for strangers. Then some cocksucker pays you for it. Look at these guys. They eat crap and drink Mountain Dew day-in, day-out. What a life."

I took a beer out of the cooler behind his seat.

"Thanks," he said and messed my hair.

"You know what they pay you for busting your ass? Ten bucks an hour. I gotchyer ten dollars right here, buddy!" He grabbed his crotch. I opened *Cally*, and felt the pull of mystery just looking at the words.

"Can you drop me off at the library?" I said. "I'm almost done with this."

"You sure do read a lot, kid," he said.

"I rectum," I said.

The Lion's Den had chains, nunchuks, leather dog collars, knives, silver chains that went all the way from your ear to your nose ring, Garbage Pail Kids cards, candy, cigarettes, lotto tickets, Guns-n-Roses t-shirts—the more faded, the better. It was a place most of us had been only once or twice. Everyone, except Cherrie, who knew the owner. He'd been in jail for selling stolen lawnmowers—the riding kind. He had a white beard and a mustache that was yellow around his mouth like he'd dipped it in the toilet. Once he hired Cherrie and her brothers to rake up the pine needles in his yard just so he could kill the grass. He reminded me of sex—he was dirty like that.

The Lion's Den was open all night in case someone came in off the interstate with a taste for badness. The owner had a tired, old bulldog whose only job was to lay by the door and sniff at people's feet as they came in. If you could talk to Cherrie without being an idiot, you could stand talking to this guy.

Talking to Cherrie was mainly a matter of listening and figuring out what to do with your face. The half smile, the cocked eyebrow, the disdainful nose scrunch: a whole box of paints were waiting to be used. I liked to bring out the "Jason Patrick" to let her know things were under control. This was my classic face. I taught it to myself last summer after watching *The Lost Boys*, because that was a cool movie, and I knew if I wanted to survive sixth grade, I needed an angle. The "Jason Patrick" was a slight eyebrow raise, a half smile, and a slow head nod—like telling your friend you got their joke, but it wasn't funny enough to laugh. Smooth.

Cherrie wanted me to buy a knife, in case Chris Strawn brought one out in the fight—but I couldn't do it. She said that made me a crybaby, too.

I dreamed that the werewolf was outside my window. It couldn't touch me, but it was always there, looking in. I was looking in, too. I told myself, you can never tell anybody. They wouldn't believe you. When I woke up, I couldn't move. For a moment, I forgot what I was scared of. I laid there and shook, and thought, *you're too good. You're too good.*

A couple days before my mom came home, Bruce tucked me into bed, touching my cheek. "Your mom's going to be alright," he said. "Everything's going to be alright." He kissed my forehead, and I closed my eyes.

"Thanks, B," I said.

That part in *Annie*, where Daddy Warbucks carries Annie upstairs in his arms, after the movies, and then he puts her nightgown on, and she's sound asleep—I always loved that. She isn't too heavy for him. She looks peaceful.

"If you ever need to talk, I'm here." He patted the blanket at my chest.

"Okay," I said, yawning.

He sat there, patting the blanket with his fingers—not in a hard way, but solid, like a Snickers bar in your mouth. I closed my eyes and thought about *Cally* and how the bachelor and the Sullivan house were haunted. The bachelor killed Cally and her friends at a dinner party, but that didn't stop me from having a crush on him. He had dark hair and blue eyes, almost like Bruce, but younger. Also, my mom dyed Bruce's hair that way, so it wasn't real—it smelled chemically, like the stuff they put in dead people so they're alive again. Even after he washed it, it smelled.

Bruce sighed. "You falling asleep?" he said.

"I'm just resting my eyes."

"I was thinking—you ever get lonely at night? I mean, real lonely, like it scares you," he said. "Cause I get lonely, sometimes. When your mom's gone."

I opened my eyes and saw blotches of light, then his face all dark. My brother was asleep in his room. I was being let in on a secret by an adult.

"If you want to come sleep in my room, it's okay," he said. "That'd be okay."

"Thanks," I said, but it didn't seem convincing enough. I wanted him to know I appreciated the gesture, because if I didn't, he might say something else. I don't know what.

"What's on TV?" I said.

"One of those miniseries you like," he said. "Wanna come?"

"Yeah," I said. "Yeah."

The next day, Rondell told me I was crowding her. She wore two Espirit t-shirts with the sleeves rolled up. Her shoulders were dry and brown. There was a piece of glitter on her bottom lip, and I watched it as she talked.

"It's like you're my shadow," she said. "You walk too close to me."

There was a part of me that shrank inside, and I remembered when my real parents got divorced. I never cried about it.

"It's not like we can't ever hang out. I'm sure you're tired of me, just as much as I am of you, right?"

"I don't know—what do you mean?" I said, imagining that piece of glitter flying away like a shooting star.

"It's just that you walk too close. I can't breathe."

"That's because you're my best friend," I said.

"Cherrie's my best friend, now," she said.

When Rondell's birthday came, she had a slumber party. Her parents didn't care if we washed our hands for dinner, or drank ten Cokes in a row. We ate pizza from Pizza Hut. We had birthday cake and candy, and I ate lots of it. No one could sleep. It was like everyone broke into dance at the same time, or screamed just to see who could seem the realest. Late at night, we got to looking at our privates.

"God," Liz said to Cherrie. "You look like a muppet."

Cherrie's privates were covered with an adult-looking tuft of hair. Instantly, I glanced at my own and was jealous.

Then Cherrie noticed that mine wasn't normal.

"What's that hanging down?" she said.

"I don't know."

"Weird," Rondell said. "Can I touch it?"

Then Rondell's fingers were between my legs, pulling my flaps of skin apart so they could see the thing better. My body flushed.

"Lay still," she commanded. For a second, no one said anything. Then she pinched it lightly. The tissue was thin and red like a tongue.

"There's a vein in it," Rondell said, using both hands now to spread it.

"Looks like a waddle," Liz said. "You know—the red thing on a rooster?"

"Gross," Kami said. I couldn't believe Rondell had invited her.

"Don't be a baby," Rondell said. "This is important."

I wanted to slap her hands and roll under the bed. I swallowed, hoping the lump in my throat would let me be, hoping maybe once I wasn't about to cry. If Kami could take it, I had to, too.

"Does this hurt?" Rondell said, pulling.

"A little," I said. "I thought everybody had one. Doesn't everybody have one?"

"Look at mine," Cherrie said, laying back, spreading her legs. We all stared at Cherrie's privates, which were dark pink. "I don't have a waddle."

"What about me?" Kami said. Her thighs were pale and freckled, and even her feet were fat. I desperately wanted her to have the ugliest one, but hers was like Cherrie's. It didn't look normal to me.

"Stop it," I said, kicking Rondell. She fell back and hit her head on the bed frame.

"Why'd you do that," she said.

"You know what," Cherrie said, excited. She rose to her knees. "It looks like a little penis—like it shrunk."

"Oh, my God," Liz said. "It does!"

"Let me see!" Kami said.

"It's like when you're really a guy, and you have a vagina," Cherrie said.

"No it's not!" I said, hoarse. I looked at Rondell for help, for back-up, but she was laughing.

"You deserve it," she said. "Shouldn't have pushed me."

Cherrie pulled out a plastic knife from under the bed. It was crusted with pizza sauce. "Let's cut it off," she suggested. "You don't need it."

"Stop it," I said. "This isn't funny."

"Why not," Rondell said, shrugging.

"I'm not playing anymore. I'm serious."

Cherrie spit on the knife and rubbed it. Then she took off her silver ring and told Rondell to lock the door. Before I could run, she grabbed my shoulders and pushed me onto my back. The other girls grabbed my legs and pinned me.

"Spread her legs," Cherrie said.

"What are you doing?" Rondell hissed.

"Mom!" I yelled, thrashing. "*Mom!*"

"Don't you want to see what'll happen?" Cherrie said. She stood over me; her nostrils were black holes.

"I'm just kidding," she said, finally. She started to laugh. "Man, you're gullible. Man."

Later we all took turns being dragged around the house in a sleeping bag till it felt like you'd suffocate, and then you'd fight your way out. Most times you were left in a dark corner and everyone hid from you. I walked from room to room. My stomach hurt. When I went into the kitchen, Rondell was sitting on the counter with a big spoon in her mouth. I climbed up next to her.

"Want some cake?" she said. "Here, take mine. I just wanted some before I start my diet."

I took a bite. Suddenly I felt hot. "Remember when we used to go to gymnastics?"

"Yeah," she said. "Whenever you did a back bend, you farted. That was funny."

"No I didn't," I said, knowing I did. "I wish we still went."

"I hated Ms. Pam. She was fat."

"She could do the splits," I offered.

"Did you see what Liz got me—a Caboodle. Now I can take all my makeup whenever I go somewhere," she said.

"That's great," I said, weak.

"What's wrong?" she asked.

I was just about to tell her I felt sick. I was just about to tell her something happened and I was scared.

Then Cherrie came in, looking red and sweaty. "Hey," she gasped. "It's your turn in the sleeping bag."

"I don't want a turn," Rondell said.

Cherrie looked at me. "It's your turn, then."

I didn't want to leave yet, but I couldn't talk to Rondell with her in the room. She wouldn't've understood. "Where is it?"

"Right there." Cherrie pointed to the doorway.

The sleeping bag was huge with fleece to keep you warm—the kind Rondell's family took camping at Lake Ouachita. I got in and rolled to the very back, and right away I felt like throwing up. Someone grabbed the sleeping bag at the end and dragged me down the hall. We turned right and they tugged faster. The carpet rippled under me, a doorjamb hit my knee; we were spinning round a big room and laughter. I heard his voice. I wondered what it felt like to die. My body kept sucking air, but I couldn't breathe. It was like I shut down. I didn't try to get out. I didn't try to get out. Finally it stopped.

KNOCKED OUT

Jane Bernstein

Avery was wounded by his parents' decision to move to Florida so soon after he and Suzanne bought a house in New Jersey. For so long, his mother had claimed that the cause of her despair was having a son past forty who was unmarried and childless. Yet even after his status had changed, and he became a husband and father both, she continued to view him disdainfully.

At least she stopped introducing him to people as a "confirmed bachelor," which for years had been her habit. "Confirmed," as if he'd gone through a course of study and gotten a certificate declaring him to be a licensed, professional single man. "Bachelor" was also a creepy name, which allowed people to affix all kinds of stereotypes on him. He was too selfish, too picky, the name suggested. He had a castration complex, was tied to his mother's apron strings, was a closeted gay.

None of these things was true. Avery liked women. They were inscrutable and erratic, but he enjoyed their company more than the company of most men, was more himself with women, he felt, wanting badly to be in a relationship, to marry and have kids—lots of them. Once, when he was in the Peace Corps in Benin, he became delirious from a terrible fever and had a dream that he was naked on a sofa and that children were all over him, suckling like puppies on a bitch. He woke, frantic and disoriented, and tried to get upright to count his teats, but his fear was so great, he could not keep count, and he cried out, in his delirium, "Feed the babies; they're starving!" His roommates heard him, and later, when he was well, "Feed the babies" became a kind of punctuation at the end of whatever absurdity they faced. To him, it was simpler than that: The dream was just his subconscious saying he was meant to have a brood, to father many children, to take care of entire communities.

When he returned to New York, there were always women in his life, at most times even two or three, though he was only capable of having a sexual relationship with one of them. ("Serial monogamist"—something else he was called, which made it sound as if he had a disorder, rather than the reality, that it was too confusing to sleep with more than one woman at a time.) So there might be one woman he was just getting to know, in the "coffee" stage, and one he was sleeping with ("the lover") who was most often becoming disenchanted with him by the time he met the coffee woman—for being work-obsessed, emotionally unavailable, empty inside, deliberately obtuse—all accusations that had been leveled at him. The problem, as Avery saw it, was that the intelligent, independent women he liked all seemed complete without him. They made better friends than lovers, which was why there was usually a woman in the "now we're friends" stage.

Things did get fouled up. Sometimes the "coffee" woman rushed things along, inviting him to her apartment for dinner. Or the woman in the friend stage was having a hard time and needed consolation, and she turned to Avery, since even as a lover, he was a *nachas*-maker, a pleasure giver, capable of deep tenderness if a woman wanted tender, though he could do Tantric or light bondage if that was more her thing.

In the spring of 1986, when he met Jonah and Suzanne, he was part of a practice on Spring Street, where the exam rooms smelled spicy from the vats of chili that simmered in the vegetarian restaurant below. The "lover" in his life was an audiology graduate student named Mindy Rothermel who brought home stray cats and often slept in her clothes, and unknown to him at the time was carrying on a torrid relationship with a deaf actor named Burl. He had just finished running the loop in Central Park and was walking west, calculating his speed with dismay, wondering if his downward trajectory was permanent, if his piss-poor time was the mark of his slow if inexorable physical decline or if he had simply gotten fat and lazy and with some effort could reverse this slide. He was not quite ready to admit how little he liked Mindy or how joyless their times when together—it was his habit to hold more tightly to a woman after their relationship had begun to sour. Instead he was thinking how much he dreaded spending the afternoon with her and her insufferable cousin from Shaker Heights, which was what he had promised to do, as soon as he was home and showered. He was forty-three years old, and unmarried, and feeling thick, stuck and slow, when he heard his name. Not "Avery," what he preferred, but "Dr. Klein!"

A stranger was calling his name—a tall, thin woman with long rippling red-blonde hair—Botticelli hair. He stepped over, struggling to place her—not a neighbor, not a patient, maybe a friend's friend—saw her face, that it wasn't quite right, her thin pale arms, and then the dog curled on the blanket. (Later, when people asked how they had met, he said, "I was walking in Central Park, and there she was—vision of loveliness!")

Her mute, panicked look pulled him closer. That was when he saw that the dog at her feet was twitching spasmodically, its eyes rolled back. Some wet beige stuff, the color and consistency of oatmeal, was on the blanket.

And this was the part that people liked best, how without hesitation he dove onto the blanket, put his mouth over the mouth of this strange dog and tried to bring it back to life, breathed and pressed on the dog's chest, wiped the dog's vomit from his face, breathed some more, and kept at it, until the woman who called his name said, "I'm sorry. Oh my God. How awful. No, really. You can stop; it's fine. She's dead."

Sometimes the women who called to borrow Avery asked where Suzanne had managed to find such a wonderful man. When she told them this story, they said, "That is *so* Avery."

Everyone except for Amy, his sister, who never fully let go of her sense of him as a grubby, socially retarded kid. When she heard this tale, she turned to Suzanne and said, "You actually *kissed* him after that?"

Suzanne hadn't. Anyway, there wasn't anything particularly saintly about his attempt to rescue the dog, Avery always pointed out. It was simply training: there's an emergency, you act. You drop to your knees; you do what it takes, no questions asked. Still, he might not have stayed once he realized the dog was dead, if it hadn't been for the alarm in her eyes, and the boy running toward them—hers obviously, the red hair was a giveaway—dirty elbows, one front tooth, big as a Chiclet.

Instinct again—Avery flipped an edge of the blanket over the dog, and the kid stopped short. "Can I sleep at Pete's?" He threw his baseball glove in the air, spun in a circle, held his hands high, then watched the glove plop to the ground.

While the mother was saying, "Your team was awesome. And you were so amazingly great," Avery kept thinking, *Your dog is dead.*

And further, that his supposed girlfriend Mindy was waiting for him. Though he silently promised he would leave the park the moment a husband showed up, he knew there was no man in their lives, could tell by her heightened enthusiasm with the boy, and the way her eyes kept darting from the lump beneath the blanket to the boy. He had to go, but he would see this out, whatever it was. It was what he did, what he was best at.

Meanwhile, the kid was bouncing, jiggling, begging. "Please? His dad said okay; he's over there." Tossing the glove in the air another time, missing it by a foot.

"Something's happened to Drinkith." Her voice quavered. She looked back, caught Avery's eye.

Avery interceded. "He may have had a heart attack."

The red-haired kid eyed him scornfully, said, "*She*," and turned back to his mother. "He has a Game Boy, Mom."

"Yes. Just…"

And he was off, this boy. His mother looked at the dead dog wrapped in the blanket and said, "That was my son. Either he didn't understand or he has no heart."

"You have a vet, don't you?" Avery wiggled his fingers in the small pocket of his suddenly ludicrous running shorts to make sure he had money. Catching sight of his hairy thighs reminded him of the night his sister jumped on him in bed and pulled up the legs of his pajamas so her girlfriend could see that he had *hair*.

He paused then, and for an instant considered simply leaving. Mindy's shrill voice came to mind, and mysterious plaid boxer shorts beneath her bed. He was tired of trying to placate Mindy, tired of restricting his life to fit into the narrowness of her existence, tired of spending entire afternoons watching her shop for shoes. He was tired of apologizing for his taste, tired of swearing he'd shave off his beard. He wanted his beard. He was tired of constructing stories designed to minimize her rage, telling her, "A man went into cardiac arrest," when he wanted to help this sad-eyed, slender woman carry the dog out of the park and into a cab and in the end tell Mindy, "A woman's dog dropped dead."

"Let me help you take the dog to your vet; he'll know what to do."

She turned to face him, revealing her silvery scars, and in the same dismissive tone as her son, said, "*She*."

He rolled the dog in the blanket. While she collected the books and gear that her son had left behind, he hefted the dead weight over his shoulder. Together they walked to Central Park West. "You're awfully kind," she said.

A cab pulled up. They edged themselves into the back of the cab and sat with the dog across their laps. The driver turned sharply, and Avery's hairy thighs brushed against her jeans. He did not think, *woman, wife*, just as he had not thought *boy, son*, when he had seen Jonah, though he'd been taken by his sweetness. They were like strangers on a dark, broken-down train, bound by a job before them, larger and more urgent than anything else.

In the vet's office, they sat beside each other, somewhat apart from the others with their living pets. While a tormented-looking cat glared at them from within his carrying case, she told him about the dead dog. Her son had gotten her at the pound two years before and named her Drinkith to go with Edith, his grandmother's name. She was very sweet, liked popcorn and radishes, preferred Jonah's bed to her own. They'd given her a voice.

Like this: *O! I slept on your bed and smelt your pajamas and drank some* eau d'toilette *and took a walk with her, and she is the most annoying person in the world. She impedes my liberty; she prevents me from eating ketchup and paper, which I love so deeply, I do.*

A terrier peed on the wall, and next on a cowering, shivering poodle.

"'Impedes my liberty'?" Avery asked.

The receptionist called, "Drinkith Sommerfeld?"

"She wasn't well educated but she read a lot," Suzanne told Avery. Then she stood up. "That's us."

Avery carried the corpse into the examining room and deposited it gently on the metal table. The vet asked the same questions Avery had asked earlier, then set out their options: They could leave the dead dog there for disposal by unspecified means. Twenty-five dollars. Or bury her at a pet cemetery. Here the road forked. Coffin and marker—wildly, obscenely expensive. Or common burial in an area of the cemetery marked with a single stone—reasonable.

Suzanne looked wildly around the small room, as if someone familiar would walk through the doorway and help her out. Nobody came, so she conferred with Avery. The coffin seemed a little overboard, but she feared the common grave was disrespectful to their beloved pet, who had been a wonderful dog, and truly Jonah's closest friend, despite his failure to register her death.

Her eyes filled, and Avery put his hand on her shoulder, and asked the vet, "Can you describe the marker for the common grave?"

The vet's assistant handed him a glossy brochure with photos and detailed burial options. Here, the common grave was described as a "shared burial area," thus making it seem as if in afterlife these dogs and cats would live communally, while the other pets in their brass coffins were doomed to solitary confinement.

"I like the spirit of this," Suzanne said.

"So do I," Avery agreed. "And your son can go to the cemetery when he's ready to go, which he will be, in time. It just hasn't sunk in."

Suzanne stepped away and began to cry. The vet's assistant handed Avery a clipboard with a charge slip and murmured, "Here you go, Mr. Sommerfeld." He reached into the tiny pocket in his running shorts and gave her his credit card. A moment later, the transaction was complete. They thanked the vet and went outside.

All these years later, Avery could not recall if it was sunny or not, if they were alone or had stepped onto a crowded street, only that he was sharing an intimate and emotional moment with a woman he'd just met, a moment so powerful that it seemed they had circumvented a whole huge early part of their courtship, the usual getting to know each other part, the "does she like me, will he call" part. They were burying the dog. They were so close that he paid and she cried big silent tears, and they were walking together, Avery with his arm around her shoulder, Suzanne's head against his dreadful stinky shirt. Avery, who had never before seized a moment, said, "Have you eaten? Why don't we get some lunch?" Then, remembering his brief nylon shorts, his hairy thighs and baggy socks, quickly took it back. "I guess that was a stupid idea."

"*I'm* really hungry," Suzanne said. "Do you like Japanese?"

"Japanese. Sure. I like Japanese."

They turned away briefly to make their phone calls. Then Suzanne took Avery to a small, empty restaurant, silent except for water trickling in a fountain he could not see. Later, he liked to tell people that Suzanne used her teeth to tear off the wrapper and split the chopsticks. When he told her he couldn't use chopsticks well—a lie; he couldn't use them at all—she decided that this was the day he would learn and had him shred pieces of the wrapper and practice picking them up. Avery struggled to hold the chopsticks correctly, cursed, defended his dexterity—he who could suture a screaming, writhing kid with perfect little stitches.

The waiter approached. Avery placed their order, and Suzanne said, "He needs a fork."

"No fork," Avery barked.

The waiter flinched. "No fork!" he promised, then quickly backed off.

"I wasn't questioning your manhood," Suzanne said.

In one day, they'd met, they'd buried the dog, they'd had their first quarrel.

After lunch, they left the restaurant and simply began to walk. It was as if walking was what the two of them always did after a late, leisurely meal. Their conversation flowed so effortlessly it would later seem to Avery that he had never talked so much to anyone, had never been so candid. He believed that he told her everything that first afternoon, that by the time they said good night, she knew all of his secrets.

It was hardly the case. Avery didn't tell Suzanne about his failures with women, that, in the end, all of them found him deficient. He didn't tell her that his moment of greatest comfort was when he walked into an examination room and said, "Hello, I'm Dr. Klein."

He never alluded to the loneliness that colored so much of his youth, or the weeping that woke him from deepest sleep on so many nights. "Idyllic" was the word he used to describe his New Jersey town. "A typical fifties boyhood," he said. "Boy Scouts, baseball, girls."

He didn't tell Suzanne that he could counsel adolescent boys with great conviction, could help them understand how complex and fluid the notion of maleness, and at the same time suspect that he, himself, was missing something fundamental that prevented him from being a genuine man.

Nor did he tell her that he spoke to his mother every day, and that her opinion, no matter how ignorant or mean-spirited, burrowed into his brain. He didn't tell her, for instance, that his mother shunned canned black olives, believing they were poison, and that, thereafter, he had always avoided them; further, that he had never questioned this belief until one of the partners from the Spring Street practice, a sarcastic blonde from Macon, Georgia, asked him why he was picking the black olives from his salad, and when he told her they were toxic, she demanded his sources. That was when he realized that he had a separate section in his brain for things his mother told him, walled off, untouched by everything he had learned in later life.

Suzanne skipped over unpleasantness just as deftly, evoking a vision of Connecticut that was made up of a lawn so smooth and green she could somersault from one town to the next. She didn't tell him that her father had moved out when she was five, and that for the next thirteen years, the only evidence that he existed were the boxes he sent at holidays, covered with so much tape she had to struggle with knives and scissors to find the odd gifts inside—forty-eight boys' undershirts one year, and the next a German peasant dress meant for a much smaller child, and a navy woolen beanie with earflaps that snapped beneath the chin, certainly not to be hers.

She didn't tell him that her father found her when she was a junior in college, and began to phone every weekend, that she could not escape his crazy, rambling calls, since he would talk to whoever answered the phone. She didn't say that her stomach knotted up when she heard his loud, hoarse happy-sounding greeting, that he would apologize for the bad connections and say, "It's because I'm calling from Kyoto." Or Santo Domingo. Or Belize City. Or Warsaw. "I'm here for a couple of weeks to meet with Lech Wałęsa about a bandage plant we're planning to build outside Łódź." He'd talk endlessly, never needing a word in response, and then, without warning, offer a word of unasked-for advice, "Don't be a number!" and hang up.

She didn't tell him that she had left school that same year, had one day stuffed some clothes into a duffle bag and without a word to her roommates, moved into an apartment over a marina office, with a man named Charlie François she'd met in a bar; that a year later, after a drunken party where she'd told Charlie François that she was pregnant, he had driven his Jeep off the road and left her on the grass to die.

Of this, all she merely said was that Jonah's father "wasn't in the picture."

It was dark when Suzanne told Avery she thought it was time to go home. When Avery asked how she had ended up in the East Twenties, she laughed and said, "Oh, I've had this place *forever.*"

She didn't tell him that her mother had chosen this ground-floor apartment because it was near a rehabilitation hospital, that after Suzanne had been put back together with pins and screws, Edith had taken her there, leaving her own new husband behind in Connecticut. She didn't tell Avery that during the long months when she lived with her mother, while her belly grew, and her days were spent in outpatient therapy, she felt so broken it seemed as if even her heart had been replaced with a ticking clock.

They stood for a minute outside her building while she scrabbled in her hand-bag for keys. She didn't remind Avery that he had been here before, that he had stood on this sidewalk, had entered this building; that she, herself, had opened the door to this same apartment and showed him to the room where Jonah's nan-ny lay, waxen and glassy-eyed.

Suzanne didn't tell Avery that she had stood in the doorway while he attended to Graça, that she had watched him draw a child-sized chair beside the bed, slowly pull the blanket back, carefully unbutton the top of her flowered nightgown, that when he had placed a stethoscope on Graça's breast, her own eyes had filled with tears, that seeing his gentleness made something glacial break inside her.

She invited him in. Catching what seemed to be her hesitance, he promised he wouldn't stay long.

When Suzanne flipped on the light switch, Avery saw bright artwork covering the walls, dioramas with amazing detail on the windowsills—a forest, a classroom, a space capsule. Mobiles dangled from the ceilings and on the fridge were photos, dried leaves, announcements, and letter magnets. Plants sprouted from milk car-ton bottoms and in paper cups, and in the dog bed, stuffed animals rested in a kind of harmony, a bear in a kangaroo's arms; an anteater nuzzling against a reclining lion. He passed Suzanne's room, paused to see her neatly hung clothing, her shoes lined up, then stepped into Jonah's room. Stars glowed on the ceiling, and there were lava lamps and strands of bulbs shaped like hot peppers and dragonflies.

He did not know that Suzanne had not been alone with a man since Jonah's birth, had not yet spent a night without her son. He saw a home that was full of life and incomplete, and beside him, a woman, who had made this home, whose strength he could see, and whose fragility he sensed, even then. Like a man breath-ing clean air for the first time in decades, he inhaled deeply, filling his chest with its sweetness, and exhaling in a slow, dreamy way. Then he stopped in front of the dog bed, lowered his eyes and said, "And the anteater shall lie with the lion in the kingdom of heaven."

COMING ABOUT

David Busis

When my Grandpa Mory made me stick a screwdriver into an outlet to test it, or climb a ladder with garden shears to get the lemons at the top of his tree, a geological process happened in my stomach. It wasn't fear. It was slower and bigger than fear. Anxiety that was always there—an inheritance from the bookish, neurotic, Eastern European Jews of my father's family—was hard-packed like coal.

After Grandpa died, I only felt that way around one other person: my middle school English teacher *cum* wrestling coach. Coach was as uncompromising on the mat as he was in the classroom. The time I herniated a disk, he looked into my eyes in a way that violated my privacy and told me that he had once wrestled a championship season after chipping a small piece of bone from his spine, and would he see me at practice the next day?

My wrestling opponents were always shorter than me. Their crotches bulged like their biceps, and their pecs strained at their singlets. My singlet fit more like a loose robe. These kids were earnest in their desire to hurt me. My goal was never to win, but to flop around on the mat for a respectable amount of time before they pinned me. I loved the feeling of returning to the bench and retreating into my daydreams.

I daydreamed constantly, about leaping like a grasshopper, crawling up walls like an ant, triggering muscle growth just by thinking about it. My fantasies always played out in a world of kids. I used my powers to save weakling boys and bovine, long-lashed girls from 12-year-old villains. I knew that adults had no need of a hero like me.

In May of 1992 I visited Grandpa Mory in L.A. with my mother. This was a few months before he got sick. I was 11, and the papers were full of stories about the riots, which took place, as far as I was concerned, in a world more distant than that of the books I loved about chivalric warrior mice. My parents had recently finalized the divorce. Nearly every morning Grandpa whisked me away, stonewalling my mother when she asked where we were going.

On this occasion he relented. We were going sailing. My mother kept trying to foist a Ziploc with my EpiPen and extra inhaler on him, but he wouldn't take it. Actually, my mother didn't care. She was only playing the part assigned to her by the men in her life. It was my father who had diagnosed my allergies, and when it came to matters medical, Mom treated Dad like a sassy native might treat a shaman: skeptical but terrified of defying him. Secretly, Mom agreed with Grandpa that my life-threatening allergies to peanuts, cats, and you-name-it were wussy and half-imagined.

I wasn't so sure. My allergies had felt pretty real when Grandpa forgot to mention that the shellfish paella from Fisherman's Wharf had shellfish—when he, in fact, assured me that it had no seafood. While I gasped at the long, slow onset of death by anaphylaxis, Grandpa acted like he was at a boxing match, cheering for me to 'fight it' and 'breathe' before reluctantly taking me to the emergency room.

As for the sailing trip, I was anxious about getting back to the house before dinner. It was my dad's birthday and I had promised to call at seven o'clock Eastern Time. I knew Dad was feeling left out back in Pittsburgh.

Grandpa settled the matter of the Ziploc by encouraging my mother to sit on the inhaler and rotate. Then he donned his captain's cap and handed me the Panama hat. I would have said something myself, but things change when you put on a Panama hat.

Grandpa had this contradictory effect on me. I'm not sure, even now, that I loved him. When he died, I had to make myself cry by imagining my dad's death and then reassigning the emptiness. But sometimes, despite the anxiety, he made me fall in love with myself. Standing beside the old man in the driveway of his ranch house in 90210, inflating my chest, tilting my head up to see my mom underneath the hat's floppy brim, I felt as fearless as any sidekick. Being a sidekick is a comfortable position. You get to share in the glory without any of the pressure.

We climbed into his 1936 Packard Bell convertible; Grandpa let me reach over him to loose a flurry of honks at Mom. She dragged open the iron gate, shaking her head as if she were actually worried—which she should have been. We screamed "Move it! Eat it!" at the cars in front of us all the way to Marina del Rey. In the froth of our excitement we missed the turnoff. I didn't mind. Getting lost with Grandpa was part of the ritual, and in my mind it made him more legendary.

The boat was called the *Morarn*, named after Grandpa Mory and his brother Arnie, who was dead. By the time we got there it was already 10. Grandpa rushed through a refresher on the rigging for me. He was an awful teacher. His lessons consisted mostly of one-word explanations:

"Mainsail, jibing, jib, tacking. Working sheet, winch. Questions?"

The correct answer was "No."

We had a hell of a time coming out of the marina. The channel was narrow and the wind was already up. Grandpa stood at the helm and bellowed commands over the water, though I was standing right behind him.

"Ready about! Hard-a-lee! No, a-lee you schmuck! Scratch that—Jibe hoooo!"

I scurried around, pulling lines almost at random. I couldn't help remembering my dad's reaction when I told him we had gone sailing a week ago. Dad said Jews didn't sail. Sailing was something WASPs did. He explained that WASPs also hunted and refinished their porches, whereas Jews hired other people to change their light bulbs. It was true: I was a terrible sailor. Things I was good at included school and oral hygiene.

We somehow navigated the channel and immediately caught a brisk westerly. The wind was pugnacious. It knocked my hat off and sent whitecaps skittering across the sea. Grey, brainy clouds covered the sun. I didn't feel cold, but goose bumps prickled up my arms. As the sloop lurched up to speed I wanted to hurl.

"If the wind holds we'll make it to Catalina before dark!" crowed Grandpa.

Catalina?

"Shouldn't we be back for dinner?"

He didn't answer. He made me feel the smallness of my worries just by squaring himself to the horizon and giving me his back. I stared, as I always did, at his calves. They were straggled with inky blue veins, glistening and tan, so big that they looked like fire extinguishers. The man had suffered his first heart attack at 26 and lifted weights ever since. On this visit, he had started taking me into his garage gym, nodding in approval as I strained to bench press 100 pounds. I always ended up pinned to the bench. He never helped me lift the bar. He thought the struggle built character.

Mom never said anything, but she approved of this. She worried that Dad was having a negative influence on my manliness, which made Grandpa Mory a corrective. For months she'd been keeping careful track of my puberty, and when it was her turn to pick up the carpool after school, she said things like, "Logan, you're getting some nice tufts coming in on those legs!" then nudged me in the front seat, as if I should take a hint.

The sky kept darkening. I was sure it would rain. I hugged myself—a gesture intended both for me and for Grandpa—and calculated how long it would take to get home.

I let my teeth chatter. "Should we turn around?" I asked, doing my best to sound like a suffering orphan.

"Turn around? It's a beautiful morning!" He pointed to a cloud blooming with orange. "Hello cloud. How are you today? Why are you standing in front of the sun?"

He lolled his hand in the spritz lapping the gunwales. "Hello water! Thanks for the lift."

This was a game we played each morning in his garden. He woke me up at seven so we could say hello to the plants. We whispered to the bluebells, so languid and wet that they seemed almost inappropriate. We bellowed up the eucalyptus, joked in Marx Brothers' voices with the cucumbers, and serenaded the tomato plants with "Volare." The game had an autonomic effect on me. I fought against my smile.

Seeing that he almost had me, Grandpa pretended to scan the water. "Hello sharks! Stay away from me today. I have a pastrami sandwich and I know how to use it!" He undid his pants and peered down. "Hello pecker." Then he did a double take. "Pecker! Why are you hiding?"

I couldn't help it. I spilled laughter like an over-boiling pot.

He rewarded me with a grin. It was a great grin, a non-negotiable grin, the one he used to schmooze the lady in the fudge store into giving me so many free samples that we didn't end up buying anything. It was the grin he used to charm the cop who wanted to kick me off the corner of Rodeo Drive, where I was selling Grandpa's lemons and running the profits back to Grandpa, who waited in his Lincoln Town Car like a pimp. It was a grin you earned by surviving heart failure at 26 and going on to live like an idiot.

He bathed me in his grin. I saw how quixotic it would be to defy it. "Hello wind!" I shouted. 'Stop trying to knock off my hat! And stop trying to make me cold!'

"Hello horizon!" he shouted. "Hold your horses. We're getting there!"

I inhaled, smelling the ancient, musky brine smell. "Hello ocean!"

He turned back towards the shore. "Goodbye Los Angeles! Goodbye traffic up the wazoo!"

"Goodbye EpiPens!" I shouted. "Goodbye inhaler!"

"Goodbye nagging mother!" shouted Grandpa. "Goodbye nagging wife!"

I racked my brain for what else we were leaving behind, and then it came to me: Dad. Theoretically, I had left him behind a week and a half ago, when we arrived in L.A., but the guilt of leaving him had made me think of him constantly. Now I was really leaving him behind, putting him out of electronic touch—on his birthday, no less.

My dad was lonely and insecure, and this made him invest occasions like his birthday with great, nearly eschatological meaning. He saw every celebration as a final test of my loyalty and love. Not calling him would have devastated him. I couldn't have articulated that at the time, but I intuited it.

Mentioning Dad, however, would break the unspoken pact of my game with Grandpa. So I pushed him out of my mind and grasped for phrases I had overhead lately. "Goodbye riots!" I shouted. "Goodbye angry *schvartza*!"

Grandpa raised his eyebrow at me. He turned again and howled in a long, game-ending yawp, "Hello Catalina!" But it was too late to avert whatever destiny I had called down upon us. We heard the speedboat before we saw it.

"Stinkpot!" we shouted together.

He had me trained. Later, Mom told me that the original *Morarn* was itself a speedboat. Grandpa had purchased it in the early '70s, when doctors and dentists still took Wednesdays off to get on the water. As soon as Grandpa learned that the gentiles at the Marina referred to anything with an engine as a "stinkpot," he had traded-in for the sloop. He couldn't sail it, but no matter: he was not going to be outdone by the *goyim*.

We turned around and saw the speedboat drifting towards us. A black man with a shaved head and sunglasses sat at the wheel. His scalp was wet with light. Another man, less dark—a honeyed walnut color—smoked a cigarette on the bench. He had a big afro. I had never seen an afro. His arm was draped around a girl with short wavy hair that shimmered with gel. She sipped a beer.

The speedboat drifted alongside ours

"Howdy!" said Grandpa.

Afro stared at us and smoked. The girl nuzzled her lips against his neck.

"You called us what?" he said. His voice was soft and wonderfully smooth, almost hypnotic. "Stinkers?"

"'I was talking to my grandson."

I shook my head. I didn't want to be implicated in this. I was afraid of these men—not just because they were black, but because I already sensed their calm, assured malice, their predator's game. In retrospect, I'm sure they meant to let us go after giving us a little scare.

Afro shook his head slowly, as if disappointed in a child. Mr. Sunglasses stared straight ahead. He wore a white tank top and I could see the contours of his arm muscles. He was so still and plastic-y that he looked like a mannequin.

"Fine day for a cruise, eh?" said Grandpa.

Afro seemed to consider this seriously as he smoked. "Fine day," he said. "Few boats."

"Yes sir," said Grandpa. Without taking his eyes off Afro, he fished around in the cooler at his feet. "Yes sir, yes sir."

Afro sucked his cigarette.

"Ain't you got nothing to say now?"

Grandpa came up with a sandwich and started peeling off the foil. His hand fumbled. "You boys hungry? Best pastrami in town."

The wind gusted and our boat gave a polite little bow to the speedboat.

Afro said, "Do I look like I'm begging?"

"No," said Grandpa. And to me he muttered: "Not yet."

Mr. Sunglasses swiveled his massive head towards Grandpa. I moved away from Grandpa imperceptibly.

"Couple of black boys on a nice boat," said Afro. "Makes a man wonder how they got the money."

The girl spoke up. "I'm cold, Lonnie. Quit playin'."

Her words evaporated without a response. Afro stared at us. Mr. Sunglasses smiled at me.

Until that moment, I had been dreaming about saving the day. I would look at the ground, quiet and unassuming. Just when I was most needed, I would jump onto their speedboat and knock out the bad guys with cartoonish "Pow!" sounds. But the smile skewered me. I felt caught. My breathing quickened.

"I can't tell," said Afro, without turning to Mr. Sunglasses. "These look like the ones that beat Rodney King? They all look the same to me."

Mr. Sunglasses shook his head. I couldn't tell if he was saying "No," or if he was expressing his deep regret about us, about everything.

Grandpa cleared his throat. When Afro looked at him, Grandpa looked down and thumped his chest twice.

"Rodney King?" Grandpa said. "Not us. I think you're looking for Hymie and Mordechai. They're on the other boat." He nudged me with his elbow.

"You're a funny man," observed Afro. He took one more lingering drag before flicking his cigarette into our boat. I stared at the butt, still smoldering. It seemed as if that butt were significant. It seemed as if I had to do something, say something, save us in real life, before the ember extinguished.

I raised my hand as if I were in class, realized what I was doing, and put it down. "I think maybe there was a misunderstanding," I said, unable to meet Afro's eye. "We always shout 'stinkpot' at motorboats."

Afro gave me a cockeyed glance. "Boy, what the fuck are you talking about?"

"Don't talk to my grandson like that," said Grandpa.

"Easy, old man."

"Fucking *schvartza*," muttered Grandpa.

"Really?" said Afro, squinting at Grandpa. "Really really?"

He grabbed the steering wheel over Mr. Sunglasses' shoulder, pulled the throttle, and rammed his boat into ours. He didn't hit us hard, but our sloop was light and we rocked violently.

Grandpa dropped his sandwich and grabbed the mast.

The motorboat gunned off, turned around, and came hurtling back at us.

Grandpa yelled "Down!" as he yanked the starboard working-sheet off its winch, but I didn't know what he meant, and when the boom swung across the deck it caught me in the shoulder. Grandpa grabbed me as I staggered towards the side, then stumbled himself. The boom came at us again and suddenly he was overboard. I was too surprised to react. The motorboat stopped and turned until it pointed at Grandpa. He was treading water, spitting it out of his mouth.

The speedboat came ripping at Grandpa. I screamed. My sloop was moving away from him, but before I could think about it, the speedboat veered left and I heard them laughing as they motored off.

When Grandpa climbed back onto the boat, dripping like a swamp creature, his teeth clacking like bewitched maracas, he made a crack about it being a shame to waste good pastrami. I didn't smile.

He punched me on the arm. He spoke as if something hilarious and expected had happened, as if he had been sitting above a dunk tank at a carnival. Finally he raised his eyebrows and whispered, "Remember the Alamo." Then he said it louder, and louder. I joined his chant, but even when we were screaming "Remember the Alamo!" I only pretended to feel roused.

A silence descended that lasted until Catalina. Grandpa shivered at the prow; he seemed small, now, in his flannel. I worked the rigging without the benefit of his commands. The clouds rolled away, but the late-afternoon sunlight was like an afterthought, vague and sapped of its power to warm. I still wanted to go home, but I was no longer keeping quiet because I was afraid he would refuse. I was keeping quiet because I was afraid he would agree. He was no longer taking me: I was going for him.

When Grandpa finally shouted "Land ho!" I felt enormous relief—so much so that I mistook the feeling for exhilaration. I called Dad from the hotel phone in Catalina, and the story became swashbuckling in my retelling. We had stood up to Afro with a doomed fortitude, then sailed to Catalina like Aeneas on his way to Italy (my mother had made me read the *Aeneid* in translation that year), bested but not smashed, our fate beckoning.

"I'm confused," said Dad. "I thought you were planning on being back in the afternoon."

He couldn't keep the hurt out of his voice. I remembered that I was supposed to call him at 6 o'clock his time. It was midnight in Pittsburgh.

"Well," I said.

And then I went through the story again, letting him guide me with "Oh's" and "I see's." This time I gave him to understand that I had been cold, nervous, and allergic—not to mention frustrated that I couldn't call him. Grandpa's stubbornness and impetuosity had endangered us both. Now I was anxious about the return trip.

In the end I ruined my good mood, sacrificed my adventure, and betrayed my grandpa for him. But it was nothing. I would have done anything not to feel the guilt of hurting him.

And yet—there was a moment I didn't tell him about.

It was right after Grandpa fell overboard. My sloop drifted through the water, steadily forsaking the old man where he treaded. The sound of Afro's speedboat faded slowly. For an instant I imagined playing out the sails, luffing anywhere, finding an island and living like Robinson Crusoe. I would lie down when I got sleepy, fish when I got hungry. I would leave my Grandpa sputtering in the water, leave my father sputtering on the other end of a continent.

It wasn't the improbability of finding an island, or of surviving for even a day, that pierced my fantasy. It was a detail: I was allergic to seafood. I could never live like Robinson Crusoe. I would choke to death on my own swollen face as soon as I tried to eat the fish I had caught. And as I gave up the fantasy, my grandfather caught my attention again. He was dwarfed by the ocean, thrashing terribly. I sighed. Then I grabbed the line and brought the ship about—not because I was some kind of hero, but because he needed me anyway.

THIS IS WHEN I LOVE YOU THE MOST

Marjorie Celona

After Thea falls asleep, Bobbie sneaks into Mr. Radcliffe's office. She finds an ashtray on his desk and pulls a cigarette from her cardigan. Mr. Radcliffe told her at dinner that he owned 4,000 novels, kept in alphabetical order by author, in special bookshelves made of birch and pine. When Bobbie asked for the pepper, she called him "Sir," and he laughed and told her, "Mr. Radcliffe will do just fine." He finished his dinner quickly, kissed Thea and Mrs. Radcliffe on the cheek, and left the house without an umbrella or a hat, although it was pouring rain.

"Swims 12 laps every night with his friend," Mrs. Radcliffe said and scooped another piece of quiche onto Bobbie's plate. "Then they drink."

Mr. Radcliffe's bookshelves reach the ceiling and are lit with halogens. The top shelves are filled with pottery and small lamps, a slinky made of brown paper, two egg-shaped rocks. He has the World Book collection but Bobbie hasn't heard of the other books, all of them hardcover. She runs her finger over *Sexing the Cherry*. On the floor, a banker's box filled with paperbacks says 'Sort and File' in careful cursive on the side. Someone flushes a toilet upstairs and Bobbie holds her breath, stubs out the cigarette and hides the filter in her hand. She sits in Mr. Radcliffe's ladder-backed chair and looks through the bills on his desk. They owe $400 to the gas company and Mr. Radcliffe has already made out a check. It is attached to the bill with a paperclip. Mr. Radcliffe is a trust lawyer. He works in a white office building on Rock Bay Road, in the same building as Bobbie's dentist.

The Radcliffe house looks like Bobbie's, which is next door. The two homes were registered in 1912 and Bobbie's mother mistakes that for being the year they were built—they could have been built any year—1879, 1901. Pitched roofs, newel posts, steep stairs, little doors—people were smaller then, Bobbie heard somewhere. Bobbie likes the doors. She likes to duck her head. The Radcliffes keep neat hedges. Their home is two stories and grey with dark green trim and a black door. Some things need fixing: the porch, the balcony, a few missing shingles. They're old houses; they lean and creak.

Bobbie is staying with the Radcliffes for a week while her mother is in Daytona. The Radcliffes are their landlords. The Radcliffes' only daughter, Thea, is a private-school girl who comes home at 3:30 and does her homework until 5:30, then practices the clarinet until she's called for dinner. She eats quietly, without scraping her fork across the large white plates that Mrs. Radcliffe warns are hot from the oven. Thea sets her alarm for 7:41 and is in the shower by 7:50 and ready for school by 8:15. She has shapely, athletic legs and a strong jaw, pale brown freckles and white blonde hair. She has an oval face and milky skin, Mr. Radcliffe's flat nose and Mrs. Radcliffe's cheekbones. Tiny eyes like she's finding fault. While Thea is in the shower, Bobbie pulls on her jeans and sweatshirt and turns her socks inside out so she can wear them again. She sits at the edge of the bed and pretends to do her hair, fiddles in her suitcase for an imaginary makeup kit.

"Mascara's on the dresser," says Thea, in a big white towel. She stands in front of her full-length mirror with her eyes closed and tugs her hair into two French braids. She takes her uniform into the bathroom and shuts the door half way.

Thea's bedroom is painted navy blue with gold stars. Thea says her mother did it last year with a stencil kit and a can of spray paint. She has an antique wrought-iron bed frame with a feather bed, white sheets with gold trim. The room's ceiling is sloped and has a window seat, where Mrs. Radcliffe set up a small foamie and sleeping bag for Bobbie the first night she arrived. She said it was where all of Thea's friends slept when they stayed the night.

"We're happy to have you here," she said to Bobbie and transferred one of Thea's bears onto Bobbie's pillow. "You're no trouble. I wouldn't want Thea alone in our house, either."

Bobbie shrugged. She and her mother had argued for days over staying with the Radcliffes. Bobbie's mother said she didn't trust Bobbie not to throw parties and make a big mess if she were home alone. "Your key. Hand over your key," her mother said, and rolled her suitcase to the curb. "Be nice to those people. Be gracious. For God's sake, be a good girl."

"I have to go soon," Thea calls to Bobbie. She steps out of the bathroom with her tie in her hand. She wears peach blush and two smudges of black eyeliner. Her kilt is hemmed above the knee and when she dips to get her backpack, Bobbie sees the white of her thighs. "I'll be home at 3:30."

Bobbie watches through the window as Thea runs out the front door and down the stairs, where Mrs. Radcliffe is sitting in the Saab with the heated seats, the engine idling, already warm.

While Thea is at school, Bobbie crawls under the hedge that separates the Radcliffes' house from hers and slides her library card under the window of her mother's bedroom. She pushes it open with her other hand. She turns over the garbage can and lifts herself up and through the window, knocking over the porcelain figurine of the tortoiseshell cat her mother keeps on the sill. She walks to the hall telephone and erases the messages to her mother telling her that she has been absent from school and makes a peanut butter sandwich. She can see her breath. She pulls the blinds and watches "Wheel of Fortune" on the La-Z-Boy. She leafs through the mail and lets it drop back to the floor.

Her mother's bed is unmade. Bobbie climbs under the covers and smells the pillowcases. White Diamonds by Elizabeth Taylor and the faint apricot of her mother's new mousse. She rolls onto her back and looks at the tops of her breasts, the hard crease from the underwire in her bra. She lifts her shirt and watches her nipples grow in the cold.

Cal. Mr. Radcliffe's first name is Cal. Bobbie finds his name funny because there's nothing to it. Mrs. Radcliffe calls him Cally. Her first name is Isadora. Cal is balding. He's a Jehovah's Witness. Bobbie's mother says that Mrs. Radcliffe is Episcopalian. "Everyone needs to find their niche," her mother says. "Jehovah's Witnesses are good at making people who feel they don't belong anywhere in the world feel that they belong perfectly." Bobbie tries to imagine if Mr. Radcliffe used to be a handsome man. Sometimes she can tell by the back of a man's head whether he was handsome in his youth. Mr. Radcliffe was thin and immature, she decides. He wore glasses as a child and had blond hair.

Last night, Bobbie asked Thea how old she was and Thea said, "13," and Bobbie calculated that Mrs. Radcliffe would have been 42 when she had Thea because she had read in Mrs. Radcliffe's journal that she was going to be 55 in June:

That's the problem with living here all my life: I am born and Cal has already been born and we both get jobs and move away—Cal first—but our parents die and so we inherit the houses and move back and everyone else has changed on our street, even the houses have changed, so many are duplexes now, but here I am, the same, and me and Dorothy swap recipes and I have her over for tea and when Cal goes swimming I draw the blinds and sit with my back straight, my butt half off the arm of the couch, my bare feet perched on the floor of this godforsaken room . . .

Bobbie's house is brown and beige. Mr. Radcliffe repainted it for them last summer. The same brown, same beige. When Bobbie and her mother moved in, he put in wall-to-wall carpet (to save the hardwood, he said) and took out the stained glass window in the front door, which he put in his basement. The walls are stark white. They have a two-year lease. Bobbie's mother is a psychiatric nurse but is on disability for a frozen shoulder. She has a cortisone shot every two months and says it does nothing.

"What if I can't ever go back to work?" she says to Bobbie when her shoulder hurts. "You might have to find your own way."

Both Bobbie and her mother like cats and have porcelain figurines of them on every surface. At night they watch "Jeopardy" in the living room and talk about getting a fish or a guinea pig. Bobbie's mother shuts the door to her bedroom and calls her boyfriend in Daytona and leaves Bobbie with the television set. She turns down the volume so she can listen to her mother, who laughs and then says, "You always say that."

At 3:00, Bobbie smoothes the covers on her mother's bed, puts away the peanut butter, and turns off the TV. She parts the blinds in the living room with her fingers and watches Mr. Radcliffe pull into his driveway with a new car—a dark blue convertible with a white racing stripe. Mrs. Radcliffe is waiting for him on the front steps with her arms out, as if she's about to catch a ball.

Mr. Radcliffe gets out of the car like an old man. He wears cargo shorts and a black short-sleeved shirt with a grey collar. His socks are pulled to the knee. Mrs. Radcliffe scurries over in heeled sandals, and they embrace. Bobbie watches Mrs. Radcliffe open the door to the new car and run her hand over the upholstery. Her hair is dyed light red and has been flat-ironed. It is chin length, but short in the back like a boy's. She wears a blue kimono jacket and capri pants. She whispers something to Mr. Radcliffe and he shakes his head, waves his hand.

Bobbie climbs out the window, slides it shut, and replaces the garbage can. She crawls under the hedge and waits until neither Mr. nor Mrs. Radcliffe is looking, then skips across the lawn. "Hi. I'm back."

"Bobbie." Mr. Radcliffe points to the car. "Mercury hardtop. '63. Like it?"

Bobbie looks at his hair, grey and white, a big bald spot at the back, and his small eyes, his flat nose. "Mom and I had a classic car calendar last year," she says. "Our favorite was the Ford Fairlane."

"Nice car. Year?"

"Oh. I don't know."

Mr. Radcliffe squints and walks around the side of the house. He reappears with an electric lawn mower, drags it onto the front lawn, and starts fighting with a bright orange electrical cord that has twisted itself like a king cobra. "Give me a hand?" he calls.

Bobbie steps forward. "Yes, sir."

"Mr. Radcliffe."

"Yes, Mr. Radcliffe." She reaches for one end of the cord and the two of them untangle, loop, and straighten the cord until it lies in a neat coil at their feet. Mrs. Radcliffe sits in the passenger seat of the Mercury, flexing her calves and watching the muscles move. The afternoon sun is hot and the lawn is muddy from last night's rain. Bobbie's mother wouldn't mow the lawn if it were wet. "Rusts the mower," she'd say.

Mr. Radcliffe plugs in the cord and adjusts the height of the mower. "Good time at school?"

"We went on a field trip," says Bobbie. She nudges the electrical cord with her foot. "To the zoo."

"Lucky girl." Mr. Radcliffe winks.

Bobbie watches the back of Mrs. Radcliffe's head as she drives. She can see a spot where the hair dye stained Mrs. Radcliffe's skin. It's small, on the hairline. She told Bobbie she sometimes works as an interior decorator, but only when she gets bored. She is 10 pounds overweight and has a manicure. Her nails are pink and an inch long. Bobbie's mother likes to make fun of her. She says that all Mrs. Radcliffe needs are a pair of white sunglasses and a headscarf.

"Bet we'll be getting a call from your mother soon," Mrs. Radcliffe says. "Must be having the time of her life." She drives with one hand on the wheel, looks in the rearview when she talks to Bobbie.

"She'll send a postcard." Bobbie takes off her sweatshirt and wads it up beside her. The wind blows through her thin undershirt. One of her bra straps slips off her shoulder and she watches Mrs. Radcliffe raise her eyebrow in the rearview.

"How old are you, Bobbie?"

"Seventeen." Bobbie clears her throat. "I failed grades six and nine." She feels a sense of pride when she says this, as if it's a swear word.

"Smart girl like you?"

"We lived an hour away from school. Two hours if the bus was late." She doesn't feel like explaining any more than that, the hurried rush out the door, her mother forgetting to give her bus fare, the apologies, the phone calls. *We're doing the best we can.*

The '63 Meteor smells like vinyl. It has cream-colored bench seats and a big black and silver steering wheel. Mrs. Radcliffe stops, and the car hiccups when she puts it in park.

Thea's private school is a brick building with stone steps and a fancy columned entrance. She and the other girls sit and wait for their parents in small groups. A girl whose kilt is longer than the other girls' sits by herself reading a book, but Bobbie can't make out the title. Thea is braiding a chubby girl's hair. She looks up, frowns at the new car, and shouts something in their direction. Her shirt is untucked and her tie is thrown over her shoulder. Some of her hair comes loose and flies around her face in soft white wisps. Bobbie wonders if she knows that she is beautiful.

"Would you get Thea?" says Mrs. Radcliffe. She taps her pink nail on the steering wheel.

Bobbie opens the car door and walks toward Thea and the girls. "Hi, Thea."

The chubby girl looks at her outfit. Thea drops the girl's braid and it unravels. "She's staying with us for like a week," she says.

"Gawd." The girl takes a tube of gloss from her pocket and rubs it over her lips.

"My mom's in Florida," says Bobbie. She looks at the girl's shoes. They have small heels and pointed toes, a buckle.

"West Palm Beach?" she says to Bobbie.

"Daytona."

"Let's go." Thea grabs her backpack and jogs to the Meteor. "Nice car, Mom. Come on, Bobbie."

Thea gets in the front seat and rolls down her window. She sits tall, her back rigid. She smells like skin lotion.

"Ice cream?" Mrs. Radcliffe swings the car around and accelerates hard.

Thea looks back at Bobbie. "Not for me."

Every night is the same: Mrs. Radcliffe carries the warm plates with oven mitts and sets them in front of Thea, Bobbie, and Mr. Radcliffe. They take turns telling one another about their day. Thea complains about needing new runners for gym class and Mrs. Radcliffe tells them she went to Dorothy's for tea and received an email about a consulting job for a couple who own a ranch.

"We went on a field trip today," says Bobbie. "To the planetarium."

Mrs. Radcliffe tilts her head and looks at her.

"That's some school," says Mr. Radcliffe. "Thea? Want to go to public school? It's only a block away."

Thea narrows her eyes at Bobbie. She moves her food around on her plate and chews longer than anyone Bobbie has ever met. While they eat, she takes her hair out of the French braids and rubs her scalp, then twists it up into a bun. Her neck is long, graceful.

"Spent the morning in meetings," Mr. Radcliffe says. "Afternoon, Jim stopped by and we played a few rounds."

The Radcliffes' dining room is the same size as in Bobbie's house, but they have nicer furniture. The table is black and shiny and has a gold runner. They have black velvet chairs and heavy drapes. The walls are off-white and decorated with pen-and-ink drawings in ornate frames—a tennis shoe, a woman with her arms around a giraffe. The hardwood has been stained steel blue. Bobbie dislikes the cutlery, which is fancy and difficult to eat with. Her soup spoon is shaped like a miniature ladle and the handle tapers to a fine, sharp point.

"'Bout that time." Mr. Radcliffe kisses the top of Thea's head and squeezes Mrs. Radcliffe's shoulder. He winks at Bobbie and leaves the room. Bobbie listens as he jangles his keys in his pocket, opens the front door, and locks it behind him.

"Good night, everybody," he calls.

Thea puts on her pajamas in the bathroom, then stands in the doorframe rubbing a cotton ball over her face. "Want some?" She holds out the cotton ball to Bobbie.

Bobbie sits on the window seat, her legs over the edge. She tugs her t-shirt so it covers more of her thighs.

Thea walks toward her in a silk camisole and yellow pajama pants. "It's witch hazel. It will help." She leans over Bobbie and rubs it on her forehead, brushes her long bangs out of her eyes. It feels cold and slimy on her skin. It stings. "I'll cut your hair for you tomorrow. If you want."

Bobbie zips open the sleeping bag and moves Thea's teddy bear to the floor. She watches Thea arrange her pillows in a neat stack behind her head and tuck the comforter under her arms. She can hear Mrs. Radcliffe cleaning the kitchen downstairs, the soft hum from the dishwasher, some music playing. The phone rings and Mrs. Radcliffe says something, then starts to come up the stairs.

"Bobbie?" She taps lightly on Thea's door. "Thea? Bobbie? Can I come in?"

"Yep." Thea yawns and looks at Bobbie.

Mrs. Radcliffe stands in the doorway, an apron tied around her waist and her hair behind her ears. There's a wet spot on her shirt and Bobbie can see through to her skin, the bottom of her bra. "Your mother is on the phone."

"Okay. Thanks." Bobbie climbs out of the sleeping bag and follows Mrs. Radcliffe down to the kitchen. It is dark except for the fan hood light over the range. The telephone is on the wall at the end of a long row of counter space. They have stainless steel appliances, a black fridge. A stack of paper and two pencils sit on the counter, a grocery list, half a loaf of rye bread. A potted plant has taken over much of the kitchen, its vines reaching to the ceiling, around the windows, to the floor. Thea told her it was a hoya, that when it bloomed, its flowers looked like they were made of marzipan.

Bobbie picks up the phone, and Mrs. Radcliffe looks at her watch and leaves the room. "Mom?"

"How're things?" Her mother's voice is loud, animated. A man is talking in the background. She can hear music, maybe slot machines or arcade games.

"It's kind of late," Bobbie whispers, cups the phone with her hand. "Where are you?"

"In the hotel bar. It's only midnight, Bob. It's not that late. How's school?"

"Fine." Bobbie wraps the phone cord around her finger until the tip turns dark.

"Okay, good. Good. Good. Hey, got you something. You'll like it. It's hot here. Hot. Are you taking care of yourself? Are Cal and Isadora being okay?"

"It's fine. Mom, hold on." Bobbie presses the phone to her chest and listens as Mr. Radcliffe's car pulls up to the house and the engine shuts off. She brings the phone back to her ear and listens to the sound of the hotel bar in the background. Someone is talking to her mother about the price of gas. "I didn't bring enough underwear, Mom. Or socks."

Bobbie's mother coughs into the phone. "I asked you if you'd packed right. Borrow some from the girl."

'She's a lot smaller.'

"For Christ's sake, Bobbie. Okay, okay. Come on, talk to me. Miss you. What have you been doing?"

"Nothing. They bought a new car. They have a nicer house than we do." Bobbie listens as Mr. Radcliffe turns his key in the lock and opens the front door. From the window in the kitchen, she can see his reflection in the foyer. She cradles the phone in her neck and pulls her t-shirt down as far as it will go. Mr. Radcliffe nudges off his shoes, puts his keys on the hutch.

Bobbie's mother takes a sip of something and Bobbie hears the ice cubes clink around in the glass. "Listen for a sec. I need you to put Isadora on."

"I don't know where she is. She went to bed."

"I need to talk to her."

Bobbie watches Mr. Radcliffe switch on the light to his office and close the door. She takes a deep breath. "Can't you call tomorrow?"

"I can't, Bobbie. Don got us this suite for two more days, he wants to stay. There's some big greyhound race this weekend. He wants to catch it. We have to call the airline."

"I thought you were coming home Friday." Bobbie picks up a pencil and draws a spiral on the grocery list. She reaches for the hoya and fingers its waxy leaves.

"Monday. Tuesday. We'll see. I need to talk to Isadora, make sure it's okay."

Bobbie digs her toe into the cold hardwood floor. "You can't ask people to do something like that. It's not polite."

"Bobbie?" Mr. Radcliffe flicks on the kitchen light and puts his hand on the counter. His hair has been combed in dark rows across his scalp and his cheeks are flushed. He is wearing brown slippers and a black tracksuit and his eyes are smaller than usual, tired and bloodshot.

Bobbie puts the phone on the counter. "It's my mother. Can—can I?"

"I'll talk to her," Mr. Radcliffe takes the phone and pats Bobbie's shoulder. "Go put on a housecoat. It's cold down here."

Mr. Radcliffe lights a cigarette and drums his fingers over his checkbook. He flips through a stack of bills and takes a long drag, ashes into a triangular marble ashtray. His office is dark except for the backlit bookshelves and a small amount of light from the window and a few passing cars.

Bobbie watches him bring the cigarette to his lips. His hair has started to dry and is sticking up in small bunches around his head. His tracksuit is unzipped in the front and Bobbie can see the hollow of his neck, red and freckled with a patch of white hair. He has a pale-colored mole above his left eye, right under his eyebrow. It looks heavy, like it's pulling on his eyelid. He licks his lips every time he takes a drag. "I left home when I was 16," he says.

Mr. Radcliffe has framed photographs of Mrs. Radcliffe and Thea on the wall behind him. Two of the photographs are black and white: a grainy picture of a boy riding a pony and a young couple holding a baby in front of a fire truck. In the photographs of Mrs. Radcliffe, she has long brown hair and wears large circular glasses. She is chubbier than she is now and laughing. Next to it is a picture of the back of a naked man with hair to his shoulders, his arms raised above his head, a clear blue lake beneath him.

"We grew up together," Mr. Radcliffe says and motions to a picture of Isadora. "She in this house and I in the one you and your mother live now. Both only children. Our parents were friends."

Bobbie rubs her feet together and shoves her hands under her thighs. The thin housecoat she found in Thea's bathroom is magenta and made of fleece. It has pink flowers embroidered on the pockets and a hood. She looks at her toenails, the dirt caked in at the edges. Her ankles have deep ridges where her socks held too tight.

Mr. Radcliffe opens his checkbook and fingers a cream-colored check. "On my 15th birthday, my father died of smoke inhalation. He was a fireman, like his father. It's what he wanted me to be. My mother had six brothers and sisters and spent her childhood looking after them instead of going to school. She was dyslexic. She was always cold. When my father died, she got a job as a social worker and started drinking vodka with breakfast. The neighborhood wasn't the same back then. It's nice now, a lot has changed. It was harder then. This was a working class neighborhood, a lot of immigrants. I walked Isadora to school every day. You didn't want to make eye contact with anyone. Isadora's family had a lot more money than we did, but they hid it well. Her father owned the bookstore on 12th and made an okay living, but it was her mother who came from money, old money, family money. These books are mostly her father's. Isadora didn't want them. She was never much of a reader." Mr. Radcliffe runs his hand over the marble ashtray, works the ash between his fingers. He closes his checkbook, stubs out his cigarette and lights another. "I don't know what to do with the paperbacks. They never look as nice on the shelves."

Bobbie inhales deeply, tries to suck in some of the smoke. "I think you have a very nice life," she says.

"I applied and was accepted to a boarding school on full scholarship for my final years of high school, Bobbie. Left my mother to sort herself out. I was no use to her. After that it was law school and the city, and I didn't come back except to visit at Christmas. My mother did okay. She met a woman about her age and the two of them lived together in the house—always wanted to ask her if they were, you know, lesbians, but I never found the words. We were close, but there were things we never discussed. Her drinking. My father. When she died, I came back to sort out her affairs and Isadora's parents had died a few years before and she was living back here—we'd lost touch over the years. I'd been married in my twenties. Isadora has been married twice. She has a son who's going to medical school in Ireland; he's about 33 now. Lives with his father over there. Nice folks."

"My father is Scottish," says Bobbie. "He and my mom lived together for a year."

Mr. Radcliffe takes a toothpick from a little jar on his desk and picks his teeth. "Do you see him?"

"Used to." Bobbie's eye is watering. She wonders if Thea is asleep.

Mr. Radcliffe offers Bobbie a mint and she takes it. "I've let everyone down, Bobbie."

He stands and walks to the bookshelf. He takes down one of the egg-shaped rocks and twists it. It opens in two halves. "When my father died, I found a three-page letter in his glove compartment. He was about to leave us. The letter was well-written, carefully written. He was lonely, he said. He was going to take an apartment. My mother and father used to come into my room at night and stand over my bed. I had the bedroom at the top of the hall, your room. My mother would rub my back and whisper, *This is when I love you the most.* She said it every night and then they would shut the door to my room. It was my favorite moment of the day." Mr. Radcliffe takes out the letter, blows away some dust and puts it back into the container. He replaces it on the shelf. "I keep things, and I don't know why I keep them."

Mr. Radcliffe runs his hand over his face. "I'm leaving, Bobbie. I've met someone else." A door shuts and someone walks down the stairs, each stair creaking loudly in the still house. Bobbie rolls the mint around in her mouth and looks at Mr. Radcliffe. He faces the bookshelf, his shoulders hunched.

"Hi." Mrs. Radcliffe pushes the office door gently with her shoulder. "It's late." Her bathrobe is white terrycloth with navy stripes. She has cream on her face and her hair is wrapped in a peach towel.

Mr. Radcliffe turns to her. "Hi."

Thea is asleep when Bobbie comes into her bedroom and zips herself into the sleeping bag. Her hair smells like cigarette smoke. She is cold from being downstairs and wraps the housecoat tight around her body. The blinds are slightly open and Bobbie can make out the shape of her house, their backyard, a telephone pole. Thea is breathing in noisy, short breaths. She has her teddy bear in her arms.

Nothing about the house is like her own. It smells musty and of furniture polish. The walls are complicated by ornate trim and fancy framed paintings. Some of the antiques look cheap. Twice she's heard the scuttle of mice in the attic; the ancient floorboards are scratched and worn. Bobbie pushes her hair behind her ears and listens as Mr. and Mrs. Radcliffe come up the stairs, their footsteps heavy and slow. Bobbie sees their shadows at the bottom of the door. Mrs. Radcliffe opens it and looks into the small room. She walks in and shuts the door behind her, glancing at Mr. Radcliffe as he walks past. The cream on her face is streaked and some of it is on the collar of her bathrobe. She takes the towel off her head and shakes out her hair, drapes her bathrobe on the foot of the bed. She wears men's pajamas with a paisley pattern. Bobbie watches her lift the covers back from Thea's bed and climb in beside her, holding both the girl and the bear in her arms. Sometimes Bobbie and her mother sleep like this. Her mother gets cold at night, sleeps with two pairs of socks, flannel pajamas; one night she wore one of Bobbie's woollen toques. She holds Bobbie, rubs her feet together and blows hot breath on her fingertips, her nose, the back of Bobbie's neck. They often fall asleep this way, intertwined, until sometime during the night Bobbie turns slowly, finds a cool spot at the edge of the mattress, shifts her feet out from under the covers, and falls asleep once more in the damp air of the downstairs bedroom. Her mother wakes, reaches for her, pulls her close, until there is no space between them.

THE DONOR'S DAUGHTERS

Katie Chase

Ashley is scheduled to take the SAT test this week, and Sam, her tutor, is looking down at his hands, soft eyes behind the Buddy Holly glasses red from crying.

"Are you sad you and Michelle broke up?" she asks.

Ashley isn't dumb. She doesn't even need an SAT tutor, but her mothers, who both work for the university—Robin as a Women's Studies professor, Cheryl in a research lab—can be forceful proponents of academic success. In the living room interview, Ashley watched as Robin was charmed by Sam's several half-master's degrees: "You're a Renaissance man!" He even, apparently, took one of her own lecture courses as an undergrad. Afterwards, Cheryl, with a straight face and teasing eyes, said, "If they'd made them like that when I was in the game, I might've stayed in it." Before her mothers met, Cheryl had always been with men. Sam has olive-toned skin and dark wavy hair, a soccer player's build and fingernails to pick a guitar. It just goes to show how gay her mothers really are that they hired him to be her tutor anyway.

Ashley knew from the start how obvious it was to have a crush on your tutor, so she tried to be his friend instead. She asked his advice sometimes, on the kinds of things she might have just asked her mothers: how to install anti-spyware on her laptop, what was the best Bob Dylan album to buy. She led him astray from flash-cards, sample essays, with innocent-seeming questions. *Are you sad you…*

"It had to happen sometime," he says. "It would've never worked out."

"You did always say she cut into your me-time."

He smiles wanly. "Talking to you has really helped. I know there has to be someone else out there for me, someone who understands me better."

Ashley does something then she always promised herself she wouldn't. Her mothers trust her not to do stupid things—or, at least, to talk it over with them first if she's contemplating one. But this time she doesn't think, she just reaches across the table and takes his hand. The way his thumb rubs lightly over her skin sends ripples through her whole body.

"You're a cool girl, Ash," he says, letting go, reaching for the flashcards. "You'll make some lucky guy a real easygoing girlfriend someday."

That night she decides to call her half-sister, Jade—two years younger at fourteen—the one sibling she's found through the Donor Sibling Search site. Jade's coming in three weeks, spring break, for a visit. They've been in contact two years now and met once in person, a year before, when Jade came to visit with her single mother, Lorraine. Jade is a sweeter version of herself, and Ashley loves her, despite Jade's sometimes cloying love of her. Jade, after all, has only one mother and is missing that second slice of bread that makes the sandwich of parental love.

"OMG, Ashley! It's like you have ESP, we're so connected. The biggest thing happened today—do you remember me telling you about that boy I liked?"

"Oh. Sure I do." Jade is always telling her about some new crush—always from her own grade, always someone she tires of just as he starts to notice her—and Ashley is always trying to keep them straight.

"Well, guess what? We started going together—my first real boyfriend! I can't wait to see you! It's so much better talking about these things in person."

"You're right. It is. You'll tell me all about him then." And what does Jade know anyway about toeing the line with your tutor? Seducing an older man? Being on the losing end of rejection?

When Ashley checks her SAT score online and announces it to her mothers, Robin says, "Oh, you'll have to call Sam! Take him out for ice cream, on us." Ice cream in wintertime is one of Ashley's favorite things.

"You think I should?" she asks.

Cheryl pats her briefly on the shoulder. "Sure, sweetie. He'll be so proud."

They meet at Stucchi's and over cones he goes on and on about how great the last Elliott Smith album is. Not a word on the ex-girlfriend, although incessantly listening to the music of an artist who killed himself is not really a sign that he's over her. "I ought to play it for you sometime," he says.

"Oh, yeah?" she says. "Well, how about right now? I'd love to hear it."

On the walk to his apartment, over old snow, she almost takes his hand, but decides against replaying that particular move. He might allow for something to happen once at his place, but that doesn't mean he wants her to be his girlfriend—he is, after all, 26 and on the rebound. She may never have gone with anyone before, but she's messed around before for practice with guys from school at parties.

They listen to the album very loud—the way he thinks it should be heard—she on his couch, he on the floor before a speaker, and that makes it difficult to keep a conversation. On the mantel of his blocked-off fireplace, he has a bottle of about every type of booze.

"I've never tasted tequila," she says. Truth: she's only had beer and wine before, and just tastes from her mothers' glasses. They ask her not to drink at parties, and she doesn't.

He examines the bottle as though for a warning label specific to this situation. "Maybe we could do just one celebratory shot. To you. Your score was all you. I know I was a terrible tutor. I always got off-track."

He shows her how to do the salt, licking the back of his hand—he's out of lemon—and the liquor burns down her throat. She really thinks she might throw up, but then it settles warm in her stomach. The tequila makes her feel suddenly very sexy. She feels his eyes on her as she walks around his room, swaying her hips, bending to pick up a CD or a book and asking him if it's good. He moves to the couch. She spies a pair of boxer shorts pushed into the corner with some dirty t-shirts. She's never been in an adult-boy's room before. It's messier.

"Come here," he says.

"What?" But she knows what. She comes and stands before him. And then, as she once made her move, he is the one who reaches out, putting his hands on her hips and rubbing lightly with his thumbs. "You're really cute, you know that?"

She doesn't agree, but *sexy*, yes—she feels wanted. "I know," she says. This is how her confident mother Robin might have responded.

He guides her to the couch beside him, and they start to kiss. He moves his hands all over her hips and thighs and butt, and she keeps hers in his nice hair. Up until he unzips her jeans and pulls them off, she's done everything before. He kisses her thighs with little licks then moves his face to her underwear. He breathes hotly and presses his tongue against her. She's embarrassed but what he's doing feels wickedly good.

"Take them off," she whispers.

"Are you sure, Ash?" he says. "Are you sure?" She nods.

When he lifts his head again to her mouth, she doesn't want to kiss him. But then he's taking his jeans off too. Pressing her hand against his boxers and then holding his hard-on has an appeal too, mostly in the way his face goes all soft and she feels totally in control. He asks her again if she's sure. That's when he remembers he's out of condoms. He could run to the store, if she wants. "I'm really sorry, Ash, I didn't plan—I mean, I didn't presume to think you would—"

She knows that if they pause she won't go through with it. She'll lose the good feeling, the one she hadn't even been close to with other boys. She says it then, "No, it's okay, don't go. I—I want to feel you inside me."

This is what Ashley knows of the donor and what is posted beside her screen name, and Jade's, on the Donor Sibling Search site:

Number M811. Born 1967. Started donating 1988. Stopped donating 1990. Irish,

English, German, Scottish. Light brown hair, wavy. Blue eyes. 6' 1", 160 lbs. Blood type O+. Medium complexion. Medical student. Protestant. Sports and classical music.

She has his stats memorized, and she knows this is juvenile, but she likes to visit this page as confirmation of him, as other fatherless children might a gravestone or the closet where a softened leather jacket still hangs. Unlike those other children, she feels no real loss, but harbors the belief that he, who doesn't love her and doesn't even know a daughter Ashley exists, is the only one who would understand why she's done the things she's done wrong when she knew better and perhaps even transferred these character deficiencies to her, as infinitesimal nicks on his strands of DNA.

Her mothers have always stressed the word "protection." Once, Cheryl had to have an abortion, and she said it affected her in ways she hadn't expected. She said she'd never want Ashley to go through anything like it—and Ashley knew this had something to do with the man, with whom Cheryl said there hadn't been love. "Just wait until you know you're ready," Robin said. "Protect your body and your heart." To hear her mothers talk of sex and love, you'd almost think those things were mere simple matters, requiring just the right decisions, the right protections, to avoid complexities.

If she were to confide in them, they would be upset but would love her just the same, as their smart and trustworthy daughter who comes to them with her mistakes. It used to be that this assurance was a comfort to her. Ashley can admit to friends now what would have gotten her made fun of back in grade or middle school: that it has never seemed strange to have two mothers. Robin and Cheryl were 35 and 36 when they had her, older than the donor—almost a baby himself, her mothers always joked. When she was little, this confused her, how a man younger than her mothers could be her "father," how any combination other than two women of roughly the same age could even produce a baby girl.

Of course, now, 16 years old, she gets it. She knows everything about it: how her mothers picked him out from the cryobank's catalogue, choosing looks in line with Cheryl's, sent in a check, and through the mail received a vial of his sperm, cased in liquid nitrogen. Her mothers' ob-gyn helped inseminate Robin, while Cheryl held her hand. This occurred, Ashley supposes, on a paper-wrapped stirrup table, underneath fluorescent lights. Across from a poster of a growing fetus, a glass jar of cotton swabs. Conceived in love, absent of lovemaking.

She sees now how everything about it could be reversed and still have much the same result, a fatherless child: how a man much older than, say, herself, a man she knew well, could, through one loveless act of unprotected first sex, successfully implant his sperm.

There's no way she can tell her mothers what she has just done.

She leaves up the donor's page and in a new tab opens her email. She has three new messages, including, horrifyingly, already one from Sam. They used to email to set up times for their sessions, or sometimes to finish a conversation about music. But now: *I hope this afternoon was as special for you as it was for me. Can't stop thinking about you… Love, S.* What she should do is, start a new email account and let this one die, alongside her contact with Sam. She could choose a new screen name, no more ashbear90; she could renew her identity. She could be, for real this time, the smart and trustworthy daughter.

Below Sam's message is a new one from Jade. The way she writes (with excitement, with innocence) about her boyfriend, makes Ashley feel happy, and envious, instead of pitying. *Can't wait 2 C U!* the message ends.

The last one looks like junk, with a subject line that reads *hi there ashbear*. But then she sees it was sent through the donor site, by someone named Megan. The message reads: *My parents recently revealed they've been lying to me all my life and apparently my dad isn't my real dad, its a piece of anonymous sperm. Well apparently a piece of that same sperm made its way inside your mom too and we're sisters. I already have a sister, and a brother too, thankyouverymuch, but I thought it would be too weird if I didn't at least say hi.*

Cheryl is the one who takes over, as Cheryl is always the one who takes over. And as usual, it is vaguely annoying but mostly a relief that she does. Cheryl might have been on the phone right now with their ob-gyn's office, scheduling tests to be conducted on a paper-wrapped stirrup table, but instead she is on with the girl Megan's parents. What might have been the central concern in their lives, a creeping accretion of cells, a not-yet-living life, has been exchanged for someone real and fully formed. After two years on the site, Ashley's found another sister, another product of her mysterious other genetic half. She feels like she created this, through Sam, and she should be grateful, enthusiastic, for the divine-seeming substitution.

At the kitchen counter, under a rare silence, Robin lays slices of tofu, as if putting them to bed, in a sesame-ginger marinade and, beside her, Ashley snaps off the ends of asparagus. From down the hall, Cheryl can be heard saying over and over, "I know…I know," and then: "Trust me, we understand how hard it can be."

Cheryl can't mean having a child through a donor or, obviously, hiding that fact and then having the dark, dirty secret come exposed. It's always been stressed, by Cheryl in particular, that their family is no different from any other, probably more loving, and nothing to be ashamed of. "Understand how hard what can be?" whispers Ashley.

"Sassy, rebellious teenage daughters, I'm sure," says Robin. "Such a *pain* to deal with. Oops, I forgot—you're my teenage daughter! Pretend I said such a *joy*."

Robin cocks her hip into Ashley's—they stand at the same height, a curvy 5' 4"—to show she's only joking. This is one, strangely important, reason she can't tell them; these jokes would have a new, cautious edge, or worse, would stop altogether.

"Don't worry, Cheryl's just working her magic," Robin says. Cheryl's plan is to get Megan here during spring break too, so all the sisters can meet. When Ashley talked to Jade earlier on the phone, her half-sis chattered on and on, guessing what Megan would be like and how much fun they'd all have.

"She sounded like kind of a bitch," Ashley found herself saying. "I mean, just through the email."

"I feel *bad* for her," said Jade. "She had no *idea*! Like, how would that *feel*?"

Jade was right, of course, and if anyone was acting like a bitch (she should be appreciative, enthusiastic), it was Ashley. "Don't tell her I said that, would you?"

"I would *never*! Ashley, you can trust me! You're my first and best sister." The response Ashley had hoped for and knew she didn't deserve. For her own part, she still hasn't mentioned to Jade anything about Sam.

Robin runs water to wash her hands, drowning out Cheryl's voice. Her dark bobbed hair streaked through with gray falls before her face, red lips against pale skin peeking through. She starts to hum a Joan Baez. Robin has a beautiful humming voice.

Both of Ashley's mothers are beautiful, but secretly, and with a consequence of rare vanity, she believes Robin more beautiful. She suspects this is weird, but she can see how Cheryl would find Robin sexy and fall in love with her. Once they had married—it was all ceremonial, of course—they sought a donor with traits similar to Cheryl's: at 5' 10", she's tall for a woman, and, like a model, gracefully and almost too slim, with strong, bright blue eyes that spark up her skin tone and in-between hair, neither blonde nor brown. Yet Ashley came out as something of a clone of Robin, and the resemblance was fortified when Ashley got her breasts and hips. She wonders if she feels closer to Robin just for looking like her.

Cheryl appears in the kitchen doorway, running the strand of her gold necklace through her fingers. "Well, that wasn't easy."

"But she's coming?" Ashley's heart picks up. She doesn't feel ready for this, not at all, but she knows Cheryl's right: the timing was perfect, and such things, if you've made yourself open to them—practically made them happen—have to be dealt with.

"Yes, she's coming. Just for a couple days. She has to miss school, but her parents thought it was worth it. She's very, very upset with them. Right now they're willing to do about anything she wants. I told them a plane ticket to Michigan is much cheaper than buying her a new car." Cheryl lets out a short laugh and folds her arms.

"You work magic," says Robin. She crosses the room to stand beside Cheryl, half a foot height-difference between, and reaches to run a hand along her back.

"Did you talk to her?" asks Ashley. "How did she sound?" From the email, she recalls, it didn't seem like Megan particularly wanted to meet *her* ever, *thankyou-verymuch*.

"No, just her parents. They only told her a month ago and she's taken total initiative, tracked down the donor number, joined the site. This is what she wants, to know where she really came from."

Ashley can't imagine going through all that in just a month. Megan must have given the whole thing almost no thought at all—how could she know so soon she really wanted to know? After all, donating a couple times a week for two years, the man may have produced dozens of offspring. That possibility has always made Ashley feel a little sick, more so now. To procreate promiscuously, without being promiscuous, and all those potential relations, wanting relationships, with her. What if there was no end to who was out there to know, no end to the consequence of knowing?

"Ashley, come here," says Robin, faux-exasperated. Ashley walks over to her mothers, and Robin takes them all into a three-way hug.

"Thanks, Cheryl," says Ashley. "This will be really great."

"You're welcome, sweetie," says Cheryl. She pulls away, with a nose toward the kitchen. "What dinner delights have you two been preparing? I couldn't smell a thing from down the hall."

I wish I'd hear something from you. Guys are the ones supposed to give the cold shoulder, you know. But seriously, I don't want you to regret or feel ashamed about what happened. Would it change things if I said you weren't just some girl to me? You're special. All those nice talks we had. I don't think I realized until it happened how much I wanted it to. I think I might even be in love with you.

This isn't happening. Clearly, he thinks that *he* seduced *her*. And now, to cover it up, he's convinced himself that he loves her. That part about her being special is probably true: he's probably never been with a 16-year-old girl before. He once confided to Ashley that he'd been a virgin until halfway through college, and though she hadn't thought that something too shameful—just surprising, in terms of how gorgeous he was now—his face had reddened and he'd looked away when he said it. Now she feels wry, unsympathetic. She can say now, for the rest of her life, that she lost her virginity when she was 16, and he probably thinks her lucky, normal, to be able to say it. Ashley isn't dumb; she knows that to answer might only turn it on again (his hands on her, his tongue). But maybe she can right this, with some degree of generosity, and make him understand that it's over.

Don't take this personally but there's too much confusing stuff going on in my life right now. I don't even know who I am sometimes. How can you love me? You don't have to say that. I wanted it to happen, but I don't think we should talk anymore. Just so you know, I'm changing my email anyway.

The day after school lets out, Robin and Ashley take I-94 to Detroit Metro airport. Cheryl said she would have come, but she had to work. That's always been the nice thing about Robin's job: she has to teach a couple times a week; otherwise, she's there. Ashley has more trust in Cheryl to meet planes on time, but she's just pleased to be in the passenger seat—now that she drives too, she hates to take the back. There's no way her mothers would have let her drive to the airport by herself, nor would she have wanted to meet Megan alone.

"Are you nervous?" Robin glances over, and just her asking makes Ashley curl her feet up on the seat.

"Let's keep driving so we can see the Uniroyal tire," says Robin. Just past the airport, along the freeway, stands the world's largest tire, once part of a world's fair Ferris wheel. When Ashley was little, the times she and Robin had to pick Cheryl up after an out-of-town conference, they'd always take the risk of being late to drive past it.

"Maybe on the way back. Jade's plane is getting in."

"It'll be great to see her, won't it?"

Jade is waiting at arrivals, with a pink rolling suitcase and bright, wobbly smile. Ashley can't believe how much older she looks. She seems to have gotten hips, and her scoop-neck sweater shows real cleavage (last time, a padded bra made up for a lack of breasts). Jade has her mother, Lorraine's, pale freckly skin and straight auburn hair, cut now into soft womanly layers. She's tall—taller—which they figure she got from the donor. Her face, though, looks 14, and something about the setting of her eyes, deep and a little wide, is the same as Ashley's, still the same, and what most clearly marks them sisters.

When Jade sees Ashley, she shrieks and the smile loses its wobble. "I knew you couldn't forget me!"

They hug; "You look gorgeous," Ashley says; and Robin stands back, "Sorry we're late, my fault entirely." Jade hugs Robin too. "I missed you!" Jade says. "I love having three moms!" This remark gets curious attention from an elderly couple, walking slowly by, each bracing the other.

"My seatmates," Jade says brightly. "The whole trip they wanted to know why I was traveling alone. Like, I'm 14!" Obviously, they can hear her, but the couple just smiles and wishes her good luck. Jade's borderline obnoxiousness can be endearing.

"Well!" says Robin. "Shall we have a seat? Are you hungry, Jade? Megan's plane isn't for another hour."

They get Starbucks, a special treat for Ashley, who normally is made to only patronize independents. "Once we get to Ann Arbor, this is over," she reminds Jade. "Oh, I don't care," Jade says. "I love the funky places you guys eat."

For two hours they sit, catching up on little things, while Robin reads the paper, pretending not to listen but smiling. Later, when they're alone, they will talk about big things, such as Jade's boyfriend. And as Ashley listens, will her face reveal her own news? If her mothers can't see it, Jade won't either, but she knows Jade wouldn't understand her reticence—aren't they, as sisters, supposed to tell each other everything, the things they wouldn't tell their own mothers?

Robin goes to check on Megan's flight, and Jade leans in. "Aren't you excited?"

"I'm nervous," says Ashley. "I just wish we could get it over with."

"Get it over with! I'm already sad thinking about when I have to go."

Robin returns to say that Megan's flight has been delayed by three hours and the agent seemed dubious the bad weather in Chicago would improve that soon. She calls Cheryl to see what they should do. Jade looks so disappointed that Ashley takes her hand. "Okay, here's the plan," Robin relays. "We're going home and making dinner. And Cheryl will come back for Megan later."

But, later, the flight is canceled and Megan is re-booked and that flight too becomes delayed. Cheryl waits at home, constantly down the hall on the telephone, and Robin is the one who brings an extra pillow.

"Goodnight, girls," she says, kissing each of their foreheads. Ashley is a little jealous that Robin kisses Jade last, that the sensation of her mother's pressed lips lifts first from her own skin, and lingers on her half-sister, who isn't really related to Robin at all.

The two are sharing Ashley's double bed. They mean to wait up for Megan. They lie facing each other, whispering—well, Jade does most of the talking, and not about Megan and the fun they'll all have, not even about her boyfriend. It's as if a promise has been made to pretend that it's just them, that everything's not about to change. That their own conceptions of their new sister, coming closer in the night, are not about to fuse together and come in between.

"Remember when my mom asked Cheryl if she missed dating guys? That was so embarrassing! I bawled her out for that later."

"Oh, I remember. How could I forget?" Ashley had been kind of mad; it had been too much like middle school, when there were rumors that she was a lesbian too and that's why she hadn't gone with anyone.

"Can I tell you something?" Jade says. "I'm kind of glad we had some time without her."

"Me too," says Ashley.

In the early morning when Ashley wakes to use the bathroom, having climbed over Jade, the heaviest of sleepers, she comes upon a tall, thin body stretched out on the couch, under an unknown blanket. Brown wavy hair, medium complexion. She wants to make some light disturbance so the girl's eyes will flutter and open, just for a second. But she knows already they will be blue. She knows this girl looks like the donor.

Megan seems like she's going to sleep the entire morning, and Robin has to leave to teach a class. Cheryl has already been at the lab for hours.

"Should I wake her?" says Robin. "I feel weird leaving without you girls getting acquainted. It would be weird for her, right? To wake up and Cheryl and I are gone, and she's in this strange house?"

Ashley is about to agree, Yes, they should wake her and do this together, but Jade says, "She's probably sooo tired! Look at her! Don't *worry*, Robin, she'll be fine. She's 17 years old!"

Ashley is getting tired of this type of argument—obviously, people don't always act age-appropriate—and she can't believe it works on Robin.

"I'm sure you're right, Jade. I just hate to miss it. I'll come home this afternoon and you'll already be friends."

Jade laughs. "Or maybe she'll still be sleeping!"

But it isn't five minutes after Robin leaves that Megan rises from the couch and pads off down the hall, as if she were awake and listening all morning, knew the layout of the house, kept her toothbrush already in the bathroom's shell-shaped holder. Ashley and Jade watch from the kitchen table, where they have Ashley's laptop and are checking out Jade's boyfriend on Facebook. They exchange a glance but keep talking like normal until she enters the kitchen.

Megan's not quite as tall as Jade and her body is much slimmer, undefined. At 17, she barely has breasts and this is not bothered to be hidden: the thin t-shirt shows her nipples. She has on basketball warm-up shorts and Adidas sandals and pulled her hair into a messy bun, and her eyes—Ashley didn't notice in the morning half-dark—are like theirs, deeply, widely set. They're blue, and flit around coldly. She doesn't smile.

"Hi!" says Jade. "I'm Jade." She stands and steps forward as if to hug her.

"Is there cereal or something?" says Megan. "I'm starving."

"Oh! Of course," says Ashley. She gets up to rummage in the cupboard for the Kashi and also brings out a banana and the soy milk. "I'm Ashley, by the way."

"Ashbear," says Megan. She eyes the carton and the cereal box. "O-kay…" She unpeels the banana. "I feel like I'm hungover. Oh, shit, that reminds me, I need to use your phone later to call my boyfriend. My cell is roaming."

"You have a boyfriend? So do I!" Jade turns the laptop to show Megan his profile.

"Cute," says Megan.

"Isn't he?" says Jade. "And he's so nice! The only thing is, he's so much shorter than me, it's embarrassing! One time, we were waiting for Lorraine—that's my mom—to pick up us from the movies, and this lady thought from behind I was *his* mom. Can you believe that?"

Megan looks amused. She turns to Ashley. "Let's see yours."

Ashley is aware that this moment is some sort of test, and she can't lie, not exactly. "Oh, me? I don't have one. Right now."

"Why not?" says Megan. "Don't take this the wrong way, but you're a hot chick."

"Wait a minute," says Jade. "You don't have one *right now*?"

"I just mean—"

"What she means is," Megan says, "she doesn't want to say. She doesn't want me to know about her boyfriends. Or lack of."

Jade's eyes go soft and she rests a hand on Megan's arm. "Of course she does! We're getting to know each other. We're bonding."

Megan folds the banana peel over the half she hasn't eaten. Her expression, if anything, is bored. Jade prompts, "So, go on, *right now*?" She looks so expectant, so supportive.

"Oh, well, I meant to tell you, last night. I was seeing this guy, it was no big deal. It's over." Ashley glances at Megan, who only raises her eyebrows.

"I can't believe you didn't tell me!" Jade turns to Megan. "She has never, *never*, had a boyfriend!"

Megan squishes the banana peel, oozing the fruit out the sides—Robin only buys organic and it's not cheap. "How long have you two known each other?" she asks. Jade doesn't answer, so Ashley does.

Megan repeats, "Two years? I've been with my boyfriend three. I didn't even tell my sister—my real sister—when we had sex. She still doesn't know. But maybe that's just what my family does, hides things from each other."

Jade laughs a little, but none of that sounded like a joke to Ashley. She says, "Since we're getting to know each other, do you mind if I ask you something?"

"Take aim and fire," says Megan. "We're bonding."

"What *about* your sister? And your brother? If they aren't from the donor—"

"I'm the oldest. My sister's about your age, Jade. When my parents wanted to have me, my dad was sterile, or so they thought. My mom was too pushy. That's what he said. They're getting a divorce. That's why they told me now."

"Oh, no—I'm so sorry!" says Jade. "That's terrible."

"Yeah, it is. I didn't know," says Ashley. "I'm sorry." She is. Cheryl's theories often pan out: Megan's family sounds much more complicated than their own. She doesn't know what she'd do if her mothers ever separated. It scares her, the small fights they have now and then—especially because they're usually over her, disagreements about things like parties and eating healthy.

"Yeah, I hate them," says Megan. "But I'm over it."

Later, when they're watching TV, Megan says, "So, do you guys hope you'll meet him?"

"Of *course*," says Jade.

"I don't really know," says Ashley, and she can feel Jade staring at her.

"Interesting," says Megan, and she doesn't share her own answer. "Which do you think he made up: sports, or classical music?"

"What do you mean?" says Ashley. "Neither."

"Oh, come on. Either he's a total geek and he said sports so he'd seem more manly, or he's a total jock and said classical music so women would choose his high-culture sperm."

"He's a *doctor*," says Jade, as if that decided it.

"Ah-ah," says Megan, shaking her head. "It said Medical Student. Who knows if he ever became a doctor. He stopped donating after two years. Maybe that's just when he dropped out of school."

Ashley and Jade are quiet. Finally Ashley says, "No, I think because he was a doctor, or in med school or whatever, he was doing it altruistically."

Jade looks confused, and Megan opens her mouth. Ashley knows what she'll say and gets to it first. "Or even just for the money. It doesn't matter, either way he wouldn't care who picked or didn't pick his sperm. He wouldn't lie."

Megan narrows her eyes at Ashley. "Everyone lies."

"Well," Ashley concedes, "most people, maybe."

But Megan isn't done. "And everyone wants to be loved. Everyone wants to be chosen. Even a sperm donor. He'll try to find us one day. The question is, when he does, will we give him what he wants? This guy who jacked off into a cup for a few extra bucks. Altruistic, my ass—you know it felt good."

Robin was going to make her special eggplant for dinner but Megan turns up her nose, so they order pizzas. "Those have soy cheese, these have dairy," says Robin.

"What's the point, anyway?" says Megan. "What's wrong with milk?"

If there's one thing Robin takes offense to, it's interrogations on her dietary decisions. Ashley catches her desperate glance to Cheryl—Cheryl who sees nothing wrong with dairy and is always on Ashley to take calcium pills. Cheryl says, "Have you talked to your parents today, Megan?"

"No, but that reminds me, I forgot to call my boyfriend. He's gonna kill me."

"Will he," says Robin.

"Be sure to call them, too," says Cheryl. "Let them know everything's fine."

Ashley watches Megan's face for eye-rolling, distance, a tight, sarcastic smile, but Megan just says, "Sure thing," and accepts a slice of dairy cheese from Cheryl onto her plate.

"Jade, you're awful quiet tonight," says Robin.

"Just tired," Jade says. She offers a small smile.

"No wonder—you girls spent hours in front of the TV. I should take you downtown tomorrow, we could get lunch, do some shopping." Robin looks quickly to Megan—oddly, as if she's embarrassed. "Or Ashley could just borrow my car. You girls don't need me to come."

"You could come," says Ashley. "There's this skirt I wanted to show you."

"The girls probably would like some time alone," says Cheryl. "You can show us the skirt this weekend, Ashley."

After dinner Megan, surprisingly, volunteers to help Cheryl with the dishes, and as Ashley, Jade, and Robin set up Scrabble and wait around the board, they can hear murmuring voices under the running water.

"She's not making this very easy, is she?" says Robin, low and kind.

Jade shrugs her shoulders. Ashley runs her fingers through the bag of letter tiles. "Let's give her the Z," she says.

"Cheryl said she was a little difficult on the ride home, at first. But I guess they ended up having a good talk. She's going through such a hard time. We can't fault her too much, I guess, for a little attitude."

Robin sounds more like she's trying to convince herself than Jade or Ashley. But Ashley knows she's right. "Maybe just the X," she amends.

That night Megan again takes the couch, and Ashley and Jade close the door to their room. Ashley puts on a mix CD she made herself that's all music, no words. It always makes her feel relaxed. Jade is still being very quiet, and she turns from Ashley to change into her pajamas.

Ashley says, "Hey, I'm sorry I didn't tell you before, about that guy. He really wasn't a big deal. I didn't love him or anything. He wasn't a real boyfriend."

Jade turns, a smile of forgiveness playing at the corners of her mouth. "If you really don't want to tell me more about him, that's okay—but only if you tell me about the one who is important! Once you've met him."

"Of course." Ashley gives her a quick hug, then leans to flip off the light.

In bed, Jade snuggles down in the covers, and the blanket pulls from Ashley's side. "You know what I think?" Jade whispers. "I think our dad liked sports *and* music. Look at Megan, she likes sports. And games—she kicked our butts at Scrabble. Look at you, you really like music. And he must have liked something else too. Something *I* like."

She doesn't say what and, actually, Ashley can't think of one thing Jade's passionate about. She's only 14. Maybe she'll become a doctor. Maybe, like Lorraine, she'll date and date and date—a novelty-seeker, someone who's always sure around the corner is something better. Someone who's always sure she can get, and deserves, better. Ashley squeezes her half sister's hand beneath the covers. "You're probably right."

"It doesn't matter if we ever find him or not," says Jade. "But I'd still like to. No matter what he's really like."

Ashley is awake, from a dream of Sam, and now she's thinking of him with a strange old yearning. Sam, with soft red eyes behind his glasses. Sam, down between her legs. She wonders if they'd only done that—if they hadn't gone all the way—she'd feel about him the way he says he feels about her. She'd never really thought they could be together, but her crush had felt special, exciting—an older man.

She climbs over Jade and sneaks down the hall to the kitchen with her laptop. She hasn't checked her old email for a while. From the living room comes a creak of the couch, and Megan's body shifts, turning from the couch's back. Ashley can't tell if her eyes are closed or open.

Ash, tell me, what is there to be confused about, with us? I know I'm older than you. But I thought you liked me. And you know how I feel about you. I hope you don't think I'm a jerk for saying this, but I wonder if this isn't really about your parents. I'd be confused about who I was sometimes too, if my parents were gay and that's what I knew.

"Still corresponding with your secret lover?" Megan is at the doorway of the kitchen, in her messy bun and basketball shorts. The sight of her at this moment is an eerie comfort, the way déjà vu can be.

"Sort of." As Ashley closes Sam's message, the words "gay" and "jerk" wink goodbye.

"Sort of? Something wrong?" Megan smirks as if she doesn't expect an honest answer. Ashley thinks of Megan's remark "Everyone lies," and the fact of Cheryl's "good talk" with her.

"He asked me if I think I'm a lesbian. Like my mothers." The bitterness in her voice feels honest, like she's letting go of a secret.

"Really? Well, what do you think? When I told you you're a hot chick, did you feel anything?" Megan's blue eyes are cold and flitting. Her whole thing, Ashley realizes, is acting like she's unafraid to say anything, but she never actually says what she's really afraid of. Ashley doesn't want to be like that; she doesn't want to be like Megan.

So she tells her. Everything. That it happened, that it was with an older man, that it was without protection. That right now, at this very moment, she could be—

"I could be pregnant." She thought that when she said it out loud, she would finally completely believe it. But still, it's only Megan—with the donor's eyes—staring back at her, not the face of a child, not an unplanned future.

"Well, so, what's the big deal? Shit happens, you can't always be careful. My boyfriend and I have broken plenty of condoms. And sometimes, I know, it just feels better without one. You're probably not pregnant, but if you are, you know you don't have to be."

"Have you ever had to…?"

"No, but I would. In a second."

So would I, Ashley realizes, though it makes her sick to remember Cheryl's pained face, her fingers threading her gold necklace, when she told Ashley about the abortion. Cheryl could have borne her, but she was too afraid, she said, that something would go wrong and she'd lose another child, one she really wanted. Ashley's mothers would want her to weigh her options, but she would just want it over with—no deliberations, no second guessing—and maybe she wouldn't even tell them. A month ago she would never have thought this possible.

"We'll buy a pregnancy test tomorrow—it's been at least two weeks?" Ashley nods. Megan adds, "And some condoms. For next time."

"There won't be a next time."

"Yeah, right. You enjoyed it, didn't you?"

"Maybe. Some of it. But I'm not doing it again," she says. "Not with him. It's just that now he won't leave me alone."

"Listen, we'll take care of everything tomorrow. Chill. Go back to bed. You people are exhausting me."

They borrow Robin's car, dropping her off first at her university office. "Okay, have fun! Call me if anything—if you need anything." Jade gets out to take the passenger seat and Robin hugs her goodbye.

"Where are we going?" asks Megan.

"Downtown, like we said," says Ashley. "We could go shopping."

"Well, there's *one* thing we need to get. At the pharmacy." Her voice is just one lilt shy of being suggestive but, thankfully, Jade doesn't pick up on it. "Then maybe some lattes. But I don't know about shopping—I'm sure your downtown is nothing compared to Chicago's. I have a better idea of where to go."

"Where?" says Jade. "The campus is so cool—Ashley could take us on a tour."

"I think we should drive by Ashley's ex-boyfriend's. Just to see it. Just to see if he's home."

"Oh! Lorraine used to drive me all the time by my boyfriend's house! Before it was official."

"But I don't like him anymore," Ashley says.

"Just to see!" says Jade. "I never got to see it, when you liked him. I missed the whole thing."

At the pharmacy while she and Jade are smelling lip glosses, Ashley sees Megan slipping to the back counter to buy the test. Then in the bathroom at Espresso Royale, Megan slips her the box beneath the stall. "Pee on this." She laughs. From the next stall over, Jade, oblivious, giggles too.

Before the bathroom's mirror, Megan and Jade open the eyeshadows and lipsticks they bought, ostentatiously applying them, smacking paper towels. Ashley watches a negative sign appear on the strip, and it's like a knot is dissolving from her belly. She's alone in the stall, her genes are still only hers, undivided and unjoined—not even shared completely by her sisters. "Jade, sweetie, do me a favor," says Megan. "Go give that cutie barista Ashley's number. She was totally blushing when he gave her her change."

"Really?" Jade shrieks. "Ashley, is that okay? Hey, are you okay in there?"

"I'm fine," she says. "It's fine. Go ahead, why not. Give him my number."

The bathroom door creaks opens and clicks back closed, and Ashley comes out and hands the test to Megan, who gives it the quickest glance. There is no sisterly hug, no squeals of relief. Her face has that bored expression. "See?" she says. "No big deal." She wraps it in a paper towel and stuffs it down inside her purse. "What? We can't leave it here. That's way too gross."

Back in the car, they circle the borders of the Diag, the center of campus where college students cross, huddled in down coats and wrapped in scarves. Spring break in Michigan doesn't mean spring. Jade chatters on about how she can't wait for college—she wants to go here, just like Ashley. But it's Ashley's mothers who've always assumed she'd go here. Ashley turns the car from campus, heading north. She takes Catherine over past Main. The houses are slightly nicer here, grad students mixed in with families. She slows the car to a stop, trying not to look over. "Well, here we are. See it all you want."

Megan says, "Get out. We're going to the door."

Ashley turns in her seat. "No, we're not! Are you crazy? I told you how he won't leave me alone."

"He won't?" says Jade.

"Trust me," says Megan, opening her door. "He'll leave you alone after this."

"He's not dangerous, is he?" Jade hasn't even popped her seatbelt.

Ashley sighs. "Of course he's not dangerous. He's just clingy, I guess."

Sam's apartment is on the main floor of a blue-shingled house. They watch Megan walk to the door. A ratty plaid couch sits on the porch, and Megan makes like she's going to lie down but just in time notices its filth.

"Should we trust her?" Jade asks.

"Should just drive away and leave her here." In her mind, Ashley can't help but picture the seduction that would take place: Megan braless, experienced, pouty; Sam unbelieving of his good luck, two teenaged girls in one month—maybe even a bonus that Megan is her sister. Ashley takes the key from the ignition. "Come on."

When they join her, Megan is all business. "Don't say a word, either of you, and stay behind me." Her knock is professional, persistent.

Sam opens the door in bare feet and jeans and a new haircut, his curls clipped closely to his head. He looks like he's just woken from a nap, his face bare, vulnerable-seeming—unless it's just that he's without his glasses. "Hi." He blinks at Megan until he sees Ashley behind her. "Oh, Ash, I'm so glad you—"

"Look," says Megan, taking a step forward, "you have to get it through your thick skull. It's over. She doesn't want you. She was only using you."

Jade, standing off to the side and looking very uncomfortable, pulls on Ashley's coatsleeve. "Let's go," she mouths.

"What is this?" asks Sam. "Ashley?"

"What does it look like?" Megan says, almost coy. "She doesn't need you—she has me now." She turns and whispers with hot breath to Ashley's ear, "Don't worry, I won't like this any more than you will."

The kiss is sudden and deep. Megan catches her with her mouth open and pushes her tongue against hers, aggressively at first, then playfully swirling it around. It is nothing like Sam's kiss, or any boy's; it feels like nothing less than a violation. She tastes of unsweetened coffee. When Megan pulls away, Ashley looks first to Sam, who doesn't seem resigned or shocked or excited but, of all things, irritated, and then to Jade, who's looking at Ashley, and only at Ashley, as if she doesn't know her at all.

That night they play another game of Scrabble. Megan's winning again, even though Robin's blatantly cheating, bending the rules so that Jade can get some words on the board. Cheryl leaves to use the bathroom and when she comes back she doesn't sit, just stands over the table, casting a slim shadow.

"What's up?" says Robin, rearranging the tiles on Jade's stand.

Cheryl brings a hand from behind her back to drop a small paper package onto the board, scattering tiles. The fold of paper towel uncurls to reveal the pregnancy test, pointing at Ashley like spin-the-bottle.

"Who does this belong to?" Cheryl crosses her arms, sets her pretty jaw. Ashley has never seen her this brusque and angry—not with her and never with Robin. "Megan? Is this yours? Is this your idea of a joke?"

"I'm sorry, Ashley," says Megan flatly. "She must have dug pretty deep in the trashcan."

"Yeah," says Cheryl. "Pretty deep in the otherwise empty trashcan."

"Sweetie?" says Robin, a hand on Ashley's arm. "Is she saying this is yours?"

Jade is staring at Ashley with her biggest eyes and filling them with tears, but Ashley can neither deny nor confirm. She is what she is and she's done what she's done and everyone can plainly see her, this new stranger at the table.

Robin says quietly, "I thought you would at least tell me."

The last word slips from her mouth as the last bead of water pulls from the tap into the sink. For a moment she and Ashley are caught in a stare, each afraid to turn to Cheryl.

Cheryl's hand plucks the test from the gameboard. She pitches it into the kitchen garbage, and then takes out their phone book, laminated with family pictures, and begins to flip its pages.

"Cheryl?" says Robin, going to her. "Cheryl, who are you calling?"

"My parents, I'm sure," says Megan. "This is not my fault, you know. Your daughter's the one who had sex and didn't tell you. And it was before she met me." She brushes past Ashley's mothers, who don't try to prevent her escape out the door. A rush of cold air comes in.

"I'm calling Dr. Gould," Cheryl murmurs to Robin, dialing.

"You know the office will be closed," says Robin. "It's late, Cheryl. Leave it for tomorrow."

"Should someone go after her?" Jade's voice is calm and newly bright but the smile she offers is the one from the airport, when she thought she'd been forgotten.

"I will," says Ashley. "I should." No one looks at her. Jade begins pushing the Scrabble tiles into a pile; Cheryl has turned her back, the phone pressed to her ear, and Robin has a hand on her shoulder.

"I didn't mean what you think," Robin says to Cheryl. "I didn't mean just me. I misspoke."

"I'm sorry," Ashley adds. She grabs her coat from the closet, prepared to chase Megan down the block. But she's only sitting on the cold stone doorstep, like someone left her there to be found.

"Megan," she announces, "you know what? You're kind of a bitch."

Megan snorts. "Like I've never heard that before. Guess what? That's the last thing my own mom called me before I left. You think you can hurt me with that?"

"So you're having a hard time. We get it. You don't have to take it out on us. On me. I trusted you." Ashley sits on the step beside her. The wind blows right through them, but she won't huddle for warmth. She won't.

"I'm sick of secrets. I thought you guys were supposed to be so *open* about everything!" Megan speaks with sarcasm, but as Ashley's learned, she may not have a truer voice. "What did you talk about, anyway, alone with my mother? When she picked you up from the airport?"

"You mean with Cheryl? I'm sure you could guess."

Maybe. Maybe the same old speech on how important it is to face your origins, your past, your blood; to know yourself through and through, before you commit to false ideas, to something you're not. The same speech she gave Ashley, over and over, the year she spent thinking about signing on to the web site. Ashley says, "You tell me."

"Just a bunch of stuff about how my dad must feel." Megan's voice is overly light. "You know, left out, like he's missing a vital connection with me. Just how I should try to be extra nice to him and understanding. Make sure he still feels included in my life. And I know that." Her eyes narrow. "I know he's my real dad, no matter what. They both did this to me. I don't love him any less than my mom."

"Of course," Ashley says. "You think I don't understand?"

"I don't need a big fake family," Megan says, looking away. "Listen, I know I'm not exactly what you were hoping for. But I'm only here one more day. Then you'll be rid of me."

No, I won't, Ashley wants to say. Now that I've found you, I never will.

Dirty Bird, bless his soul, was a friend of mine.

Six-foot-one. Solid as brick. A man among boys. He owed his nickname to his distinct scent and aversion to bathing.

Dirty Bird, at 15, was the youngest kid I knew with a job. He cleaned out stoves and mopped floors at Domino's Pizza on Dekalb Avenue. Domino's, he told me, was the only place in all of Brooklyn where the workers were on good terms with their manager. A man could clean at his proper pace, as he wanted. He paused and fixed me with an expectant stare after he said this, hoping I'd understood him. He had arms so muscular they fought the elasticity of his sleeves, biceps thick and perfectly sloped.

There was power there.

His work shirt was Domino's blue and Dirty Bird dingy. He never washed it, which made it all the more comical that he had put effort into stitching his given name in big letters above the Domino's logo on his right breast: "EARL." He wanted to matter. A lot of us did.

I was 13 and getting a taste for importance too. When I fell into daydreaming about mattering—typically I was a sports hero or a man pushing a terrified child out of a speeding car's path—I'd always end up thinking about Haagen-Dazs ice cream. My mother brought it home only once a year because it cost so much. It sure *tasted* like it cost more, and whenever my mother splurged for it I'd get happy, deep-down-inside happy. Just to feel that way was incredible; so strong a feeling it was almost tangible. It was the kind of sensation that when you get all grown-up you wish you could still have. But I wouldn't even imagine that feeling. I'd imagine being the Haagen-Dazs, inspiring that type of nervous adulation and desire inside people—oh they wanted you so bad, they just needed to have you.

It was August, 1989. We were hugging the curve of the final turn from Summer into Fall. It was a time of poverty and turmoil in my life. Even the Yankees were unraveling and leaning toward last place, though not there yet. The overmatched duo of Bucky Dent and Dallas Green split the managerial duties; short-on-talent who-the-hells like Alvaro Espinoza, Wayne Tolleson, and Greg Cadaret manned the diamond. No star power. Rickey Henderson went and got himself traded mid-season. To make matters worse, the Mets (the Mets!) were gobbling up all the space on the back page. But Don Mattingly was still an All-Star, at the top of the league in a handful of categories, and on his way to a fifth consecutive Gold Glove award. He was, separate from the Yankees and alone, keeping me sane.

COMMUNION

Jason England

Every afternoon I'd go by Domino's at about three, when Dirty Bird got done working. I'd stand outside the pizza factory (you couldn't be from Brooklyn and call Domino's a "pizza shop" or "pizza place" without great shame), rifling through the sports pages of *The New York Post*, scanning boxscores and sometimes moving forward to the gossip pages. I didn't have anything more to care about. Or else I didn't know what more to care about. Or else I did and had already trained myself not to know.

Dirty Bird would come out, sweaty and smiling. Soon as he spotted me he'd nod and ask the same question:

"How them boys doin'?"

"They suck more than a whore."

Dirty Bird worked hard, and he smelled like it. Which was really something, because he normally smelled so terrible. Who could forget the time Father Evans sent him away from Church? His body must not have known soap and water for weeks and weeks, and we all smelled it: from the back row of pews up to the pulpit. There was no refuge from it, no pinching your nostrils together or shifting location helped. It was like his odor was stalking us.

Father Evans took to the aisle while we sang the opening hymn. Feet shifted, books closed, coughing broke out the way it always does like it's contagious. Heads turned and eyes followed his path to the back row, where he halted before Dirty Bird and said quietly, "The Lord's House is one of purity not filth, Earl. Cleanliness is, indeed, next to godliness." Dirty Bird met Father Evans' eyes, shrugged, and left. If that had been me I think I would've cussed Father Evans to hell, or at least cried. But Dirty Bird was so much more decent than anyone else. He was a good person.

My mother was never around. She worked a whole bunch, two jobs at a time, and she was still young enough to get up her energy and go out with her friends. She'd become transient, and our apartment was not so much a home as a place to go back to.

There was one time earlier that year I made peanut butter milkshakes, my mom's favorite, to surprise her when she got in. I came home from school, plugged in the blender, got everything ready. By nine PM she still hadn't shown. Didn't make it in until very late when the only things left were two empty glasses and me asleep on the living room floor. She had her own life to live, apart from me and my needs and loves and good deeds.

I'd pass the days in August alone, lying on my back in the living room. I'd stare into the faded white of the ceiling and imagine Don Mattingly, his demeanor. It would be the same whether he'd just taken the collar or hit a three-run homer. He'd never showboat. He'd never mope. He'd never complain. He'd been nagged by a back injury all season and I pictured him before games, stretched out on the rubbing table with his eyes closed, tired and sore, all worn down, a quiet, noble warrior. At 13, I was so unsteady and alone that I gave my faith to him all the way. He mattered so much to me.

I would go for walks early in the afternoon, usually three blocks from where I lived on Atlantic Avenue, up to Fulton Street. There were crowds of young people dressed in crisp clothes, ironed and new all over. There were music stores, a mall, and a movie theater; it was easy to lose myself. I could move between different shops, weaving in and out of crowds of people, and pretend to have a purpose: examining cassette cases, trying on fitted baseball caps, contemplating a movie, my anonymity completely endurable.

The late afternoon was reserved for Dirty Bird, a person who accepted the responsibilities of friendship. He would listen as I scrutinized the sports pages, snarling in inconsequential arguments as though the fate of the world was decided by the scores and Don Mattingly's batting average. On really hot days he would walk with me to the corner store and buy me a soda, sometimes a bag of chips, without any prompting. There was a way he could do those things unlike anyone else I knew. His charity never demanded my guilt in exchange.

When we went to the park right down the way a little from Domino's, where all the guys would be, Dirty Bird made sure to pick me first for his basketball team. I was too short to shoot over anyone, too thin to make my own way, and too awkward with my hands to dribble. There were so many better players. Much, much better.

We'd win anyway, Dirty Bird was so good, so tall and solid. He would bull his way into the paint, and once there he turned all buttery and slick, drop-stepping, swiveling, and sliding to the basket. The ball dropped delicately through the hole. He punctuated every score by pointing to the logo on his dingy shirt and exclaiming: "DOMINO'S DELIVERRRRRS!" the way lumberjacks on television yell "timber." When Dirty Bird played baseball you wanted to watch him, what he could do with a bat. His swing was almost flawless, maximum power with minimum waste motion. He swung so sweet and easy, but when he made contact with a ball: SMASH!

There weren't many things Dirty Bird couldn't do well. He was Mr. Everything.

I saw Dirty Bird's home on August 12th. I remember because it was a week after Don Mattingly had his 17-game hitting streak snapped, and I was all twisted up inside with something that was not quite sadness. I woke up in the middle of the night and went out into the living room. I wanted to stare up into the ceiling, maybe picture Don Mattingly, not be so alone. Instead my mom and some strange man were in there kissing, half-on half-off the couch. The strange man's big hands were like claws on my mom's breasts; they grabbed and tore at her shirt until the dark brown of her skin showed. She pulled her body up to his and pinned herself hard against his chest.

Dirty Bird lived on the bottom floor of a nondescript three-story apartment building. It was the kind of building you could walk past a million times and never notice. We went in through the front door and his father—diminutive, bald, and pudgy with a huge black moustache—greeted us.

"Ahhh, what the fuck, Earl? Who is *this* you done drug home with you?"

"My friend Albert. I'm gonna fix us some lunch."

His father looked at me and sighed.

"You two better not fuck up my kitchen, man."

We were silent. A toilet flushed in another apartment. I could hear a television on in a room somewhere to our side. Dirty Bird's father looked up into his face and jabbed a plump, stubby finger into his chest.

"You gonna get rid of them snakes today too."

"Nah," said Dirty Bird. He shook his head several times from side to side. "Nah."

"I ain't asking, I'm telling your ass."

"Why?"

"Because ain't no snakes living in my house, getting big and hungry, eating shit up."

"Come on, Dad."

His father walked away, back into what I assumed was his room, and slammed the door behind him.

"I ain't getting rid of my snakes," Dirty Bird said to me as we walked into the kitchen. "He must be crazy."

For lunch he fixed us up some spaghetti, which was actually elbow macaroni with ketchup on top. The kitchen was filthy. Dishes were piled high in the sink. Empty jars and cans were scattered all over the counter top and floor.

We ate at a dirty table, out of dirty bowls, with dirty forks. Dirt, dirt, dirt, Dirty Bird and me.

When I was done eating I pushed my bowl away from me, toward the center of the table. Seconds later Dirty Bird did the same, and then stared off toward the sink.

"My dad is wack," he said.

"My mom too," I answered. "She's a slut."

Dirty Bird got up from the table and added our bowls to the pile in the sink. I could still hear the television somewhere in the apartment, louder now.

"I'm bigger than him," he said matter-of-factly.

I was not, in fact, bigger than my mom, but roughly the same height and much skinnier. I looked down at my feet in shame.

"He touches my snakes, I'm putting him in the oven at work. I'm baking him like a pepperoni pizza."

I imagined what it would be like to kill my mom. I thought maybe I wouldn't even miss her, just buy myself a Nintendo and play Pro Wrestling all day. I'd choose "King Slender" and finish my opponents off with the back-breaker. When I pinned them for the three count that graphic would flash across the screen: "Winner is you!" It would be that easy.

"You want to see something secret?" Dirty Bird scraped the last of the elbow macaroni out of the pot and put it in a bowl he grabbed out of the sink. "Let's go." He led me out from the kitchen, swift steps but careful, past his father's room, then another room, down the hallway to its end, where he stopped in front of the last door before the bathroom. I was still a few feet behind, apprehensive.

He cupped a hand over his mouth and whispered: "*Quick, come here.*" When I joined him at the door he put down the bowl and pointed at the knob. "Go ahead. Open it." Uneasy but intrigued, I reached out for the knob. I turned it with an exaggerated slowness, hesitating inside. I pushed it open. It was too dark to make anything out, not the contours of the room, not its contents. I looked back over my shoulder at Dirty Bird for advice or an explanation. What did he expect me to do now? Go in there? Before he could tell me, something shot out at me, *shooom!* a huge blur, some sort of creature, knocking me to the ground. It pounced on me, on top of me, fast, foul-smelling, moist, and massive. My mind went wild with panic and I thought the thing was swallowing me up. I went to scream but Dirty Bird's hand blocked my mouth from opening.

"Shhhh," he said as he pulled the thing off of me.

Once I gathered my focus I recognized the thing was a naked man, solid and tall as Dirty Bird, loose-necked with dull, dark eyes so that he looked drowsy and disoriented. Drool spread across his face as he flailed against Dirty Bird's grip. He twisted and I saw a long scar on his back that ran all the way from his ass to his shoulder blade. His penis dangled and swung in a way that made me at once embarrassed and disgusted. He was that rare kind of creature who inspired both pity and scorn in your heart, so that before him you felt utterly human—sympathetic and evil, your emotions moving in a natural, unobstructed flux.

Dirty Bird wrestled him to the floor, dragged him into the room, and came back out for the bowl. He brought that in too, then shut the door. He turned and went down the hallway, retracing the way we came, toward the front door and out, and I followed, still stunned, silent and wide-eyed. We stood in front of his building. I was glad not to be inside, and I never wanted to go back. The sky had turned dark; the sun was somewhere way down behind the buildings. We stood without talking and watched the empty street. I wondered whether my mom was back on the couch, eyes full of fury, pulling and panting like an animal.

"That was my brother Eric. He's a retard."

I could live in my own screwed up world pretty easily, but to visit Dirty Bird's was another thing entirely. While he talked I kept picturing him in the park, crowding a square chalked over to mark home plate, a wooden bat slung over his shoulder like an axe, a kind of hero to me. Then I pictured him wrestling with his naked beast of a brother.

"I feed him," he said, looking past me, down the block, into a different line of thought. "I ain't giving up my snakes."

"Where did that scar on his back come from?" I didn't want to let his brother slip away just yet.

"My dad beats him sometimes. Hits him with the extension cord. Or else he can't stop him." He shook his head and smiled. "I'm the only one who can stop him."

"You're strong as hell, man. Crazy strong."

"I know," he said. "Always been that way."

"Whose Streets? Our Streets! What's coming? War!" Some 8,000 people, mostly black, took to the streets of the Bensonhurst section of Brooklyn on August 31st, chanting, toting signs. Fists thrust in the air, faces scowled up, voices loud with indignation. It was the "Day of Outrage," a confrontational protest of the murder of Yusef Hawkins, a black teenager who had been beaten and then shot by an all-white mob in an all-white neighborhood. It had happened nine days earlier, in my own borough, to a boy like me or Dirty Bird or anyone else I knew.

I sat with Dirty Bird in the park, reading him the news coverage of the march. It was Friday, the first day of September. In 11 days Don Mattingly would celebrate his 1,000th game in California, against the Angels. He would go four-for-four and hit a homerun. The next day I'd celebrate with Dirty Bird—drink sodas in the park and eat a really big sandwich from Ziad's Deli. Not a care in the world. But today was dismal, the park was empty, and a somber force was pressing down on us.

"The Reverend Herbert Daughtry said 'the wonder of it all is that New York has not exploded.'" Every quote I came across was ominous, heavy on my tongue. Dirty Bird stood over me, half-heartedly dribbling a basketball, his face pulled in tighter than usual.

"My dad says white people are evil. They want to wipe us out."

I kept reading:"According to an eyewitness, alleged gunman Joey Fama shouted,'To hell with beating him up, forget the bats, I'm going to shoot the nigger.'"

"That white boy wouldn'ta shot me. I woulda taken that gun right from him, I woulda decked that white boy in his mouth 'til his teeth broke."

"Listen to this lady, Viola Plummer:'Do you know how many millions of blacks have been killed? From this day forward, for every black child we bury, we are going to bury five of theirs.'"

Everyone seemed wrong to me, talking about war and exploding and turning my Brooklyn into something so ugly, even uglier than the murder had already made it.

"I don't know," Dirty Bird said. "You might could hurt some white boys for revenge but not kill them."

"Would you beat one up?"

"If he was racist."

"How would you know?"

Dirty Bird looked down at me in surprise, as if I had hit upon something he never once contemplated. He turned away from me and dribbled the ball a few more times, thinking.

"With something like that you know. You could *feel* it, don't you think?"

I wasn't sure. I didn't think it was so simple and detectable a thing. And I certainly didn't want to believe that all white people were inherently and intentionally malicious. There was already enough to fear in life, enough that I couldn't escape. To believe in that kind of evil would smother me. I wanted to tell Dirty Bird all of this, to explain it, but all I could come up with was:"I *know* Don Mattingly ain't racist."

A half hour later we were still idling around, debating and sorting through a morality that was totally confused, when a white guy walked into the park. The man was forty or thereabouts, graying at the temples, a brown bag of groceries tucked under his arm. He passed in front of our bench and glanced quickly at, then away from us. To Dirty Bird it was a disdainful glance.

Dirty Bird sprang from where he stood and threw a lightning bolt of a punch at the man's face, knocking him back and breaking his grip on the groceries, which scattered when the bag hit the concrete. A jug of milk busted open and a white stream spread out and rushed toward me. I followed it all the way under the bench as the man, stunned and afraid, scrambled to his feet and took off running. "You don't own this park!" Dirty Bird shouted. His words were sharp, earsplitting. "This is our park," he said, his voice trailing off a bit. He turned to me and muttered, "Our damn park."

That's how it was then. That brand of vehemence, that kind of all-around senselessness, blind rage, and fear. It's quite unfathomable to me now. What Dirty Bird must have felt that day is something long ago lost to me. I couldn't even care a penny's worth about the Yankees or a bowl of Haagen-Dazs ice cream anymore. What I latched on to, embraced wholeheartedly with immeasurable passion, has now become easy for me to relinquish. There was once that unbridled enthusiasm, since blunted by age, or maybe gradual wear, or heartbreak. All gone now.

That Sunday Dirty Bird showed up at my apartment building and rang my bell, something he'd never done before. I got dressed, went downstairs and saw him standing there, tired and slightly hunched over, as if he'd carried two of himself through the streets on his way over.

"I need a favor."

We walked five blocks west on Atlantic Avenue to the church, Father Evans' church, a place Dirty Bird would not enter. I understood, because in addition to being decent, he was also very proud. He stood outside, across the street from the old brick church, reddish-brown and not at all magnificent or holy-looking, while I went in and sat through the service. I came back out, 30-40 minutes later, and crossed the street, one hand gingerly cupped over the other.

"Thanks, Al," he said, taking the wafer from my hand. It was a little damp with sweat from my palm and had lost its crispness. We stood there, like we'd stood in other places all over Brooklyn, on other blocks like that one, looking up and down the street, sometimes for direction or just a thing to do or talk about. I watched the churchgoers leave mass and go their separate ways, spreading out toward lives I could only imagine and would never touch.

"My dad snuck in and threw my snakes out," Dirty Bird suddenly said. I gave him a solemn, sympathetic nod in response. He lifted the wafer to his mouth, closed his eyes, and slipped it in. Slowly, gently. He crossed himself, opened his eyes again and stared out over the street.

"It's cool you like Mattingly the way you do."

"Yeah." I shrugged and looked down at my sneakers.

"My dad don't know a thing about nothing."

"Nah. He's old, though."

"I know. It's not that…" He paused, extended his arms in front of him, and balled his hands into fists. "You ain't supposed to hurt people," he said, shaking his head and unclenching his hands. "I shouldn'ta hit that man."

I looked up from my feet and turned to Dirty Bird. I didn't want to ever let that moment go, the way he was and how I felt around him, but it was already gone. He started off east, back toward our neighborhood, and I followed. When we reached my building I stopped and Dirty Bird halted momentarily; we gave half-waves to each other. I'll never forget the loneliness, to feel so strongly about someone and not even muster the courage to hug him, to give a full wave, to step outside of myself. He turned and kept on, hands in his pocket, back slightly hunched. Striding long and strong, he disappeared around the corner.

That was before a lot. Dirty Bird hadn't knocked up a simple girl with a plain face. He hadn't locked himself into that kind of draining life. His brother, Eric, hadn't died from choking on a hot dog. My mother hadn't torn up her knee and I hadn't started working my own two jobs to help put food on the table. Brooklyn hadn't seen blacks and Jews at each others' throats in Crown Heights. Back then I'd talk up Don Mattingly until I was out of breath, and Dirty Bird would score baskets and shout "DOMINO'S DELIVERRRS!" like a lumberjack. Things were still growing in us, not dying out. It was 1989, in Brooklyn, and faith was justifiable.

CHAPTER 1

The puppy asks: "Why can't I run down the stairs barking?"

I say:

The cat disappears.

GOOD DOG

Sherrie Flick

CHAPTER 2

The puppy says: "I'm misunderstood and underappreciated. The problem is you don't listen to me."

I say: "Sit. Stay. Stay. Stay. Good dog."

My 15-year-old daughter disappears.

CHAPTER 3

The puppy is always ready to go. The answer is: Yes! (always, an exclamation point) no matter the question.

Unless the question is rhetorical, like:
"Do you understand when I say no, I mean no?"
"Did you hear me?"
"What the fuck?"

Then the answer is wagging a tail; the answer is licking.

CHAPTER 4

The cat was here one minute, full of big fur and belly and then she was gone. Vanished. Not like she was hiding or crouching somewhere in the cobwebby rafters, but instead de-particleized on the spot. Gone.

CHAPTER 5

The puppy asks: "Why can't I chew the antenna wire for the clock radio? You don't even use that clock radio anymore."

I say:

The cat doesn't reappear for two days. Then she's there, slinky by the dog bowl, picking through the stray kibble like an overweight debutante.

The puppy says: "Hey, that's *my* food."

My teenaged daughter is still gone, not so much disappeared like the cat, but instead refusing to come home because I am stupid.

The puppy agrees.

CHAPTER 6

The puppy says: "You really need to lower your voice when you say no. You aren't convincing to me. You aren't convincing to anyone."

CHAPTER 7

The puppy prances, dances like a tip-toe ballerina at the end of his leash. He looks over his shoulder. He smiles and says: "I am so fucking happy."

I say: "Watch your mouth."

The cat disappears again.

I think it's drugs.

CHAPTER 8

The puppy is sleeping now, curled up like a little beanbag chair. The dog wasn't my idea, but he's moved in, and some days he's the only one who talks to me. He's naïve and innocent, really.

The cat is wise.

My teenaged daughter has slammed the door of her room. Her TV is blaring. No, that's not right. She's still unfound.

The police have been called.

CHAPTER 9

The puppy asks: "Why can't I lick your ice cream spoon? I love you."

I say: "Sit. Stay. Stay. Stay. Good dog."

WAKE

Kevin González

It's New Years Day and I'm on my godfather's Dusky doing 5,000 RPM on the North Sound of Virgin Gorda with a mechanic named Michael Jackson at the helm. He's shoved the twin Evinrude controls all the way down on the console, and I keep trying to sip my beer, but it spills all over my face until there is nothing but dead wind left inside the bottle. A boomerang-shaped key glides past our starboard, and scattered marinas dot the port side, with their schools of masts rasping the sky, and the unrelenting logos of petroleum empires stenciled against the green backdrop of the mountains. The other night, my father mistook the orange Gulf sign at Leverick Bay for a full moon. He was drunk and wearing his sunglasses, hitting on a young bartender from St. Kitts.

"Look at that moon, Bertha." He pointed with his entire arm. "It's as full as I am with lust for you."

"Who Bertha, mon?" she said. The "t" cut through the name like a razor. In the Islands, they swallow their contractions and say *mon* instead of *man*. If Batman lived here, for example, he be Batmon. "I not Bertha, mon. I Martha. And that no moon, mon. That the gas dock."

This week, I've visited every marina in the North Sound—Biras Creek, Saba Rock, Leverick Bay, The Bitter End—and learned the name of nearly every bartender therein. Back in my mother's apartment in Puerto Rico, a stack of college applications lies untouched on my bed, though I suspect she may have already begun to fill them out for me, unwavering as she is. This is a test run: if Michael Jackson says the engines are tip-top, I could be home tomorrow. He's zigzagging the boat to avoid cracking any of the moorings that peek out like turtle shells throughout the Sound. We're spilling a heavy wake at the anchored motoryachts and the dinghies that loll a few yards behind them as if tied to leashes. The waves look like carpets being unrolled for royalty, and the crew of a bobbing trawler is screaming at us to slow down, but Michael Jackson doesn't care. He's got a big check coming if the Evinrudes hold up, and it looks like they will. He starts singing "Billy Jean" and moonwalking in place, but he never lets go of the wheel, and the twin controls pressed down to the console never come up. The underside of his belly prods out from under his t-shirt, and the wind rips into his afro, vacuuming the lyrics into the Dusky's foam-trail: *The kid is not my son.* It is almost noon, and we're flying past The Bitter End as if we're deliverymen late for a funeral with a cabin full of flowers.

Ten days ago, no one believed me when I announced that the boat had sunk. I was coming down the hill from our hotel room, and saw a tilted bimini top in the slip where we'd docked the night before, but no boat beneath it. The ropes were still tied to the pier, but the pleats had ripped off the gunwale and lay floating above the Dusky, almost motionless, with the other ends of the ropes still lassoed around them. Floating too were the white seat cushions that were always loose because their buttons had rusted, the zip-up bottle holders from Tortola, the empty Bud cans we'd thrown on the deck during the trip, the free jug of Pusser's Rum we got when we gassed up at Sopper's Hole, a quarter-full bottle of Pennzoil, and, surprisingly, even the Igloo, full of saltwater and beer. There was a block of ice hovering like a cadaver, melting away, changing shapes. A round lifesaver was sunk halfway, tilted at a perfect 90-degree angle, as if half its insides were rotten. The tanks were leaking gasoline, which pooled within the seawater, and it looked like the boat was bleeding rainbows.

My father and Yasser were sitting at a table next to the bar at the Lighthouse. Yasser was eating breakfast and my father was drinking a Cuba Libre, which meant he'd already drunk two or three screwdrivers and, perhaps, a preceding Cuba Libre as well. He'd gotten up before seven that morning and he'd flicked on all the lights in the room and raised the volume on the TV as high as it would go, just to get back at me for eating his sandwich. Our first port of call, fifty-seven miles east of Fajardo, is always Crown Bay in St. Thomas, where they make my father's favorite roast beef. Yasser and I always eat ours on the spot, but my father safeguards his. He wraps the cellophaned sandwich in a grocery bag and tucks it in the Igloo and, at night, takes it to the hotel room, and then he puts it back in the Igloo the next morning. This goes on for days, and he never eats the damn thing. Yasser and I had stayed up late the night before, and by the time the bars closed, there was nothing to eat but my father's sandwich. Yasser didn't want any, because it had three-day-old mayo and he didn't trust it, but I tore into it. When my father realized what I was doing, he jumped out of bed and began gnashing his teeth, screaming that his sandwich was sacred. He demanded I give him what was left, which was most of it, and he sat on the edge of the bed and ate the whole thing. The whites of his eyes blazed like neon lights in the dark. He was still breathing heavily when I fell asleep. "I will never, ever, ever forgive you," he said.

"The boat sank," I said.

My father sipped his drink.

Yasser didn't take his eyes off his plate. "Hey," he said. "Do you wanna eat crabs tonight? Because if you do, the chef said you have to order them now."

"Fuck the crabs," I said. "The boat sank. It sank!"

They both grinned and looked up at me, as if expecting a lame punchline.

"Fine," I said, and pulled out a chair. "It didn't sink."

We kneeled on the pier and looked down at the Dusky, trapped beneath the gaudy film of diluted gas. Even the bimini top had gone under by then, and the empty beer cans had begun to drift.

"I just saw it when I came down the hill, like half an hour ago," Yasser said. "It looked fine. What the hell do I do now, Hector?"

"Well," my father said, "you get it out."

"How?"

"With a liftbag. Hire someone to do it, then find a mechanic. I'll be right back." He hobbled away, and I knew he was going back to the bar, because that's where he goes whenever he says he'll be right back. Yasser and I went to the marina office. The dockmaster was a middle-aged British blonde with leathery hands and a handheld marine radio latched onto her belt. We told her our twenty-five-foot fish-around cuddy-cabin Dusky with twin Evinrude outboards had just sunk in slip B-17. She didn't seem impressed.

"So, Lady," Yasser said. "How you get it out?" His English is terrible.

"Liftbags," she said. "Underwater Safaris has them. But that's the easy part. What you need is a mechanic on the spot, when they lift it, and maybe he'll be able to salvage the engines."

"Where you get mechanics?" Yasser said.

"There's only two outboard mechanics on the island. One's at Biras, the other's at Bitter End."

"What is their name?"

"Bozo and Michael Jackson."

"Can I use your phone?"

"I'll call," she said, flipping through her Rolodex. "I'll say it's an emergency. Which one should I call?"

"Both," Yasser said.

"They don't like each other."

Yasser shrugged. "Call which one you want." He leaned on her desk and pouted his lips. "What you do today for dinner?" he said.

She looked up from the Rolodex and studied his face. "Excuse me?" she said.

"I will like to thank you for your help, sweetheart," Yasser said, "with crabs."

"I'll be right back," I said.

The bar at The Lighthouse is shaped like a sailboat, and my father was sitting at the bow. He was the only customer, and he was already drinking Chivas. This is how he does it: a couple of Screwdrivers when he gets up, then it's on to Cuba Libres until the Coca-Cola gets too sweet, and, finally, Scotch for the rest of the day. He can drink an entire bottle, but I've never seen him stumble or vomit or make a scene. And he never eats: especially in the Islands, because by the time he's ready for dinner all the restaurants have closed.

He was talking to the bartender, and before I sat down, she reached into a cooler and pulled out a Heineken, opened it, and set it on top of the bar. My father dragged out the stool next to his and patted it. "Update me," he said.

"Yasser's trying to fuck the dockmaster," I said. "But she's not into him."

"Well," he said. "I've been investigating many things." This meant he'd just bombarded the bartender with a bunch of questions and was getting ready to relay the information. "The Virgin Gorda Carnival starts tonight," he said, and sipped his drink. "Some reggae bands from Jamaica are playing, but it's in Spanish Town, so we need to rent a car, because the taxis are murder. There's some guy named Speedy who rents Jeeps, and Martha here is getting a hold of him for us."

I glanced at the bartender, who was slicing lemons, and took a sip of Heineken. "Well, the dive shop here has liftbags, so they're going to get the boat out, and they're trying to find a mechanic."

"The fucking bilge pump," my father said. "I told him before we left. You heard me, I told him to check it. There's a little ping-pong ball sensor in there that sets off the pump when the water gets too high. I bet you anything the ping-pong ball was rotten and it didn't float. I told him to check. He has no idea what he's doing, you know."

My father sold the boat to Yasser when he was getting divorced from my mother, just so she couldn't claim it. He'd bought it in Florida after winning a big case in '87, and the day after, he came home, put frying oil in the burner to make some french fries, fell asleep, and burned down our apartment. My mother pleaded with him to return the boat because they needed the money to rebuild, but he didn't, and they never got along after that.

Yasser doesn't have a feel for the boat, nor does he take care of it the way my father did when it was his. All the fenders are partially deflated, and the ropes don't match in length or color. He's afraid to take the boat out unless my father is with him, yet he insists on maneuvering it, though he always smashes it into docks, and he skitters all over the marinas before he's able to plant it in a slip. My father and I call the boat "Baryshnikov" since all it does is prance around like a ballet dancer when Yasser's at the helm. He doesn't even know how to talk on the VHS, and his sense of direction is nonexistent. Whenever we arrive at an island, he walks up to the first person he sees and says, "Excuse me, where are we?" just to piss my father off, since my father knows exactly where we are at any given time. After the divorce was final, my father tried to buy the boat back for what he'd sold it, but Yasser wouldn't sell.

"What did he say to the dockmaster?" my father asked.

"That he wants to give her crabs, sweetheart."

"No, but did he complain at all? He knows the marina's liable. We'll sue when we get back home." My father always talks about doing things he never gets around to doing. He often threatens to write letters to the *San Juan Star*, the slender English-language newspaper that nobody reads, in response to things that bother him, but he never does. I've heard him say, for example, "I was driving through Old San Juan, and you wouldn't believe how run-down that huge fountain in front of the Capitolio is—it doesn't even have water in it," or, "I hate all these people who build $100,000 homes on government land in Piñones—they're goddamned rich and they're squatting," and he always caps it off with, "I'm going to write a letter to the *San Juan Star*." I like to tease him about it.

"I mean," my father continued, "Yasser's paying for the marina's services. They're supposed to have someone on duty, watching the boats, making sure no one breaks into them, that they don't fucking sink. Think about it: Baryshnikov sank in the middle of the morning. There should have been someone watching. It's neglectful."

"Definitely," I said. "You should write a letter to the *San Juan Star*."

"Fuck off, Tito," he said. He took a little tube of Orajel out of his shirt pocket, squeezed some onto his finger, and rubbed it inside his mouth. He'd had a toothache since we left. "Hey, did you see those two girls over there, having lunch? They're about your age."

They were sitting outside, right across one of the arcs that divided the indoor and the outdoor parts of the restaurant, and they had temp Rasta tattoos on their lower backs. They were obviously from the States, and, like most white girls do when they come to the Islands, they'd gotten sunburns and braids. "If I was your age, I'd be over there buying them a drink right now, before one of these dirty island guys gets to them. Look at those tattoos," my father said. "They're looking to get laid."

"Well, I got Camille at home," I said, knowing well that he knew my girlfriend. We'd been together for six months. She hadn't wanted me to come on this trip.

"Come on," he said. "You're too young to be faithful. Here, take the card and go buy them one of those frozen drinks those girls go crazy for." He pulled my grandfather's MasterCard out of his wallet. The three of us have the same first and last name. My grandfather is at the Presbyterian Hospital in San Juan—yellow, dying.

"Maybe later," I said.

"They won't be here later," he said. "Come on, don't be such a pussy. As your Dad, I order you to go talk to the two little sluts over there."

"You're not my Dad," I said. It was a joke we had, which started with a card I'd given him for Father's Day. It said: *Anyone can be a father, but it takes a special one to be a Dad.* My father told me he wasn't a special one. He said that serial rapists, axe murderers, military dictators, all kinds of horrible people could be fathers: It was just a biological accident. *Dad* had more to do with being there to watch the son grow up. My father's father hadn't been a Dad, and neither had mine, so it was something we had in common. We were both also only children.

"Fair enough," he said. He looked at the girls again. "As your lawyer then, I advise you to buy two frozen daiquiris and escort them to that table." Two months ago, my father got me off the hook from a DUI because he was old poker buddies with the circuit judge who was on duty.

"You're not my lawyer," I said. "You're still disbarred." This was true: Because my father had not tried a case in years, he'd stopped paying his Bar Association fees, and they revoked his license. He has been living off my grandfather's MasterCard and the money my mother paid him when she bought his half of the apartment.

"Either you go over there and buy those girls a drink, kid, or I'll go over there and tell them every little thing you don't want them to know about you," he said, and started to get up. I knew he would: He never bluffs, and he loves to embarrass me in public. He's not shy, and he can be the most charming man in the world when he makes an effort. I ripped the MasterCard from his hand and pushed out of my stool.

Picking up girls in the Islands is a breeze: All you have to do is be straightforward, and avoid flowering shit up. I walked over to their table with the MasterCard in one hand and my beer in the other, leaned on one of the green plastic chairs, and said, "Hey. I'm Antonio, and I'd like to buy you girls a drink." I exaggerated my accent, but spoke eloquently. They looked at each other and giggled, and I sat down before they said anything because I knew I was in. It's a simple thing, really: What girl who isn't old enough to drink in her own country is going to refuse a free frozen drink on a tropical island?

They were sisters: one of them my age, the other a freshman at Columbia. They were from Baltimore, staying on a chartered sailboat with their family. I was Antonio, a parasailing instructor from San Juan, who was headed to Yale, early admission, in the fall. It's a thing we do when we come to the Islands: Yasser is always Augusto, my father is always Ramón, and I'm always Antonio, though I don't take it as far as them. Sometimes, in the mornings, when we set off for the next island, women would wave from piers, or from the decks of cruise ships, or from chartered motoryachts, and yell, "Augusto!" or "Ramón!" My father and godfather would grin at each other and say, "Shit, I wonder who she's calling to?" and we'd speed off into the open sea.

The girls had a strawberry daiquiri each, and we flirted and made plans to meet the next day. They told me the name of their sailboat, a fifty-foot Beneteau, and pointed to where it was moored. There was a plastic seat cushion from Yasser's boat drifting towards it, and, from where we sat, it looked like a dead stingray, belly-up on the water. I told them I'd be around the bar for the next few days, gave them each a peck on the cheek as they left, and returned to my father.

"Give me the card," he said. "Speedy's come through for us." I handed him the card and he forwarded it to the bartender. My father always finds somebody else to run his errands. "So, what they packing?"

"A fifty-footer, Moorings charter, bareboat." Bareboat meant they had chartered it without a captain. "I guess the Dad knows how to sail."

"You pick up their lunch tab?"

"No," I said.

"You're not my son," he said. "You have no class. No wonder you never get laid in the Islands." He shook his head. "Where'd they moor?"

"Out there," I pointed at their sailboat. "It's called 'Uhuru.'"

At this, Yasser walked into The Lighthouse, stood behind us, and put a hand on my left shoulder and the other on my father's right one. "So, Hector," he said. "You want to buy the boat now? It's officially for sale."

My father spun his neck to look at Yasser and chuckled. "Any luck?" he said.

"Well, they're lifting it up pretty soon, charging me a fortune. I left messages for the only two mechanics to come. Bozo and Michael Jackson, can you believe that shit? This place is a circus."

"What about the dockmaster? Any luck with her?"

"Ah? No. Nice liftbags, but she knows my real name," he said. "I figure we'll be here for a few days, right? I called Monica and told her to fly down. She might come tomorrow." Monica is Yasser's mistress. She's over twenty years younger than he is, and works for American Eagle, so she flies free. My father says it fucks up our trips when she's around, since Yasser can't be Augusto.

"Well, while you've been out there doing nothing," my father said, "we've been finding out all sorts of things, and we have great news. The Carnival starts tonight, it's in Spanish Town, and we have a Jeep. And Tito's got two rich gringas with braided hair and tattoos who will be joining us."

"You do?" Yasser's eyes lit up.

"No," I said, and sipped my beer. "The tattoos are fake. Where's the phone? I need to call home."

Virgin Gorda is only about a hundred miles upwind from Puerto Rico, but calling long distance is a pain in the ass, because the operators are incomprehensible. It took fifteen minutes to place a collect call to my mother, who was upset instead of sympathetic.

"What do you mean the boat sank?" she said. "What'd you do to it?"

"Me? Nothing," I said. "It sank. It just sank."

"Well, you're still coming home in a week, right? That'll give you four days to finish your applications. Did you start the essay yet?"

"Don't worry, there's plenty of time."

"Have you called your grandfather?" she asked. "He's not well, Tito. You shouldn't have left. It's so irresponsible of you and your father to just take off like that, when that old man is so sick. I don't know how your father could just—"

"Okay!" I said. "Listen, this call is costing you a fortune. We'll be back in a week, if not before, all right? I've got to go help them get the boat out. Bendición?"

She sighed. "Que Dios te bendiga, mijito."

The applications on my bed are all for Ivy League schools that I won't get into. Colleges have been bombarding me with mail for the last year, all because I got a high score on the PSAT. If my GPA was over 3.5, I'd be a National Merit Scholar, but I've coasted along with a middling 2.9. The application for the UPR, where I want to go, is not due until February. Both of my parents, as well as Camille and my college advisor, think I should go to college in the States, so I've decided to apply to the impossible ones. Camille really is headed to Yale, early admission. People in school have no idea why I'm with her, or, rather, why she's with me, because we have nothing in common. While she's conducting National Honor Society meetings on Friday mornings before school, I'm out in Bondi's station wagon, getting high, listening to Israel Vibration. While she's representing Canada or Finland or Djibouti at Model UN on weekends, I'm sitting on the bench at a basketball game, sweating away a hangover. In school, while she's raising her hand to recite integrals in her AP Calc class, I'm sitting in the back row of Algebra, writing notebook after notebook full of poems to give her, which is something no one knows. I couldn't believe the bitch refused the charges when I called.

The divers from Underwater Safaris lifted the boat in less than an hour. The hardest part was sliding the yellow liftbag under the keel, but once they started emptying scuba tanks into the valve, the boat rose like a bubble. They used an electronic pump to drain the water that remained inside. Yasser and I dried the anchor and battery hatches with a handpump, and we sprayed WD-40 on everything. My father sat on top of the Igloo on the dock, nursing a Scotch in a plastic bottle, yelling out instructions and tossing us beers when we asked. Underwater Safaris brought a machine from Spanish Town to siphon the watered-down gas from the tanks. They left the inflated liftbag under the hull of the boat to make sure it didn't sink again, and Baryshnikov looked as if someone had tried to wrap a yellow ribbon around it but came up short. Then, the mechanics showed up, at the same time, and we could hear them arguing as they made their way to slip B-17.

"Who the owner of this boat?" one of them demanded, and Yasser stepped forth, extended his hand, and shook both of theirs. They introduced themselves: Bozo, Michael Jackson. They both had bristly beards and were the same height, but Bozo was thin and Michael Jackson wasn't.

Michael Jackson pointed at Bozo. "What you doing calling this fool, mon?" he said to Yasser. "He don't know what he do. I the best mechanic here."

"No way, mon," said Bozo. "You don't listen to him, Captain. I seen him burn down a engine. A 200 Mercury, mon. I seen him burn it down over Gun Creek."

Yasser smiled. "Okay, which is better of you two?" His English really is terrible.

"I tell you, Captain," Bozo said. "This man here, he crazy. He think he Michael Jackson, mon, King of Pop. Let me check your engines. You ain't got time to waste." He took a step towards the boat.

"I ain't burn down no engine, mon," Michael Jackson said. "This fool just jealous cause I hook up with his girl at Maddogs. He a clown. He ain't shit." He poked Bozo in the shoulder.

"You don't fucking touch me, mon," Bozo said, and shoved Michael Jackson with both hands. Michael Jackson lost his balance and fell into the water, and his head barely missed the platform of the Hatteras docked on the other side of Baryshnikov. The water splashed up on the pier, and my father got wet, which rarely happens on these trips.

We all looked at Bozo without saying anything: me, my father, Yasser, and the two divers from Underwater Safaris. "Shit mon," Bozo said, and picked up his tool-box and took off running down the dock.

"I fucking kill you, mon," Michael Jackson said, his head poking out of the water like a buoy. He propelled himself onto the platform of the Hatteras and stood on it. "Come back here, fool."

Yasser smiled. "Well, Mr. Michael," he said. "You get my job today. No burn down no engine, okay?"

"I'll be right back," my father said.

The road in Virgin Gorda is like a roller coaster track. The island, if you look at an aerial map, looks like a dumbbell: One of the ends is the North Sound, the other is Spanish Town, the Capital. The thin middle is all hills. Yasser and my father made me drive the Jeep and risk the foreign country DUI. I'm young, they always say, and, while Yasser has his political post to worry about, my father simply can't drive because of his bad eyesight. Michael Jackson was able to start one of the engines on the spot, after putting in new fuses, but the other needed a part that had to be sent for. My father used the MasterCard to rent the Century Tree Villa, which had a private pool overlooking Leverick Bay, right by the marina. There was a three-night minimum, and we figured that a mechanic who thinks he's Michael Jackson would take at least that to fix a boat. Plus, my father said, it was Carnival weekend, so we might as well spend three days in Virgin Gorda regardless, before going on to Anegada, our next port of call.

We parked in a lot full of cars, across the street from a huge tent that had thousands of people inside it. There were long parallel tables full of artwork and t-shirts and food and drink vendors, and once we passed all that and came out on the other side, there was a patch of grass with makeshift bars and game booths on either side, and a stage on which a reggae band was playing. We went to get a drink at one of the bars: a tall metal table, behind which were two bartenders, several coolers, and about a dozen bottles on a smaller table. The bartenders kept all the money in their pockets. My father ordered two Scotches, for him and me, and Yasser ordered a Finlandia on the rocks, which meant the crowd had energized him. He started talking to a tall Island girl with a gap-toothed smile. My father drifted to the next table, where they were playing some sort of game, and I knew he wouldn't be able to resist gambling for long. I started walking towards the stage. Everyone had a plastic cup or a glass bottle in their hand, and they were all smoking cigarettes or weed or both. I still couldn't believe Camille hadn't accepted the charges when I called. Someone spilled beer on my sandals, and it trickled down between my toes. Someone was calling someone else's name, and it took me a few seconds to realize it was mine.

"Antonio! Antonio!" One of the sailboat sisters, the youngest one, ran up and put her arms around me. "What's up?" she said. "What you doing here?"

"Waiting for you." I smiled and ran my fingers through my hair.

"We begged, and our Dad actually let us take a cab from the marina." She said this like it was some sort of miracle. "Ohmygod, we just had these shots at one of those bars over there. Liquor 43, you ever tried it? It's like orange Nyquil with a kick. I can get you one, they don't card."

"I'm good. I got a drink." I raised my cup and jiggled it lightly. The ice cubes hit the plastic sides. She looked at it, surprised.

"What is it? Can I try it?"

The older sister came up behind me and whispered something indecipherable in my ear, and then backed up to look at me. "So, you know where we can get some?" she asked.

"What?" I said. The little sister took a sip of my Scotch and made a sour face.

"Grass!" the older one said, leaning into me. "You know anyone here?"

"Sure," I said. "How much?" She pulled a fifty from her purse, bent it twice, and handed it to me. I gave it back.

"Stay here," I said.

In the Islands, a dime bag costs six bucks, and the stuff is better than San Juan's. I had only smoked it twice, with a bartender from Tortola named Zeus, in the back of a bar where women took off their tops and signed them, then left them tied to the wooden rafters on the ceiling. At the Carnival, I just asked the first guy I saw smoking.

"Dude over there," he pointed. "Camouflage hat. He Speedy. He hook you up."

Speedy didn't ask any questions. I gave him twelve dollars and he gave me two bags and some papers. "And thanks for the Jeep, mon," I said.

"Yeah, the Jeep," he said, as I walked away. "That kid so fucked-up. He call the spliff the Jeep." The people around him burst out laughing.

The Ivy League sister rolled and sparked the first one, and we passed it around, watching the band play Marley covers. Both girls danced only from the hips up. The younger sister was in front of me, and I kept glancing at the temp tattoo on her lower back. It looked like two dolphins sixty-nining in yellow, red, and green. After the joint burned to a roach, the Ivy League sister went to find a bathroom, and the younger one began to lean her back against me. I put my arms around her waist.

She turned her neck and looked at me and bit her lip, so I went in, and she kissed back. She kept leaning into me, and I kept my arms tight around her waist, our upper bodies dancing. "Don't say nothing to my sister," she said, pushing into me.

When the older one returned, she hugged us both and complained about having to piss in a port-a-potty full of flies that stunk like shit while some dudes watched her. I loosened my grip on the little one, because if there ever was a mood-stopper, I'd just heard it. "Now I'm ready for a drink," the older one said. "What about you guys?"

"Sure," I said. "What you girls want? I got it."

"A beer," the younger one said. "And a shot. That 43 Nyquil liquor thingie."

"I'll help you carry," the Ivy Leaguer said. And, to her sister, "We'll be right back, don't go anywhere." She grabbed my hand and pulled.

As we walked to one of the bars, I saw my father, still sitting at the game table, throw both his hands up in the air as if he'd just lost a bet. There was a small crowd gathered around him, nothing unusual. Yasser was nowhere to be found, not that I was looking. The girl and I stood in line to order drinks.

"I'm having such an awesome time," she said. "Are you?"

"Yeah," I said.

"Hey, you know what Uhuru means in English?"

"Freedom," I said. I'd seen Black Uhuru in concert with Bondi. "Why?"

"You wanna make out?" she said, and laughed, and made eye contact.

When the younger sister found us, she yanked the older one's braids so hard that her lower teeth scraped my tongue and cut my lip. "What the fuck, you bitch?" the Ivy Leaguer yelled, and slapped her sister. I thought, briefly, about Camille: the way she slides her hair back on her head using only her pinky, ring, and middle fingers. All the locals stopped what they were doing to laugh at the two white girls going at it. The younger one turned around and began to run away. The older one didn't even look back at me. She just ran after her sister, cursing. I stood still for a few seconds, until they disappeared into the crowd, then turned to face the bartender and ordered two more Scotches.

I brought my father a refill and stood behind him while he played the game. I could see, as I approached, that he was down. It was a complicated game, and it took me a few minutes to understand what was going on. The player got three ping-pong balls for $10 and had to toss them onto a board with holes in it, and each hole had a set number of points, and you had to get to a hundred. You could buy an extra ball for $5 if you didn't get to a hundred with the first three. The first toss usually earned you at least 50 points, and so it seemed that reaching a hundred would be easy. But then, the points added up very slowly—you got two points, five points, half a point with every toss—so you had to buy extra balls. Finally, after you reached a hundred, you had to play a game of five-card draw. There was a sign behind the booth that said, in big red letters: FOUR OF A KIND WINS $2000. I doubt that's ever happened. My father got a pair of queens and won five bucks, which was like a sixth of what he'd spent getting to a hundred. He got up from the table.

"It's a scam," he said, as if I hadn't figured it out myself. "They let you win your first hand, then they take you to the bank."

"No shit. You should've at least kept one of the ping-pong balls for the bilge pump thing. Why the hell did you play that? You know those things are scams."

"No, it should be illegal. There should be some kind of commission regulating these things, you know. I'm an idiot who has money to throw away, but there are other people. They see that sign that says you could win a thousand and they get sucked in, and it's impossible to win."

"I know," I said. "You should write a letter to the *San Juan Star*."

He chuckled and put his arm around me. We began walking towards another bar, and we saw Yasser in the crowd. He had his arm around the gap-toothed girl, and they were talking to an older couple.

"Augusto!" my father called out to him, and he motioned for us to come over.

"Yes, where have you gone?" Yasser said. He turned to speak to the girl and the couple. "This is the best man, of course, Ramón. And this is usher number one, Antonio."

"And this!" Yasser said to us. "This is the beautiful Wanda! We have been getting engaged tonight!"

My father and I looked at each other and grinned. Wanda had an Adam's apple.

"And these!" Yasser continued, "Are Wanda's much wonderful very great parents! Mr. and Mrs. King, like the royalty! The royalty of Virgin Gorda! They keep giving me their daughter's hand for married. I have told them you are good friends with Mr. Speedy, Ramón, yes? He is the cousin of Wanda. You will be best man, yes?"

The couple shot us a suspicious look. My father shook both their hands. "Yes, of course. Speedy and I are good friends. Friends for a long time." He stopped to look at his watch. "Will you excuse us? We'll be right back."

The Virgin Queen was less crowded than the makeshift bars at the Carnival. My father was having another Scotch, and I had a mellow buzz, so I'd switched back to beer. It stung every time I sipped it, because the sisters had cut my lip. We had walked right past a closed jewelry store on the way to the bar, and my father stopped by the window to look at the watches, like he always does when we come to the Islands.

"Next trip, I'm getting that Submariner with the blue dial," he said. "I miss that fucking watch." He used to have one, and he told everyone it was stolen at gun-point. Once, drunk, in a rare moment of vulnerability, he told me the truth. He was in Boston, arguing a case in the Appeals Court, and after the case was over, he'd met a woman in the lobby of the Four Seasons, and he took her to his room. The next morning, when he woke up, the woman was gone, and so was the watch. The door was cracked open, and there was a fresh turd floating in the toilet. He called it the time he traded a Rolex for a piece of shit. When he returned to Puerto Rico, he had to make up a story for my mother.

"Why don't you just get it on this trip?" I said. "Get it over with."

"No, not yet." He looked at his Casio. It was just after 2:00 a.m. "When I get the Pateks, I'm giving you one, you know. As soon as you pass the bar. I don't need both of them." My grandfather has two Patek Philippes, which I have only seen once, in the wall safe of his mansion. I honestly don't see the point of walking around with something so expensive on your wrist. My grandfather has pancreatic cancer, and they've just diagnosed some stricture, and it's too late for surgery. They put him in the hospital the day before we left.

"I don't want it," I said. "You can wear one on each arm if you want. It doesn't matter to me." When my father was my age, my grandfather told him if he studied law, he'd set him up with a good job. After he passed the bar, my grandfather gave him a clerk job and paid him minimum. "You know I'm not going to law school," I said.

"Well, you don't know that yet, Tito," my father said. "You're almost as smart as me. Maybe someday you'll be smarter. If only you got off your ass every other day."

"It's the genes, mon," I said, and raised my beer. "Not much to look forward to, mon."

"So," my father began, "you think your grandfather—"

At that moment, three men with black stockings over their heads, wielding Uzis, rushed in and told everyone to shut the fuck up and get the fuck down. One of them stood by the door, one of them jumped over the bar, and the last one opened fire at the ceiling, and everyone in the place got on the ground, except my father, who didn't move. The one by the door kept yelling to the one behind the bar to hurry up, but he was having problems opening the cash register, so he unplugged it, picked it up, and took off running with it down the beach. The other two followed. It happened in less than a minute. Everyone got up and left without paying.

Because it was such a good night for business on the Island, I guess the Virgin Queen wanted to make up for what they lost, so they stayed open. My father and I remained in our spots, though we were instantly sober from the rush of adrenaline. I looked at the zinc roof and studied the small arrangement of bullet holes, shaped like a seven. My father stared at the top shelf. "You ever had Blue Label?" he said.

"Yeah," I said. "Every Tuesday, after polo."

He ordered us both a drink, not a hint of humor.

"Mom says I shouldn't have come on this trip," I said. "That we shouldn't have come."

"She's probably right." He took a sip of Blue Label, but he didn't react to it. "But I don't want to be there. You know, he'll find a way to fuck with me, even with a tube stuck down his throat."

"It's good," I said, holding up my glass.

"It's all he ever drank," my father said. "Well, here. Let's drink to him."

Our glasses met and we drank. "Hey, maybe you'll become born-again," I said. "Like Mom."

"Nothing like three big black men with Uzis to put it all in perspective," he said.

As we were leaving, a white-haired Englishman walked right up to us. "Excuse me," he said, very properly, to my father. "We think we have the assailants trapped under a house. Would you be so kind as to come with us? We want to drive them out, and we need you to guard the north lawn of the property, in case they come your way."

My father looked at me for a second, then back at the Englishman. "Excuse me?" he said. "You're telling me that there are three men with automatic weapons trapped under a house, and that you want *me* to stand guard, in case they *happen* to come my way? These men have Uzis, and what do I have?" He searched his pocket and came up with the Orajel. "I have this little tube of Orajel, old chap. What should I do when they come at me? Orajel them to death? I don't think so. I'd rather have another drink."

The Englishman stormed out. We finished our drinks and went looking for Augusto and his groom to be.

The crowd at the Carnival had dwindled, and, instead of a band, loud recorded music poured out of the speakers. Yasser was sitting at one of the makeshift bars, drinking vodka on the rocks, his arm around Wanda's waist. All of the ice in his drink had melted, and it had overflowed onto the metal.

He got up from the stool when he saw us. "Ramón! Antonio! Have you heard? Terrorists! Terrorists with Uzis have taken Virgin Gorda." Word of the hold-up had apparently gotten out, but neither my father nor I were willing to explain any of it to Yasser, not at that point. "I'm happy you're not shot. Good health! Good health for everybody!"

My father leaned discreetly into Yasser. "You know, you're engaged to a man," he said in Spanish. "A man dressed as a woman."

"No?" Yasser said, and looked at Wanda. He leaned over and grabbed her crotch. Well, *his* crotch. Wanda jumped out of his stool and spilled his drink. "Yes," Yasser said. "Yes, let's go."

On our way across the undulating road, Yasser kept asking where we were and what had happened. I was laughing, but still shaking. My father, on the passenger seat, asked how I was doing.

"I sure as hell could eat a sacred roast beef sandwich about now," I told him.

"You know, you're still not forgiven for that," he said.

"Can somebody please tell me what has happened?" Yasser yelled.

Soon after we returned to the villa, someone began knocking on the door. My father and I were lying in our beds, watching TV. Yasser was in the other room, sprawled on a king-sized bed, which he would share with Monica during the coming week. The knocking began to sound more like punching. My father answered the door, and I heard my other name being called, so I peeked out of the bedroom, in my boxers.

"You Antonio?" a white, middle-aged man wanted to know.

"Who the hell are you?" I said, snooty.

The man took a step into the house. He held up a bunch of flowers. He threw them onto the tiles. Some of the petals broke off. He pointed at the wrecked bouquet. "What the fuck is this?" he said. "Who the fuck do you think you are?"

"Antonio," my father said. "I think this man is coming on to you. Should I leave you two alone?"

"You stay out of this," the man said.

"Is this a joke?" I said, to both of them.

My father put his hands inside his pockets. He took a deep breath and looked at the man. Then, he looked at me. "Antonio," he said. "I think I better leave. This man clearly wants a taste of what you gave those girls. I hope they didn't wear you out, it looks like he could go all night." I had not told him anything about seeing the sisters at the Carnival. I had no idea what was going on, but my father's words pushed the man over the edge. He charged me, arms extended face-high. I jumped over the living room sofa, opened the sliding door, and ran half a lap around the pool. The man stopped and stood at the opposite end, knees bent, ready to sprint again.

"What the fuck you want?" I said.

"I'm gonna kick your ass, you little Puerto Rican shit."

"What for, man? What the fuck I do to you?"

"What the fuck did you do to my girls?" he said. "That's the fucking question here."

My father walked up behind the man. Yasser had gotten up, and was standing behind my father. "Look," my father said. "It was just some innocent, friendly flowers. What's the big deal? He's just a kid. Want to know the truth? He didn't even send them. I did. I sent them for him."

The man ignored him. "Tell me," he yelled. "What the fuck did you do?"

"Sir," Yasser said. "Sir, please, please go. This boy is not good. You give him much too stress for his sick, sick heart." My father and Yasser had to be at least 15 years older than him.

"Bullshit." The man started around the pool, but my father tripped him and he fell on his face. I'd already taken off in the opposite direction. My father kicked the man hard on the side. Yasser kicked him too.

"That's my kid," my father said. "My kid. He didn't touch your girls, you dumb fuck. You hear me. He didn't fucking touch them. You touch him and I'll kill you. You understand? I will kill you. Now get the fuck out."

The man got up slowly. He looked at me. "You stay the fuck away from them," he said. My father and Yasser grabbed him by the shoulders and walked him to the door. I followed far behind. I went to pick up the flowers, and noticed a note buried in the stems:

Dear Uhuru Girls:
It was wonderful to meet you both
Kisses, Antonio
PS: Century Tree Villa, up the hill

"You're an asshole," I told my father, after the man had limped away.

"What?" he said. "It was a nice gesture. Classy. It's not my fault the guy's a red-neck, you know. I'm just trying to help you out."

"Well, fucking don't. Okay?" I turned back into the room, clutching the note. I lay in bed, and read it again. It was beautiful cursive. What got me: the two little sails in the middle of "Kisses," the three little cups in "Uhuru." The way that, like a reckless suicide note, it had no final period.

Uhuru was gone the next morning. Monica came down from Puerto Rico, and Yasser chilled out, and my father and I went drinking around the North Sound. We did not return to the Carnival, nor did anyone come looking for us. Eight days passed before we finally got the part Michael Jackson needed to fix the engine. We drove to the airport at least ten times, waiting for the package to come on a flight from Puerto Rico, but not once did it occur to us to buy a ticket to go home. The man in the Hatteras next to Baryshnikov told us, one night, that he'd surprised some skinny nigger with a beard fucking around with our tanks—that's how he said it. The gas-siphoning machine had to be brought back from Spanish Town, and Michael Jackson kept saying, between songs, that he was going to kill Bozo. My father bought five ping-pong bilge pump censor balls, had them gift wrapped at the same place where he'd bought the flowers, and gave them to Yasser as a gift. The masked assailants were caught after holding up a bar in St. Marteen, several hundred miles southwest. They were pulling jobs all over the Caribbean. I have sat, drunk, each night, with a new notebook, writing poems for Camille. I want to give her everything when I come home. The first night my father saw me doing this, he asked what I was writing.

"Your eulogy," I said, and he never asked again.

This week, the days have flowed into the nighttime without us noticing, except for yesterday, when we sat at Biras Creek, drinking Champagne, toasting to a new year, watching the hazardous hills bleed the sun until there was no glow echoing off the Sound. Though we've cruised from bar to bar in water taxis, downing single malts and overtipping on a card that doesn't belong to us, the immediacy of disaster has kept us sober. We have not called anyone and there is no way to reach us: This is an island with two ends that look like giant wings, but what little is between them is tied to the bottom of the ocean.

The boat's keel digs into the water like a blade. *Billy Jean is not my lover.* Michael Jackson gives me a nod and looks back at the wake the boat is tracking. He asks if I want to bring it in, and I dock it on the first try. My father and Yasser are waiting by the slip, and Michael Jackson throws them the lines.

"Everything good?" Yasser asks.

"No problem, mon," Michael Jackson says.

"Everything good, Tito?" Yasser looks at me.

"Perfect," I say.

Yasser has just dropped Monica off at the airport. My father has returned the key to the villa and left Speedy's Jeep in care of the bartender. I have left both engines on. While Yasser writes Michael Jackson a check, my father and I load the things into the cabin. The Evinrudes purr like resuscitated beasts.

After we've unknotted the pleats and pushed off, and after we've zigzagged past the moored sailboats in the bay, and after we've each opened a beer, Yasser points the bow towards the channel between Prickly Pear and Mosquito Island.

"Off to Anegada!" he yells over the wind. Anegada is the sharpest edge of the Bermuda Triangle. It is bound by the famous horseshoe reef on all sides, and its highest elevation is only twelve feet above sea-level, so you can't see it until you're on top of it.

My father looks at me. His eyes are flooded, as if his eyeballs too have sunk. How could he not love his father?

I put my hand on Yasser's shoulder. "That's enough," is all I have to say. He looks at me, then at my father, and he understands, so he turns the wheel the other way.

Our wake looks like the tail of a cloud: shaking everything up from underneath, unsettling the plane of the surface. The wind, this time, is on our backs, and the waves are pushing the boat down the Sir Francis Drake Channel, trying to hurry us home.

BELOVED CHILD

Diane Goodman

I know Aiko is frying the bacon in her wok, using chopsticks to turn the pieces without even looking at them thanks to her inherited skill and grace. Not a drop of grease would dare splatter upon her. Gil is in charge of lettuce, lovingly wiping down each leaf with a wet paper towel as if he were bathing a newborn child. He also keeps his eye on the wheat toast browning in the toaster oven. Donny is in his Barcalounger in the living room, reading some impenetrable book, underlining passages key to him which he will quote during lunch. He is puffing on an unlit pipe.

I am not there yet but I know it is exactly as I imagine it, this preparation of our Saturday "family" lunch. Aiko had said 'Avocado BLTs' so I said I would bring the avocado and the tomatoes, as soon as I finished my long swim at the university pool. Aiko had said 'no, no, I can get them' with the odd urgency that I never quite understand when I offer to help. But I'd insisted because if I bring nothing to the Saturday lunch, then I am nothing but a family guest.

Normally when I am swimming, I am pleasantly lost and not thinking. That's why I swim in the pool instead of in the ocean because the ocean has no walls to turn me back and I need the freedom of turning back. In the pool, Bruce Springsteen sings in my head. But today, thanks to Veronica Smiley, I was thinking about why Gil's desk isn't covered with pages for the draft of his book on Thoreau. It is summer and Gil is an assistant professor at University of Miami; he spends his summers writing this book, which he hopes will find a publisher before he comes up for tenure. He has three more years. In the locker room today, Veronica—Gil's department chair—asked me how his book was coming and it occurred to me that I didn't know. It also occurred to me that I didn't care because if I cared I would probably know but then what propelled me through the water was trying to figure out why I didn't know. I seem to care about that.

It is nearly noon when I get home and I am almost late so I run up the stairs, taking two at a time, breathing in the gorgeous smoke of bacon. I undress in my kitchen, throw my wet tank suit into the sink and slip on the t-shirt and shorts I'd draped over a kitchen chair before I left. I grab two tomatoes and put them in a bowl with the avocado I'd left to ripen on the windowsill for just this occasion, and a lemon. I am starving. My hair is wet and tangled and I smell like chlorine.

Donny is a very large imposing man but no one ever calls him Don or Donald. He has a buzz hair cut, a goatee and one pierced ear, in which he wears a small silver cross although he claims not to be religious. He is thirty-five years old and does not have to work. Aiko and Donny have been married for over five years. They met six years ago at the university library, when Donny was a graduate student and Aiko worked at the circulation desk so she could take dance classes for free.

Donny keeps most of his past a mystery and all Gil and I know is that his parents died in a hotel fire somewhere in Europe while he was here writing a dissertation on T.S. Eliot. When he inherited their fortune, he quit school and shortly after, married Aiko. He is an only child. So is Aiko. Gil has an older sister named Loretta. She is paralyzed, in a wheelchair, and lives with Gil's mother, RuthAnn, in Phoenix. I have never met them.

We all live in the house Donny owns in Coral Gables: Aiko and Donny downstairs, Gil and I upstairs. Donny continues to educate himself and thinks we are his students. Gil teaches Freshman Composition, an introduction to literature course, and one section of his specialty, 19th-Century American Literature, where he gets to spend some time talking about Thoreau. Gil loves to be outside. He and Aiko take lots of long walks around the campus when I am at work and Donny is either reading or taking his afternoon nap. They "commune" with nature, they say, loving its "grandeur" and its "sadness" and "yet its hope." They use these words and phrases not as if everyone does but to point out that everyone does not. Donny does not seem to hear them, and usually I just plug Bruce Springsteen back into my head. I tend to gravitate toward "Born to Run" at these times and there's no irony in this.

I love to swim. I love the power of my body when it moves through the water, the small satisfying breaths, the pushing toward something and the return, pushing and returning, freedom with boundaries. I would do little but swim and cook if I didn't have other obligations. Aiko still takes dance classes at the university and she takes care of Donny. She is Japanese-American, slim and sturdy, delicate but not the porcelain doll you would expect. She is freckled, especially across the bridge of her upturned nose, and she has gleaming blue-black hair that is cut in layers to her shoulders with bangs that are always just casually touching her almond eyes. She has a deep voice that is a surprise coming from such a heartbreakingly beautiful girl. Her mother still lives somewhere in Japan. Aiko talks about her mother often, about how she misses her. When this happens, Gil nods in complicity and often says "I understand. It's the same for me. Phoenix can be as far away as Japan" and I turn my face away so I can roll my eyes as Aiko says, "I know," because it is not the same at all. Phoenix is a four hour plane ride away from Miami. In the three years that Gil and I have been together, he has never gone to visit his mother and sister. Not once. But he loves to suffer their absence.

Suffering absence is what binds Gil and Aiko, what suspends them above the ordinary world.

I go downstairs and walk into Donny and Aiko's part of the house without knocking as is our way and pass Donny reading in the lounger. I say hello. He reads, *"in my beginning is my end"* and I say "that sounds right" and go into the kitchen, into the scene I imagined, and also into the heavy quiet leftover from last Saturday's lunch. Gil has laid all the washed leaf lettuce out on clean paper towels and is going for the toast. Aiko is draining the perfect bacon. I go to the sink to wash my tomatoes. No one says hello, not even me, but then Gil asks, "How was your swim?"

"Wet," I say, and, angry at myself for saying it, turn on the water. I wish Gil wasn't so handsome; it makes me angry and more sarcastic than I want to be. Lately, his whole being has become unbearable. He has a perfectly sculpted face, like a model's, with the strong jaw, the high cheekbones, the dark blue eyes and naturally pale, almost see-through, skin. His teeth are perfect. He has straight blonde hair that he is always pushing off his forehead, a gesture that was for a time endearing. He wears huge square tortoiseshell glasses that he really needs and which make him even more handsome and more unbearably so because on someone else they would look ridiculous. He has cultivated this look of eternal sadness, even when he's smiling. It makes me sick.

Gil and Aiko are close friends, much closer than Donny and I are but it's necessary to all of us: Gil is an empty receptacle that I could never fill and so I am relieved that he and Aiko have the kind of relationship that lets them feed off each other's never-ending grief: they are both the children of dead minister fathers. Sometimes their sorrow can be trying, often annoying, but at least I have a career which provides hours of escape. Donny is home almost all the time but he is not interested in the constant amorphous sadness that permeates the rarefied air Gil and Aiko breathe; in fact, somehow he doesn't even seem to notice how bound up they are in their shared melancholy.

Whatever is going on now has been going on for a while, or at least for a week. At last Saturday's lunch, tuna melts on rye, I looked over at Aiko while she was laying the farmhouse cheddar slices onto the open face sandwiches, while Gil was holding open the broiler door, and saw she was crying. I said, "Aiko, what's wrong?" and she said "My father was a minister" and then I said "I know" because we all knew that and then I said, "so was Gil's" which was something else we all knew but that they both always loved to hear. In Japanese, Aiko's name means *beloved child*. It was the name her father gave her.

That day I had brought a homemade lemon remoulade I'd mixed with dill and capers; we were going to spread it on the rye before the scoops of tuna went down. But, as usual, I was almost late and Gil and Aiko had gone ahead and assembled the sandwiches before I got there. I'd said, "Oh, but what about this remoulade" and immediately Aiko went to the refrigerator and produced a lovely platter of crudités that she had prepared earlier.

"So you knew I'd be late?" I said.

"I didn't want your spread to go to waste," she answered, in a low small voice that said she was clearly upset about something but whatever it was, no matter how grave, she was still thinking of me.

That kind of sacrifice is pure Aiko; family first, her own troubles later. She had a way of relaxing her grief so that it made room for more timely obligations that needed to be fulfilled, like laundry, bill paying, or slicing vegetables for remoulade. Aiko's father died seven years ago, Gil's eleven, but they both live in the wake of those deaths as if they had just discovered them. Before he met Aiko, Gil kept his grief going through a career in literature which provided endless opportunities for personal sadness and Aiko, I imagine, nurtured hers out of honor and private necessity. But then they found each other and their friendship took their combined sadness to an entirely new level, one that made them almost happy. But I was so tired of being confronted with all that old sadness all the time so I stuck a carrot into my remoulade and put it in my mouth so I did not have to inquire any further. By the time Donny came in from the living room and started quoting from Robert Frost, Aiko's tears had gone away.

Today Aiko asks me if I want her to slice the avocado that I am in the process of slicing. The kitchen is not small but it is small enough for all of us to see what each one is doing. I rub a cut lemon on the slices so they won't turn brown. Then I add some salt and pepper. I say nothing because she is not expecting a response. She knows the answer but she can't help herself. I begin to slice the tomato and it spurts all over my t-shirt, seeds and juice. I am the executive chef at the South Miami Country Club. I have to be at work by 2:00. I am always covered in food.

Aiko and Gil instituted our Saturday lunches two years ago, a few weeks after Gil and I moved in upstairs. They won't let me cook anything for the lunches, and wouldn't even let me help if I didn't insist on doing something. They say I shouldn't have to do the work I do at work in my own home.

I met Gil three years ago when his department hired the country club to cater their Christmas event. I stopped by on my way to work to check on the catering staff and Gil was there early too because he was in charge of drinks. He had pitchers of iced tea, and bottles of wine coolers and beer that he had put warm into a silver serving bin. I saw him struggling with the ice and walked over; I took the big bag, threw it on the ground three times to break up the cubes, and then poured the ice over the warm bottles. Gil was not embarrassed by what he called my expertise; he was grateful and relieved. He said, "Wow. You're small but really strong" and I said, "Not a big deal. I have to do this stuff all the time" and we got to talking and before I could leave, he'd asked me out for the next night. I said yes because Gil was handsome, because I had the next night off, and because I had been in Miami for going on two years and had not met anyone other than the staff at the country club. Not that I'd had any opportunities to make friends. I lived in a room off the kitchen at the Club, and I swam in their pool at 6:00 a.m. before the members arrived. The rest of time, I tested recipes, met with vendors, supervised the budget, oversaw the parties, and cooked. The country club was a stepping stone for me; I had just finished culinary school when I took the job and believed I'd be moving on to another place in another city at the end of three years. Living at the club allowed me to save the money I would need to really launch my cooking career.

On our third date, Gil took me to a very dark restaurant for dinner where the hostess and the waiters knew him by name. He rented a room in a house in Coconut Grove and didn't have a kitchen, which didn't matter since he didn't cook, and he ate nearly all his dinners in this place. By the time our entrees were served, I knew a lot about him: the story of his dead father, his disabled sister, his suffering mother who lived far away in Arizona. I knew he played tennis, loved the Miami Dolphins and why he'd gravitated toward Thoreau. In the candlelight, he was beautiful and his sorrow was seductive and I stayed with him that night in the single twin bed in his small room. It was summer in Miami and the air conditioner was old and weak but when I woke up in the morning, I was freezing. It only took a few seconds for me to realize that I was freezing because at some point between sex and waking, Gil had wet the bed. While I was trying to gracefully wiggle out of his embrace, he woke and immediately started crying. I know for some women, all of this—the pee and the tears—would be a deal breaker but it wasn't for me because I peed in swimming pools all the time and assumed everyone else did, too, and when Gil held me very tightly, seemingly unaware of how his embrace forced me deeper into the wet sheets, and thanked me over and over again for understanding, for being who I was, I immediately absorbed the idea that I was a person who could rise above someone else's humiliation, who could understand.

And now I hear Aiko thanking me for the avocado and tomatoes, as if I'd brought them to her as a gift. I ignore her, as we assemble the BLTs. Aiko has torn basil into the mayonnaise, a trick she learned from me. Gil spreads it on the toast and then adds the clean lettuce. I lay the tomatoes down, then the avocado; Aiko adds the bacon, a bit more basil mayo, closes the sandwiches and slices them through with a Ginsu knife. She calls Donny in for lunch and he lumbers to the table with his book, lifting a large bag of potato chips from the top of the fridge that only he and I will eat.

"My father loved bacon. He would eat it on almost anything. On Sundays, he would put a scoop of vanilla ice cream on a waffle and top it with maple syrup and crumbled bacon. And then I would do it just because he had done it. Like father, like daughter. His beloved child. His illness lasted too long," Aiko says. I am certain that she and Gil talk about their fathers every Saturday while they are preparing our lunch and that it is the remnants of their memories that darken the kitchen by the time lunch is served. Perhaps this new bolder sense of dread in the kitchen is just the product of deeper and more personal exchange. Usually Gil will follow Aiko's inevitable comment about her father with one about his own but today he just sits there, staring at his sandwich on the plate.

But then Aiko picks hers up to take a bite and Gil does the same. Aiko eats in the most irresistible way, half perfunctory and half passionately, and both aspects of her eating have a profound effect on me. Between culinary school in France and trying to make a name for myself through the country club restaurant, I have tasted nearly everything only to discover that while I have a sophisticated and sensitive palate, there are a lot of foods I don't especially like to eat. But I always want to eat everything Aiko is eating just because of the way she eats it, even unusual Japanese delicacies her mother sends that smell like dead fish or wet mud or eggs gone bad. I am certain that even though Aiko and I are eating the exact same sandwich, hers tastes so much better than my own.

"What do you think it was that God could have been thinking?" Aiko asks.

"*In his end was his beginning,*" Donny says, paraphrasing from the book, which is open on the table in front of him. He passes me the chips. I take three, stack them up one on top of the other, place a piece of bacon that fell out of my sandwich on top, and bite.

"I ask myself that all the time," Gil says, ignoring Donny and responding to Aiko, "it's excruciating." I didn't really hear him say this last line because of the extraordinarily loud crunching in my head but I'd heard him say it so many times before that I recognized it by the way his mouth moved and how his shoulders slumped. And by the way both he and Aiko lowered the sandwiches they held in two hands into their laps and then lowered their eyes. The adult children of dead ministers, they were grieving.

I slam one of my bare feet onto the other, hard, to punish myself for thinking that, and try to remember that there was a time when I truly, genuinely, felt Gil's loss and wanted to try and fill it. But I cannot make those memories return to me so I change the subject.

"So Donny, what are you reading?" I ask.

"Rereading. *Four Quartets*. Eliot. So if everything leads to the present, to this moment, pointing to now, what is the beginning? Everything, right? Everything is the beginning. Every second. Aiko's father's death, Gil's father's death, their lives, these BLTs, all of it." He polishes off his sandwich and begins to look around for another. Aiko has one ready on the counter behind her and spins the top half of her body around like the dancer she is or was meant to be, lifts it, and spins back to put it on his plate.

I wonder why Donny does not include his own dead parents in that litany but then I begin to understand. He does not want his sorrow to be present. Satisfied by my own deduction, I celebrate by taking a big bite of my sandwich and a slice of avocado slips out and joins the tomato spots already on my t-shirt. Aiko jumps up as if I am on fire.

"Club soda," she says, heading to her fridge.

"Old shirt," I say, "don't bother," but bothering about others is what Aiko does best so now she is pouring the soda onto my shirt and rubbing at the green stain with a paper towel. I am thinking it would be good for her to have a child, someone she could take care of who, unlike Donny, would respond to her constant need to care.

"Excruciating," Gil says, again, as if we had all sat silently since the first time he said it. "He had to pee all the time, or at least he felt like he did. But he couldn't. So he would moan, and then scream for hours until the doctors gave him something to make him pass out. I did not understand what God could have been thinking."

"In his end was his beginning," Donny says, "like a baby. Wailing. Helpless. Waiting. Peeing. Aiko, a beer?"

"Yes," she says, rubbing the last of the avocado out of my shirt.

Even though I don't want her to be wiping my shirt, even though the shirt is old and thin and I would be happy to throw it away, I am helpless to stop her. Silently, I am wailing and waiting and hoping that my end is not in my beginning because if Donny and T.S. Eliot are right and the beginning is the present, then my beginning is right now here in this house in Miami and I do not want it all to end here. At least not here, in this kitchen, at the family lunch. I do not want this to be the rest of my life.

I look at Gil and see that his sandwich is still in his lap and he is nodding his head, as if he is agreeing with Donny, or Eliot. Or just having one of those conversations that he often has with himself. I stare at him, will him to look at me. I know he knows I am waiting but he will not look up. If Aiko looked at him, I think his head would snap up so fast it might go flying off his shoulders. I think I see a drop of spit fall from his lips onto his lap but then I realize it is a tear. I want to slap him.

When Gil and I met, he had been friends with Donny through the English Department; although Gil was a new assistant professor and Donny was a grad student, they were the same age and gravitated toward each other quickly. Gil had not met Aiko, though; he'd just heard Donny talk about her, about her beauty and her homemaking, her easy happiness and her obedience. "She sounds like a paper doll," Gil had told me. He said he was surprised that Donny would have such an old-fashioned wife, someone so young who was so content to just take care of him. Gil said he was lucky to have me, someone with a career, with ambitions and a sense of humor. I was pretty sure Gil didn't "have" me but I liked him fine and living with him had given me a life outside of work that I had little trouble getting used to. In the beginning of our relationship, despite the periodic crying jags, we had the kind of excitement and fun all new couples have, everything we did—from movies to dinners to bike rides on Key Biscayne—seemed as though we had invented it, our sex life was sweet, on my nights off, we watched videos until the early morning and before going to sleep, had breakfast in bed. We didn't seem to notice our life together morphing into routine but I like routine and I like order; plus, I wasn't home very much because of my work schedule and when I was, it was easy to hold Gil, to have sex, to tell him everything was going to be all right. It made me feel good to have someone other than my country club staff depend on me. Gil believed in me and that made me feel good, too; it made me happy to know that I had the kind of power to lift away sadness, that with just a few words and the pressure of my hands on Gil's back, I could make things better. And I thought everything would be all right: I was young, twenty-seven, but even so I'd had enough life to know that every bad or sad thing that happened to you was not the last thing that would happen to you. I was living proof.

We had been living in the room Gil rented for nearly a year when Donny offered us the second floor of his house and we went there for a drink, to see the place and discuss the possibilities. Aiko set down a tray with flutes of champagne and sushi she'd rolled herself and told me she'd had a dream about me before she even met me and she put her hand on my knee and squeezed, perhaps to make sure I was real. She said she knew I would be coming to her before I ever appeared, that we were meant to be family. I don't usually trust that kind of hocus pocus but I was moved by what I thought was her sincerity; plus, at that time, I thought she was this caged wife who needed a friend.

A week after we moved in, Gil came upstairs from having helped Aiko bring in her weekly load of groceries. He had stayed to help her prepare a dinner they would be eating that night while I was at work and he said he had been wrong about her. She wasn't just this young passive girl living in the dark ages. She was more than that. She had depth. Her father had also been a minister. He understood her.

Now I seem to be the one not understanding much but instead of slapping Gil for crying in the middle of our "family" lunch, I thank Aiko for laundering my t-shirt and stand up to do the dishes but Aiko reads my mind and says no. It is not so hard to read my mind because the same thing happens every Saturday: I stand up to do the dishes and Aiko says no. Now Gil has stood up and is at the sink running the hot water, having barely touched his lunch. Donny is back in his book, asking what's for dessert.

Last month was Aiko and Donny's five-year anniversary. I insisted they celebrate it by having dinner at the country club. Of course Gil would join them and it seemed less pathetic of him to be with them on their anniversary if I was at least partially there. Plus, I wanted to cook a "family" meal.

I planned a special five-course dinner, things that are not on our menu, and I meant to cook it all by myself while my sous chef managed our dinner rush. I started with a seared foie gras, drizzled with a balsamic reduction, finished with pink peppercorns and warm blackberries. I came out shortly after it had been served. Donny's plate was empty, wiped clean with some of our homemade French bread. Aiko had taken one bite and Gil had taken none—he was moving the berries around his plate, coating them completely with the reduction.

The first thing I said was, "Hey, I thought this was supposed to be an anniversary celebration," but other than Donny nodding his head in agreement, no one said anything so then I said, "Oh, I'm sorry! I should have thought about the foie gras. Not everyone likes it," except I knew Gil loved it and I'd seen Aiko eat way more controversial food than goose liver. But she said, "No, it's lovely. It's not that," but she did not say what it was so I nodded my head and went to the kitchen to prepare the salad.

I tossed microgreens with a fig vinaigrette and then topped each salad with crispy pancetta and a poached quail egg. When I appeared at the end of that course, it was the same scenario. *So then if it's not the food, what is it?* I was about to say but the folks at Table 26 began applauding when they saw me.

"This carrot-ginger soup, it's gorgeous," a woman in a white sheath dress said.

I smiled a grateful thank you.

"You are a wonder," her companion stated, still clapping.

I let the sous chef and the line cooks finish preparing the anniversary meal and I stopped going out to check. Aiko always carried with her white cards that had her name and phone number embossed in blue; she sent one back at the end of the evening but I was pan-frying a trout with one hand and flipping a pan of baby vegetables with the other so the waiter stuck the card into my apron pocket.

When I got home that night of the anniversary dinner, Gil was not there. I knew he'd fallen asleep on Donny and Aiko's couch, as he often did when I was working. I knew Aiko had covered him with an afghan she had crocheted. I undressed and then remembered Aiko's card in my pocket.

It said, *you ARE a wonder and we love you.*

Who loved me, I mused, stretching out alone in our king-size bed and hoping for a long dreamless sleep. Donny liked me well enough, thought I was funny, but dismissed me in the way he dismissed everyone—with patience and some good humor. To Donny, we were all sort of necessary impediments to his private literary search for truth. But Donny liked having an audience, and a home and a schedule; he liked to eat and drink and be around people when he wasn't reading. I suspect he also liked having sex with his beautiful wife but about that I was not entirely sure: they never touched, displayed affection, shared inside jokes. I didn't see any passion there, which didn't necessarily mean there wasn't any passion there, except anyone could see the passion Donny had for books. He loved reading. And he loved talking about what he was reading to the people who were around. I was pretty sure he loved his dead parents and that he did not love talking about them. In that way, I understood him.

Gil loved me with a kind of relief I grew accustomed to. He needed a lover, and that I could be, but he also needed a mother, a protector, a sympathetic ear and although it was easy enough for me to go through these motions, I did not care for him the way he imagined I did because I did not want to love anyone in the way Gil imagined love should be. But that is what made us such a great match: immersed in literature, Gil made assumptions and presumptions about how my actions translated into what he wanted to believe I must be feeling; he embraced his theories as truths and they made him feel superior and sure. My knowing this had the same effect on me and so we co-existed peacefully. I was not demanding in any way because I did not need much. I kept his secrets and didn't chide him or flinch when he cried, wet the bed, stayed silent for days on end. I knew he trusted me and could explain away my vague detachment through his interpretations and my clear presence, which he believed was a sign of devotion.

Aiko loved me because she dreamed me, because I was evidence of her powers. And because she believed she had created me, she could turn me into anything she wanted me to be at any time. That's what made me a wonder.

At today's lunch, though, I am wondering what I am supposed to be. Aiko and I are going through our usual tug-of-war about the dishes but I am missing something. Something new. I can feel it.

"Don't worry about the dishes," Aiko says to me, as she does faithfully every Saturday, "you need to get ready for work." Gil is soaping up the sponge; he's already filled the wok with water. Aiko has given Donny a stack of Oreos which could only mean that she did not have time to bake and that makes me suspicious.

"What did you do this morning?" I ask, because she always bakes on Saturday mornings so we have something homemade for dessert after lunch.

"I had an appointment," she says. "Do you want some Oreos?"

"No, thanks," I say, "an appointment for what?" I am slight and bony and love any kind of dessert more than just about anything else so my refusal and my follow-up question make everything even more awkward and uncomfortable.

Aiko puts the package of cookies down and looks at me.

"Let's have it," I say, because now we both know that I know something is going on but she just shakes her head and looks down. Gil is washing the dishes in water so hot that I can see the steam rising off his wet hands and I know they are burning. There is pain in those hands for sure.

Donny eats two Oreos at a time and asks if there's any milk. Or, better yet, he says, can someone make coffee?

"Anyone can make coffee," I say, and walk toward the kitchen door. "I have to get ready for work."

" 'Go, go, go, said the bird: human kind/Cannot bear very much reality,' " Donny reads.

"Amen to that," I say, and leave.

Suddenly I realize that I have been waiting for a sign. I have been waiting for something or someone to tell me it's time to pack up and go, to leave the country club and move on. Maybe to New York. To work with the real chefs—Mario Batali, Bobby Flay, maybe even Eric Ripert. I have proven myself at the country club but I need to know more. I need real instruction, real inspiration. And mostly now I know for sure that I need to get away from Gil, and from Aiko. I think today's lunch is my sign: something is happening and I realize that it's something I don't want to know, not because it would hurt me but because I sense impending drama that I do not want to witness. I want out and when I say it out loud—*I want out*—all my anger and frustration seems to fade away. I get into the shower and think that tomorrow, before I go to work, I will work on my resumé. I start humming some Bruce Springsteen, this time "Sherry Darling," and this time out loud, not just in my head.

When I am dressed in my chef whites and nearly ready to go, I hear Gil coming up the stairs to our part of the house and I think I am fine, happy in fact, so I start to go to the bedroom door to greet him but then immediately find myself back in the bathroom and closing the door. I turn on the hair dryer, even though I have already dried my hair. I hardly need to start sweating now, before I get to work and the real sweat behind the line will begin, but I do not want to listen to Gil now. If the sound of his footsteps could make me retreat, then I know the sight of him will bring back all the bad feelings my epiphany and shower just washed away, which would make all the good feelings I just had not real. Maybe I do want to know what's happening with Gil and Aiko? Except that I think I don't. And yet, I feel as though I want to murder someone.

I know he is sitting on our bed and hope that he will get tired of waiting for me and go back downstairs. I turn off the hair dryer and wait for a few minutes. I hear nothing and am relieved. When I emerge from the bathroom, my head hot and sweat coming down my hairline and sliding into my ears, he is still sitting on our bed with his hands folded in his lap and his eyes downcast. Same as it was before, except without the sandwich.

"I'm sorry," he says.

"For what?" I ask, and sure enough, my anger is so palpable I think I must have a fever.

He looks at me as if I should know the answer and then looks down into his lap again.

"I am sorry about all these downcast eyes," I say, trying to make a joke that even I don't find funny.

"I don't know how to explain…I'm sorry. It's just that Aiko and I, only we really…"

"Hmmm, must be lonely for you two," I say, and then because suddenly I am about to implode, "in The Dead Ministers' Children's Club."

Either Gil is not fazed by my nastiness or he does not hear me. "Yes," he says, and when I don't respond, "this is excruciating" and I feel the avocado BLT threatening to come up, and then he says, "I'm sorry. I wish I could make you understand." But I do understand. Perfectly. Gil and Aiko have made a pact to dwell in a cave no one else can enter. They are the children of dead fathers who were ministers and the shelter of their grief protects them, makes them smug. I get it.

I say, "I'm late" even though I'm not, and I leave.

I drive to the country club fuming but not really knowing what exactly is bothering me. This is my way out. I should be relieved. And I am because I am tired of Aiko and her sanctimony. I am bored with Donny. And I do not love Gil. So maybe I feel guilty about lying, about pretending, and maybe that is what is bothering me so much. In our first year together, when we lived in his small rented room and were getting to know each other, Gil and I spent time talking about our pasts, our families, our fears, the things we said we had not told anyone else ever; as I got to know Gil better, I knew he had probably told lots of people his secrets but I had been telling mine for the first time. Then I was done talking and wanted him to be done, too. I wanted to move on, to live in the present, in the now. I was very busy with work and when I was off, I wanted to swim, go to the movies, the beach, drive down to the Keys, go to restaurants and have great chefs cook for us, drink wine, watch the sunset. I wanted to ride bikes, plant flowers on the little balcony off the room, listen to music, play cards. I wanted to have fun. By the time I realized that Gil wanted none of these things, that he only wanted to keep talking about his past, his father, his sister—or he wanted to read and then talk about the way what he was reading related to his past, his father, his sister—I was so tired, I didn't have the energy to leave him, to find myself another apartment or a new guy. It was just easier to stay.

"No matter how much you talk about the past," I had said, "it stays the same. You just hurt yourself." I knew a lot about this: my mother died when I was fifteen. But it didn't matter: I had been a teenager and she was a single mother—not a minister father—so it didn't count. When I told Gil, I left out the details; I thought death was enough. But it was not. To Gil, my grief seemed thin and without punch, almost silly. He probably didn't even tell Aiko.

Reservations in the dining room are full for tonight so when I get into the kitchen, I call a meeting to see what kinds of specials we can offer that can be prepared quickly and will last for the whole service. Normally, I already know what kinds of specials I want to serve—this is my kitchen and ultimately the responsibility for all the dishes falls on me and that's how I like it, how it must be. This kitchen is my child: I conceived it, created it. I take care of it and devote all of my passion to tending to it, nurturing it, making sure it is the best it can be. But tonight, like even the best parent, I am weary and distracted.

Tao suggests something braised, a spicy pulled pork over polenta that can sit on the stovetop all night and just be ready to go, and I say yes right away and send him off to prepare it. Harriet, my sous chef, asks if we can do a pasta entrée special, something like gnocci in lemon with asparagus and olives. Harriet makes the most glorious gnocci. Beautiful, I say, and she goes off to make the dough. She is smiling and I realize that my staff, too, are like my children, even though many of them are older than I am. But it is my job, my responsibility, to guide them while making sure they can be confident on their own. I hand-picked them when I started here and despite the difference in our ages and levels of experience, we grew into this kitchen together. I can be tough and I can be critical but mostly I think I am loyal and supportive. I know I am as proud of them and what we do together as I can be.

I think that two specials might be enough for tonight when our intern, shy Marie, blurts out that the Ahi looks beautiful and asks if she can create an upscale entrée-size salad with it and when I say yes without even thinking, she literally runs into the prep kitchen before she thinks I have a chance to change my mind.

I have frightened her, though I am not sure why. I thought my enthusiasm was obvious, but she ran away. I wonder how Marie sees me and then it occurs to me that I don't know how Aiko or Donny or even Gil perceive me now, other than as someone who doesn't understand. Donny would never presume that I could understand the books he reads or the things he says; to him, I'm the cook who lives upstairs with his old colleague, the professor. I know Gil perceives me as someone who is not Aiko, someone who cannot understand the significance of the past. And Aiko? She must perceive me as an extension of herself, since she thinks she created me, the part of her she thankfully does not have to be. So it seems as though there is a lot I do understand and yet I feel confused, a bit lost in my own life.

Dinner service goes smoothly despite the big crowd and the Ahi salad runs out after twenty orders because it is such a big hit. Marie approaches me timidly at the end of the service and apologizes: she is so sorry she ran out of the special.

I tell her don't be silly—everyone loved it—and then she thanks me. For trusting her. For my faith in her. I see her arms moving toward me, like she wants to reinforce her gratitude through a hug, but then she must think better of it and puts her hands in her apron pockets fast.

"What don't I understand?" I blurt out, and she literally recoils.

Marie is small and shy and very young. She has an obvious fear of authority so I think that even if I was on my knees and kissing her feet, she would still be afraid of me. Perhaps more. She is the wrong person to be asking this question to but everyone else is busy shutting the kitchen down and I need an answer now.

"This isn't a trick, Marie, honestly. I just need to know: is there something I'm not getting?"

She says, "Chef, I'm sorry, but, uh, I don't know what you're talking about" and her lips are quivering.

"Do you trust me, enough to tell me what's going on?" I don't think it's that Gil or Aiko don't trust me. I think it's more that they have a secret that they want to keep to themselves.

"Nothing's going on," she stammers, "I'm sorry, Chef."

"Sorry about what?" I say. What was Gil so sorry about, sitting on our bed with his hands in his lap? What is there to be sorry for this time? What are the people I am with every day doing that they keep apologizing to me for? "Tell me what you're sorry about." My voice is thick and dark and rising.

"Um, well, I don't know," she says, and I see her struggling to figure out how to say what she thinks I want to hear. She loves her internship, is hoping it will turn into a full-time job when she finishes culinary school. She does not want to get fired. And although she could not know this now, I love having her here and have no intention of firing her. I am living in two worlds, the one where I am battering a fragile cook who has made a fantastic salad tonight, and the one where no one will tell me a truth I realize now I desperately want to know.

"Tell me the truth," I say. "Just blurt it out."

"This is your kitchen, Chef. And you're a genius. Everyone thinks so. I am so lucky to be here. But tonight was...different. Weird. Because normally you don't talk much to us, you don't really need to, I guess. I mean you need us, yes, you do, but it's also like you don't. You're quiet, you're concentrating. Everyone always says that you're in your own world, but in a good way, you know? But by yourself, so we were just surprised that you needed us to help. To help you. That you asked us for help."

I never saw this coming. Or what came after it.

"Thank you, Marie," I say because I need to put her out of her misery, "the salad really was gorgeous. We're going to run it as a special all summer. We're going to call it *Marie's Summer Ahi Salad.*"

"Oh my gosh, thank you Chef," she says, and I think she might faint. "Thank you so much, I don't know what to say."

"Great, go on now, help the others shut the kitchen down," and she literally skips off like a child.

One morning when I was fifteen, I got up to go to school, just like every other morning. My mother was in the kitchen with her nurse's uniform on; she sat at the table with me drinking herbal tea while I ate my toast and told me that today she would not be able to drive me to school. She said she had an early meeting at the hospital and I would have to take the bus. Sometimes I took the bus, and my best friend Allison and I would chew as much gum as we could before we got to school and had to spit it out so taking the bus was fine with me. My mother walked me to the door and pulled on the lapels on my jacket. She said I was a good girl, which was something I already knew, and kissed me goodbye three times, which was our habit. Then I walked to the bus. When I got home, around 3:00, there were two cars in my driveway: my Aunt Sue's and a police cruiser. My mother's bedroom door was closed and when I went toward it, the police officer gently pulled me back because my aunt was crying too hard to stand up.

My mother had crushed a bottle of Valium into the morning tea she drank while I was eating my toast and when I left to catch the bus, she got back into her bed to die. After that, something important shut down in me. But I didn't know what I no longer had, what had vanished along with my mother, and I have never told anyone the truth about this.

When I get home, I am surprised to see Gil in our bed. He is reading. It's nearly three in the morning. When he sees me, he puts the book on his lap and takes his glasses off. He has no shirt on and his chest is milky white, like an old man's. I can see some of his veins and I wonder if he is completely naked under the covers. I stand at the end of the bed and stare at him for a couple of seconds, trying to figure out which one of the things in my head I want to let out first:

I understand.

Here is the truth.

What on earth is going on?

But before I choose one, he says, "Aiko is pregnant."

I am sorry.

Here is the truth.

Is that what all this fuss is about?

"Wow," I hear myself say. "Wow. That's great. When is she due?"

"Around Christmas."

"Boy or girl?"

"We don't know yet."

"Oh. Oh, boy." I take off my chef whites and the sweaty bra and panties beneath them.

Gil is staring at me, though not at my nakedness.

"They'll be great parents, Donny and Aiko," I say. "Here's to the next Beloved Child."

"You don't understand," Gil says.

"I'm going to take a quick shower," I say, which is true because I am heading into the bathroom, and then, "I'll be right back," but that part is a lie because I am already gone.

Heeber checked his watch again.

People hustled by—past the flickering tiki torches, on into the restaurant. Laughter came from inside and music. Yet here he stood out front, alone in the muggy night air. The valet, a hungry-looking kid with shabby epaulettes, had twice approached. Heeber waved him off. He'd been warned that they were going to try to fleece him down here and he'd been on his guard since the move.

Another look at the watch.

SAMBA

Derek Green

You expected this of locals. But his own boss, Ellis—an American—had told him to be here at a certain time, and here he was. What got Heeber was that he'd wanted to go shopping, buy his wife a souvenir. She lived stateside, he *missed* her. But Ellis had claimed there wasn't time before dinner. This was earlier, at the golf course. Heeber had dutifully rushed home, changed and rushed here by taxi, only to wait alone like a fool for more than half an hour.

Tears stung his eyes. When the valet approached again he growled that he didn't want any help.

Nine-and-a-half minutes later Ellis's Grand Cherokee pulled up, tiki flames dancing in the windows. The valet hopped to the door. Ellis poured himself out, followed by Luciano, a junior engineer, local personnel. Both were beet-faced, laughing. They'd been off drinking somewhere.

Heeber raised a hand in half-hearted greeting.

"Hi, Mr. Ellis," he said. "Is Simons coming?" Simons, Ellis's friend from sales, had rounded out their foursome earlier.

Ellis walked a pace ahead of Luciano, palms upturned, a Mafia guy from TV. His smile was draining fast. "Jesus Christ, Heeber. Look how you're dressed!"

Heeber looked down. Shorts, t-shirt, sandals. It was hot. He looked back up.

"You're wearing a damn *Tigger* t-shirt, Heeber!"

"But you said casual, Mr. Ellis. I—"

"Casual, Heeber, not kindergarten. God *damn*." Ellis had cruel blue eyes. Pale, animal-like. Heeber often found it hard to look at the man.

Luciano leaned in. "I do not believe they will allow you without a collar-shirt."

Ellis regarded Heeber for an extremely unpleasant moment, then turned to the valet, barking something off in Portuguese. The kid turned in the direction from which he'd just come.

"I don't have to go in, Mr. Ellis. I mean, if there's a dress code or something."

"Christ, you're here already. Just wait."

Ellis himself wore black slacks and a golf shirt, hardly dressy. What got Heeber was that the t-shirt had been a gift from his four-year-old boy last Father's Day; he'd worn it out of homesickness, a way to feel closer to his wife and son.

The Cherokee came rolling back up. Ellis opened the liftgate and rummaged around in back. He came out with a wadded up Hawaiian shirt.

"Here. Wear this." He threw it Heeber's way. "Consider it a gift."

The place was called a *churrascaria* and here you ate Brazilian-style. An army of waiters cruised the dining room with skewered meat, fish, chicken, sausage. Heeber liked his meat and potatoes but some of the food here was scary. Last time he'd seen a cart being pushed around with a fish on it the size of a man, toothy head still attached. You could lose your appetite. Crossing the dining room, Heeber was aware of eyes on him in the ridiculous shirt. The thing reeked of Ellis's musty cologne and stale sweat.

They were seated.

"Isn't Simons coming, Mr. Ellis?"

"He's coming, Heeber." Ellis studied the menu without looking up. "He had a couple things to take care of, is all."

So. There was time for Simons to take care of things before dinner. Heeber made the mistake of glancing at Luciano, who wore his usual idiotic grin. At the golf course there had been no one else for Heeber to talk to and now the guy thought they were best friends.

"Did you find for your wife the gift you were looking for?" Luciano asked.

Heeber inspected the silverware in front of him. They used weird forks down here with only three prongs. "I'd rather not talk about it, Luciano."

"Answer the kid's question," Ellis snapped. The cold eyes were on him again. "Don't be an ass."

Luciano smiled awkwardly. "The souvenir? The CD of samba music?"

"I didn't get them yet," Heeber answered. "There wasn't enough time."

A waiter trundled up behind a bar cart, the way they did here. Ellis pointed at each man in turn. "*Caipirinha*?" he asked. "*Caipirinha? Três caipirinhas, por favor.*"

"Not for me," Heeber said. "Coca Lite, no ice?"

The waiter placed the warm can before him. Heeber wanted to make a joke about not drinking, as his wife had taught him. But Ellis sat motionless, jaw clenched, and the three of them watched in silence as the waiter sliced limes with a sharp-toothed knife.

Simons materialized, rubbing his palms together.

"Everything's lined up for later, gents." He collapsed into the seat beside Ellis and looked across the table. "A*loha*, Heeber! Check out the shirt on you."

"You think that's bad," Ellis said, "you should've seen what he had on earlier. Goddamn Tigger t-shirt! I had to give him that thing so we could get in."

"Tigger?"

"You know, the cartoon. 'The wonderful thing about Tiggers—'"

"'—is that Tiggers are wonderful things!" Simons turned back to Heeber. "Grrrr!" he said.

Everyone, including Heeber, laughed. Then Ellis kept laughing, so hard that tears swam into his eyes. He had trouble ordering another round of drinks and Heeber thought: it's not *that* funny.

Waiters arrived bearing meat. Heeber was just starting in when Luciano came to life. "Ah, look," he said. "*Coraçao*! You must try here the *coraçao*. Is in all of São Paulo the best!"

"Hey, I got an idea," said Simons. "Let's try the *coraçao*!"

They waved the waiter over. He carried a skewer studded with lumps of meat that looked like old blisters.

"Ah! *Espectacular*!" Luciano kissed his bunched fingertips like a Frenchman. "This you must try, you must try."

The waiter bowed toward Heeber. Ellis nodded, grinning. He said something in Portuguese. Heeber smiled. "What are they, Mr. Ellis?"

"Chicken hearts, Heeber." The waiter scraped half a dozen onto his plate. Heeber gripped the edge of the table as the things plopped down, God help him, like the meaty droppings of some small carnivorous jungle beast.

They were crammed into a taxi. Simons to his right and Ellis up front were singing—drunkenly, off-key. "The Girl from Ipanema," a song Heeber had liked till now. On his left Luciano stared from behind a dumb grin. It was a workday tomorrow yet they were showing no signs of slowing down.

They entered an area of seedy buildings and garish light. Heeber squirmed and asked where they were going. No one answered. They sang another song. Finally the taxi stopped and deposited them in front of a bar with a blinking sign that read BLACK'S.

Heeber paused on the sidewalk as the others started for the steps.

"What are you waiting for?" Simons asked.

In the window glowed a neon girl with breasts like bananas.

Heeber forced a smile. "I think I'll just grab a taxi home, guys."

"Come on," said Simons, "we'll only be a couple hours."

Ellis observed in silence.

"No, that's okay, you guys go on." Heeber retreated a couple steps. "I have to work tomorrow."

There was some mumbling, then Heeber heard Ellis say, distinctly, "Fuck him. Let him go." He and Simons headed for the door.

Luciano touched Heeber's elbow. "Mr. Heeber, do please come. Is fun to look. You do not have to *fack* any of the womans."

Heeber snatched his arm back. "I said I'm not *going*."

Of course the cab had left. Heeber stomped away with no clear destination. Why had he agreed to dinner with Ellis and those guys in the first place? What was he thinking? What he didn't get was why Ellis hated him so much. He worked hard, he did what he was told. But that wasn't enough. You had to drink and chase women with the man.

Ellis!

Just the name made Heeber tremble. He kicked at some loose chunks of pavement; he spat.

That was when he heard a voice.

"*Tudo bem?*"

Heeber looked around, then down. Swaying along beside him, a little off to the side, was a boy—short-haired, barefoot, brown as a nut. It occurred to Heeber that this might not be the safest place to go for a walk. The boy cast a watchful eye down the street, where a patrol car waited at the curbside, green lights swimming overhead. Heeber let out a breath.

"English? Merican?"

"Go away," Heeber said. "I don't have any money."

"Ah, *Merican*. You need money? Change from dollars to *reais*?"

"No."

"Okay," the boy said. "How about souvenir. You like the souvenir?"

Heeber peered down at the kid. "Souvenirs?"

"Yeah, man. Souvenirs. Real nice, man. Nice deal!"

"Where?"

"Very near. *Tudo bem*, man. Real nice. Follow me, you."

"Well." Heeber glanced again in the direction of the patrol car. He licked his lips. "Okay, let's go."

The kid led him along for another block then down an alley. About half way down, right in the alley, they came to a storefront. The word *Bodega* was etched on the window and beneath that, *Umbanda*. The boy opened the door and beckoned Heeber to follow.

Potted palms sagged in the corners and oddly-shaped bird cages hovered overhead. Heeber bumped into a rack of outdated postcards. Behind the smell of dust and disuse lurked something else—something strange. Smoke, maybe, or incense. The boy vanished into a back room. A minute later he returned with a woman in tow. She was taller than Heeber, dressed in a flowery African skirt, strong-looking, black as lava. A hemp blouse strained across her large breasts—an amazon, Heeber thought, amazed.

"May I help you?" she asked in plain English.

"I guess so," Heeber said. "This boy, he said something about souvenirs?"

"We have souvenirs," she said. "We have works of art. Also we have animals: piranha fish or pet monkey. How about a tarot reading? Your fortune told? Ouija? Talk to the spirits?"

"Just souvenirs," Heeber said. "Something for my wife, you know, something really Brazilian. Maybe a woodcarving of a parrot. I saw one of those at the airport once. Or some Brazilian music CDs if you have them. I don't want any garbage that's gonna fall apart or not work, though."

The woman turned and left for the back room. The soles of her feet were pale and cracked like parched earth. From behind the counter, the boy stared, and Heeber thought of the pet monkey the woman had offered.

She reemerged and to Heeber's surprise placed just what he'd been looking for on the countertop—a small wooden parrot like the one from the airport and a stack of several CDs. But Heeber knew that to show approval with these people was to invite swindle.

"Do these even work?" He turned the CDs over. Beach scenes, pretty girls. On each was a single word: *samba*. "I wanna hear them. Play them for me."

The woman wagged a finger in his face. "You take off wrapper, you bought CD."

He examined the wooden parrot. "This isn't even hand-carved." He shrugged. "So how much for everything?"

"Fifteen *reais*."

About five bucks—less than he was actually willing to spend. "Too much," he said.

The lady raised her shoulders. "Is late," she said. "Ten *reais*."

"Better." Heeber took care not to let them see how much money he had in his wallet.

"Would you like," she asked as he paid, "to cast a spell?"

"A what?"

"A spell. Good, bad. Perhaps to bring luck to a beloved one. Or to place the evil hex on some enemy for sweet revenge."

What was this mumbo jumbo? Heeber smiled. "Boy, do I ever know someone I'd like to put a hex on."

She made an accommodating gesture. "Costs only six *reais* to place the evil hex on an enemy. Is on special this week! Makes you feel real nice."

Two bucks. Now *there* was a bargain. "How do you do it?"

"First, you provide to me a personal item of the enemy. Then at midnight, I call upon a demon to place the evil hex." She waved her hand. "Is all very simple. You don't even need to be here."

"Well—" Heeber said with a laugh. "There's not much chance of me getting my hands on—" He stopped short, fingering a button on the Hawaiian shirt. Ellis's cold blue eyes stared out at him from the dark. "Okay," he said. "What the hell!"

The African woman was confused as he passed the Hawaiian shirt over the counter. "But this is yours, no?"

"Trust me," he said. "Hex away."

She brought the shirt to her face and breathed in deeply. "Ahh," she said, her voice low and greedy like a man's. "Sweat. They *adore* sweat. Is very precious to them."

"Keep it," he said, surprised by his bitterness. "Consider it a gift."

"I am supposed to warn you, mister. Exu of the Seven Crossroads, the dark being on whom we are calling, is restless and impulsive. Once called upon to perform evil he is not easily controlled." She shrugged. "Is just only fine print, though. Almost never there is trouble."

At first he'd felt real nice. The souvenirs were a bargain and the hex a good gag—a couple of bucks to rid himself of the ugly shirt and have a laugh at Ellis's expense. But there was something about the African woman's warning that troubled him now. Now, riding home in the taxi, he decided he'd been fleeced after all. Worse, he'd done it to himself! In front of his building he quarreled with the driver over the fare. Upstairs there were no messages from his wife. He put the souvenirs on the table beside the bed and tried calling her. The phone rang and rang and finally, feeling abandoned, he gave up.

In bed his heart raced. Ellis was in the room, insulting him, ordering him to do humiliating tasks—polish his golf balls, press his wrinkly slacks. The African woman was there too. She had thrown off her skirt and straddled Heeber, her great breasts in his face, the cracked soles of her feet beneath his calves. The bed rocked and groaned as they made love to pulsing jungle music. Ellis squatted in the corner, wagging his tongue obscenely, taunting them. The music grew louder and more frantic. Heeber smelled blood and heard the panicked beating of wings. There were flashes of light, like bulbs exploding in his face. Someone cackled with laughter; someone else screamed.

Heeber sat up with a lurch. The salty meat, the Diet Coke—it had him all worked up. He warmed some milk in the kitchen but drinking it he had a thought. What if Ellis wanted the shirt back in the morning? It was like him. Heeber could imagine being teased mercilessly for not having the thing, a fresh torment. He poured his milk down the drain and began to pace. Now he wanted to find the African woman and demand the shirt back. For a long time he walked back and forth in his little kitchen, telling himself to calm down, and cursing Ellis and the power the man had to make his life miserable.

He was late to work and poorly rested. He slipped past some locals gossiping at the *cafezinho* cart and ducked into his office. There was a rap on the door and Heeber looked up as if he'd been at the desk for hours.

"Mr. Heeber?" It was Daniela, the office secretary. "Are you unwell, sir?"

"I'm fine, thank you. I'm actually quite busy, however, so if you don't mind—"

"It is just that…have you not heard?"

Heeber's eyes narrowed. "Heard what?"

"Oh, my God. You have not heard!"

"*What?*"

"About Mr. Ellis. That last night he is in the city assaulted by robbers?"

"You're kidding me."

Her eyes grew round. "No, I am not. His car was, how you say, hijack?" She touched her temple. "When he is fighting they hit on him against the head with a pipe."

"Is he okay?"

"I believe he is alive but no good."

Something scaly raced down Heeber's spine with icy feet. Was it possible?

"Simons from sales," he said, "and what's-his-name? Luciano. They were both with him last night. Were they involved?"

"No, sir. Mr. Ellis, he is all alone now going to home when he becomes attacked."

After work Heeber caught a cab to the American hospital. Ellis had a private suite overlooking a leafy park. Walking in, Heeber passed a little conference room by the door. Ellis. Even sick he got all the best perks.

The man himself lay beneath hospital sheets. He was connected by wires and tubes to a wall of machinery and a constellation of hanging bags. His eyes were ripe plums and a goose egg had grown on his forehead. At bedside stood his wife. Blonde-going-gray, pearls, a company wife.

She looked up as he came in. "Oh, hello," she said. "You work for Hank, don't you? Matt, right?"

"Rob," he said. "Rob, uh, Heeber." He cleared his throat. "How is he?"

She shook her head. "At first he seemed okay. He was joking, teasing everyone. You know how playful Hank is."

Heeber knew all about it.

"But then this afternoon he had an awful fit of some kind. The doctors says it's like that sometimes with a—a serious head injury." Her hand came to her mouth. "Oh, we've never had trouble here before! Just last night Hank had dinner with friends then went back to the office to work late. You know how hard he works."

"Yes." Heeber cleared his throat again. "Hard."

Ellis's bruised eyelids fluttered. "Claire? Are you here?"

"I'm here."

"Don't leave," he said, "okay? Who were you talking to?"

"Your friend, dear. David Heeber, from the office."

The feral eyes turned toward him. "Heeber? What the fuck are you doing here?"

Sweat broke out on Heeber's forehead. "I came to visit when I about heard your—accident, Mr. Ellis."

"Accident? Christ, this was no accident. Just what the hell is going on here? Why are my eyes black? Where's all my money? Heeber, what the hell did you do with the goddamned shirt?"

Ellis's wife looked stricken.

"Heeber, do you hear me? I want it, bring it to the office or to the golf course if you have to."

"You see," she whispered, "he says crazy things."

"Like all mixed up," Heeber said.

"Claire, are you here? Don't leave me!"

144

"I'm not leaving, dear. I'm right here."

"Heeber," he said. "*Heeber!*"

"Yes?"

Ellis climbed up on his elbows. "Listen to me, you—" Suddenly his head jerked back and veins popped out like hard blue cables in his neck. The machines chirped in alarm. Ellis made strangling noises; spit sizzled along his lips. His wife gasped. A doctor rushed in, a nurse. Heeber fled.

He muttered his address to the cab driver then stared out at the hellish cityscape. What was going on? It was a gag, a harmless joke! True, if anyone deserved a hex it was Ellis. He was a hateful, lying man. But Heeber hadn't imagined him jerking around like a fish in his bed. And what, by the way, was *he* doing? Rob Heeber, a decent, God-fearing American, believing in the hocus pocus of foreign people!

On the dashboard stood a cloth doll clutching feathers and voodoo beads—a little pagan shrine right there in the cab. It was this place, Heeber thought, these people. They were to blame! Ellis was to blame! Forget the hex, Heeber thought. Ellis was an American—he was corporate. This made his mugging newsworthy. The African woman would see the news, put two and two together, figure out who Heeber was. She and the boy would track him down, blackmail him, and ruin him at work.

He rocked in his seat; he groaned.

The driver glanced at the rearview mirror. "You okay, mister?"

"Just drive," Heeber said. And then: "Wait a minute. Do you know where Black's is?"

The driver grinned. "Ah, Black's."

"Take me there."

"Is real nice, Black's. *Real* nice."

"Just shut up and drive!"

He wandered the streets. Nothing ever looked the same way twice in this city, as if the place shifted and changed shape nightly. He walked up dead alleys. Where was the little boy now that Heeber needed him? People would take notice—a white man with money walking these streets alone. He began to sweat. He stopped and looked around, walked a few more blocks. He was ready to give up when he stumbled into an alley. Halfway down was the sign: *Bodega. Umbanda.* Was it the woman's name?

The place looked different this time, shimmering and hot, lit with a hundred candles. The boy, perched in his place behind the counter, gawked, a wicked imp grinning in weak light. The woman listened to Heeber's story with a look on her face like *he* was the weird one here.

She crossed her arms. "You ask for the evil hex. The evil hex, it works. But now you ask me to undo it?"

"That's right, reverse it. Call the whole thing off. It was just a crazy mix-up."

"Is not so easy. Exu of the Seven Crossroads is very, very powerful. Didn't I warn you? Didn't I tell you that when you ask for evil to be done, you—"

"Yes, yes, you warned me! I don't want to hear it again!"

She stroked her chin and Heeber found himself staring at the awesome swell of her breasts, his dream coming back now, embarrassing and arousing at the same time. The woman said something to the boy in Portuguese; he grinned at Heeber and replied at length.

The woman turned back. "There is one possibility. To reverse the hex, first you must retake possession of the shirt, buy it back from me. Then at midnight in your home—it must be your own home and it must be at midnight—you will destroy the shirt by fire as an offering."

"You mean burn it? I live in an apartment. I can't set a fire there."

"Look, you ask me to undo the hex. If you're going to tie my hands..."

"All right, all right, skip it." He took out his wallet. "How much to buy back the shirt?"

"Is one-hundred *reais*."

"One-*hundred*? That's almost forty dollars!"

"To reverse hex is a different story. Costs a little more."

"So that's how it works?" Heeber threw each bill on the countertop. "You charge two dollars to *place* an evil hex but *forty* to take it back. Pretty clever."

The woman showed her palms. "Is the market rate, mister."

The little boy disappeared into the back room. A minute later he scampered back with the horrid shirt.

At the door, Heeber turned. "What if it won't burn?"

"Don't worry, is polyester. It should burn. Real nice."

Heeber downed three warm milks, one right after another. Then he climbed a chair to remove the battery from the smoke alarm on the kitchen ceiling. He opened the windows in the living room. In the bedroom the wooden parrot stared at him with an evil countenance. He slapped the thing from the nightstand. The bathroom window was jammed shut. Heeber seriously considered breaking the glass, going so far as to wrap his fist in a towel. But what if the neighbors heard? In the end he used a heavy book to pound the jamb until the window gave. Damp tropical air flooded the little bathroom. Now he waited.

Music from the next apartment bled through the cheaply constructed walls. Heavy on the drums, tribal and crazy. It played on and on. When his watch read five till midnight, Heeber placed the shirt in the sink basin. Then he realized that that he had no fire—he didn't smoke, he didn't have a lighter. He scrambled to the kitchen and opened empty drawers looking for matches that weren't there. How much time did he have? The African woman hadn't said. He panicked, then looked at the stove. He rolled up a paper towel, held it to the hot coils.

Back in the bathroom he touched flame to the shirt. The nasty thing began to move in the sink, squirming, alive with tiny worms of fire. Soon tarry smoke filled the bathroom. He realized that it had been a mistake to open the windows—the neighbors would smell the smoke. The shirt writhed like something dying in the sink basin.

When he left the bathroom the phone was ringing. It was his wife.

"Rob, is that you?"

"I've been trying to call all week," he said.

"Rob? Are you okay?"

"I'm fine."

"Are you sure? You sound strange."

"Strange? Why would I sound strange?" A laugh escaped from high in his throat. "I live in a third world hellhole full of insane people where you can find a witchdoctor on every corner but you can't eat dinner in a fucking t-shirt. I have a boss that treats me like crap. I hate my job. I hate my life. How could any of that possibly *bother* me?"

"Rob, you're scaring me. You're not making any sense."

He paused. "It's been a strange week. I miss you."

"I miss you, too."

"It's this place," he said. "I hate it."

"Poor Rob."

"I hate it, I hate it!"

He skipped work next morning and went straight to the hospital. Stepping from the elevator, he ran into Simons. The man's face sagged like loose clothing. "Hey, Rob," he said quietly, "how's it going, buddy?"

Rob? Buddy? Since when was Simons so friendly? Heeber asked how Ellis was doing.

Simons shook his head. "Not good."

Well, there it was. He'd been fleeced again.

"It's the damndest thing, isn't it?" Simons asked. "How everything can change overnight?"

In the room the wife stood beside the bed. Now a tube ran from Ellis's nose to the back of his head. He seemed to be asleep.

"You're back," Ellis's wife said. "He was asking about you."

"About me?"

"He's so close to the men who work for him."

The doctor entered. He was tall and brown, Brazilian-looking, yet spoke English like an American. He nodded at Heeber without curiosity and told the wife he wanted to speak to her. Heeber offered to leave.

"No," she said, "stay. I'm sure Hank would want you to."

They followed the doctor to the sitting area. He described Ellis's condition and how it had worsened overnight. The tube in his head was called a shunt, he said, and it was draining fluid from the brain. The wife hid her mouth as the doctor spoke of things Heeber knew nothing about: left temporal seizure disorder, epileptic fugue, postictal disorientation.

The shunt was only a short-term fix, which was why they were recommending an operation. It was not a lobotomy, the doctor stressed: just a procedure intended to stop the seizures long enough to fly Ellis home safely. Head injuries were like that, he said. They could take a turn for better or worse at any time. For now, the doctor said, the important thing was to keep him calm and avoid upsetting him. He did, however, warn that there was a chance the procedure would fail.

"Fail?" the wife said. "Oh, my."

"I'm confident everything will turn out well. You might, however, want to call any friends or relatives in the area. The nurse will let you use the phone in my office."

She thanked the doctor and turned to touch Heeber's hand. "Will you stay while I make a few calls? You've been such a help."

Heeber agreed and she left.

"This operation," Heeber said, "do you really have to do it? There's no other option?"

"I doubt he would survive a flight home without it."

"Tell me the truth, Doc. Is it risky?"

The doctor considered the question. "Quite," he said finally.

The doctor left and Heeber returned to the bed alone. Ellis was awake now, stirring. "Claire? Is that you?"

"No. It's me."

The eyes rolled toward Heeber. They were different now, strawberry-speckled, weak. No ice there, no cruelty. Ellis was scared, you could see it in his eyes. "Heeber? Where's Claire?"

"She had to go make some phone calls."

"You won't leave till she gets back, will you?"

Heeber promised to stay.

Ellis had become old overnight. Shriveled, unmanned by injury. The word *chickenhearted* came to mind. He did, however, seem much nicer this way.

"Why did Claire have to go make *phone* calls, Heeber?"

"Because," he said, "they're going to do an operation on you."

"An operation?"

"Yes. On your brain. They're going cut your head open and do a lobotomy on it."

"A lobotomy?" Ellis clutched Heeber's hand. "On my *brain*?"

"The left lobe part," Heeber said.

"The left lobe? An operation? Is it dangerous?"

Heeber leaned close enough to feel Ellis's warm breath—close enough to kiss the man. "Quite," he said.

The eyes grew wide with fear; Ellis actually began to sob.

"Don't worry," Heeber said, wrenching his hand free in disgust. "I'll be here with you the whole time."

ALL THEM CRAWFORDS

Honorée Fanonne Jeffers

Floretta come over here this morning. Early this morning 'bout seven but I been up since five-thirty. You know I get up early. I get up and I make me some rolled oats for breakfast to keep me regular. It take me a little while to get to the kitchen with my cane but I like to make my own breakfast. And then after I eat my rolled oats, I sit in this here easy chair and I reads my Bible. Every day God send, I reads my Bible. Then I think on the Lord a little bit and how He have been so good to me. I look out the window from time to time.

It was after breakfast so I musta been here reading my Bible and then here come Floretta, knocking on the door. Say Junebug called Charmane four days ago and told her he was getting out yesterday and come get him in the afternoon. You know Floretta some kin to her. Charmane is Floretta's sister child.

Junebug told Charmane, come get him at the jailhouse and bring the children, too. Why he want his kids to see him that way, I sure don't know.

I ain't expect Junebug to end up on the chain gang, neither, but he sure needed it. I don't care what they call it nowadays. Jail, prison, it still the chain gang to me. Same thing. And that Judge ain't give Junebug as long a time as he should 'cause Junebug robbed that man. Poor Mr. Lee Coker. He ain't deserved to be robbed.

But what you expect? That's the kinda stock Junebug done came from. Them Crawfords. You know I use to live up the road from them. Right up the road. Me and J.W., we was way older than Junebug's daddy. The daddy and my Buster, they the ones come up together. We lived out there on that place 'bout twenty years when Junebug daddy and mama moved out there. That was before they did the paving out to County Line. Before J.W. died and my daughter Mary moved me into town.

Junebug daddy won't no good. That man used to stay gone for weeks and then come home to beat up on the mama, get her big, then be back out in the road. He treated that woman a scandal. Making babies and ain't never worry 'bout feeding them. Ain't bring no food in that house. Child, that woman and them kids was hungry. It ain't make no sense how hungry they was. Living on that good land, but that man ain't never go out in the fields. He ain't even try to grow nothing, just hunt and fish when he feel like it, and the mama, look like she thought she was a white woman 'cause she ain't know one thing 'bout running no house. Ain't keep no garden, no pigpen, a hen house neither. She ain't know how to chop no wood. J.W. had to teach Junebug how to do that.

Oh, pretty. Yes, ma'am, the mama was pretty. Hair down to there, but no sense.

They call theyselves sharecropping, but them white peoples sure won't getting no shares, and folk won't doing no sharecropping no more, not by then. I don't know who owned that land, but I believe some of Mr. Tommy Pinchard Jr.'s kin.

Me and my husband did some sharecropping back in the day for Mr. Big Thom but we bought us some land from his son, Mr. Tommy, long time ago. Long, long time ago. Mr. Tommy wouldn't sell us that piece of land we had farmed. He give us a different parcel to buy and we couldn't grow much except a garden but it was ours. Junebug's mama and daddy had that good bottomland. They was sorry, though. Wouldn't do nothing. I can't tell you how many baskets of peas and okra and collards I left out by the gate for Junebug mama, especially when she was big. Every winter when we killed a hog, I bring her some fresh chitlins and pig feet and side meat, too. Sometimes even some pork chops.

Come summer Junebug and them walk up to the house every day to eat. You know I couldn't see them children starve. How I'ma meet Jesus and I let them kids go hungry? They had the free breakfast and lunch come school, but in the summer, they was hungry.

They be up by the big pecan tree that stand on the property line, acting like they was playing, but I know all they doing was rooting in the dirt, waiting till dinnertime. 'Cause they know I got some cornbread in the oven and some pinto beans in the pot.

I call out there to them. "Y'all hungry?"

"Yes, ma'am, Miz Jolene."

"Come on up here and get something to eat, then. Come on now, and don't forget to say your blessing."

"Yes, ma'am, Miz Jolene."

Junebug's mama just ain't had no spunk. Ain't no way I woulda let some breath and britches be rolling on top of me and ain't gone feed me and mine. Little puny woman she was. She ain't had no business having all them babies by that man with her puny self. That's why she died like that. Just wore out. You shoulda seen the blood come outta her before she died. Baby died, too, blue in the face. Lord have mercy.

I was there with the midwife. The mama couldn't afford no hospital. They was letting in colored by that time, but she ain't had no money for a doctor. We had to burn them sheets. Umph, umph, umph.

Mr. Cruddup ain't never say 'bout paying to bury the mama, but everybody know Mr. Cruddup paid for it hisself.

Me and J.W. had took Junebug and them down to the funeral home for the wake. You know the daddy won't nowhere to be found. We had to search for him to get him to the funeral. Sorry nigger.

Junebug was so broke up. He won't but 'bout ten or eleven, and trying not to cry but looking so sad. I tell J.W. to take Junebug and them to view the body and then I take Mr. Cruddup aside and ask him how Junebug's daddy was gone pay for a funeral. I thought maybe we could take up a collection down to church, don't you know? Mr. Cruddup ain't say nothing, just ask me to sign the book and say he got another funeral he got to attend to and, *Excuse me, please, Miss Jolene.* But won't nary other body laying up in that funeral home. Mr. Cruddup just ain't want to tell me Junebug's daddy couldn't pay for no funeral.

Mr. Cruddup, that's a Christian man right there. Let me tell you, Mr. Cruddup put that woman away right. Nice, nice casket and flowers, and a gravestone down to the cemetery. Junebug's mama ain't left nothing to pay for that. I know, 'cause the insurance man used to come 'round, but she ain't even have fifty cents twice a month to pay him. Man just stopped showing up after a while.

Preacher give such a sermon. When I go, I sure hope somebody do right by me like Preacher did Junebug's mama.

"Who can find a virtuous woman? For her price is far above rubies."

Talk 'bout crying? Child, when that man started talking 'bout how a good woman do right by her man, you better hear me. Every woman up in that church was crying. And when Preacher say, if you got a good woman, you better keep her and treat her right? 'Cause the Lord hath gave her to be a man's helpmeet all the days of his life? I just floated to my feet and I raised my right hand. J.W. was sitting on one side of me and Junebug on the other.

I was thinking 'bout J.W. and how when we was young, had been married 'bout three years, I got big with Mary. I was all swole up, couldn't see my feet or nothing and I walked 'round in a pair of J.W.'s old boots with the laces undid 'cause I ain't even feel like bothering.

J.W., I guess he got tired of me being tired all the time. You know. At night when we get ready to lay down. You know what I mean. But let me ask you this: who gone want a man jumping up on top of you when you got a baby kicking and poking you from the inside? And you so wore out all you want is sleep? And you thinking 'bout how you got that way was some man jumping up on top of you in the first place? I told J.W. he better go on with hisself and leave me alone.

Well, J.W. started going out to the juke with his friends. Coming back late, smelling like liquor. J.W. ain't try to bother me no more at night. I was glad at first, but then when I get up in the morning to fix his breakfast, J.W. always say he ain't hungry. Same thing at suppertime. Now you know a man not wanting to hug up on you at night might not mean nothing, but when he don't want your food he stepping out on you. Cause he got to be eating someplace.

So one Sunday morning, J.W. had done been out the night before. He ain't even beat daylight home and child, I was so sleepy, 'cause that baby had kept me up just swimming 'round in me, but I get up outta the bed and try to look pretty. I put on my blue flower dress but I can't get in my regular shoes. I fix J.W. breakfast before we supposed to go to church. Ham, eggs, biscuits, grits with butter in the middle. Coffee black like he like it.

I go and I stand over the bed and I say, "J.W., get on up and eat, baby, 'cause we fi'in to go to church." He don't say nothing.

"J.W., honey, ain't you hungry?" I keep calling his name. I start begging him to get up and eat the food I had done cooked for him. Putting my pride to the side and tryna be sweet. Tryna be a good wife, but he don't move and I think on how I have stood up in front of God with this man, the way I am standing over that bed. I think on how I'ma have to be with J.W. for the rest of my life and I just feel like crying. 'Cause my mama and daddy had told me when I wanted to marry J.W. that I could go on 'head if I wanted, but don't be coming back to they house. They had wanted me to be a schoolteacher, and they ain't like J.W. no way. He ain't have nothing to begin with, 'cept his good looks.

I think on how I was a smart gal but I left school early to marry J.W. and after three years with him, I ain't even remember half of what Teacher had taught me down to school. I don't talk proper no more like I used to back when me and J.W. was courting.

I start praying.

"Lord Jesus," I say. "Lord Jesus, I done tried to be a good wife to this man. I done kept his house clean. I done cooked his meals. I done went against my mama and daddy to marry this man. Now I'm making a baby for him and can't go nowhere and I ain't gone never be a schoolteacher. I'm calling on you, Lord Jesus, to help me."

Seem like God don't want to hear me. I don't feel no Spirit coming on and I just keep praying, looking for a sign, but don't none come. It go on like that for a little while. Finally, J.W., he roll over on his back and half rear up out the bed.

"Woman, can't you see I'm sleep? You better shut up that damn noise!" Then he fall back on the bed and close his eyes like he so tired.

I stand there a while more and then I go into the kitchen and I get that pot of grits off the fire and I go back into the bedroom and stand back over J.W. I pour them grits real slow on his chest. Then J.W. hollering and he jump up cause them grits is burning him. He run 'round the room but I throw spoonfuls of them grits at him and some of them catch him.

He say, "Stop it, please! God knows I'm sorry, Jolene! God knows I am!"

After them burns on his chest healed, I ain't had no more trouble from J.W. We was happy for fifty-three years and he ain't touched nary other drop of liquor to the day he died. And he ate his meals at home.

I was thinking 'bout that morning when Junebug daddy was sitting up at the front of the church crying and carrying on through the mama's funeral like he had been a good husband to that woman. Tryna hug up on the children and they slipping out his arms like greased pigs. Junebug wearing this tired look like he already a grown man. He look disgusted at his daddy acting a damn fool 'cause everybody in that church know that man won't nowhere to be found when the mama bled to death and her little baby died, but he got the nerve to show up and be carrying on. Wouldn't feed them kids, couldn't pay for his wife's funeral, but the daddy got on this good suit. Look like he had gone to Milledgeville and got it. Mr. Cruddup coming out his pocket for that woman's homegoing and who knowed where Junebug daddy had got that good suit from? I was thinking if the mama had stirred her up a pot a grits for that man like I had did for J.W., they coulda been happy.

After the mama died, things just went along. Junebug kept on going in school. He wanted to quit and start working, but I asked him, what's a little boy like him gone do for work?

He was smart in school. Knowed his figures real well, but he couldn't spell too good, and I helped him with his reading. I remember when J.W. used to pick him and the rest up in the morning and drop them off at school, and then come back with them in the evening. That was when J.W. worked in town at the sawmill. They won't sending the school bus out to County Line, not to pick up no colored children, they won't. They would ride them white children up and down the road in that school bus, but not no colored children. They was supposed to have let the colored children sit in the school house with the white. That's what the law said, but you know they found a way 'round that. Them white peoples started theyselves a Christian academy for they kids. *Christian*. That's what they called it.

Junebug daddy was staying with that trash from Madison by then, the one he had them outside kids by. That dog had a baby in every stroke, seem like. He ain't come home again for more than a day or two every so often, not after the mama died.

You ain't know Junebug daddy had them outside kids by that tramp? Child, where you been? Everybody know that. Two or three of them. Before the mama died, the daddy used to be up to the juke with that tramp, buying her drinks and fried fish sandwiches like his real family won't at home starving. Honey, hush.

Floretta told me Junebug's daddy be down to the Legion even now, tryna get him some womens. Floretta say he was down there two weeks ago tryna talk to that gal of Butch Paschal. That gal fast anyway. Ain't but nineteen, and she gone have a belly full soon, mark me. Floretta say that Paschal gal had on a skirt so tight if she'da farted it woulda ripped in two, and there go Junebug's daddy rubbing his hand on that gal. Whispering up in her ear. Old enough to be her granddaddy and still chasing tail, like he can do something with it if he catch up to it.

Just from what I hear. I'm still spry, now. I get 'round, but I'm too old to be down to the Legion on Saturday night getting into foolishness, and it's a good thing. Might get cut with a straight razor the way they be carrying on. You never heard such a boogaloo from way down the street. The music—I can't even get to sleep. They be sinning on Saturday and then be having the nerve to come to church the next morning.

Look like Junebug was tryna be different from his daddy. He was making him some good grades in school and looking after the rest of his brothers and sisters. They was raggedy, but I had showed Junebug how to wash out they clothes in the tub. He kept them kids clean, and they was still getting the free breakfast and lunch at school. Junebug's mama ain't had no spunk, but she did raise that boy with some home training. He always come up to the porch in the evenings after school and speak to me.

"Hey, Miz Jolene, how you this evening? You need me to do something for you?"

"Naw, sugar, I'm fine. You go on back home and get your lesson out. I'll see y'all at dinner."

Just to have something to do, he'd go out to the garden and pick out my weeds for me. Every Christmas, Junebug got together something to give me, too. One time, he had went down to the dime store and bought me some of that Jean Naté perfume. I don't know where he got the money, but he ain't steal it. I know that.

He got drafted right outta high school. I don't know what he thought he was gone do in the middle of a war. Sit down on his corporation, I guess. He won't no bad boy, though, and he looked out for his brothers and sisters. He had them send me the check every month when he was gone over there, and I took care of them for him.

When he get back from over to the war, he and that gal Charmane got married and seem like he was gone be fine, but right off, I knowed something was wrong, 'cause all he wanted to do is lay up there on Charmane and eat her outta house and home. Don't nobody eat more than a man won't work. Seem like a lazy man just got more appetite. She did try, though. She sure loved herself some Junebug. Got a good job at the peach pie factory. She stayed off the welfare, you can say that much for her.

Laying up on Charmane and smoking them reefers when he come back from over there. Putting babies in her and complaining 'bout how they had did him wrong, drafting him. That's all he got good for. Complaining 'bout the white man and making babies and smoking them reefers. What he got to complain 'bout? He was eating. If anybody shoulda been complaining, it was Charmane. She the one working at the peach pie factory.

Then when they start making that crack, Junebug smoking that, too. I guess them reefers ain't work on him no more. Next thing you know he on the chain gang.

I thought the service was supposed to make a man outta you. I don't like no war, neither, but the President had said. Won't that enough? They was making good money in Vietnam, when back in the day, it was plenty of colored mens cleaning outhouses in the war. You ain't see them complaining.

My boy Buster fought the Germans. Junebug's daddy got outta that, but Buster went on over there.

Look at that picture. Won't he pretty in that uniform? Won't but twenty in that picture. That boy sure know he could sing. Aw, he used to love to sing! He had all them records. Nineteen forty-four, the Army sent him back, said he had something wrong with him. Shock or something. He come back from the war and used to wake up screaming. Said the Germans was coming to get him. Used to get up in the middle of the night and turn on the light in me and J.W. room.

"Mama, Mama, they here again!" Buster just be shaking and trembling. Sweat just be running down his face.

"Buster, calm down sugar," I say to him. "Mama ain't gone let nobody get to her baby."

"They coming through the door, Mama! They coming!"

He fine now, though. He live out there on me and my husband's land. He kinda quiet and keep to hisself. He ain't never get married but he fine. He damn sure ain't end up on the chain gang, I can tell you that.

Child, them young kids, they was just different. Complaining on the TV 'bout they don't want to go to no Vietnam. Maybe them white boys ain't had enough sense to stay off the TV but them colored boys shoulda knowed better. Let them white boys be stupid if they want to, 'cause this they country. But colored boys suppose to have more sense. And what's wrong with colored fighting side by side next to white and ain't nobody getting lynched? Look like they ought to be proud to go over there for they country and get a check to send back home to they family, but naw, they won't proud. They was on the TV, screaming and burning they draft papers. Hair just as nappy, talking 'bout they ain't going. All them niggers need haircuts. I used to be so shame and mad I just turn it right off.

Junebug mighta complained, but at least he did his duty, and when he come back, he sit with me every week. He come every single week to sit with Miz Jolene. Even after him and Charmane got married and I moved into town, he come and find me and he sit with me. He was here right before he got sent up to the chain gang.

When he started smoking that crack, oh, he got so skinny. Make me want to feed him a pork chop that boy was so skinny. His clothes be clean and pressed and he smell all right, but his eyes be red and he fidgeting. He seem calm, but what he say make me think he be out his head. And he too skinny.

"Miz Jolene, I got me some big plans. I'ma be a musician," Junebug say.

"A what?"

"I'ma be a musician. I'ma play me the piano. Start me a band. Like Thelonious Monk back in the day."

"Like who? Junebug, how you think you gone be in a band, baby? You ain't never even learned to play no piano."

"I'ma learn, Miz Jolene. And then I'ma be rich and famous. One day, I'ma come pick you up for church Sunday morning and ride you 'round in a big car. A Cadillac or Mercedes or something like that. I'ma travel the world, only this time, I won't kill nobody just 'cause the white man tell me to."

"Junebug, you don't need to have no big car for me. You want to make Miz Jolene happy, you get yourself a job. You get yourself a job, baby, and help Charmane raise them kids."

"Yes, ma'am, I'ma do that, Miz Jolene. But I got me some plans."

"Junebug, baby, why don't you go on in the kitchen and fix yourself a plate? Mary come over here and cook for me this morning. She made me greens and some nice baked chicken. It's a sweet potato pudding in there, too. I know you like that, you always liked you a sweet potato pudding."

"No, ma'am, I ain't hungry. I got to go anyway. I got to be making my plans. Thelonious Monk."

Talking all outta his head. Then he kiss me on the cheek and leave.

I thought Junebug was gone be different, but them Crawfords like that. Junebug's daddy ain't shit. The daddy folks won't shit. All them Crawfords. Won't nary one of them hit a lick at a snake if it was rolling toward him in the dirt. They just gone get bit and die. All them sorry ass Crawfords.

Tyrone and Bootsie, though, they the ones started that robbery. They always been in trouble. The devil just in them. You wonder what they mamas was thinking when they made them, but Junebug ain't had to follow along behind Tyrone and Bootsie. He coulda had his own mind. One thing I always thought I could say 'bout Junebug, he ain't never been no troublemaker. But I guess a idle mind and the Devil just be waiting. See now, if he had took hisself to church and prayed once in a while and got hisself a job and helped Charmane raise them kids, he woulda stayed off the chain gang. And them reefers and that crack ain't help him none.

Taking advantage of Mr. Lee Coker like that and the way he been good to Junebug and them. I ain't the only one used to feed Junebug family. Mr. Lee Coker had that big cornfield and he always brought over what he ain't use. That cornfield ain't half as big as it use to be 'cause he had got old and won't farming but a little corner, but he still used to be making that moonshine. He ain't sell it to nobody no more. He say he just made it for his rheumatism. The police ain't even bothered him 'bout it, even though he gived away a few jars, too.

Junebug told the Judge at the trial that they was just tryna take Mr. Lee Coker's moonshine. I guess they was gone try to sell it to get some money for some more of that crack. They musta been high already 'cause don't nobody have to buy moonshine no more. You can go right down to the Six to Twelve and get some liquor right off the shelf. You ain't got to be a criminal no more to get you some liquor, if you grown.

Him and Bootsie and Tyrone had worked it out in the truck. They was gone park down the road and walk back up to the house so Mr. Lee Coker wouldn't see the lights from the truck. Then break in and grab him and hold onto him and make him tell them where he kept his still, but when they got there, they had done forgot 'bout Mr. Lee Coker's old hound dog. He won't young enough to bite no more, and Mr. Lee Coker ain't hunt no more with that dog, neither, but that dog sure could bark and he wouldn't stop. Junebug, he said he wanted to leave right then when he heard that dog barking, but Bootsie and Tyrone said they won't gone leave without the moonshine. So Tyrone come up on the dog and kicked him and kept on until he stopped barking. Bootsie broke in and grabbed Mr. Lee Coker but then the old man had that heart attack.

Junebug ain't even try to run like Bootsie and Tyrone. When Mr. Lee Coker had grabbed his chest, them two other devils just left him like that with Junebug. Just left him. Bootsie and Tyrone, they was running back up the road to the truck when the police caught up. When that dog ain't stop barking, before Tyrone had kicked him, Mr. Lee Coker had called the law on his telephone.

I bet Junebug ain't thought to rob that man. That's why the Judge give Bootsie and Tyrone thirty years for Mr. Lee Coker dying from that heart attack. He just give Junebug five years cause he stayed there with Mr. Lee Coker. The judge knowed Junebug ain't have no real meanness in him. Junebug just a natural fool, that's all.

If that boy had stayed hisself in the service he wouldna ended up on the chain gang. He coulda made him some good money and bought him and Charmane a house, and he wouldn't be dead, neither. Charmane told Floretta Junebug called her up and said he was getting out yesterday. That ain't sound right cause he ain't did but six months on the chain gang, but Floretta say Charmane got herself up yesterday morning, anyway, and the children, too, so they could drive down there to the jailhouse. When she showed up, the peoples at the jail had to tell her Junebug had hung hisself. Floretta say Charmane just fell out, she was so upset.

Child. Child.

Junebug down there to Mr. Cruddup's funeral home. I guess Mr. Cruddup gone pay for that one, too, 'cause you know that gal Charmane ain't got no money to pay for no funeral. I sure hope the new preacher give a good sermon for Junebug like old Preacher did for Junebug's mama. These young reverends, they don't go back to the Word enough for me, but I'ma be there, though, if God say the same.

Pass me that there spit cup, sugar. No, on the floor over there. Thank you, ma'am. I don't know why Mary don't put it over here with me. I sit here everyday in this easy chair and she still don't put it over here next to me. She act sometimes like she ain't got the sense God gave a goose, that's my heart, though. She got her own grands and great-grands now but she still come see 'bout her mama. I'm just grateful somebody come in here and bring me my snuff but I think Mary hide my cup. She don't like me to dip but I don't care. J.W. dead and I ain't kissing nobody these days. I'm past grown and I do what I want. Mary's my heart, though. I could be out there in the county home, losing my mind and laying up in my own mess and getting to like the stink.

Praise Jesus, I still got my faculties. Uh-huh, the Lord sure do bless. You right 'bout that.

ORLANDO

Samuel Ligon

Nikki turns eighteen between Hagerstown and Cumberland, the Potomac out her window a fat black snake. She celebrates with a joint in the Greyhound's bathroom, blowing hits out the spring-hinged triangular window as the bus rattles across Maryland. When she left Providence this morning, Buckley's money was in her paraphernalia pouch at the bottom of her leather backpack, the safest place she could think of until she had to pee around New London and realized the money could be stolen. Now it's two fat rolls in the front pockets of her jeans. Thinking about the money makes her want to touch it again, smell it. She knocks the cherry from the joint out the window and stashes the roach, then pulls out Buckley's money—her money—and counts it one more time. She's still rich, still worth twenty-three hundred bucks, more than anyone she has ever known.

Out on the sleeping bus, Nikki settles into her window seat and puts on her headphones, the only other person in her row a weathered nun leaning against the opposite window asleep. Nikki calls her the smoking nun, because she lit one cigarette after another out of Baltimore as she read a hardback book called *Breathing Lessons*. At least she didn't try to make conversation. Nikki doesn't know what she'd say to a nun. Since Baltimore, she's been listening to *Life's Too Good*, by The Sugarcubes, but skipping that song "Birthday," holding it off until this moment, stoned, alone on the bus in the first minutes of finally being eighteen. Now she hits play and listens, the diesel smell around her, the Potomac—and she knows it's the Potomac because she asked the driver—still unwinding out her window, the bus and Nikki heading for Pennsylvania, Ohio, Kentucky, Tennessee, all these places she's never been, Bjork saying, 'They're smoking cigars. They lie in the bathtub,' the greenish light inside the bus perfect with the music and her buzz, thirty-five hours until Austin, another place she's never been, and her cousin Melanie, Nikki's whole life waiting to happen. When the song ends, she rewinds it and plays it again. And again.

'Today is a birthday. They're smoking cigars.'

She wishes she had a loop tape of this song to send her to sleep in the green light of the Greyhound going west. Last night, Friday night, she was with Buckley and this chick Maya, up all night on ex, before taking the money this morning. And though it's almost impossible to believe, she only met Buckley yesterday afternoon, a nice enough guy whose drug money has allowed her to get out of

Providence and spend her birthday in all these places she's never been, though each place will be inside this bus or ones like it she'll transfer to in Pittsburgh, Columbus, Nashville, and somewhere else, which, when she looks at her schedule she sees is Dallas. She hopes Buckley won't take the lost money too hard, hopes he won't get into some kind of drug trouble over it. A rich kid at a snotty art college, he probably won't suffer much. She'll pay him back with interest is what she'll do, maybe won't even spend much of it. Maybe none. Who knows what's waiting in Austin?

When she bought the first ticket in Providence sixteen hours ago, she picked Orlando because she wanted someplace warm, and figured there would be jobs at Disney World, another place she's never been, but after transferring in New York City, Nikki got the idea to call her cousin Melanie, to tell one person in the world she was alive somewhere, but also hoping Melanie would say, *Why don't you come to Austin?* which is exactly what Melanie did say, Nikki not caring she couldn't get a refund for the unused portion of her ticket to Orlando, just buying a new ticket and getting on a new bus going a new direction an hour after getting off the phone in Baltimore.

Luck does change—she can feel that—all these people gone from her life forever, Frank, George, Buckley, new ones, better ones, out there waiting. And she hasn't seen Melanie in two years. She rewinds the tape again, touches the money rolls in her pockets, listens to her birthday song, the whole country out her window, the smoking nun coughing and thrashing, dying across the aisle, Nikki so tired after days without sleep and wracked from the ex and all that beer, but wanting to stay up just a little longer on the best day of her life so far, wanting to remember forever the green light inside the bus, the diesel smell, the music, the money, the Potomac out her window a fat black snake.

The driver shakes her awake, saying, "Catherine," Nikki surprised he remembers the name she told him. "You have to get off here," he says. "Pittsburgh." It's three in the morning, two hours sleep leaving her worse off than if she'd stayed awake. She steps down into a bay of running, stinking buses and waits to retrieve her Shipping Container, the box they made her buy in Providence to put her plastic garbage bag into, the box making everything she owns bulky and harder to carry than the garbage bag.

Inside the terminal, people wait on orange plastic chairs attached to each other in rows under dim fluorescent lighting that makes everyone look sick, wasting. She smokes a cigarette. A drunk homeless approaches for a smoke, the stink of b.o.

and liquor and shit radiating off him. She gives him one only if he promises to get away from her, to leave her alone, which he promises. Then he lights the cigarette and sits next to her.

"I got half a mind to double up on the backstretch," the homeless says. "Church. China. Like that."

Nikki moves her box and backpack to another row. She has to stay awake thirty more minutes. She puts her headphones on, takes The Sugarcubes out of her tape player, the homeless sitting next to her again, his stink all around. "You think you're better than me?" he says as she fumbles to pop the Pixies into her Walkman. She drops the tape onto the grimy tile, and as she reaches down to pick it up, the homeless says it again, only this time he grabs her arm above the elbow and holds her like that. She snaps her arm free. "Don't fucking touch me," she says, pulling her backpack onto her lap fast and opening its front pocket. She's got a Buck knife in there, a three inch lock blade. She touches it, feels people in the terminal watching them, watching her.

"Go on. Git," a black woman says, standing in front of the homeless. "Leave that girl alone."

"I don't need help," Nikki says, and the black woman says, "You don't, huh? Good for you," and the homeless says, "I got just as much—" and the black woman says, "You got nothin'; look at yourself," and the homeless says, "If the holy spirit," and the black woman says, "Get up go," and the homeless raises himself and shuffles away, mumbling.

Nikki takes her tape from the floor and pops it into the Walkman. She hits play and the Pixies start into "Bone Machine." Even though she didn't need help, even though people end up fucking you one way or another, she nods thanks to the black woman, who sits in the opposite row. The black woman nods back, but doesn't smile, doesn't seem to want anything. Some people are like that—dignified—but not many.

The music only Nikki can hear makes the bus station unreal, as if the people smoking and waiting and poor in the hollowing three a.m. light exist only for her to see, as if she's the only real one here, which, in a way, she thinks, she is. The only one that matters. And on the first line of the chorus, she can never tell if the lyric is, "Your bones got a little machine," or, and she likes this better, "Your bones got a little mush-y." She's all by herself with the music, the other people actors performing for her or part of some bigger play or movie she can't see, that she herself is part of, inside of, that she herself's the star of. The black woman across the aisle works a complicated yarn craft, knitting, crochet, needlepoint, the woman as self-contained as Nikki. As Nikki now is. Because right now—and maybe this will change—she feels free of the hatred she's wasted on George, who suddenly seems as irrelevant as the actors here in Pittsburgh, making a brief appearance in her life, then gone for good. Is it possible she's no longer angry with him for leaving her in Providence like that? She fell honest to God in love with him, ran with him from Manchester and her mother to Providence, where he disappeared less than four days later, abandoning her in a city where she knew no one. She's spent all these hours, days, weeks, some significant portion of her life, hating him for fucking her over like that, but now that she thinks about it, if it hadn't been for George getting her out of Manchester, she never would have made it on her own more than six months in Providence, never would have met Buckley and taken his money and ended up in this crazy room in Pittsburgh, waiting for the next bus, all these extras walking through their brief scene in her movie, the Pixies singing, "Your bones got a little mush-y," and she thinks, Yeah, no shit, they did, but they're okay now, realigned and strong. Holding her up just fine. And it's still her birthday and everything is still out there waiting, and even though she's wicked tired, she could not feel better. As if it's better to be in this crappy bus station in Pittsburgh than anywhere in the world. As if there are going to be places like this the rest of her life, waiting rooms she'll sit in on the verge of something. On the verge of everything.

And on the next bus, this one three hours to Columbus and another transfer, she once again has her side of the aisle to herself. She doesn't know how she could be so wired. She's slept, what, two of the last forty hours? It's like the ex is still kicking, though the last bump she did with Buckley and Maya was twenty-four hours ago, so that's impossible.

She wakes to the sound of a familiar cough, and when she cranes her neck it's the smoking nun, two rows back. The couple in front of her are moaning, making out under a blanket. Fucking people. She wakes again in Columbus, hazy daylight, gets her box and waits for the transfer to Nashville, which is supposed to be famous for Elvis or some other dead asshole everybody loves for reasons Nikki can't comprehend.

Dude gets on the bus that evening and she knows from the corner of her eye he's heading right for her. There's only a handful of seats left, one beside the smoking nun, who made the transfer in Nashville, too; she sat in the seats across the aisle again and smiled at Nikki like they were old friends, Nikki half smiling back, looking away, not wanting old friends on the bus, especially a smoking nun who seemed to be stalking her. The dude continues down the aisle until he stops at Nikki's row waiting. She moves her backpack from the seat beside her. She's been on buses thirty hours, driven through a thousand states, can hardly believe it's the same birthday. Dude sits himself but doesn't sprawl into her space, Nikki keeping her headphones on, though her second and last set of batteries died hours ago.

She's been sleeping and dreaming all day, half dreaming when she's awake, lulled by the motion of the bus. The dude doesn't stink or try to make conversation; he's got a paperback book folded over itself in front of his face. What she's been trying to figure out in her dreams is what to do with herself in Austin, what to make herself into. She'll have to find a job, sure, and something better than washing dishes like she did in Providence. Now that she's eighteen she can get a waitressing job, which might not be great, but at least she can make some money. That's just short term, though. What she's decided, without quite knowing she's decided it until now, is that she's going to go to school to become something, maybe a music teacher, even though she doesn't play an instrument, but when she asks herself what she's interested in, what she likes, the main answer keeps being music. Maybe she'll be a reviewer, attending concerts, listening to albums, telling people what's good and what sucks. Or—and she hardly lets herself think this—she could sing in a band. She's got a list of band names she adds to when she's trying to go to sleep—Piss Factory, Popes on Dope, and Mary Got Knocked Up being her favorites. Maybe she'll finally get a guitar and learn to play.

Dude beside her pulls a cigarette from his jacket pocket, never taking his eyes from the book. He smells like soap or shampoo. He looks at Nikki, holds up his cigarette. "You mind?" he says. They're sitting in the smoking section. Nikki shakes her head, looks out the window. She'll have to get her GED, but how hard can that be? And Austin probably has some kind of college. The other thing she could do is become a chef. Four rows behind her, in the back three seats by the bathroom, a woman's been yelling at her two kids since Bowling Green, Kentucky. "Breece," she says now, "touch your sister again and I'll touch you, hear?"

Nikki doesn't have any brothers or sisters, just Melanie, who's three years older than Nikki and as good as a sister, maybe better, everything they've been through, Melanie's mom's death, Nikki's mom's life.

"That's the last warning," the woman says, and Nikki hears scuffling at the back of the bus. Dude beside her turns in his seat to look, then resettles himself and blows smoke over his paperback, shaking his head.

"Trash," he says.

Nikki watches his reflection in her window as he turns to face her.

"The way people raise their kids."

He's twenty, maybe twenty-two, with long black hair parted at the side, big square hands.

"Breece!" the woman screams as the kid runs up the aisle, "get back here," and she scrambles after him, a chunky girl in lime green stretch pants, not much older than Nikki, catches him half way up the bus, and carries him—maybe five years old in short pants and a plaid suit jacket—silently thrashing against her to their back seat. And when he says, "Bullshit," in his little boy's voice at the back of the bus, it sounds like "Booshit."

Nikki looks at the dude beside her, who's looking at her, and they laugh.

"Kid's right," Dude says.

Nikki reaches for a cigarette and lighter in her backpack.

"Man," the dude says, "if she was my mom—"

Nikki hears the south in his voice, how he says mom "mawm."

"—I'd call it bullshit too."

He smiles at her. "I'm David," he says, and Nikki says, "Catherine," glad he's not named Jimmy or Bobby Lee, surprised she cares before deciding she doesn't.

"I've got some Black Velvet here," he says, pulling a flat bottle from his jacket pocket. "We can mix it with a little Coke."

"Sure," Nikki says.

David pulls the Coke from a brown bag at his feet, opens it and drinks. "We'll drink it half way down," he says, passing it to Nikki, "then pour in the Velvet." Nikki drinks, hands the bottle back. He's got a little scar over his left cheekbone, under his eye, like a fingernail indentation, a crescent. Like he's been marked, touched by something. Otherwise, his skin is flawless. He's wearing a Ramones leather jacket but doesn't come off tough or posing. Nikki likes how fat his lips are, or not fat— fleshy. And smooth. Not all cracked up. They look like Mick Jagger's back when he was cool.

"That's what you get for riding the bus," David says.

Nikki takes the spiked Coke and drinks.

"Sea of trash," he says.

Nikki can't remember riding a bus with her mother, certainly not across country, but if they did, she knows they would have been the trash. She hands the bottle back. "Sounds snotty," she says, and he says, "Shit," tipping the whiskey with a laugh in his eyes, his grin making one deep dimple in his left cheek as he lowers the bottle and says, "Takes one to know one, right? I mean, I'm pulling for the kid."

"Maybe you should rescue him," Nikki says, taking the bottle and another drink.

"There should be somebody doing that," David says, "shouldn't there?"

Nikki shakes her head when he offers the bottle.

"You're right, though," David says. "A guy who junks his car in Nashville for bus fare home's got no business calling people trash."

"Breece!" the woman in back shouts, and the boy runs again, his suit jacket flying behind him. David raises his eyebrows, grinning, his bottom middle teeth overlapping like David Bowie's, and they burst into laughter.

"You gotta love him," he says after the mother drags the boy back to his seat. "You just gotta," and Nikki thinks he is exactly right.

"He's running away from it," he says. "From her. Damn trash having babies they can't take care of."

"Is that how it was for you?" Nikki says. "Your trashy mother chasing you down?" and David says, "A little trashy, maybe, but there's degrees to it. Don't get me wrong. I like that kid—like a beagle scratching to get out his cage."

"But his mom's just trash," Nikki says. "Not like yours."

David squints at her. "Hey," he says. "I didn't—"

"More like mine," she says, and David says, "I didn't say that," and Nikki says, "I said that," but she can't remember her mother chasing her down, except a pathetic, predictable attempt once Nikki was already gone from Manchester, her mother sending just two letters, thank God, the first forwarded by Melanie and telling Nikki she had one chance to come home, within two weeks—or stay the fuck away forever, the second coming after Christmas, this one sent to Frank's place, where Nikki was staying in a semi-permanent way. She'd sent her mother a letter with Frank's return address on the envelope, telling her she was happy and fine in Providence, going to school, meeting people, just newsy shit, a bunch of lies, the only thing ever worth giving her mother, her mother of course waving the cancer rag in Nikki's face with her reply, exactly as she'd been doing since the mastectomy, practically blaming Nikki for her sickness, or if not blaming, promising that she was Nikki's future, drunk and diseased even though the cancer had not recurred by the magical five year mark or even now—Melanie would have told her if it had—ending that final letter by telling Nikki she prayed night and day that Nikki herself would never get the cancer that had ruined her own life, prayed day and night that Nikki could be happy, though she herself could never be now that Nikki had gone and left her sick, left her to die all alone in a dirty apartment on Spruce Street, men and boys selling drugs on the sidewalk outside her building, and even though she prayed for Nikki's happiness—Nikki not knowing where all this praying bullshit was coming from—she would never be able to forgive Nikki for—and here began a numbered list, items one through seventeen, which Nikki decided not to read, being familiar enough with her crimes against her mother. And so maybe Nikki's mother has been chasing her for years. But not anymore. She's done thinking about her, anyway, wasting herself on worry and hate.

She takes the bottle from David and pulls a long drink. "Come on," she says, "talk about something." She wants to hear his voice again, wants to forgive him for calling the fat girl trash.

"Like what?"

"Like, you know, what you do."

"About what?"

"About anything."

David tells her he works for his father repairing appliances in Little Rock—how it's only the rich people who bitch about bills—but that he wants to partner with his uncle who owns a billboard company and cleared half a million last year.

"Billboards?" Nikki says, and David says, "You know. Truck stops. Restaurants," and Nikki says, "Signs?" and David says, "I know, but he's heading for a million bucks this year. Who cares how?"

Nikki doesn't know how anyone could dream of owning billboards, unless maybe they were going to paste up pictures of fat families mooning the highway, say, or that image of Johnny Cash, sneering and flipping off America.

She's about to tell David that, about Johnny Cash, but he says, "You gotta make your money somewhere, don't you? It's just like anything else," and Nikki says, "Like being in a punk band?" and David says, "Depends on how you think about it. Maybe it's like that."

"No it's not."

"Who'd want to be in a punk band anyway?"

"You would," Nikki says. "With your Black Velvet and leather coat," and David grins and says, "Maybe a metal band," and they trade band names until David convinces Nikki he has no taste in music whatsoever. How shallow she is to judge people solely on their musical taste or lack thereof, especially when this David so clearly understands the little boy Breece at the back of the bus running from his white trash mother. And at least he has ambition. At least he wants to do something. To be something. But no, Nikki thinks, he just wants money like everyone else. She's kind of drunk. She can't tell if she feels bad for judging this David or for misjudging him, thinking when they first started talking she could maybe like him, feeling a hint of that rush she felt with George at first. But she's just tired is all, tired and stupid, thinking without even trying, without meaning to, that what?

she's going to get off the bus with this guy in Little Rock and start some kind of life there in love? Not that she really thought that, but doesn't she know better than to even start down this path? Christ, she's not a kid anymore. Plus, she's got her own money now. Buckley's money, she thinks, but no, it's hers. Besides, what difference does any of this make? She's going to Austin, to Melanie.

She looks at David sitting beside her, the scar under his eye, how smooth and sort of glowing his skin is.

The little boy flies up the aisle.

"Crap dang it, Breece," the mother calls and she tears after him, carries him back thrashing against her, the boy looking right at Nikki and saying, "Booshit."

"Like the central bank," David says hours later and halfway through the second flat bottle of Black Velvet. "The federal reserve."

Nikki takes the bottle he offers, trying to pay attention after the long string of lies she's told, that her father's a musician, classically trained, her mother dead, that her roommate at Brown overdosed on sleeping pills and vodka right before Christmas and how Nikki found her body all bloated on the living room floor two days later, what a freak out that was, to see your best friend glassy-eyed and stiff, naked, the smells in the room overwhelming, and how Kara—that was her name—haunted Nikki's dreams even now, David saying, "Jesus, that's awful," making Nikki feel bad about lying as they pulled out of Jackson, Tennessee, though for awhile it felt like singing. Without the lies, she has nothing to say and has stopped listening as well, except in snatches.

"Nobody really knows who's pulling the strings," David says. "It's like the free-masons."

Nikki hands him the bottle, excuses herself, and walks to the bathroom, the little boy Breece and his mom and sister on the back bench seat watching her walk toward them, the mother's eyes pointing different directions, the sister, maybe three years old, perched in her lap with big eyes on Nikki and a lollypop in her mouth, lollypop smeared on her face and the front of her white dress, Breece the boy beside them holding a stuffed dinosaur, biting his thumbnail as he watches Nikki reach for the door handle, the mom saying, "Somebody's in there," and Nikki nodding, says, "Oh," and stands in front of them facing the door waiting. She feels something on her ass, jerks her head to see Breece pull his hand back to himself. "Hey," the mother says, rapping the boy's head with her knuckles, "hands to your-self." Nikki smiles at the mother, but can't tell if she's looking at her or not. She looks up the aisle to see David twisted around watching her, feels the hand on her ass again, and jerks around, Breece looking up at his mother, saying "Sorry," as the mother raps his head again and says, "Sorry don't feed the bulldog."

Nikki moves forward, out of Breece's reach and stares at the floor. She's trying not to touch the seats, trying not to disturb other passengers, but she's drunk and the bus is wobbling. She's a little sick. She walks back to the bathroom and reaches for the door, figuring to alert the person inside that somebody's waiting, but when she lurches against the handle, it turns and the bathroom is vacant. She looks at the mother, who ignores her, then slips inside, locking the door behind her.

She sits on the toilet and breathes. Should have brought her water back with her. Touches the bumps of money in her pockets, takes out her half joint, but doesn't light it. She feels drugged, fucked up. Did that David slip her something? But no, they've been drinking from the same bottles. She pushes open the triangle window and sticks her face as close to outside air as she can. It doesn't help. Finally, she pukes in the toilet, but almost nothing comes up, and she realizes she hasn't eaten in days. That's the problem. Somebody knocks on the door. 'Just a minute,' she says, sitting on the toilet and breathing. Maybe she's feeling better. When she gets back to her seat David's talking to the smoking nun.

Just an hour to go until Memphis and food, but the thought of food makes her stomach lurch. David offers the bottle. She pushes it away. He resumes his conversation with the nun, something about celestial reasoning. Isn't that some kind of soup? Nikki takes a sip of water. She's going to throw up again. She concentrates on the seatback in front of her. It feels like the time she was six years old and threw up so many times in a row on New Year's Eve her mother had to take her to Elliot hospital. They were still in the house on Salmon Street, where Nikki lived the first eight years of her life, before the annual relocation from one shitty apartment to the next on Spruce or Hanover, her mother still a secretary at Velcro, an office manager she called herself, before Melanie came to live with them, but Melanie was there that night, their mothers—twin sisters—at a party somewhere, in the bars, wherever, and Nikki started throwing up around ten o'clock, cheese doodles and orange soda and hot dogs, and felt okay for about ten minutes after, Melanie telling her she was fine, that she'd eaten too much too fast, and she wanted to believe it because they were going to stay up until midnight to watch the ball fall in Times Square, which Nikki had never seen, imagining the ball some kind of zipper handle falling and tearing the old year off the new one about to begin, time laid out flat in Times Square, the old year waiting to tear and flutter away like the page of a calendar, but then she threw up again and another time and didn't care about watching the ball fall, had to stay in the bathroom because she couldn't stop throwing up.

And Melanie couldn't track down their mothers on the phone. She fed Nikki crackers and ginger ale in the bathroom, but Nikki couldn't hold anything down, kept falling asleep between throwing up, her skin burning with fever.

Melanie helped her into a cool tub, where she shivered and threw up all over herself. Melanie got her out of the tub and wrapped her in towels on the bathmat. Nikki threw up on the floor. Finally, her mother was there, picking her up and carrying her to the back seat of Aunt Patty's car, holding her as Aunt Patty drove them to the hospital. Her mother must have been drunk, but Nikki couldn't recognize it then. She threw up the last time in the emergency room lobby, before being lifted onto a gurney and wheeled into a curtained-off space where a nurse poked her with an IV needle, a doctor shining a light in her eyes, pressing on her stomach, her mother saying, "She's okay, right? Is she okay? She's okay. Is she going to be okay?" the doctor hushing her, touching Nikki's body, Nikki wondering if maybe the doctor would marry her mother.

When she woke, the first thing she noticed was the IV tube attached to her arm, running up to a clear bag on a pole over her head. Then she saw her mother slumped in a green chair beside her bed, sleeping with her mouth open a little, the most beautiful woman in the world in her violet silk blouse and black skirt, freshwater pearls almost matching the flawless skin over her collar bones, a beautiful princess Nikki hoped she would someday become. She woke a few seconds later and smiled at Nikki. "I knew you'd be okay," she said, "didn't I?" coming to Nikki's bed to lie beside her, but now Nikki can't imagine this memory is accurate, that her mother was ever capable of waiting for Nikki to wake and be okay. The memory must be a lie she created to convince her seven or eight year old self her mother was decent and normal, the inaccurate memory now stuck with her, unquestioned all these years buried, to come back on a bus somewhere between Nashville and Memphis where Nikki is going to vomit again.

She pulls herself up, says, "I have to—" and David looks at her, the nun looks at her—the nun a turtle, some kind of reptile—and David scrambles out of his seat. She makes her way to the back of the bus with her water bottle. No one's in the bathroom this time, thank God, real or imagined. She pukes in the toilet, wonders if Breece and his mother and sister are listening. She's going to have to smoke that joint. She can't tell if she has a fever. Only a hit or two, just enough to settle her stomach. She blows four hits out the window, then drops the roach outside and takes a few sips of water. It can't be food poisoning because she hasn't eaten anything. When she gets back to her row, David stands and the nun says, "Are you okay, dear?"

"Fine," Nikki says, sliding into her seat.

"Here," the nun says, handing David something across the aisle. "Give her this."

David hands Nikki a rice cake.

"Thanks," Nikki says.

"And no more liquor," the nun says. "Okay?"

"Okay," Nikki says.

And the nun says, "No more liquor for her."

She must have slept through Memphis because she wakes with the rice cake still in her hand, damp, as they pull into Forrest City, almost eleven o'clock in Arkansas, not yet midnight in Providence, still her birthday no matter what time zone she's in. She hears the sounds of people getting on and off the bus, then they're moving again. Still drunk, exhausted, high, she doesn't feel like puking anymore, but keeps her eyes closed after squinting at her watch, the image of her mother as an object of beauty beside her hospital bed lingering. What other lies has she made of her past? She thinks of Maya and Buckley and her, the three of them in bed last night, this morning, two days ago, whenever it was, fucking on ex, how she could tell Maya and Buckley were made for each other, a sort of gauzy halo around them, but now, half drunk, half hung over, starving in a bus she's been on forever, she knows Maya and Buckley have as much chance as anyone—none. She thinks of David talking earlier about his year in Daytona framing houses, Nikki asking if he ever got down to Orlando, to Disney World, and David saying sure he did, and he could take Nikki there, too, if she wanted to go, and for Nikki to have let herself be pulled like that, by his hands or lips or scar, or whatever she thought he could promise—if even for a second, pulled like a robot, a dog, oblivious to the pulling current—scares her, makes her wonder if she has any control of herself at all. She's going to have to watch herself from now on, if she wants to—to—what? Be okay? But no, she wants to be so much more than okay, she wants to be, she wants—

She sits up in her seat and feels dizzy. David sleeps beside her, his head tilted back, face to ceiling. Across the aisle, the little boy Breece sits next to the sleeping, smoking nun, picking his nose and staring at Nikki, as if he's been waiting for her to wake. She smiles at him.

"Bitch ass," he says, almost a whisper.

"What?" Nikki says.

"Bitch ass," Breece says as quiet as the first time.

Nikki shakes her head, puts her index finger to her lips. "Don't say that."

"Shit bitch," he says.

Nikki twists around and raises herself to look back to the bench seat, but it's empty, as are most of the seats. "Where's your mother?" she whispers across David, and Breece whispers, "Shit bag."

Nikki looks back again, but the seat's still empty. She scans the other rows behind her. No sign of White Trash Mother. She stands, works herself around David, who moves his legs in his sleep, and squats in the aisle by the little boy who stares at her, picking his nose. "Hey, Breece," she says. "Where's your mother?"

"Dong," Breece says, and for the first time he smiles at her.

"Ding dong," she says. "Where's your mom?"

"Gone," Breece says.

"Gone? In the bathroom?"

"Hell in a handbag."

"Don't move," Nikki says. "And stop picking your nose."

At the back of the bus the bathroom's empty. Did the mother get off somewhere and leave the kid alone? What kind of shitbag must she be? Nikki walks up the aisle, stops by Breece and says, "I'll be right back," and makes her way forward, weaving with the motion of the bus, no sign of the mother anywhere. Is Nikki going to have to be responsible for this kid because she fucking found him, because she discovered he's been abandoned? She's going to Austin. To Melanie. The nun can take the kid. Probably already has. She's not stopping now that her life's about to start. But after the driver turns the bus around, maybe she'll sit with the kid in a depot somewhere, until the mother or someone can be tracked down. Maybe she'll take care of him while somebody finds somebody he belongs to. Not even her own shithead mother would—but then Nikki sees the mom in the third row aisle seat, the little girl's head in her lap, both of them asleep. A wave of relief washes over her, thank God, but something else too. Almost like loss. Proving how fucked up she is, how aimless, but isn't she going to Austin? Doesn't she have a plan? She stands looking down at the mother. "Nun's got the boy," a man says from the seat behind Trash Mom. "Wanted to get the baby outta the smoke."

Nikki walks back down the bus and crouches by Breece, who sticks his finger in his nose the minute he sees her. "Come on, Breece," she whispers. "Let's sit in back."

Without looking, she knows he's following. Less than twelve hours to Austin, she's wide awake again, ready. She sits on the bench seat, Breece beside her, his naked leg below his shorts touching her jeans.

Breece cups her ear with his hand.

"Asswipe," he whispers, and Nikki cups his ear and whispers, "Motherfucker."

"Fuck pig," Breece whispers back.

"Cock-a-doodle-doo," Nikki says.

She's surprised to discover the smoking nun's rice cake in her hand. She breaks it in two. "Here," she says, handing Breece half. "This is my birthday cake."

Breece looks at it, looks at Nikki. "Can I eat it?" he says and Nikki says, "Of course you can eat it. It's my birthday, isn't it? I can cry if I want to, can't I?"

"You gonna cry?" Breece asks, his big eyes roaming Nikki's face.

"Of course not," Nikki says.

Breece examines the rice cake. He take a bite and spits it on the floor. "'At tastes like old dust," he says.

"So don't eat it."

He raises himself to his knees on the seat beside her and whispers in her ear, "Big butt birthday bash," and Nikki whispers, "Thank you, Breece," and Breece whispers, "What's your name anyways?" and Nikki whispers, "Nikki," and Breece says, "Shit pile," the South in his voice making it sound like Shitpal.

"That's right," Nikki says. And she laughs.

"Shitpal," she whispers back, and Breece giggles, says it again, the bus mostly dark, humming along south, taking her farther and farther away, drunk David and the smoking nun in front of her waiting to disappear, Little Rock and then Dallas about to pop up and fall away, Nikki safe at the back of the bus swearing with a five year old, all these miles gone behind.

STOLPESTAD

William Lychack

Was toward the end of your shift, a Saturday, another one of those long slow lazy afternoons of summer—sun never burning through the clouds, clouds never breaking into rain—odometer like a clock ticking all those bored little pent-up streets and mills and tenements away. The coffee shops, the liquor stores, laundromats, police, fire, gas stations to pass—this is your life, Stolpestad—all the turns you could make in your sleep, the brickwork and shop fronts and river with its stink of carp and chokeweed, the hills swinging up free from town, all momentum and mood, roads smooth and empty, this big blue hum of cruiser past houses and lawns and long screens of trees, trees cutting open to farms and fields all contoured and high with corn, air thick and silvery, as if something was on fire somewhere—still with us?

That sandy turnaround—always a question, isn't it?

Gonna pull over and ride back down or not?

End of your shift—or nearly so—and in comes the call. It's Phyllis, dispatcher for the weekend, that radio crackle of her voice, and she's sorry for doing this to you but a boy's just phoned for help with a dog. And what's she think you look like now, you ask, town dogcatcher? Oh, you should be so lucky, she says and gives the address and away we go.

No siren, no speeding, just a calm quiet spin around to this kid and his dog, back to all the turns you were born, your whole life spent along these same sad streets. Has nothing to do with this story, but there are days you idle past these houses as if to glimpse someone or something—yourself as a boy, perhaps—the apartments stacked with porches, the phone poles and wires and sidewalks all close and cluttered, this woman at the curb as you pull up and step out of the car.

Everything gets a little worse from here, boy running out of the brush in back before you so much as say hello. He's what—eight or nine years old—skinny kid cutting straight to his mother. Presses himself to her side, catches his breath, his eyes going from you to your uniform, your duty belt, his mother trying to explain what happened and where she is now, the dog, the tall grass, behind the garage, woman pointing. And the boy—he's already edging away from his mother—little stutter steps and the kid's halfway around the house to take you to the animal, his mother staying by the side porch as you follow toward the garage and garbage barrels out back, you and the boy wading out into the grass and scrub weeds, the sumac, the old tires, empty bottles, rusted car axle, refrigerator door. Few more steps and there—a small fox-colored dog—beagle mix lying in the grass, as good as sleeping at the feet of the boy, that vertigo buzz of insects rising and falling in the heat, air thick as a towel over your mouth.

And you stand there and wait—just wait—and keep waiting, the boy not saying a word, not looking away from the dog, not doing anything except kneeling next to the animal, her legs twisted awkward behind her, the grass tamped into a kind of nest where he must have squatted next to her, where this boy must have talked to her, tried to soothe her, tell her everything was all right. There's a steel cooking pot to one side—water he must have carried from the kitchen—and in the quiet the boy pulls a long stem of grass and begins to tap at the dog. The length of her muzzle, the outline of her chin, her nose, her ear—it's like he's drawing her with the brush of grass—and as you stand there, he pushes the feather top of grass into the corner of her eye. It's a streak of cruel he must have learned from someone, the boy pushing the stem, pressing it on her until, finally, the dog's eye opens as black and shining as glass. She bares her teeth at him, the boy painting her tongue with the tip of grass, his fingers catching the tags at her throat, the sound like ice in a drink.

And it's work to stay quiet, isn't it? A real job to let nothing happen, to just look away at the sky, to see the trees, the garage, the dog again, the nest of grass, this kid brushing the grain of her face, the dog's mouth pulled back, quick breaths in her belly. Hours you stand there—days—standing there still now, aren't you?

And when he glances up to you, his chin's about to crumble, boy about to disappear at the slightest touch, his face pale and raw and ashy. Down to one knee next to him—and you're going to have to shoot this dog—you both must realize this by now, the way she can't seem to move, her legs like rags, that sausage link of intestine under her. The boy leans forward and sweeps an ant off the dog's shoulder.

God knows you don't mean to chatter this kid into feeling better, but when he turns, you press your lips into a line and smile and ask him what her name is. He turns to the dog again—and again you wait—wait and watch this kid squatting hunch-curved next to the dog, your legs going needles and nails under you, the kid's head a strange whorl of hair as you hover above him, far above this boy, this dog, this nest, this field. And when he glances to you, it's a spell he's breaking, all of this about to become real with her name—Goliath—but we call her Gully for short, he says.

And you ask if she's his dog.

And the boy nods—mine and my father's, he says.

And you touch your hand to the grass for balance and ask the boy how old he is.

And he says nine.

And what grade is nine again?

Third.

The dog's eyes are closed when you look—bits of straw on her nose, her teeth yellow, strands of snot on her tongue—nothing moving until you stand and kick the blood back into your legs, afternoon turning to evening, everything going grainy in the light. The boy dips his hand in the cooking pot and tries to give water to the dog with his fingers, sprinkling her mouth, her face, her eyes wincing.

A moment passes—and then another—and soon you're brushing the dust from your knee and saying, C'mon, let's get back to your mother, before she starts to worry.

She appears out of the house as you approach—out of the side door on the steps as you and the boy cross the lawn—the boy straight to her once again, kid's mother drawing him close, asking was everything okay out there. And neither of you say anything—everyone must see what's coming—if you're standing anywhere near this yard you have to know that sooner or later she's going to ask if you can put this dog down for them. She'll ask if you'd like some water or lemonade, if you'd like to sit a minute, and you'll thank her and say no and shift your weight from one leg to the other, the woman asking what you think they should do.

Maybe you'll take that glass of water after all, you tell her—the boy sent into the house—the woman asking if you won't just help them.

Doesn't she want to try calling a vet?

No, she tells you—the boy out of the house with a glass of water for you—you thanking him and taking a good long drink, the taste cool and metallic, the woman with the boy at her side, her hand on the boy's shoulder, both of them stiff as you hand the glass back and say thank you again.

A deep breath and you ask if she has a shovel. To help bury the dog, you tell her.

She unstiffens slightly, says she'd rather the boy and his father do that when he gets home from work.

In a duffel in the trunk of the cruiser is an automatic—an M9—and you swap your service revolver for this Beretta of yours. No discharge, no paperwork, nothing official to report, the boy staying with his mother as you cross the yard to the brush and tall weeds in back, grasshoppers spurting up and away from you, dog smaller when you find her, as if she's melting, lying there, grass tamped in that same nest around her, animal as smooth as suede. A nudge with the toe of your shoe and she doesn't move—you standing over her with this hope that she's already dead—that shrill of insects in the heat and grass as you nudge her again. You push until she comes to life, her eye opening slow and black to you—you with this hope that the boy will be running any moment to you now, hollering for you to stop—and again the work of holding still and listening.

Hey, girl, you say and release the safety of the gun. You bend at the waist and gently touch the sight to just above the dog's ear, hold it there, picture how the boy will have to find her—how they're going to hear the shots, how they're waiting, breaths held—and you slide the barrel to the dog's neck, to just under the collar, the wounds hidden as you squeeze one sharp crack, and then another, into the animal.

You know the loop from here—the mills, the tenements, the streetlights flickering on in the dusk—and still it's the long way around home, isn't it? Wife and pair of boys waiting dinner for you, hundred reasons to go straight to them, but soon you're an hour away, buying a sandwich from a vending machine, calling Sheila from a payphone to say you're running a little late. Another hour back to town, slow and lawful, windows open, night plush and cool, roads this smooth hum back through town for a quick stop at The Elks, couple of drinks turning into a few—you know the kind of night—same old crew at the bar playing cribbage, talking Yankees, Red Sox, and this little dog they heard about, ha, ha, ha. Explain how word gets around in a place like this, Stoli, ha, ha, ha—how you gave the pooch a blindfold and cigarette, ha, ha, ha—another round for everyone, ha, ha, ha—three cheers for Gully—the next thing you know being eleven o'clock and the phone behind the bar is for you.

It's Sheila—and she's saying someone's at the house, a man and a boy on the porch for you—be right there, you tell her. Joey asks if you want another for the road as you hand the receiver over the bar, and you drink this last one standing up, say goodnight, and push yourself out the door to the parking lot, darkness cool and clear as water, sky scattershot with stars. And as you stand by the car and open your pants and piss half-drunk against that hollow drum of the fender, it's like you've never seen stars before, the sky some holy-shit vastness all of a sudden, you gazing your bladder empty, staring out as if the stars were suns in the black distance.

Not a dream—though it often feels like one—streets rivering you home through the night and the dark, that déjà vu of a pickup truck in the driveway as you pull around to the house, as if you've seen or imagined or been through all of this before, or will be through it again, over and over, man under the light of the porch, transistor sound of crickets in the woods. He's on the steps as you're out of the car—the lawn, the trees, everything underwater in the dark—and across the wet grass you're asking what you can do for him.

He's tall and ropy and down the front walk toward you, cigarette in his hand, you about to ask what's the problem when there's a click from the truck. It's only a door opening—but look how jumpy you are, how relieved to see only a boy in the driveway—kid from this afternoon cutting straight to go to his father, man tossing his cigarette into the grass, brushing his foot over it, apologizing for how late at night it must be.

How can I help you?

You're a police officer, says the man, aren't you?

Sheila's out on the porch now—light behind her—a silhouette at the rail, she's hugging a sweater around herself, her voice small like a girl's in the dark, asking if everything's all right, you taking a step toward the house and telling her that everything's fine, another step and you're saying you'll be right in, she should go back inside, it's late.

She goes into the house and the man apologizes again for the hour and says he'll only be a minute, this man on your lawn pulling the boy to his side, their faces shadowed and smudged in the dark, man bending to say something to his son, kid saying yes sir, his father standing straight, saying that you helped put a dog down this afternoon.

And before you even open your mouth, he's stepping forward and thanking you for your help—the man shaking your hand, saying how pleased, how grateful, how proud, how difficult it must have been—but his tone's all wrong, all snaky, all salesman as he nudges his boy ahead to give you—and what's this?

Oh, he says, it's nothing really.

But the boy's already handed it to you—the dog's collar in your hand, leather almost warm, tags like coins—the guy's voice all silk and breeze as he explains how they wanted you to have it, a token of appreciation, in honor of all you did for them.

It's a ship at sea to stand on that lawn like this—everything swaying and off-balanced for you—and before you say a word he's laughing as if to the trees, the man saying to put it on your mantle, maybe, or under your fucken pillow. Put it on your wife, he says and laughs and swings around all serious and quiet to you, the man saying he's sorry for saying that.

Nice lady, he says—and when you look the boy is milk-blue in the night, cold and skinny as he stands next to his father—man telling how he made it home a little late after work that night. Was past nine by the time he got around to the dog, he says, dark when the two of them got out to the field—the boy with the flash-light, himself with the shovel—almost decided to wait until morning, didn't we?

He nudges the boy—startles the kid awake, it seems—and the boy says yes.

Anyway, says the man, couldn't find her for the life of us. But then we did. Not like she was going anywhere, right? Took us a while to dig that hole, never seen so many stones, so many broken bottles.

He turns to the house behind him, the yellow light of windows, the curtains, the blade of roofline, black of trees, shrubs. He lets out a long sigh and says what a fine place you seem to have here.

You say thanks—and then you wait—watch for him to move at you.

Any kids?

Two boys, you say.

Younger or older than this guy here?

Few years younger, you tell him.

He nods—has his hand on his boy's shoulder—you can see that much in the dark, can hear the sigh, the man deflating slightly, his head tipping to one side. So, he says, like I was saying, took us a while to get the hole dug. And then when we go to take the collar, the dog tries to move away from us—like she's still alive—all this time and she's still alive—all those ants into her by now, imagine seeing?

He hums a breath and runs his palm over the boy's hair, says the vet arrived a little later, asked if we did this to the dog, made us feel where you're supposed to shoot an animal, slot right under the ear. He reaches his finger out to you and touches, briefly, the side of your head—almost tender—smell of cigarettes on his hand, your feet wet and cold in the grass, jaw wired tight, the boy and his father letting you hang there in front of them, two of them just waiting for whatever you'll say next to this, man clucking his tongue, saying, Anyway—helluva a thing to teach a kid, don't you think?

A pause—but not another word—and he starts them back toward the truck, the man and the boy, their trails across the silver wet of the lawn, the pickup doors clicking open and banging closed—one and then the other—engine turning over, headlights a long sweep as they ride away, sound tapering to nothing. And in the silence, in the darkness, you stand like a thief on the lawn—stand watching this house for signs of life—wavering as you back gently away from the porch, away from the light of the windows, away until you're gone at the edge of the woods, a piece of dark within the dark, Sheila arriving to that front door, eventually, this woman calling for something to come in out of the night.

THE ANTICHRIST CHRONICLES

Andre Malan Milward

In the months before the lake disappeared, I began having lunch every day with my high school guidance counselor. It was early in the semester, a few weeks into my final year of high school, and I'd taken to eating my lunches with her because Joby, my one real friend, had a different lunch period. The counselor's name was Susan and she had the undeserved surname of Cox. It was a name for pranking and practical jokes, a name to be yelled over the intercom by juvenile delinquents during the Pledge of Allegiance, as Robbie Toobler had done the previous spring: "Ms. Cox I need your help! I think I'm in love with you! Ms. Cox aaahhhh…" We became friendly after I mistakenly barged into her office looking for the school nurse and ended up talking right through my fourth-hour trig. But we spoke less as student and counselor than as neighbors on barstools. She must have realized that since she didn't recognize me the first time we met I had to be a slacker of astronomical proportions, one of the doomed and futureless, destined for a life mopping floors at Shop 'n Go, for the avoidance of all things class reunion. And perhaps because of this, she seemed to let her guard down in front of me.

That day, the day Joby first started suspecting her father of following her, Susan and I were talking about Mr. Hudson, the 8th grade English teacher who'd hanged himself earlier in the week. Susan was spending a lot of time at the junior high helping out. Underequipped to handle the aftermath, the principal called for reinforcements, and in Susan he found the right person. Tragedy and general ill fortune were her bread and butter. She was three times a divorcee and her daughter, Jeanie, had a prosthetic leg from the time a doctor's knife slipped during surgery and severed a nerve he was trying to spare. When I asked how she helped the shaken students, she replied, "I don't hold their hands," steeled by her scientist's sense of sympathy. "I listen. Best thing you can do. How can you ever try to reason something like this to kids?" I nodded as the memories of Mr. Hudson slowly stretched back to life inside my head. I'd had him in 8th grade for a month before I was pulled out and switched to the remedial English class. Thinking of him after he was gone, I remembered all sorts of things I hadn't thought of for years, all that matter that lies dormant until someone has taken his life: how he was always reading in his classroom after school let out; the way he encouraged his students to call him Jim; his gait, the somber milling of a dreamer. She shook her head and nibbled on the small block of cheese that, along with a Granny Smith apple, she ate every day for lunch. "Still, it's sad, you know. All those kids, most of them deal-ing with death for the first time. You should see them, Tom. They walk around the hallways like ghosts."

"Yeah, like ghosts," I said, wondering what I must have looked like myself walk-ing down the hallway, eyes down, trying to survive those terrifying five minutes of anarchy between bell rings unmolested as the gauntlet of high-fives and ball-grabbing swallowed up those around me.

Just then there was a knock on the door and Joby popped her head in.

"Hey," she said. She had that look about her, up to no good. "Let's get out of here." Like junkies sick for truancy, we'd developed a bad habit and being so early in the school year we were cutting with a frightening regularity.

I looked at Susan and she threw her hands up. "I don't want to know anything about it."

And with that Joby and I took off down the hallway, ducking out a side door, skulking past Mr. Mineo, the ever watchful parking attendant, and dove into her car, where we both crouched for a few seconds. We waited until he circled around to the other side of the parking lot and then left. When we reached the street and zoomed away from the school, we shouted triumphantly, extending our middle fingers out the window, and Joby turned the music up full blast. She had on a tight red shirt purchased on a recent trip to Kansas City. The shirt was made to look old-er and less expensive than it was, projecting a silhouette of Lenin flanked by the hammer and sickle. Her finger- and toenails were painted black and she'd drawn little anarchy signs on the white tips of her black Chuck Taylors. "Fascists," she said, looking at our school shrinking in the rearview. Joby spoke in the language of those stuck in a state of permanent revolt. When asked, she'd identify herself as a Socialist, but as far as I could tell her platform was a hodgepodge of leftist ideas designed to get a rise out of anyone over the age of thirty. I lacked her passion. Apathy was the bedrock of my ideology, a veritable third rail. Despite this, we'd become friends through high school's strange process of natural selection. Physi-cally we were opposites, too. She was tall and bone-thin, pretty even, with straight brown hair and a long angular face—intimidated the hell out of most boys—and I was short, a little pudgy, invisible but for my big-ass head. We were, Susan liked to tell me, quite the pair.

Joby sped through town, headed toward her family's house. Her family's gi-gantic house. Her folks were loaded, a fact she resented more than anything else, the unwashable stink of her own privilege. She lectured constantly about the evils of capitalism and yet drove the SUV her parents gave her for her 16th birthday with no sense of irony, with reckless abandon.

The house was part of a private development that bordered the lake that would disappear in a matter of months. We often went to the lake on these afternoons, to smoke-up or talk, taking refuge from our families and school, though today we found ourselves just wandering throughout the house, looking for anything to distract us. I followed behind her, looking down at the back of her Converse, where she had scratched off the *All Star* and written *Anarchy* in black marker. Aimlessly we went from room to room picking things up—home-decoration magazines, antique clocks and wooden pieces, pillows embroidered with passages from the Bible—sometimes commenting on them before setting them back down. When we were bored with one room, we went to the next. The house was huge, but more than that it was hugely empty.

"Where are your parents?" I finally asked as we stood before the closed door of a room I knew was her father's office, though I'd never been inside before.

"They're out. Mom's garden club meets all afternoon and you know my dad," she said, touching the knob of the door.

What she meant was that her dad was rarely home anymore. In fact, beyond a few pictures on the walls, I'd never actually seen him. Apparently he once owned a small livestock farm outside of town and made a fortune selling the sperm of a prize bull. As Joby told it, coming into all this money was a sign, so he sold the farm and moved his family here, where, born again, he took up the cause of a church of growing notoriety. He spent most of his time and disposable income developing an ongoing series of videotapes called *The Antichrist Chronicles*, which he sent to people selected from the phonebook—the "chosen," as Joby referred to them—trying to show the myriad ways we had failed God in hopes they'd hightail it for church. Judging from booming attendance rolls and the increasing number of highway billboards that read HELL IS REAL and REPENT AND BE SAVED, the operation was a rousing success.

I was curious. I'd never seen one of the videos before, so when I said, "Show me one of his tapes," it seemed to give the afternoon a sense of purpose. Joby eased open the door, slipping inside, and quickly shut it. When she appeared again, she was holding a videocassette. We went down the hallway to the TV room, where I plopped into one of the beanbag chairs.

"This'll be on volume thirteen but it's not edited yet," she said, loading the tape into the VCR. "He's going to start transferring them to DVD soon. Keep up with the technology, you know." She punched a button on the remote and the unsteady picture spilled over the television. We sat quietly as the camera zoomed in on a man bent over a moped chained to a parking meter. I wasn't sure what to make of it until he removed the gas cap and shoved his nose deep into the hole. He huffed the fumes for a good thirty seconds before his legs gave out and he fell to the sidewalk.

"Your dad filmed this?"

"I don't know, maybe. Could be any whacko from his group."

"Do they just wait around for stuff like this to happen?"

"Pretty much," she said, hitting the pause button, which froze on a close-up of the man's face. He looked, I remarked, happy.

"I guess that's sort of their point, right?"

"Whatever. They're crazy, if you ask me. You know, sometimes I swear he's following me with that fucking camera. Seriously, no joke." She hit the eject button. "This is creeping me out. Let's go to the lake."

The town where we lived was a small agrarian community in central Kansas, not far from Salina. "The Center of the Center of America," as the welcoming billboard on the edge of town announced. In recent years most of the small, independent farms had gone bust or been swallowed up by corporations and developers. Or worse, they were given small governmental subsidies *not* to farm their land. No one could really make a living on the subsidies so most had foreclosed or turned to agritourism to stay afloat. This was what accounted for our amazing number of pumpkin shooting ranges, shitty Kansan vineyards, country hayrides, and corn mazes in the shape of famous Kansans like Eisenhower and Amelia Earhart. All this to avoid foreclosing or watching their tenable land waste away unused, though sometimes even this was not enough, which had given birth to our other great industry: the production and consumption of crystal meth. This was rural Kansas, where Mom and Pop farms were giving way to Mom and Pop methamphetamine labs. Where the divide between rich and poor was a gulf and, with few exceptions like Joby's neighborhood, the streets were lined with doublewides and the cheap bourbon flowed like water. This was a town where everyone knew each other, but no one wanted to admit it.

My dad and I both worked on the weekends. On Saturdays we'd head out early to grab a bite at Ma's Diner before the rush and afterwards he'd drop me off at Shop 'n Go, where I'd spend six hours mopping floors and bagging groceries, while he went onto his job at Alive With History! The crown jewel of our agritourism boom, Alive With History!—part museum, part amusement park—was comprised of a series of historically recreated farms from different time periods that together told the history of Midwestern agriculture on nearly 600 acres of land. My dad was an "historic actor," which meant he pretended to farm and delivered an informative spiel on farming techniques of the period whenever a tour group arrived. When the park opened, he started out on the "Bleeding Kansas" 1859 farm, and in a few years moved up to the post-Civil War 1870 farm, and now had made it to the post-Industrial Revolution 1920 farm. For fear of sinking further into the dross of coollessness, I'd never told anyone this, even Joby.

After my shift I usually walked over to SUNFLOWER'S, where Joby worked as a line cook. I sat at the bar sipping pop, talking to her on her breaks, waiting until she finished. It was an awful place, an unfortunate knockoff of Hooters that not so cleverly punned on our state flower, but Joby didn't seem to mind it much. The monstrous sign outside depicted a buxom blonde with triple-D sunflowers for breasts. Today I was seated next to a couple from the Northeast who, I gathered from eavesdropping, were driving to California and had mistakenly come in looking for local color, not realizing it was a boobs-and-wings joint. They were staring anxiously at the menu when Joby tapped on my shoulder. A white apron, mottled by sauce and grease stains, hung from her neck. The woman next to me scoffed to her female partner, "Look, they actually have salads in Kansas."

Joby leaned over, an inch away from the woman's ear. "Yes we do, but we smother them in gravy," she said and walked off.

I followed her out back and she lit a joint by the Dumpster. "All through?" I asked, and she nodded, balling up her apron and dropping it to the ground. We were exhaling little plumes when Jonas walked outside from the kitchen with a bag of garbage. He bussed tables there and occasionally attended our school, but he'd been suspended so many times it was hard to tell if he was actually enrolled anymore or not. Every month or so, just when I thought he'd surely been expelled, I'd see him walking the hallways or sleeping on his desk in class.

"Hey," he said, looking at Joby. "What're you doing?"

"Nothing," Joby said. "Gonna walk around or something."

Jonas had shaved his hair into a Mohawk, though the remaining swatch was trimmed so close that it looked less punk than military. He laughed and put up his hands. "Oh, sorry, didn't mean to interrupt anything." He was almost a foot taller than me, but I wanted so badly to bruise him in the shins right then.

"Fuck off, Jonas," Joby sighed languidly, like the chorus of a sultry song about a never-ending summer. Our friendship had always been asexual, something that seemed to confuse those around us. "Come with."

Smoking another joint seemed to put us in a mood to walk around, so there the three of us were, watching the lights from the bars and pool halls switch on.

Neon bands of light snaked through the dark and the smell of ozone singed the air. Men in newly bought cowboy hats practiced their strut around town, wearing multiple turquoise rings and belt buckles the size of championship boxing titles. It had been a brutal summer, the heat unyielding, and even now in mid-September we wondered when it would cool. The landscape was dominated by long stretches of sunflowers that would only disappear when the heat broke. We walked through town saying things like, "It's too hot to smoke," but did so anyway.

Paranoia was a major buzz kill with the local ragweed we smoked, and later when it was full-dark Joby said again that she thought her father was following her. She was convinced he had started planting microphones and miniature cameras in her clothes. "That's the kind of shit they do in totalitarian regimes," she said, her eyes wild. I tried to calm her, telling her we'd leave, but she wouldn't settle down.

When we got back to the parking lot where Joby was parked, Jonas wiped his nose on his shirtsleeve and held out his hand, saying, "Wanna try? Won't make you paranoid as weed." In his palm sat an 8-ball of the ice-like chips that had provoked the President's drug czar to compare what was happening in rural parts of Kansas and Missouri to the crack epidemic that plagued inner cities in the '80s. Joby was looking down the neck of her shirt, trying to find some means of surveillance, and only looked up at Jonas's hand after having found none, smiling.

"Phew, I think I'm clean."

When I was three, my mother came home from work, fixed my father dinner, and put me to bed. Then, that night, after my dad had fallen asleep in front of a Star Trek rerun, she packed a bag, left the house, and disappeared. I say disappeared because there was never a note or phone call, never a reason or explanation, just the reality: she was gone, vanished. I knew all this only from the bits I'd been able to pull out of my father when he'd had a few drinks; without one he'd tell me I was adopted. There were no pictures; all evidence of her existence was gone. I remembered so little, a form mostly. We'd lived in Kansas City then, where my dad was a Lit professor at UMKC, but after it was clear she was never coming back he moved here to get himself together. His uncle, Mort, owned a little bar in town and we stayed with him a while. Dad spent most of his days drinking at the bar with Uncle Mort, where he developed his habit. For a large part of my youth he collected unemployment and lived off of savings. When Uncle Mort died though, my dad sold the bar. He only began working at Alive With History! when the money was nearly gone. The only traces of his former life as an impassioned lecturer of poetry survived in fragments, popping up unexpectedly, as in notes he'd leave on the kitchen counter: *This is just to say: I've ventvred to the store. Shall retvrn henceforth, ioyovsly, Redcrosse.*

It was several Saturdays later, in early November, that the lake disappeared. From our table at Ma's Diner my dad rattled the newspaper. "You'll never believe what happened." I was looking down at my plate, trying to discern if the black flakes floating in my yolk were cigarette ash or pepper, and mumbled back, asking what's up. When he didn't respond, I looked at him. His mammoth eyebrows dwarfed his eyes, and he'd long since stopped trying to control the Einsteinian flair of his wild gray hair. He was wearing a black t-shirt with a picture of Leonard Nimoy under the heading *What Would Spock Do?* and he was grinning, holding the front page of the paper out for me to see. As the wave of intrigue moved across his face, he looked like a mad scientist from some old Universal horror film on the brink of major discovery, of something that could either save the world or end everything.

After breakfast we went to see the lake. I studied the article as my father drove Uncle Mort's old truck, a big pewter tank of a thing that would survive long after the asteroid hit. I was slow to realize that it was our lake—Joby's and mine, the one by her house—that had vanished. The article said officials weren't sure what had caused the strange occurrence.

"What do you think happened?" my dad said, shaking his head. "What happened to all that water?"

"No idea," I said, folding up the paper and dropping it into the foot well. "Aliens," I offered, and before I could take it back the word was suctioned from my mouth like a losing lottery ball. He said nothing, but I could feel him bristle at my sarcasm.

My father was a Believer.

We arrived to find a growing crowd of rubbernecks looking at the hole where the lake had been only yesterday. There was a post-Apocalyptic air about the place that seemed to fit with the pre-millennium angst the country was working through. The lakebed was swampy with mud, sailboats stranded in the muck, and dead fish lay quietly decomposing in profile. The stench was awful. The local news media were live on the scene, updating the fact that they had no new information minute by minute. It was dizzying; the headline *Water Stolen!* ran on tickertape around my head. In the distance, all around the perimeter of the hole, were the huge lakefront homes like Joby's and behind them was a new development of condominiums. I studied the crowd but couldn't find her in the swath.

My dad looked at the lake in awe. "Where the hell did all of it go?" he said quietly.

It was hard for me to imagine my dad in that other life. Some of my earliest memories involved the two of us dumpster-diving, rummaging through rot and stink, for things people had thrown away—so unwavering was his commitment to avoiding work. As scavengers for the debris of other people's lives, we populated our house with their unwanted memories, those possessions whose histories we'd never know. The house was still largely made up of them, even though things were different now. In some ways he was better, and in others he'd never been worse. I knew there were parts of himself he never let me see, parts that were pushing him farther away from reality, deeper into space. I watched him glance over his shoulder as he pulled a silver flask from his pocket. Raising it to his lips, he held it there like a microphone: "Star date: zero, zero, dash, one, nine, nine, nine. We have successfully discovered the site of a failed Klingon attempt to end life as we know it on this strange planet. So much like Earth," he said, then stopped, with a pause that would give Shatner a boner, "but entirely different."

Susan looked at her reflection in the glass that framed a Van Gogh self-portrait, inching close to the painting and pulling down the skin below her eyes so that she looked like a basset hound. "Jesus, I look like hell." She was telling me about the trouble she'd had trying to get her daughter Jeanie's new prosthetic leg; they'd driven to Kansas City three separate times for fittings that failed her five-year-old's stub. There was a picture of Jeanie on her desk, a pretty sprite of a girl with blonde hair and a smile that could move millions of boxes of cereal.

Susan's face bore the topography of a hard life. She was pretty, though. Very pretty, in fact. She'd broken the hearts of many high school boys who feigned mental instability and interest in college just to sit in her office, so I felt lucky to be whatever it was we were. "So have you thought about schools," she said, picking up the apple on her desk and tossing it to me. She'd been doing this lately, asking me to think about college.

"No," I said, and lobbed it back to her.

"Where do you think you might like to apply?" She underhanded it to me again.

I threw it back. "Did you hear about the lake? It disappeared."

"What part of the country do you think you'd like to be in?"

"They have no idea what caused it."

"There are only two more chances to take the ACT. Have you signed up?"

190

"Do you believe in aliens? My dad actually thinks they might be mixed up in this."

"It's important you sign up to take the test, Tom."

"My dad says they could have a strong interest in our water supply because of the high iron content."

"Colleges will not accept you if you don't take the test."

"He says there's an outside chance they might give the water back," I said, as Susan caught the apple we'd been tossing back and forth the entire time. "But it's best not to get our hopes up."

"Your father," she said, setting the apple on her desk. "And what does a professor think of his son not wanting to attend college?" It caught me a little off guard, this lie. Like everyone else, I'd told her he still taught. I said that he was leaving it up to me and she nodded, eyebrows raised, sighing. She looked at the file on her desk with my name on it, and then up at me, and said, "Tell me about your mother."

"I have to go," I said, standing quickly. "Class," I nodded towards the hallway.

She rolled her eyes, saying she needed a cigarette, like it was an invitation or peace offering, but this time I would not follow her outside.

After school, Joby and I drove to her house and walked to the lake. There were men in rubber suits that looked as though they should have been handling plutonium, though they were just tossing the dead fish into big yellow barrels. The smell was horrible, pestilent, the ground still muddy. There were people walking around the lakebed in fly-fishing boots and, for a reason lost on me, hardhats. They were setting up surveying equipment.

A small group of onlookers still crowded the perimeter and Joby spotted her father amongst them, filming, so we quickly walked the other way, a half-mile on the abandoned baseball field where a minor league team once played years ago. The advertisements lining the outfield wall were all faded and the field had grown over with dead sunflowers, scrub, and brush. Joby took a can of black spray paint out of her bag and went over to the fence, spraying over advertisements for athlete's foot salve and simonize, writing little enigmatic anarcho-haikus like *This is Terrorism; Fuck Nazi Sympathy; Anarchism is the Union of Lovers*; and the classic *God is Gay*. Afterwards we walked over to home plate, where the grass was thinner, and sat down. She lit a joint, took a couple puffs and passed it to me.

"Out here, everybody's crazy with looking for something," Joby said. "I swear, sometimes I think it's only God or drugs that ever finds them, though." She pulled her long brown hair back tight and let it fall down her shoulders. "Like my dad. He thinks this all has to do with God." She motioned with her chin in the direction of the barren lake as I passed the joint back. "He's been out there every day with his video camera recording what's happening. Gonna put it in one of his stupid tapes probably." She flicked the ash off the tip of her Converse. "At dinner he talks about God's judgment, that He took the water to punish us for our sins." She laughed sadly, shaking her head. "And people wonder why I'm the way I am. It's like how they say preachers' daughters are the most rebellious, only my dad's not a preacher. He's a psycho."

"Your dad's not a psycho," I said. "Look at my dad. He didn't do anything but watch 'Star Trek' for an entire decade after my mom left. Barely even spoke to me. That's messed up," I shook my head. "Your dad, he's just religious."

"What he is has nothing to do with religion," she said, and she proceeded tell me about their last attempt at reconciliation a few years before. At her father's urging, she'd agreed to go to one of his church's rallies, not knowing exactly what it would entail. That night he drove a busload of followers all the way to Lawrence on the night of the big KU-Mizzou basketball game. There were thirty or so others from the church and they congregated in the parking lot outside the game, holding signs and posters, waving them at fans who walked past. "I still remember the one I was holding. It was right after Oklahoma City and mine had a picture of the Federal Building after the bomb exploded under the heading my father had written in black marker that morning: *God's Wrath for Gays*. Everyone was holding something similar—pictures of the Challenger exploding, of Mathew Shepard, aborted fetuses. It was horrible, you should have seen people's faces—the way they looked at us."

"Jesus."

"Exactly," she said. "I knew then there was no hope for us." She took a last drag and let the nub fall to the dirt. "The thing is, he wasn't always like that. He was once just a farmer. But that was a long time ago." She put her head down and shook it, then looked up with sudden conviction. "You don't understand. These people aren't harmless, Tom—they elect presidents, for Christ's sake."

Later that night when I arrived back at the house, I found my dad sitting on the couch, dressed up as crewman Scotty from 'Star Trek.' This, strangely enough, was not abnormal. "There's my boy," he said in a faux-Scottish accent that was a conflation of Irish, Australian, and Jamaican. I'd almost forgotten about the convention that weekend in Kansas City. He'd been going to these things ever since I could remember and liked to try and get into character a day or two before—he could be almost Method about it. I'd heard stories about how he once went to a convention as Uhura, dressed in blackface and drag. "That was Toronto '77," he'd blushed.

"You could get away with that then. Boy, that was a great one, though. You should have seen it, Tommy—thousands of Canadians saying 'ooter space.'" I could smell the Scotch on his breath and saw the tumbler, nearly full, tilting half off a coaster bearing the likeness of George Takei. On the television ran a special about how the 1969 moon landing was faked. This was heresy in my father's house, but he seemed to watch with the interest of an interloper, a sports coach who's snuck into the opposing team's gym to see what plays they're going to run. The TV flashed the familiar pictures of Neil Armstrong beach-balling across the lunar surface with the voiceover: "Notice that the flag isn't moving. Our expert scientists attest that the shadows are reversed from normal—they're *physically* impossible." The screen switched to show a man standing in a NASA-type control room.

My father drained his glass in one throat-searing funnel, then leaned forward and started rocking, trying to get some momentum off the couch. I gave him a little push and he rose, banging his knee against the corner table as he left the room. I turned my attention back to the television, where I learned that the moon landing was actually filmed on a Hollywood soundstage, simply a strategic bluff to scare off the Russians as our countries fought to determine whose galactic balls were bigger. "Interstellar brinksmanship," the host called it with his slithery English accent. "Imagine," he said, slowly raising a hand up to the wall of clocks, monitors, and glowing buttons behind him, "the repercussions."

I flipped the channel and caught the tail end of the national news. More about our virtuous bombing of Serbia.

"What are you watching that for?" my dad said from behind me when he returned. "Turn it back to my show."

But it was too late; the moon-hoax special was already over and the familiar opening music of our local news began. There was a breaking story about the lake. That entire week people had been speculating about what happened, flooding the editorial pages, and to try and quell the fervor the mayor called a press conference. The news anchor explained this as the screen showed the stout mayor trotting out a team of white-coats to address the media. Without wasting a moment, the lead scientist offered a logical, if unusual, explanation for the strange phenomenon: a sinkhole formed when water eroded the limestone deep underground and created pockets in the rock. The entire 23-acre body of water disappeared into one of these sinkholes, worming deep into the ground below town. In what seemed a stab at humor, he grinned, analogizing: "Think of a plug being pulled on a bathtub."

"These guys don't know similes from metaphors, their asses from sinkholes," my father mused, shaking his head.

When the press conference finished, after my dad had had another drink, I helped him upstairs to his room, where he plopped down on the bed.

"Are you drunk?" I asked.

"I am," he grinned, stretching out the declaration, "not."

I sat at the foot of the bed, the only spot free from the piles of creased sci-fi paperbacks littering the surface. "Tell me about Mom," I said.

"Nothing to tell. It's just you and me, kid. I grew you in the basement like a sea monkey."

"What happened to her?"

"Moved to Mexico. Joined the circus. Perished in a fire at a mental institute."

"Dad!"

He was quiet a minute, eyes closed. He shook his head back and forth and began humming some sort of Irish ballad. Then his eyes opened abruptly. "I am not drunk," he said, raising a single finger. "I'm a romantic. I'm a poet. I am the bard of agriculture!" His voice was strained, and he lowered his hand, accidentally knocking over a stack of books that were at his side. He gave a little shrug, as if to say *That's life*, and turned off the lamp on his bedside table, filling the room with darkness.

With winter's descent, the question dividing most of the town was what to do about the lake. After the geologists and surveyors gave the okay to work, there was still the matter of cost. Because the lake was private property, the subdivision's residents were saddled with the burden of fixing it. Some estimates were as high as $5000 a household. Factions formed within the subdivision: those who thought the city should assume some of the cost; those who thought the lake should be filled with dirt and turned into either park or parking lot; people who wished to move; and the few, like Joby's parents, who could afford to pay and were willing to do so, whatever the cost. To further complicate the matter, the cold weather meant that it would be spring before anything could be done about it. The papers covered the drama daily. Even the major circulations in Wichita and Kansas City began carving out space for updates on the lake, for our little town, this theater of the absurd.

Susan and I were sitting in her office discussing the drudgery of the holidays when school resumed after break. We were oath-less and irresolute in the New Year, this new millennium. She told me about Jeanie finally getting her new prosthesis, how on the way home from the hospital they composed a new song: "All I Want For

Christmas Are My Two Front Feet." "She's such a good sport about it," she smiled. I told her about how my dad and I settled for watching *It's a Wonderful Life* with gigantic twin mixing bowls of instant mashed potatoes settled on our laps.

Before the bell rang, she said, "I need some fresh air," meaning she wanted to smoke, so we left. As I followed her down the hallway, a few students looked at us, whispering to one another or laughing. Susan didn't seem to notice and I thought them jealous. Secretly, their jeers made me feel good. Outside it was cold. I put on my black stocking cap and she pulled up the collar of her coat. She took out a cigarette and rifled through her purse for a lighter. I could make out the callused and yellowing tips of her fingers and suddenly wanted to touch them. Her hair wisped around her face in the wind. Her ears were already red; I offered her my hat, but she declined. "You know," she said, holding a hand to block the wind. "You missed the ACT exam. I checked the roll." She spoke out the side of her mouth. I shook my head. Great, she's gonna start this again, I thought. "If you just take the damn thing you'll at least have some options." I didn't have a good excuse for not taking the test, other than that I didn't want to take the goddamn test. That, and because Joby and I had plans for the next year that didn't involve college. "Higher education is indoctrination," Joby liked to say. Relieved of the burdens of schooling, she planned on leading the Revolution from a studio apartment in central Kansas, and I planned to be right alongside her, still working at the Shop'n Go most likely. Apathy, remember. I'd accepted my lot. I told Susan this and she said, "That's the most bullshit excuse I've ever heard."

A group of kids walked past us. One of them waved at Susan but she didn't see.

"I mean, why do you want me to take the test so bad anyway? What do you care?"

"Because I want you to get the hell out of here!" she said, throwing her hands onto my shoulders. The emphatic outburst took me aback and the commotion caught the attention of the kids, who turned to look at us. Quickly, Susan took her hands away. "You don't want to end up in this place," she shook her head. "You should see what else is out there." She told me there was only one more test next month, the last before applications were due. "Promise you'll take it," she said. I didn't know if I meant it, but I told her I would, so that she would smile.

As with many vices, the beauty and bane of crystal meth is its simplicity. Anyone who has Internet access and the will to shoplift from the drugstore can manufacture it. It was a serious problem in our town. All of a sudden iodine, camphor oil, and cold medicines were flying off the shelves, stuffed in the bottoms of lint-filled pockets and the crotches of unchanged underwear. Those with more gumption stole the anhydrous ammonia tanks from farms. And it wasn't just the poor and desperate who were making it. People were paying their mortgages, financing their farms, and saving for college funds or retirement. It was making fortunes for suppliers and taking the hair and teeth of the addicted. I knew all of this and yet Joby's habit happened right underneath my nose.

One night late in spring, when the weather had finally started to warm, Joby invited some people over to her house. Her father was out of town for the weekend at a religious convention in Kansas City and her mom—silently sympathetic to Joby's misery—agreed to house a party, this anti-prom. Joby invited about twenty or so of us, including Jonas, and her mom greeted us at the door with an uncertain smile, a look that seemed to say *Don't trample my flowerbeds and please use coasters.* Inside, cold 30-packs of beer were stacked like bullion. People were talking, playing music they were too cool to dance to, and trying to find a vacant closet to fondle one another in. Joby wore a red shirt with Che Guevara emblazoned on it and she'd paid a salon to put her hair in dreadlocks. Later, when most people had passed out or fallen asleep, Joby told me to follow her. We were both pretty soused by then and she pulled me by the hand to her dad's study. It was the first time I'd been inside. There were several bookshelves lined with videocassettes flanking both sides of a messy desk.

"Check it out," she said, pointing at the bookshelf closest. "They're of the lake." I looked closer and saw they were dated consecutively. "He's been filming every day since it disappeared."

"No way."

"We can watch it if you want," she said. For a long minute we were quiet and then she moved closer to me, within a few inches, and said, "You can stay here tonight, you know." She began rubbing her hands against my chest. This surprised me. I didn't know what to do; I didn't do anything. She rubbed harder, then leaned into me. Still I didn't move. It must have been like hugging a 2x4. I'd had this dream before, where Joby confesses she's really loved me all this time and we make love and live happily ever after, but I was frozen, as though anything I might say or do would make her stop. Then she kissed me, our lips bumping together awkwardly. "Do it with me, please. You'll like it."

"I don't know," I finally managed to say, eyes still closed.

She leaned closer, laughing a small amorous laugh, and bit the lobe of my left ear. "Please, Tom. It'll be fun." I inhaled the cocoa butter scent of her skin and for a moment it made me feel good, but quickly the smell turned oppressive, falling over us like a gigantic blanket dropped from a distant ceiling, trapping me.

"I can't," I said. "I don't have a condom."

I heard her breath catch and she pulled back from my chest, her scent wafting away. When my eyes opened, I saw she was holding a small baggie. Quickly, she stuffed the meth back in her pocket and lowered her head, rushing out of the room. I let her go, standing still for a minute, confused. I didn't know what to say, so I snuck out to the deck to get my head together. There I watched the soft glow in the sky that precedes the sun in the early morning. There was just enough light to make the ground visible. I traced the circumference of the empty hole below me. The ground of the lakebed was fully thawed now, deep and cavernous, like the site where a meteor had tried to end the world.

As I leaned my elbows on the wood railing, a flicker of light from the trees caught my eye. I looked down below me and saw it again, a glint, like the face of a watch momentarily catching the sun. I squinted. It was still quite dark and I tried focusing my eyes, but I couldn't quite make it out. Then I saw it again, the little flash, several yards away from the first. "Who's there?" I called out. There was no response and all I heard was the shuffling of bodies moving past limb and leaf.

I went inside to find Joby, to tell her that people were prowling around, and when I walked downstairs I had to step over the bodies of sleepers splayed and passed out on the basement floor. Joby and Jonas were sitting on the carpet, backs to the wall. She looked at me, expressionless. Jonas had his arm around her. "Tom, you gotta take a hit off this," he said, holding out a CD case with several thin dust lines on top.

"Don't," Joby said, holding back his arm. "He doesn't have a condom."

The morning after Joby's party I slept through the last ACT exam, and the morning after that the school fired Susan. Joby delivered the news in a note passed during chem. I asked to go to the bathroom and rushed to Susan's office but it was too late; her stuff was already cleared out, as though she'd just vanished. Joby arrived a minute later. "I saw her earlier, loading boxes into her car before school." These were the first words she'd spoken to me since the party.

"What'd she say?" I asked, stepping inside the empty office and looking around. "Didn't she say anything?"

"That she was leaving."

"Is that all?"

"No, Tom. She said she loves you."

"Fuck you."

She was still mad about the other night, but a kindness seemed to come over Joby then. She exhaled heavily. "She said with the school year almost over she was strongly encouraged to leave now and spend the summer looking for other employment because 'her conduct had not been professional.'"

"Professional? What the hell does that mean?"

"You tell me," she said. I looked sharply at Joby for the first time, but couldn't muster a word, and then turned my attention back to the vacant room. I wanted to ask if Susan said to tell me anything, then felt stupid and young for thinking she might have. Joby moved closer, touching my shoulder. "Come on, let's cut out."

Outside, as we ran for Joby's car, Mr. Mineo was noticeably absent. I'd never seen him miss a day and for a fleeting instant I thought it had to be related to Susan. I pictured the two of them in a car, fleeing this awful place together. Joby said we needed to talk, that she had something to tell me. She asked where I wanted to go. "To the lake?"

"Head out toward the highway."

She took her foot off the gas and our speed dropped sharply. "I'm not taking you to find her. She's gone. Get over it."

"Just drive."

She looked as if about to object, but only eased back onto the accelerator. Periodically I gave directions, telling her to switch lanes here, to make a turn there, and soon we were sitting in a parking lot. "Mind if I ask what the hell we're doing at this place?" she said. I told her to follow me. Begrudgingly, she obliged, removing a flaccid cigarette from her jeans as we walked towards admissions. After I paid, we entered into the 1850-style frontier town that served as the gateway to the farms. We passed different trade booths and crafts stores, places where you could watch horses being shod or glass blown, where you could dip your own votives or mint bronze coins. Joby regarded the people dressed in the oppressive period costumes they'd sweat through all summer, unimpressed. We walked to the south end of the miniature town and caught a tram to the 1920 farm, passing the 1859, 1870, and 1900 farms in a slow succession of agrarian history.

We exited the tram and walked past a reconstructed farmhouse and paddock to a wooden fence on the edge of a cornfield, where before a crowd of school children a man leaned against one of the early mechanized plows.

He looked tired in his worn brown trousers and heavy boots. He removed his rumpled period hat and wiped his brow, smiling at the kids before him. "Hot enough for you?"

"I don't understand why we're—look, I have to tell you something, Tom."

"That's my dad," I interrupted.

Joby looked confused. "I don't know what you're trying to pull, but we really need to talk."

"Seriously," I said. She looked away from me at the man with the crazy hair, wielding several stalks of corn. He saw us and waved before delivering his short monologue on what farming was like in 1920, not long after the world had become modernized. Business industries were creating new innovations that would forever make farming easier and more productive, he told them. What he didn't say was that these were the same innovations and developments that would eventually make it near impossible for family farms to exist today. He seemed at ease, smiling at the kids as he handed each child a cornstalk. "Well, you ain't no use to me standing around like this," he said, assuming a countryish accent. "Now listen, I need your help. My wife," he said, motioning toward the white farmhouse, inside of which was a woman who cooked authentic meals for tour groups to sample while delivering her own speech on the woman's role in running a homestead. "Well, the missus is expectin' some corn for supper. I'm running behind today, see, and need your help. Who here knows how to husk corn?" The kids looked at one another, clueless, and he proceeded to show them, first tearing off the corn from the stalk and slowly folding back the layers of husk to reveal the corn-silk-covered kernels. The kids struggled to do the same, looking surprised when they unearthed the yellow vegetable. My father smiled as he walked up and down the line, offering encouragement, so comfortable talking to them. He looked amazingly functional, as he often did despite the disease. Without nerves or edge, this must have been what it was like all those years ago teaching students at the university.

When it was over, my father momentarily broke character, unable to resist telling the children to "Live long and prosper," and Joby and I walked away.

"Why did you bring me here?" she asked.

"Don't know," I said, mumbling something about truth.

She didn't ask me why I lied to her about my dad, perhaps because she didn't have to; she must have known we tend to believe what we need to.

As we walked back to the tram and through the town to the parking lot, Joby revealed her own secret. She told me that she applied to UMKC in the fall, just to keep her options open, though she never mentioned it to me. She was sorry, but she'd been accepted and was going. I watched our feet move as we walked in a strange syncopated rhythm. "Aren't you going to say anything?" she asked. I thought of a story Susan once told me about how Jeanie sometimes still felt the leg that was gone—that when Susan got her ready for bed Jeanie would take off her prosthesis and point to the air below her kneecap, saying, "My leg hurts, Mommy. Will you rub it?"

"You need to quit that junk, you know," I said. "It'll ruin you good."

She didn't respond, didn't say anything until we got to her car, asking if I needed a ride. I told her I was going to wait for my dad's shift to finish, that it was almost over. We both seemed to sense the finality—that whatever connection we'd had would never be the same—and understood the lack of fanfare with which it arrived.

After she pulled out of the parking lot, I noticed the headlights of a black SUV, identical to Joby's, turn on. The light shining right at me, I couldn't make out the driver but had the feeling I knew who it was. It was a cool evening. Small buds from a flowering tree floated in clusters through the air, and for a second it seemed that if I were just waking up now I might think it was snowing. I stood there looking at him, a silhouette in a hulking car, knowing I was being filmed, and stretched out my arms.

We are all reversed in some ways, our lives shading backwards like the shadows on the moon. We're fed-up and off-kilter, a little crazy or too spacey, poisoned by the lake water in our soil and drugs sprung from our towns, and yet we find ways to inch forward despite our best efforts not to. And so, soon began the summer, my first as a high school graduate. These were the three months I found myself still pushing mop and broom over the floors of Shop 'n Go, whispering for customers to watch their step when someone accidentally dropped a bottle of wine or juice, setting up my yellow cautionary signs and moving the wet mop head in circles, watching the maroon stain spread and dilute, as though something—some sign—might reveal itself in the mess. This was the summer I wrote long letters to Joby that came back unanswered in envelopes stuffed with pamphlets requesting donations for the Zapatistas, Amnesty International, and Serbian civilians who'd lost limbs in the NATO bombing. This was when my dad and I went to see the lake every week, watching as they slowly refilled it with water; a time when I'd finally open the brochures of nearby community colleges to see what they offered. This was the summer I was so alone I could barely stand it, thinking of Susan and Jeanie, Joby, my mother—all those women—imagining where they might be, what they were doing. And though I knew that if I didn't leave soon the town would swallow me forever, I hated myself for not having been able to. This was the summer I returned home from work each day hoping to find a videocassette lodged in the mailbox, a tape we could watch, that would reveal all our sins and transgressions, so that then we might finally be free from them.

CREPUSCULAR

Dustin Parsons

Cougars are crepuscular. I only recently learned what this word meant. I am filled with the anxiety that accompanies this knowledge, and so I repeat the words as I spend my morning walking the eyebrow of dense cottonwoods that line Miller's Creek. I've said the word *crepuscular* so many times it fails to come out naturally. It could also be the cold that is freezing up my mouth. The freeze has pulled up the pools of water in the footprints I'm following from my previous patrols, and the walking is easier.

As sheriff, I am bound to track down this painter if no able-bodied volunteers or professionals can be reasonably paid to do so. But with only one arm I am at a distinct disadvantage. The lack of a shotgun or rifle. My inability to balance through deep brush. Difficulty running.

Those first two patrol days were frightening. Dawn and dusk, I carried my pistol in my good hand knocking aside brush. The cottonwoods had given up their leaves and the ground was sloppy wet. My boots grew heavy, and my face chapped. I often thought I heard noises around every fallen log.

Today, I do not draw my pistol as I walk. The freeze has perhaps given me a sense of safety, like I might be the only dumb animal out and about on a day like this one. I turn around a thicket and find my first definitive trace of the cougar: one of the temporary dens where she has stashed a doe. The hind legs are nearly gone but the rest is neatly intact save the neck wound. These are the woods I used to hunt as a young boy. Grandpa dropped us at the highway and drove round, finishing the six-pack he was on, to meet us two miles down the creek on the lease road near some tank batteries he checked. My brother and I stomped through trying to scare up quail and dove. We shot up trees when we got bored. We stomped on rotted logs and fried up dried out briar patches with our lighters, but they fizzled out with a small trail of smoke. The cold air swept around groves of trees and skipped off the creek water like sharp stones. I think about that a lot when I walk the patrol.

At home, after patrol, I find Beth still in bed. The morning shifts leave me awake and jittery, and I pull the Old Grandad from behind the hall closet coats. Some of the coats are still Suzanne's, and Beth won't go near them. They are large and synthetic and patched and still smell of her. I have to duck my head in to get the bottle and I try not to linger but it's tough. I keep a spare bottle in her coat pockets. Suzanne kept tissues in every pocket when we were married. They were tucked into her purse, in the cushions of the couch when she watched football on Saturdays, into romance novels tucked under the bed. Beth has cleaned more tissue up from the house than anything else. Except for these coat pockets, Beth has finally gotten them all.

Beth is the age a daughter of Suzanne and I might have had if we'd had children. I arrested her father after he held a shotgun to Carl Lest's head outside his house, but she's never mentioned it. I asked him to let Carl go, and he had, and I asked him to put the gun down and he did. I did not cuff him those ten years ago, and I remember avoiding eye contact with that small high school kid watching me take her father away. Her mother moved back to Colorado with her sister, but Beth stayed after high school in the house her mother bought after her father was arrested. It is off my route, but I walk by it now as a regular part of my beat in the night.

Now she is lying in bed. She sleeps hard, like a beating put her down. I'd forgotten how the young sleep, like there is nothing but themselves in the world. After some time she stirs and I start the coffee. Her father was a fighter—drunken brawls with other men in town. He lost a son, and Beth a brother, to a farming accident, and he was never the same after. I hear he's due out soon.

"I didn't hear you come back," she says. She covers her face with the meager sheets when she talks. She must be freezing with only that small cover in such a cold room, but she doesn't shiver.

"Maybe I didn't leave," I say. I am sitting in a chair in a far corner of the room, the arms loose and the legs uneven on the wooden floor. I sit up and the chair scoots. The curtains are just plain blue, threadbare, letting in a great deal of the day's light. The carpet on the floor is stained. After Suzanne left me, this was temporary. It has now been a five-year lease. I tell Beth to stay where she is and I walk to the kitchen and take the percolator off the burner. The bubble on top has long since clouded over with residue—one of the items on Beth's list to replace.

Beth came to me in response to an ad I put in the county newspaper to clean my house a few days a week. After the car wreck and the loss of my right arm, I had to start at square one—writing, feeding myself, brushing my teeth—all the simple things I'd once been able to do were little impossibilities now. I passed out from exhaustion after taking a meal. Cleaning, after Suzanne left, was bad enough. After I lost my arm it became unbearable.

I pour coffee and drop milk and sugar in for Beth. When I return she is putting shirt and pants on, the same she'd worn here the night before, and begins cleaning the bedroom.

"You aren't on duty," I say. I set the coffee on the bedside table. I feel the sheets and they are still warm.

"Neither are you. You should practice the board," she says. The board is a palette with circles in it that I tap with my fingers to gain coordination in preparation for a lifetime of left-handedness. I don't see the point, and hate this time in the morning when she shifts back to the employee.

"Did you have any luck today?" She is still folding discarded shirts from the floor, the right sleeves pinned cuff to shoulder. The room is bright but I open a window for the direct light and Beth looks out at the street through it, walks over and closes the curtain again.

"I found his den," I say. "Or one of them. He'd dragged a doe there." She finishes with the shirts and I follow her out of the room and into the kitchen. Her jeans are loose on her—she is so slight as to worry a man, her body like a lever. At night she absently caresses my shoulder where my arm has been separated from my body. In the day, she can't look at it.

"What happens when you find this thing," she says. "Are you good enough to kill it before it kills you?"

I tell her the likeliness of the old painter attacking at all are slim, and how a few shots, even if they don't connect, will scare it off. "Besides," I say, "the traps will get him before I do." I have seven steel traps set at intervals with fresh meat in them. Part of my job involves replacing the bait periodically but it is getting expensive and I am having my doubts about the effectiveness of the bait and trap method. I set each one by hand—large cages cold to the touch. I put loose brush over them to make it feel like a den. So far I've caught some very large and angry raccoons and a few skunks, but nothing else.

"Are you coming back tonight? I have the night shift and patrol." I take a few steps to her and she puts her cup in the sink. She nods and moves to go.

"There are the dishes to do," she says. "And this place needs a dusting."

I walk the creek again that evening, and it is a mile and a half round trip from town. By the time I am back from the traps and the creek bed it is fully dark and the kids have already begun to cruise Main. A parade of trucks and old beaters line the highway circling back on one another. Regular intervals of honking and shouting. It's like time has stopped, and all of this could have happened thirty-five years ago when I was eighteen.

I have loosely followed the highway out and back in, but now I take the side streets to steer clear of the traffic. My accident, the one that cost me my arm, also cost me my license. I fell asleep going over a bridge and rolled the squad car. I was drunk and on duty and the judge thought the best way to preserve both the dignity of his police force and punish me after my recovery was to make me continue to walk the "checkout" beat. So twice a night—9 p.m. and 4 a.m.—I walk along the businesses in town in the same order I might have driven it years ago, and check for anything unusual. My first stop is the park, the pool, and the baseball diamond. The water has been drained and the edges of the pool are chipped white paint peeking out of the tarp that covers it. Laverne Whipple lives across the street. We've been there a few times for domestic disturbance since he won that $18,000 in the lottery a few years ago. All the emergency calls are handled by Locker, Pete and Art now. I read all about it in the reports they submit. I'm still the sheriff, with a sheriff's paperwork, but for a cop my day is very ordinary.

After the park I walk the alleys behind Central Well Service, Cheyenne Roustabout, the grocery store, and Gantz Grain Company. By itself, near the railroad tracks just one block south of the highway, the elevator looms over the town and I put my lone hand on the side of the concrete silo and feel the cold it gives off. The storefronts of downtown face the highway and I can hear the echo of horns and kids, but there is a dark peace to the route. In a few hours, the kids of Ransom, Kansas will pack it up for parties in the country and the streets will be calm again except for the cattle trucks.

I shine a flashlight in the corners behind dumpsters at the quick shop and scare up two possums. I check the doors to be sure they are locked. Everything at this time of night is closed up except Tony Vandegriff's body shop, where he is still working on his dragster. I can hear his music as I pass behind the shop, see the barrels of old parts and empty cans of primer and paint. In the next block I come upon a couple of kids behind Howard's Bar who are waiting for someone to come out so they can beg them to buy beer for the night. This is another thing that hasn't changed in all these years.

Mike Carl and Blake White aren't bad kids. They are sitting on the boxes with empty beer bottles in them, talking and smoking a cigarette. They are both in high school. They still haven't seen me when I turn the corner and I clear my throat. Blake's car is down the alley about 100 yards. Mike puts out the cigarette, and their laughing stops, but they don't run. There is country music playing in the bar, but nobody has come out.

"Are you boys waiting for something?" I shuffle toward them slowly. Both boys look down.

"Relax," I say. "Do you have another one of those?" I point to the wasted butt on the ground with my single hand, and both boys forget to hide their stares at my folded and pinned sleeve. Blake takes out another cigarette and gives it to me, and I light it with my zippo.

"So what are you boys doing out here?" They are smart enough not to lie, and tell me they shouldn't be there. That is all I want to hear, and after a few drags I stomp out the butt and ask them to move along.

Mike heads for the car, but Blake still stares at the sleeve. "Does it hurt?" he asks. I see an honest curiosity in his face, almost like concern mixed with a lack of fear. The little breeze kicked up brings with it the smell of the dumpster and stale beer from the empties at our feet. It is cold and both of us are standing bent over at the back slightly, like being huddled over a barrel fire that isn't there.

"When I wake up," I tell him. This is perhaps the most truthful I have been with anyone about it. I am disarmed by such a young man asking such a direct and genuine question. "My shoulder itched for the entire stay in the hospital, and even when that went away there was always a tenderness. Now it is just in the mornings. Feels like a bruise. A deep bruise."

"My grandfather lost his legs in Korea," Blake tells me. His hair is high and tight, like Mike's, and his face is covered in acne. Mike stands by the door to the car but says nothing. "He used to have to drag himself to the bathroom after grandma died."

I nod because there is nothing more to do, and Blake nods in return and walks to his car. His sweatshirt is hardly enough to protect him from the cold wind that is now finding its breath, and they get in the car and drive away. I look up at the cloudy dark sky and take out the bottle from the morning and take a long drink and I can feel my legs for the first time the entire night. They are tired and wobbly but they'll get me back to the station.

At the dispatcher's office I get the reports from Jeannine, and take them down the hall, past our three empty cells to the computer where I slowly type out my summaries of the reports to submit to the state. The rest of the deputies are on call or out on patrol, so my small desk in the corner is quiet. The walls are yellow and the concrete walls make the holding area feel cold.

It is as strange as you might expect to be the sheriff of a town you grew up in. I've responded to a domestic violence call from my high school best friend's wife. Ansel had Peggy by the throat, and I had to deal with that. I worked my father's farm accident when he died. I've seen my ex out with Walter Baines while on patrol. I'm always in the shadows observing these events—even when the sheriff is there cuffing a friend or burying a father. Like I'm two different people at once. In a town this small it turns out to be a job where you are suspicious of everyone, and they, no matter your history, are suspicious of you.

The report Locker filed includes a notation about an old classmate of mine, Carnie Lawson. Carnie and I used to hunt when we were kids, and I remember taking my first drink of his dad's schnapps with him when we were twelve—I thought all alcohol was like that: smooth peppermint that flushed my cheeks. The first sip surprised me but it wasn't long into the bottle we were both drinking like pros, long indignant slugs that lodged in our throats, and we wanted to take off our coats in that cut cornfield in January because of the heat of the alcohol, and the gun felt right in my hand and instead of more reckless I felt controlled, moored to my numb shoulders. I've heard people say they drink to get that feeling back of the first time. It feels true inside of me, and though I don't dare take another drink with Jeannine at the desk, I press the bottle to my leg in my pocket.

Locker picked up Carnie in a bar fight and had to drive him home. Seems harmless so I file it and move on.

I am anxious in bed when the day has already started. There is daylight peeking out of the blue curtains and Beth has been here all night. I try to remember if I thought about her last night while I was out on patrol, thought about her in my bed by herself, but I'm certain I did not. She is here now, and warm under the sheets, and the morning walk through the creek and the surrounding cottonwoods was cold and boring. I've put away my gun the past few trips. I was so tired then, and now I try not to press my old body to hers for fear of waking her and because I am somehow disgusted with myself for her being here. These moments pass when she wakes up and we are able to share that small amount of time between her waking and my sleep. The next four days for me are nocturnal. My body makes the adjustment easy because I hardly sleep even on normal nights. But the first morning is the hardest.

Beth sleeping. I might be a proud man to have dinner with her in Hays or Dodge City, but here I just feel old and ashamed. I've seen her on the street when she is picking up dinner for the shut-ins she works for. She cleans their houses and takes care of them, and for a moment I consider that she must think of me in the same small way. She is quiet on the street but always sure of herself. Even when she can't say hello there, when she knows people are looking, she breaks my heart.

When she wakes it is with a start. Her legs kick out and her body arches—she might be falling in the dream that wakes her. Even with her startle she is not fully awake, and she presses into me and I wince because it is against my shoulder, my missing arm. It is tender again, like a scratch rubbed raw.

"I'm sorry," she mutters, still asleep. I tell her it's okay.

When she finally wakes up, I am still lying there, awake, looking at the ceiling and the flashes of reflected light that shoot across my vision when cars pass outside. The throbbing has decreased and I have warmed to comfortable. Beth stirs and comes slowly awake. She begins the absent rubbing of my shoulder with her fingertips, and it is a feeling of excitement that crackles in my body, like an exposed nerve. I tell her not to stop in the quietest voice I have.

"Do you reach for things and realize that part just isn't with you anymore?" Beth asks this question with sadness, like she already knows. The truth is I don't. Not anymore. It is hard to forget but it does go away. I tell her that if the arm could be reattached I'd probably find it more of a pain in the ass than anything.

"Will you be back tonight?"

"I'm visiting my father in Larned," she says. She's told me this before—she says she goes to the state prison to see him, but her car is in her driveway and I can feel that she just stays in her mother's house, pacing and closed off to the world.

I rebait my traps and make my way across the creek and through another field— this one a fallow field the farmer is collecting government money on. The grasses are the old short-grass prairie variety that needed just a little seeding to take off. It is several different shades of green that sway and make one uniform shade of prairie. As I walk through it there are small bits of concrete, brick, and rock in the field, the foundations of an old farmhouse that must have been here long ago. It must have given the undercutter hell when the farmer used to work the land, and it now makes sense why this field is fallow.

I also find another den, one that comes with my first sign of scat. The dens are beginning to take shape around a bridge on the highway; a place I never thought to look, for the traffic and the noise. I begin the walk in and see the glow of a fire in the distance, just inside the town's limits. I don't run well, but I begin to jog to the city limits to catch sight of the fire, and turn on my radio to hear if anyone has responded.

Art and Pete are on duty and have already blocked off the roads and are amongst the onlookers, keeping them away. The volunteer fire department has been called and will be on-site soon. The family is accounted for, sitting on the curb. The fire has moved to the second floor, and the flames are leaving bottom floor windows and being pulled into second-story windows like red rivers, and I think of Bobby Dale's tattoo of a girl with flaming laces in a corset on his forearm.

This is the first time I've been *on scene* in some time, and the same panic fills me. We move vehicles out of the line of the fire, and set the fire hoses on the adjacent house. It is Walter's house, and I see my ex-wife walk out with her coat in her hand. Walter follows Suzanne, his hand on her back. They do not see me, and they join Walter's children from his first marriage on the sidewalk watching the fire consume their neighbor's home.

Beth is here also. I see her down the street coming from her mother's house across town. My radio squawks and the second fire truck arrives. The crowd parts for it and Pete and I begin to direct it in. Several people look at me as I ask them to move. They look at my sleeve. They move without taking their eyes off of me.

The fire blazes for one more hour before it finally begins to die. The smoke continues, and there is still the risk of a flare-up. The crowd has, in the fading light from the fire, begun to return to their homes. Art and Pete have returned to patrol, and offered to take my checkout route leaving me behind to keep an eye on the house with the pony fire truck and three volunteers. The house is still standing, but it won't for long. All there is left is to wait for the smoke to stop. This was easier when I had a prowler, or a bottle. I'm without both.

Beth comes towards me, and I put my lone hand in my pocket. I have the feeling that Suzanne is watching from one of the dark windows of Walter's house, but they took the kids and went to Walter's mother's house. Suzanne left me because of my drinking, and hasn't looked back, and I've always had the feeling she'd began an affair with Walter even before we finally divorced. They worked together for so long in his restaurant, I can't help but think it is no coincidence. This is a quiet town, and I know I don't have a memory of most of it. We fought in close quarters at dusk. We fought with whispers at dawn. When she asked, I slinked out almost on my tiptoes. When she sold the house to move in with Walter, she did so with a lethal quiet. It was so quiet I can almost pretend it didn't happen.

The truth is I don't begrudge her happiness. I miss her presence, but not her. I keep her coats because it is easier for me to feel like someone else might still be there to need them, even when nobody is.

"How is your father?" I say. Beth stops near me. We face the smoldering house and smoke trails out of my mouth as I say *father*. I feel tense around her, like the first time she approached me in my home to kiss me. She'd been pulling newspapers from the corners of rooms, and her sad face lifted for a second when she saw me trying to turn the water off to the sink with the same hand I held the coffee pot in. She reached across me to turn it off and pressed her body near my empty side, unafraid. I almost dropped the percolator.

"I didn't go," she answers. "He'll be out soon enough anyway."

The smell is acrid around us. The inside of the house is glowing with a pulse, and I can see the life being sucked out of the windows and roof. But that pulse is dying.

"The day I came to your house, the day I arrested your father," I say, "I don't think I even looked at you. It was too hard to do anything except take him in."

She nods.

"You've never gone to see him, right?"

She nods again. She is crying, little sobs overtaking her shoulders.

"What happens when he comes back? When he comes home?" She is nearly unable to make words, and cannot look at me. "What happens when he sees me for the first time?"

I have no answer. The water from the hoses has pooled in the yard, and they reflect the clearing sky and the stars. Two old men stand away from us thirty feet, and they begin to walk back to their respective homes. The volunteer firemen have returned to their pony truck, and a neighbor brings them coffee. There is action around us, and I feel this might be the first time since I've lost my arm that nobody is looking at me.

In the morning I grab meat from the butcher—he saves scraps from the slaughterhouse for a discount. It is time to load the traps. The cooler I take it in is slung over my shoulder and chest and hangs at my armless side. It sways back and forth like an arm as I walk. Today I load the traps quickly, sloppily, and make my way to the highway where I so often started my hunting as a child.

The fire kept me the entire night, and there had been no flare-ups. The house seemed to slump as the smoke decreased in the night, and the streetlamp cast a downward glow as though it was telling ghost stories, the pits of the house's front windows empty, and dark, charcoal makeup slashing up the face. It scared me.

The smell of the creek is pronounced near the eddy at the highway overpass, and a few collected piles of river trash have developed in these shallow pools. I can see beer cans and plastic wrappers. The bridge itself is only about fifty feet long, rusted underneath. It is due to be replaced soon. I sit for a moment at the creek edge, on the cold ground with my back against a tree.

Having one less arm I think about balance a lot. About symmetry. About everything it takes to keep one upright. I am upright more often now than I have been in some time. Everyday I find myself falling or tripping fewer and fewer times. Even sitting here I feel settled. My legs are healthy and strong and tired. The traps are set and I know Beth won't be back.

I find myself without a bottle, and without a drink. It has been one full day, and though I know it will get worse, right now I don't feel my body needing it.

I look up and see the bridge's rivets and its curved steel girder. Beneath it the cougar steps slowly from tall grass. It is a beautiful animal, a lighter brown than I thought it would be. She is a mistake here in this place, but she belongs in this time between darkness and light. The cougar is magnificent in a pale glow. Its mouth and muzzle are white, and it steps high and slow out of the grass tucked into the overpass.

I should reach for my gun. She has seen me and walks across my field of vision on the opposite side of the creek. I can see every press of matted fur. I am light and I can't feel my fingers. They are numb and light, and I should be holding my gun. She is enormous—the size of a greyhound with the weight of a predator. I lower my hand and touch the handle of my pistol, just my fingertips on the grip. I think about killing her, what a shame it would be to see her dead on the ground. I do not grab my gun. My hand balances on the grip and I watch her watching me. Part of me wants to see her hunt—the reckless abandon of a predator so superior to her game. Never more than now do I think the traps could never work—this cougar could never trust what is already dead. I can't help but think of what Beth will think of my dead body. What Suzanne will think. This cougar is a magnificent animal. Magnificent in her full and whole body. Magnificent.

GOLDEN RETRIEVERS

Matthew Pitt

Even before August, summer was smothering the dogs of L.A. June's heat wave shocked Orange County. The forecasters laughed it off. It'll peter out, they predicted; but it didn't. A tractor-trailer filled with Pacific fish jackknifed in July, leaving Hollywood and Vine smelling of mackerel and eel and smelt roe, a foggy, murderous scent the street cleaners couldn't erase. A scent the dogs could neither locate nor escape from. They ran down Gower beside their owners, actors trying to shed water weight in the heat. They ran across bridges that rose above rivers; when the dogs saw the barren riverbeds they howled. Their tongues swelled as they begged licks of Evian from their masters' palms.

Then came August 5th—and the meltdown of Susie Light's Hollywood career. On the evening of the 4th, Susie shut out the lights at Peticular Bliss, her kennel for the dogs of stars. She'd just finished preparing sixty meals: fifteen low-cal, eleven no-fat, nine vegetarian, and twenty-five more assorted rations, all done up with capers, coated with twists of lemon, and spooned into colorful, Fiesta-style ceramic bowls. The next morning Susie knew something was wrong by the smell outside the bedding area. Food. Food? But the dogs always ate what was given them. She unlocked the door. A pulse of heat lurched at her. Her hair fizzed, her lungs felt thin: The air inside was grim and splintered with stillness.

Susie walked the aisles, pawing fur, checking for heartbeats, holding her breath in hope of hearing theirs. A minute later, a recorded, eerily perky, female voice filled the otherwise silent room. It came from Ab's suite. Ab Doberman, a Pinscher belonging to an aerobics instructor who taped two shows for ESPN2: *Lose the Fat!* and *Living With Fat*. The instructor insisted that Ab wake up in the morning to her programs. Susie approached Ab: His rangy body lay stiff on the carpet and his face was a queer void, though his nose was still slightly moist, like a stick of butter left out to soften.

She bent down and petted his fur. You liked Desert Palm Bottled Water mixed with a protein supplement that made it look like split pea soup, and you liked to hear your owner feeling the burn. Could you be dead too, baby?

In the following weeks, Susie received measures of exoneration. The SPCA of SoCal and the LAPD reached similar conclusions: The air conditioning unit had been left on when Susie locked up the kennel; it had simply conked out during the night.

Susie Light wasn't delinquent in paying her electric bill, or negligent in her duties. The city removed her license from probation.

The first September breezes redeemed the stale air; mercy followed. Most of the actors dropped their lawsuits against Susie. Others failed to show at the courthouse. Susie did show, each time wearing the same gray suit, a spindly yet animated frock, a lilac pinned to the lapel. In her mirror the gray seemed louder each morning she wore it, as though the fabric were feeding off her skin. She bought Snickers from a machine in the courthouse for comfort.

Though it was the stars who sued, it was the Jamie Farrs and Conrad Bains who seemed to suffer. Those who hadn't fared so well in the wake of fame—the actors surviving on residuals—who seemed truly disconsolate from the loss. They were the ones Susie couldn't face.

"I think I need to cut my losses," Susie was saying over iced tea to her old friend Clara, late in September. Clara was what Susie had longed to be: a television actress, only one step away from her dream of cinema. The other friends in their group from high school, all of whom had also wanted to make it big, regarded Clara with the very mix of awe and protracted envy she'd hoped they would. Only Susie had remained close to Clara: The others now felt puffy and bucolic beside her. Not that they were doing poorly. But L.A. is a town of earthquakes as much social as geological. Imbalances in clout are documented overnight, rifts in status between friends, institutionalized.

Clara smoked cigarettes with scrabbling intensity, like a dog stripping leftover chicken bones. She'd once been the group's prude, delusional with duty. Now she was wildest and fairest of them all. Her voice had gone gruff, and this drop in register gave her pleasure. The thinner Clara became, the more fiery she had to sound, so producers would know she wasn't just some softhearted fuck from the sticks they could push around. "I don't think you have losses to cut, Sooz."

"I agree," Clara's manager said. Clara had brought her along for advisement. "If anything, now's the time you franchise." The whole incident felt unreal, almost playful. Litigation in L.A. was like a bad review of a smash hit: not to be taken seriously. "We just gotta handle it delicately. Who was your biggest client? Your biggest *name* client?"

"Johnny London."

Clara's manager stroked the rim of her water glass. "London's tough. He's in Tunisia wrapping a picture, but he'll be back soon. I happen to know he shares a joint checking account with his personal assistant. And she owes me huge. I'll have her draw up a check for $10,000 to Animal Relief Shelter. I'll tip some hack at *Variety* to it, they'll write a big spread on Johnny's humanitarianism in the face of sorrow. By the time London gets wise to his pooch dying, his ass will be so well-licked from the good PR, he'll think it was his idea to kill her off."

London's pooch had been a basenji. Johnny had visited her at the kennel only once in a year. "Might I ask how you 'happen to know' these things?"

"Susie," said Clara's manager. "Take my hand, squeeze it. Trust what the hand is saying. The kennel mess couldn't have happened in a better climate. Politically, I mean."

"I don't want good politics. I think this is a sign to go. Get out."

"And do what?" demanded Clara, to no response. She stamped her cigarette out, eyes narrowing to the width of fingernails. Life here was tough on Clara, and would be tougher without Susie. She'd once told Susie she was too busy finding work to enjoy her own accomplishments: "I have to live vicariously through the people living vicariously through me."

Back in high school, Clara had also been the only one in their circle of friends to believe in God. Now faith had found the others—Gina with her prayer group, Kay and Ray with their AA. Clara claimed to have given up on the Church entirely. "But I've been advised not to rule out Scientology," she had said. "It's like a pre-approved platinum card. You don't dismiss the offer."

Roderick Kim strolled by their table. He had blue eyes, a sharp chin, biceps that seemed to be fighting through his lemon-green T-shirt. Susie had been to his place once, to bathe his Australian sheepdog. This was years ago, when she told clients she had to introduce herself to the dogs on the dogs' home turf. Her method empowered and relaxed them. The actors lapped this up, the servile artistry of it.

Initially Susie used her house calls to reveal her acting ambition. She tried to work it in naturally, hoping the celebrity in question would ask what had brought her to L.A. But that never happened—so Susie resorted to reciting famous film lines to the dogs, in earshot of their owners. Or more transparently, leaving her number on the backsides of head shots. She often dreamt of how her discovery would unfold. With Roderick it went like this: She'd pick up the latest script he was working on—a romantic comedy set in Prague, perhaps?—its pages tossed everywhere. Roderick would be having ego clashes with his leading lady, and when he saw how naturally Susie read the lines, he would grab the phone, demanding the role be recast for her. He would lean into Susie on the couch—the flickers of candle flame flanking her face would draw him in—and he'd kiss her. The morning after they would laugh together gently, trying to recall each detail for the inevitable profile in *People*.

In fact there was no morning after, or night before, Roderick was in-between projects, and he used track lighting. His house was Venice typical, a chimera of clashing cultural milieus, party favors from the booty of various forgotten and ruined empires. One of his bookshelves was lined with editions of the "Idiot's Guide To" series; others were filled with the companion "For Dummies" volumes. Roderick recited Shakespeare at the Mark Taper Forum like a demigod; what a disappointment witnessing the dropped foliage of his original thoughts. Even his dog had seemed embarrassed.

Australian sheepdogs were the most perfect specimen, Susie reflected—but bloodhounds and fat bassets, oh, they were her favorites. She'd had four bassets in her care at Peticular Bliss. None had survived; they were heavy panters, which probably contributed to their death.

Clara checked her watch and nudged Susie. "It's time for the opening. We have to hurry if we want to be late."

That August night at the kennel, it had risen to 110 degrees. Only nine of sixty dogs had survived. Fifty-one dead friends. "Okay," Susie said, rising slowly. "How much do I owe?"

They drove south. As they approached MacArthur Park, Susie tuned out Clara's monologue; she watched joggers leave their cars at the park entrance, leash their dogs, and run toward the poplars and cedars. She tried to admire the leaves on the trees, aglow with sunshine, edges slightly polar with deposits of off-white pollen. But dogs kept catching her eye. She watched them all—some heeled, others throwing all of their weight and happiness into the run.

Clara's Jag idled at a red light one block from the park. Looking into the passenger-side mirror, Susie watched a mastiff move behind her. Its jowls jiggled as it strutted a slow line, like some prisoner at sea walking a plank with fierce, final dignity. Then it was out of sight, having suddenly dissolved behind the mirror's blind spot. Susie waited for the dog to reappear. It didn't. She thought she heard the mastiff's claws scrape the concrete, saw the flesh dent its ribs when the dog drew a deep breath, but of course she did not hear or see these things. When the light turned green, Susie scoured the area. There was no sign of the mastiff, no sign it had ever been there…

She might never forgive herself. What would that mean? Susie had failed herself before; all those mistakes eventually tunneled under the range of her consciousness. Eventually. What would it take to make this mistake seem insignificant, too?

"This is so exciting," Clara squealed. "I can't believe I'm about to watch a first-run film *beneath the earth*." Mann Underground, a subsidiary to Mann's Chinese

Theatre and the Hollywood Walk of Fame, was opening today. It was indeed the world's first movie theater located inside a subway station. It had THX sound to block out the rumble of subway cars, and little windows in the doors, so customers could take a break from the film to watch people getting on and off trains—or so passengers getting on and off the trains could peer in and try to recognize famous people not watching movies.

Clara had been invited to the premiere, a remake of a 1979 disaster film. The two descended an opalescent gray staircase past the checkpoint. Susie hung back, making sure she seemed an innocuous "plus-one," not a lover (Clara's career wasn't strong enough to survive lesbian rumors). They strolled into the embassy of celebrity flesh, Susie drifting, Clara exchanging clerical kisses with her peers, throwing discretionary waves to the audience, which was held back by an embankment of bouncers.

Liz Phair, Beck, and members of Pavement were strumming guitars and drinking Coronas, secluded in a corner of the subway station. Liz sang harmony in burnt orange taffeta, to Beck's lead: "*You say I'm a bore / Not your cup of tea / But you've been an Elysian Encounter / An Elysian Encounter to me…*"

The premiere went off without a hitch, technically speaking. The soundproofed walls worked. The projector worked. The headsets worked too, though most of the guests discarded them early to talk shop. But halfway through the film, Susie saw something possibly terrifying beyond the theater window; trick of light, maybe, though it seemed real enough to smell. A murky bauble of bronze fur. A dog. But no one else had seen what she had. Had they? No. So she let the disaster movie play on and the players speak through it and the new L.A. subway roll on through all the satisfied talk and pomp of the Hollywood elite.

Susie found the incidental habits hardest to break. Ordering squeeze toys online. Running a lint roller over her clothes. Fridays—when she'd buy food for the dogs—were worst. Her life had made sense on Fridays, comparing vitamin supplements at Trader Joe's, watching baggers gather the purchases she paid for on borrowed wealth. She'd listen to the receipt churn from the register; spending so much on frivolities made her feel like an actress.

"Uh, ma'am? Excuse me. Your card has been declined."

She stared dumbly at the store clerk. He must be new. Trader Joe's knew who she was. They knew Susie took care of Oscar winners' wiener dogs, movie execs' Great Danes. This kid needed a lesson in respecting clout. Then it struck her. She slid her hands into one of the bags. Her fingers traced the frozen liverwurst entrees, which prevented heartworms and contributed to coat sheen. There was no reason to buy this. It was September 27th; all the dogs were now ashes or buried bones, and reason for any of this had long since left.

"None of this is for them," Susie said. "None of them, really, are mine anymore." The store clerk trained a casual smile toward her; this must be how policemen look at the women who've just been punched blue and deserted by their boyfriends. She felt too embarrassed to return it all. She felt pressure to return the clerk's smile. She felt the thinness of the paper sacks.

October began cool. The temperature dropped (71 at night, 74 during the day). Softness resumed. Clara called Susie each day. Encouraging her to shop. Drive. "Walk, even, if that's what it takes."

"I'll be fine, really. My checking account's still pretty flush."

"This isn't a money call. If it were, then fuck, I'd just promote you to producer."

"I don't work on your show, Clara." Susie readjusted her phone. "What's this really about?"

"This is a health call. You need to let go. Inner turmoil doesn't cut it in this town. Confession and memory don't either: You have to explode. Do something flip. Show don't tell. Exaggerate your confidence."

"Maybe I should get back into acting." Susie was half-serious, though Clara often ran through the list of her friend's physical features—"sharply arched brows, eyes too dark and bracing, that whole wise thing you've got"—working against Susie, preventing her from having The Look.

Clara was worried for her friend. "I don't want you to be like Mike," she said.

Mike? Mike? The name lingered in her mouth—oh God, she meant Michael! Susie hadn't thought of her old friend in years, regarding him as some light confectioner's treat that gave her pleasure long ago. He'd been part of their group, the oddest and softest of them. And being a boy, the most useful. He'd been the one boy allowed to commiserate with the gaggle of girls. He'd given the girls' collective ego a knuckle; his devoted presence persuaded many a popular male senior that these were the girls to try and score with. The girls to blow part-time paychecks on.

When the girls became seniors with cars, they graduated themselves to the nearby college town, towing Michael along. A bright nervous face rushed suddenly to Susie's mind—Michael's, and Michael's quick, chattering feet—such a dancer! So good he prompted competition, prompted Chet Baker to cut in on the two of them one night at a frat house. Chet was dark and powerful, and moved with a rusty swivel to his hips, his groin hemming her in. Chet kissed Susie when he wanted to, his tongue darting down her mouth like a sloppy banana squeezed from the skin. From time to time she'd look up at Chet—named after the famous trumpeter, though his lips held no fraction of the skill, the dexterity, the tenderness. Still, Susie felt flush; she was a trophy of desire. His desire. She would let this man cave her virginity in, topple the last remnant of this stupid, boxy innocence she couldn't wait to rid herself of.

"How did you hear from Michael, Clara? Did you call him?"

"What are you, kidding?"

"Right, okay. Well, when did *he* call? What is he doing these days?"

"Stand-up. In Vegas," Clara said, sucking in smoke. "Vegas, can you believe it?"

"Do you have his number?"

Clara said she'd misplaced it. Susie could tell she *hadn't*—an actress is the sum of the style of her lies, and only the childhood friends of the actress were familiar enough with that style of deception to call it in the air. Finally, Clara relented. "I'll give it to you, but I don't think he's a person you should be speaking with. He's a real idiot mess."

"What do you mean?"

Clara blew a tray of smoke into the phone receiver. "I mean Michael's like a boy with a ball. He throws it, uh, in the woods, and it's lost. But instead of just finding a new ball, he chases it into the woods, uh, looking for it..."

Susie stretched her arms, the receiver still in her hand. She looked at the clock, wondering, if these were long-distance calls, how much sooner she'd cut Clara off during rants. Susie didn't care how far Michael had fallen, or what talent he was, in Clara's judgment, tossing away. He was just a name and a voice Susie had lost track of, and now wanted back. She sought only simple reconnection with the man, and that was all. Well. Maybe reconnection and a drink. And maybe a show. Maybe a dance; maybe. Maybe. More.

Though they hadn't spoken in nearly a decade, Michael answered Susie's phone call as if he'd been waiting on hold all this time. After three phone talks, Michael agreed to visit. They'd meet at Union Station; he refused to take a plane in from Vegas. "Flying into Los Angeles is like staring at your own smile in the mirror. You're seeing too much forced nicety at once."

Susie respected his complaint, at least associatively: To her, Las Vegas was a wasteland on life support, intubated on electric sunlight and slot machines, arid of charisma, underscored with a population far too vulgar to see that they were lost souls.

Michael stepped off the train and sniffed the air; Susie took cover in the crowd, in case she wanted to back out. An old valise hung over his shoulder, blue, half-empty, veined with wrinkles. She took in his faded penny loafers, the long shelf of his nose. She drew close to hug him. It was a long hug, one she refused to stop. Finally he pulled back, complaining his bag was too heavy.

"So where are we taking me?"

"Public premiere of a new subway stop in East L.A. The seventh mile."

"I thought L.A. was The Last Mile."

He was speaking with a hard tone, the clipped efficiency of a failed traveling salesman. But wasn't he here, weren't they together, because of how well the phone conversations had gone? She ruffled his head. "Your top is thinning."

"That's okay," he countered, maneuvering from her touch, "my bottom is thickening. Hey, thanks! You helped me walk right into that one. Truth is I've been killing myself for new material all summer, and getting *nada nunca.*" Susie forced a smile. But she could see where he was headed: jokes. They began to compare fitness regimes, but Michael took the opportunity to toss off self-deprecating one-liners: "I'm so abusive to my body, my liver had to pick me out of a lineup. My only form of consistent exercise is passing kidney stones. When I tried to donate my semen to the sperm bank, they told me to take it to a pawn shop..."

She managed to stop him with a compliment. "I like that one best."

"Really," he wondered. "Because that one I'm still playing with the wording."

They continued toward the turnstiles. A tejano band struck up a ballad in the subway well. Susie gobbled up Michael's hand with her own; it felt more relaxed than she'd expected. "Still dance?" Michael shook his head. "Oh, come on. Bullshit. A man can't teach himself to stop dancing once he knows he's good." She led him down the stairs, eager to grandly descend, but he wasn't kidding: He moved like a lumbering bear. "Michael," she said finally, eyeing his nose, releasing his hairy hand.

"I told you. I'm no dancer. I don't work out. I don't do anything anymore that isn't bad for me or good for tourism. Usually both. Susie, I'm not even Jewish anymore."

"What are you talking about?"

"No fooling." He showed Susie his Nevada driver's license. "I'm no longer Michael Yonah Resnick; meet Mike L. Resno." Three years ago the manager of the Mirage had offered him a spot opening for Nick Fike, on the condition he adopt a *nom de plume.* "My heritage threatened the goyim from Provo. They were all convinced that if the Son of God were to choose the Mirage as the site to stage His second coming, then the funny Jew onstage would find a way to stab Him before He could get His first parable out. So I've been officially gentilized by Nevada." As he spoke, light flashed from around a bend; the subway was pulling in. When its horn blew, Michael pretended to have been shot: "Watch out! They got me! I'm coming apart, I've come unjewed!"

Susie backed off. Her brow furrowed. She was listening to Michael, Mike L., trying to figure out whether he was going to kiss her. Through his routine, she'd made a point of touching him, or pollinating his ego with well-placed laughter. In the crawlspace of time from the momAe amtrak to the first mordant rumbles of the Red Line, Susie recalled how starkly Michael had once loved her. In high school, in the mash letters he'd written then, and the increasingly desperate notes in college. And now here she was, pining for *his* affection to no avail, waiting with empty lips for a train.

As their train came to a halt, Susie pressed her front teeth against her lower lip. She wondered—would she see a dog again? The first time in this station with Clara, she had spotted what had seemed to be a golden retriever jump into the subway well, dart in the direction of the cars, only to leap from the well and over the turnstile, before vanishing. But it was all impossible. Some leprosy of her senses had afflicted her; she'd recover. Only it happened again. This time at the North Hollywood station, on her way to have her hair done. A different dog, darker, fuller plume in the tail, but still a retriever. It had sat patiently among the waiting passengers, not seeking scraps of food, attention, anything. Finally the train had arrived—and that was when the dog bounded into the stairwell and darted down the tunnel, trying to outrun the momentum of the train. It had left a calling card of hair and heat on the platform's edge. Surely it hadn't survived. But how had it gotten there?

Suspicious of her mind, but always a fan of a fair trial, Susie began to weigh the evidence. Perhaps it had been another kind of animal—a rat or cat, or even just clothing blown by wind? Or some blasé promotion...light FX from the engineer's car, visual ad copy for a new family film? But the trades would've hyped such a stunt to death—she wasn't that out of the loop. Madness, above all, was the affectation of enhanced or depleted perception, corroborated by no witness other than the afflicted. Was she headed there?

Michael egged Susie onto the subway car. The Red Line shot into the tunnel like a panic, a slippery riot, bound for East L.A.

Michael proved a devoted companion. He took Susie's tension and doubt over her career and threw it far away. He kept her out of her house, kept her in the moment. In East L.A., they sat on a new bench already pocked with graffiti and knife grooves. They sat, just so, for two hours. The jet set arrived for the ribbon cutting, surveying the station. Some were there to have their hands immortalized in wet clay beneath the turnstiles. Michael watched, giggling. "This damn town. It kills me. It took me all of two months interning in 'the 'Bu' as Ed Frietland's piss-ant to realize I couldn't bring myself to live here… Why haven't you figured it out yet?"

"Michael, I love L.A.!" He eyed her. "Well okay, love is strong. How about despise affectionately?"

Michael sipped Sprite, waiting for more of an explanation.

"Have you ever had to stop yourself in mid-curse? Your whole day has gone to shit. Like anarchy had a fire sale. So you drive to 7-11. Maybe buy a scratch-off. You take your coin out, shake your fist and scream, 'If this Lotto ticket doesn't fucking come through!' Even while some of you secretly *wants* to lose, you're so used to it. But you scratch the ticket…and it's a twenty-dollar winner. L.A. fucks with my head and heart, sure, but just when I'm about to jaywalk across rush hour Sunset…Boom! It hands me a twenty." She toyed with the disposable camera he'd brought. "It retrieves itself to me."

"Retrieves. How do you mean?"

She laughed. "I said 'redeems.' L.A. redeems itself to me."

"No. You said 'retrieves.'" Susie blanched. She covered her face with the camera. Michael's face seemed small through the lens, distant and unattainable.

"So what's great about Vegas?"

"What's *great*?" He turned away and chewed his straw. A street vendor selling tapas made it halfway down the subway stairs before bouncers dragged him back up, kicking and screaming. Michael turned back around. "On any given night," he said, "someone else is a bigger loser than me."

The celebrities orated gangtags they saw on the wall with an errant flourish. "*Somos locos y que,*" read a leading-man, leaning into his cocktail. "Such a beautiful language they have. So romantic, so peaceful."

"This is great; in weeks this station will be littered with undesirables, riffraff."

"I plan to give change—but only to the well-spoken ones."

"Oh, me too."

Michael smiled as he eavesdropped, a forced, squirmy smile. "With all the free pub and cameras, I'm surprised I haven't spotted Clara. How is she anyway?"

Susie shrugged. Just where to start with Clara? The hit show? The Emmy nomination? The makeover and body sculpting? "Clara is, uh, in a word, superior."

"Yeah." Michael set down his Sprite. "And I bet she's the first to tell you."

"At least that means I'm the first to know." Now it was Susie with the squirmy smile. "But she worries these days about self-inflation. So get this…to stem her ego, she stayed at a monastery the other month."

"You are joking."

"Wait, it gets better. So she arrives, right, and from the moment she walks in, she's giving the holy men there all these assignments and special requests."

"Priceless. I can see her now. 'Uh, excuse me, Brother. Do you think I could possibly get my monasticism *on the side?*'" Michael shook his head. "So our girl Clara turned into one of these?" he asked, indicating the antics of the celebs.

"She's probably as close to a confidante as I've got, Michael. Her concern for me is deafening. She'd give me half of anything she owned." Susie mashed her lips. "Having said that—yes. She has. Clara is absolutely a Beautiful Person."

"What does that make you?"

"Lumped with the other ninety-nine percent of Los Angeles—Part of a Beautiful Person's Entourage. A sidekick."

"Don't sidekicks deserve sidekicks of their own?"

She looked at Michael. *That* was the kind of one-liner she'd been hoping to hear from him. Was it lust she sensed—hopeful, anxious, light flask of lust—peeking through all his talk of friendship and warm reunions? She'd lured Michael away from his world. Back into a city he hated. So surely, surely, the two of them should get a little sex out of this raw deal. Maybe, but she sensed something else: coarse enjoyment. Some part of him was glad to see her alone, aimless, spineless, confused. But his coldness only made her lean closer, splash hot breath against his cheek when she spoke. Susie believed the body more courageous than the mind. She'd dated a man years ago that she'd lived in fear of sometimes—but at night she never hesitated, in sleep, to pull the covers off of him when her feet got too cold. The mind slipped into timid lapses, rote response. But the body was tropical, dense and prolific. Ready, always ready, to churn forward, even at risk of her mind's protests. Though the mind thought all day, it took it years or, sometimes, a lifetime, to recognize what the body had known all along.

After Chet, Susie had lost the patience to seek out a mate who coddled, who offered up decency beyond the bed. After Chet, Susie begged off Michael and men like him, and found herself drawn only to lovers who could circulate damage. Lovers who cornered and claimed, spoke only when speech was the final alternative to sleep.

What was she chasing? What end result had she had in mind?

They bought tickets for the 3:15 show at Mann Underground. Susie sifted through her purse, in case Michael wanted to pay for both tickets—which he did not.

Maybe she hadn't sifted long enough.

Seven Ugly Sundays was playing. The plot was claptrap, something about buzzards carrying hazardous waste, with a bit of revenge and a girl sewn in between AK-47s and dialogue abstaining from plausibility. Michael pulled off Susie's headset. "Ever seen a grown man cry?" he whispered—though he didn't need to, everyone else in the theater was involved in full-throated discussions, trading up, making deals, wearing the mark of the good life on their faces. "One more 'violent male bonding' scene should just about do it to me."

"I've given you more culture than you can handle, huh?"

"Sweetie, Vegas is twice as medieval as this place." She watched him shift in his seat. His belly was round and soft, like a scoop of sherbet. "We better hope they never institute a reapplication process for statehood. Our domiciles wouldn't stand a chance."

"Hey, it's a smile. I thought you'd lost it."

"I still have it," Michael said. "But you're right, I usually save it for shows. It's a Mirage smile."

"You make a lot of money out there."

He let his hands nap on his belly. "I do alright." She asked if they tipped well and he nodded. They must love you, she said, you must be good. "They tip me because they would hate to be me." The sound of villains getting iced leaked from their headphones, a guttural sweep of exit wounds, claustrophobic gunplay. "I get money for the same reason Salvation Army Santas do: People pay me to remind themselves they're blessed. People pay for my life because they don't have to live it. I've got a career because I'm one of life's great washouts."

"I'm unemployed," Susie said, "because I take my job everywhere and can't put it down." They looked around; no one was shushing them, not a body in the theater seemed to care.

"So how about that job? Clara gave me her version of your story. Two versions, actually. The first just depressed me, the other made your life sound like a Kafka novel."

"Right." Was it Clara's way to exaggerate because she was an actress? Or because it got results? *The Drama of the Gifted Child.*

"So where's the truth lie?"

The end credits began to advance, the names evaporating in a crawl from the top of the screen. Never before had Susie wished that a movie like this, a piece of escapist trash, would stretch on. "Nowhere in particular. It just lies."

"Listen to you. Timing, cadence, killer material to boot! You could do what I do in a minute! Just the right blend of stage presence and eviscerated esteem."

Clara complained to Susie—each chance she got—that she was misreading signs. "He lopes in and dashes your heart apart every weekend. You keep dressing for a first date; he shows up looking like he's come to paint your house." But Michael had loved Susie once, a thing Clara didn't know. The feeling had gone missing over the years, true, but Susie was sure she could retrieve it.

In time, though, Susie grew less sure. Grew sick of Michael's sexless attention. She was tired of washing her sheets for his weekend visits, only to have him sleep on the couch. She was tired of him apologizing for bringing half-wilted flowers, apologizing for falling asleep in the middle of movies, apologizing for being the kindest man she knew at a time when she couldn't seem to recognize kindness; or worse, a time when she tried to stare kindness down, burn holes in it, ignite it into something else.

During Michael's last visit, they made the mistake of buying wine. Michael made the mistake of holding her hand all the way through a Police LP, the same one they'd listened to back in high school, in Susie's bedroom. She set down her glass; Michael refilled her. She was going to do it, touch him, just as soon as it got to "Invisible Sun."

"I think the rest of the band should've seen a messy breakup coming," he suddenly scoffed. "Anyone that willfully calls himself Sting vants to be alone."

"And I guess that makes you the reverse," Susie said, breaking away. "You gave up your goddamn name to get in bed with Andy Williams and Siegfried and Roy."

She checked the wine bottle: empty. The peace and pleasure they'd felt a moment ago seemed to have slipped away, a chained dog gone madly free from a tight backyard.

Michael turned the turntable off. Gordon Sumner's voice warbled to a halt. "What about you? You still call yourself Susie Light. I don't even remember what your real last name is. I mean, if you're really so okay with losing the kennel, and okay with your acting dreams sinking into the La Brea Tarpits while you prop her majesty Clara's head up for public appearances, then why keep the fake name? Why not give that up?"

Oh, why does anyone let dead dreams possess them?

Susie stood. She emptied her ashtray, a legacy from Clara's last visit. Clara had inspected Susie's house with disdain, scorning her efforts to spruce it up for Michael, scorning Michael for playing games with Susie, scorning Susie for letting Michael continue them. "I don't know—hope?" She wondered if he'd call this time when he got back to Vegas. She wondered if she wanted him to. She wondered why it was not in Michael's power, or hers, to take themselves seriously.

November fizzled on, for the most part, incidentally. The summer heat was a distant memory. A few celebrities wore white ribbons shaped like dog collars, or halos, to honor the victims of the kennel incident. But who could recall, exactly, who the victims had been? Los Angeles was perceived as a harbor for disaster; in fact it thrived on the contrary: L.A. gorged on recovery, it was in love with the belief that single acts of temperance could wash away all excess.

Midway through the month, the final lawsuit against Susie was summarily dropped. The actor's agent had caught wind that "granting forgiveness" was in with 18–24-year-olds. Johnny London sent a fruit basket thanking Susie for all the attention. Susie called Clara. "I don't want to do it, Clara, so tell your manager thanks from me…"

"Linda? You got it. See, what did I say? All woe works itself out here. Linda's a real golden retriever."

Had Susie forgotten to wake up this morning? "She's—she's a real what? I don't understand."

"Golden retriever. One of *those terms* you forbid me to use. It's LA-LA slang for execs who fetch the goods. The ones who roll their sleeves up, swim through the cesspool of a project everyone thinks is doomed, and surface with an Oscar between their teeth."

After the good news about the lawsuits, Susie found herself afraid to stand still. She feared she'd float away with the slightest wind. There was nothing to prove, nothing demanded of her. For the first time she had no ties to this city, and for the first time, she found herself truly terrified of it. She would have to find out if there was a sum to the parts of Los Angeles, any sum at all. Or was it just parts?

Only dogs stabilized her now. Cigarettes and dogs. She'd begun hunting for their sight. Their trace. Any dog would do. She loved them all so much—plaintive beagle eyes. The pugs' fractured mugs. The burning loyalty of setters. Scotties, those bluish blessings. How a boxer's stomach scratches across an uncut lawn, making the grass softly hiss.

When she thought of dogs she thought of Michael. How he'd come to L.A. without an agenda. How he'd left without a kiss. When he'd been here, much had felt right. She'd forgotten the weight that was supposed to have been pinning her. Their time together had been like some trailer to a kind of movie she thought she'd never pay to see, but found her heart racing for all the same. She'd always presumed she would use dogs as her key to stardom. They would unlock the door for her, and then she'd give them up. Someday she'd groom the right terrier, nurse an ill greyhound back to health, which would lead to a producer or casting agent re-sculpting Susie's life into the mold of instant fame. They would discover her. Conan O'Brien would marvel at how she got her start. The humble beginnings from which she'd phoenixed. *After seeing your movie*, he'd say, *I find it hard to believe you were ever just a dog lady.*

But she *was* a dog lady. This was the plot twist she hadn't counted on. The dogs were the sum of her parts. At some point, caring for them began to give her pleasure in a way that headshots and auditions no longer did. The narrow bend of her dreams had shifted without telling her first.

The day before Thanksgiving, Clara invited Susie to the Pacific Ocean. On the deck of a pier, another offshoot of Mann's Chinese Theater—Mann Overboard—held its Grand Opening. The banner struggled to keep still for the cameras as DC-10s roared above, rocking and bending it in rude salutation. Wind whistled in Susie's face. If it had been this cold in the kennel, even for an hour, they all might have lived to see morning.

Roger Hewlett strolled by to say hello, refusing to walk away until Clara and Susie congratulated him on his People's Choice Award. Craig Capshaw waved his fork, a triangular piece of flapjack at its point waving in syncopation, like some miniature windsock. Alsie Ajay, who later that month would insinuate Clara's lesbianism in *The Hollywood Reporter*, hugged her now through her stole, as though a warm embrace in the present could erase future acts of spite.

Susie peered at her food. Her crêpes were gray. The birch syrup was dimpled with bitter clots and tasted like mildewed chocolate. Clara hardly touched her soapy oatmeal and blonde orange juice, transfixed as she was in the meandering sophistication of this power breakfast. Susie clasped her hand. "Tell me again— why do we eat here?"

Clara thumbed through Susie's hair and regarded her as a piece of clay. "It's not so bad. What doesn't kill you only makes you stylish." That was the end of that examination. Over the years, they'd shared pointed words, moments where they seemed on the outbreak of discovering crucial flecks in the other. But it would never happen in front of cameras. Publicity's promise was a kind of alchemy, molding people into alloys of their purer selves. True stars knew how to walk a banana path to stay in focus for a camera. True stars followed Tinseltown's rules to the letter. Susie was not that—no matter how much she'd dreamt of becoming it—she was no true star.

A soft flash of color, a khaki gold, lit up beneath the table just in front of Susie. This was unsurprising. It would be a retriever. Pacing beneath tablecloths. It would go unnoticed but for Susie; it would seem to be in search of a toy or ball, something to fetch, but would soon grow tired, about to give up the game in disgust, its tongue hanging close to the ground like a flag at half-mast. Susie was used to all of this; the retrievers must belong to someone, but she'd stopped wondering whom—from fear the answer might prove too logical. She needed, in her life, leaps. Sighing, she gulped Volvic and watched. This dog moved with fantastic fluidity, maneuvering past celebrities in small steps like a typist tittering on a keyboard. He went unnoticed, and seemed to be everywhere in the room at once, a strange figure that didn't belong at, but couldn't be removed from, the party.

The patio at Mann Overboard was loud, but Susie's head was louder, flush with the quizzical diction of new knowledge. Some loss allows its victims to kick it under the carpet, to, thanks to memory's weak range, eventually lose the loss, and its nagging persistence. All other loss proves perilous when ignored; at every turn it demands resistance, stance of character, hope for better days far into the hummable beyond…

The retriever was at Susie's feet, eyebrows arched like broken dashes. Ignoring her crêpes, her syrup, but not her eyes. She nuzzled his soft curly nape with her lips. "Yes boy," she said, "oh God yes, bring him back."

HAIR'S FATE

Donald Ray Pollock

When people in town said inbred, what they really meant was lonely. Daniel liked to pretend that anyway. He needed the long hair. Without it, he was nothing but a creepy country stooge from Knockemstiff, Ohio—old people glasses and acne sprouts and a bony chicken chest. You ever try to be someone like that? When you're fourteen, it's worse than being dead. And so, when the old man sawed off Daniel's hair with a butcher knife, the same one his mom used to slice rings of red bologna and scrape the pig's jowl, he might as well have cut the boy's ugly head off, too.

The old man had caught Daniel playing Romeo in the smokehouse with Lucy, Daniel's little sister's carnival doll. Daniel was giving it to her good, making believe she was Gloria Hamlin, a snotty, bucktoothed cheerleader who'd spit chocolate milk on him last year in the school cafeteria. "Boy, that's Mary's doll," the old man said, when he jerked the smokehouse door open. He said it matter-of-factly, like he was just telling his son that the radio was calling for rain, that the price of hogs was down again.

To make matters worse, Daniel couldn't quit, or even slow down. Trapped in the bright July sunlight pouring in through the open doorway, he was at that point in his fantasy where Gloria was begging him to split her in two with his big, hairy monster; his poor hand couldn't have stopped if the old man had chopped it off and thrown it to the dogs. With a shudder, he unloaded his jizz all over Lucy's plastic face, the crooked orange mouth, the bobbing blue eyes. Then, like an omen, a black wasp glided down from the rafters and landed gently on top of the doll's fake blonde hair.

"That's Mary's doll," the old man repeated, his voice revving up this time, trembling with static. He stood there for a minute, looking down at the doll Daniel still clutched in his shaky hand. The wasp began struggling to pull itself loose from the sticky hair. "I always knew you was a retard," the old man said, reaching over and squashing the insect between two callused fingers. Then he pursed his lips and shot a stream of brown tobacco juice on Daniel's bare feet, something he loved to do to all his family at impromptu times. "Now zip up and get rid of that goddamn thing before your sister gets hold of it," the old man said. "I'll take care of you later."

Stooped over with another disgrace, Daniel carried Lucy down to Black Run and threw her into the muddy water. He watched her float down past the cable that marked their property line, then walked slowly back up through the field to the slab house. Maybe he was turning into a sex fiend like his Uncle Carl, he thought. He pictured himself in the nuthouse on the hill over in Athens, sharing a padded cell with his crazy uncle, trading sick stories about the good old days, arguing over who gave the best blowjob, Barbie or Ken.

For the rest of the afternoon, Daniel warily watched the old man strut around with a fifth of wine like the Prince of Knockemstiff, the kind of windbag who showed no mercy and killed blood relatives for an extra sack of corn. Finally, near suppertime, he called Daniel into the kitchen. The rest of the family was already gathered around the Formica table with the bent leg so they could benefit from the old man's royal blathering. Daniel's mom nervously polished one of her lard buckets and Toadie, the little brother, kept sticking his tongue on the fly ribbon that hung from the ceiling, while the sister, Mary, stood still as a tree in front of the window.

The old man walked in a circle around Daniel, scratching his chin and looking the boy over as if he were a prize shoat at the county fair. Finally, he stopped and pronounced, "You need you a goddamn haircut, boy."

Daniel, his heart sinking like a stone, took a deep breath, and resigned himself to the scissors his mom kept in the kitchen drawer. But then, in a surprise move, the old man whipped out the long knife instead and shoved his son down in a chair. "You goddamn move, I'll scalp you like an Injun," he said as he gathered up a long brown lock of Daniel's hair in his fist and began sawing close to the scalp. He was like that, the old man, full of mischief when everyone else was down.

It was like being in the electric chair, Daniel would think later, though without the pleasure of dying, or even a last meal. But with specks of his blood splattered all over the cornbread, and hair floating in the soup beans, who was hungry anyway?

Later that evening, Toadie skipped out to the rotten picnic table under the hickory tree where his older brother sat brooding over hair and hair's fate. All summer, Daniel had dreamed of stepping onto the school bus after Labor Day with his hair hanging down to his shoulders. The scene was as clear and vivid as a movie in his head, and now the old man had taken it away. "You look like a dern lightbulb," Toadie said, running a broken plastic comb through his own greasy locks.

"Shut your mouth," Daniel said.

"You was ugly and now you're real ugly," the little brother said.

"Want your ass kicked?"

"Mary wants her doll back," Toadie said, determined to rub it in.

"Tell her it ran away."

"That ain't the truth and you know it," Toadie said, though a crinkle creased his forehead as if he were trying to imagine it. "How's Lucy gonna run away?"

Daniel stared across the hills behind the house. The red sun was sinking like a giant fizzing bomb behind the Mitchell Cemetery, where hair continued to grow, undisturbed by butcher knives and old men. "She hitchhiked," he told his little brother.

That night, while lying in bed and listening to the old man cuss some rock and roll band playing on the Ed Sullivan Show, it suddenly occurred to Daniel that anyone, even he, could be a hitchhiker. He'd had it with hick hairdos and lard sandwiches and having to make up movies in his head while the old man hogged the TV. When Ed called the rock group out for an encore, Daniel heard the crash of a bottle against the wall. "Might as well watch niggers as listen to this shit," the old man yelled at the TV. The boy ran his hands slowly over his head, searching out each tiny gash that had been made with the knife. Then he rolled over and began planning his escape.

A few days later, Daniel walked to Route 50 and stuck his thumb out. It wasn't long before a white semi speeding past suddenly downshifted to a stop, the air brakes screeching, the trailer bucking and hopping on the asphalt. The truck driver's name was Cowboy Roy. At least that was the name spelled out in ragged black electrical tape on the rusty doors of the cab. "I ain't really no cowboy," he blurted out before the boy even got settled in the seat. Pulling back out onto the highway, he went on to confess that he'd never actually been on a horse either; that, in fact, he was allergic to horsehair. "Everyone's got their cross to bear, I reckon," the trucker said, pushing back the black ten-gallon hat that sat on top of his round, sweaty head.

Cowboy Roy was on his way home to Illinois. He was fat and wore tight coveralls that threatened to split open every time he hit a bump in the road. His feet were encased in pointy brown cowboy boots. A set of shiny spurs hung from the mirror. To make up for his allergy to horses, Cowboy Roy did other manly cowboy stuff, like drink cheap whiskey from a pint bottle and chew stringy tobacco and write songs in the tradition of Marty Robbins.

Daniel didn't say anything. He figured the man had as much right to call himself a cowboy as the movie stars on TV. The trucker rattled on about the best way to build a campfire in the rain. It suddenly occurred to Daniel that out here on the road you could be any damn thing you wanted to be. You could make up a new life story for every stranger who offered you a ride. You could be a Boy Scout without a single badge, a millionaire without a pot to piss in, a cowboy without a horse.

"So," Cowboy Roy finally said, "where'd you get that haircut? Cops do that to you?"

"Nah, my old man," Daniel said.

"Damn, he musta been highly ticked off," the trucker said. "What the dickens got him so riled up?"

Daniel, thinking of the day in the shed with Lucy, hesitated as he tried to think of a good lie. "He caught me with his girlfriend," he finally said.

Cowboy Roy gave a low whistle. "Well, that'd do it," he said. "But pap or no pap, I'd shoot a man down like a dog that scalped me like that."

"It weren't like I didn't want to."

"So you ran off instead?" the trucker asked.

"When I go back, I'll have hair clear to my knees," the boy vowed, staring out the dirty windshield.

Just as they crossed over into Indiana, Cowboy Roy gave Daniel a red snot rag to tie around his neck, just like the one that he wore. "So people will think we work the same spread," he explained. Then he handed the boy a harmonica to play while he sang a song he'd just thought up. Puffing out his cheeks, Daniel raised the mouth harp up to his lips, then noticed a thick glob of tobacco juice oozing from one of the reeds. "I don't know how to play," he told the trucker.

"Shoot, just blow on the damn thing," Cowboy Roy said. "You know how to blow, don't you?"

"Yeah, I guess so."

"I'll bet you do," the fat man said with a grin.

"What's the name of the song anyway?" the boy said, banging the harmonica on his knee, trying to knock the spit out of it.

"It don't have no name,'" the trucker said, "but it's the best dern love song I ever wrote."

They traveled across the bottom edge of Indiana, past sleepy cornfields and remodeled Indian mounds and small towns still decorated with sagging Fourth of July banners and painted rocks. Cowboy Roy broke out a pint of redeye, and before long Daniel's head felt as fluffy as a paper cone of cotton candy. The trucker began talking a mile a minute about driving straight on through to Mexico. He said they could become bandits and hide out in a smoky cantina with a servant boy who would worship them in return for scraps off the table. He described young Miguel in minute detail, right down to the tiny purple birthmark on his lower stomach. Then he pulled a small plastic bottle from his coveralls and shook out some white tablets. "Here you go," Cowboy Roy said, handing Daniel two pills.

"What are these?" the boy said.

"Them's trucker's lifesavers. They keep you awake, make your dick hard as blacktop. Longhairs call 'em speed."

Daniel recalled once seeing a photo of an actual speed freak in Mrs. Kenney's health class at school. Her brother, a prison guard in Kentucky, had sent it to her. The teacher claimed the man was only thirty years old. His skin was drawn tight as a drum over his grinning face. "Once you start on that stuff, you're like one of those space comets that don't ever stop," the woman warned the class that day, as they passed around the picture of the pale stick with the brittle heart. Daniel looked down at the white pills the trucker had given him, then tossed them in his mouth and waited for takeoff.

Cowboy Roy was an independent trucker, but drove much of the time for a big slaughterhouse in Illinois, delivering meat throughout the Tri-State area. He'd seen enough filth to give up eating most flesh altogether. "It just breaks my heart to see some mom stick a hot dog in her baby's trap," he told Daniel. His favorite food now was pork and beans. "Eat 'em right out of the can," he said, "just like the cowboys do." He'd inherited a little spread; and as they crossed over into Illinois that evening, he invited Daniel to spend the night. "It gets pretty lonely at the ranch ever since Mom died," he said, his voice cracking just a little.

Daniel was surprised that the landscape didn't change after they left Ohio. He'd always thought of every other state as an exotic world, but so far everything he'd seen was as dull as a Lawrence Welk tuba special. In the meantime, though, the pills and whiskey turned him into a regular chatterbox; and before he could stop himself, he told Cowboy Roy the whole sad story of Lucy and the butcher knife.

"Sounds kinda kinky to me," the trucker said. He lit the butt of a skinny black cigar he'd stashed behind his ear, and blew a cloud of smoke in the boy's face.

"It woulda been down to my shoulders by the time school started," Daniel said, shivering with a speed rush.

"I never cared much for dolls myself," Cowboy Roy said. "Hell, they just lay there, you know what I mean?"

"My little cousin's got one that talks when you pull a string," the boy said. He rocked back and forth in the seat, unable to hold still.

"It's a shame they don't sell live ones," the man said, mashing his bloodshot eyeballs with his fist.

Eventually, Daniel and the trucker dropped the trailer off in a potholed parking lot outside a warehouse on the edge of a small town. Then they drove on for another hour or so; and near dark, the trucker pulled down a long, secluded driveway lined with pine trees. He parked the semi in front of an ancient house trailer that had "PONDEROSA" spray painted in big red letters across the front of it. "I got twelve acres here," the trucker told Daniel as they stomped through the weeds to the trailer. "We could put on a rodeo if we took the notion."

Stepping up on some cement blocks, he pushed a key in the door and shoved it open. "It's ain't no dude ranch, but it's good enough," he said, beckoning the boy inside. The trailer smelled like a closet full of bad times. All the windows were shut, and it must have been a hundred degrees inside. Black flies crawled on the walls. A flaky brown snakeskin was stretched out on the kitchen counter. Daniel looked around at the empty whiskey bottles and pork and bean cans lying on the floor. The shabbiness of the trailer suddenly choked him up, made him think of home.

He asked Cowboy Roy for another pill. "I can pay for it," Daniel said, digging some crumpled singles from the front pocket of his jeans. The sixteen dollars was all the money he had left from selling blackberries that summer. He'd picked them in the bottoms down past Pumpkin Center, then walked door to door all over Twin Township peddling them for thirty cents a quart.

"Shoot, pardner, your money ain't no good here," the trucker said. "What's mine is yours." Digging the bottle out of the front pocket of his coveralls, he uncapped it and gave Daniel two more pills, then flopped down on a sagging couch. "You think you could pull these boots off for me?" Cowboy Roy asked the boy. "My poor feet's killin' me."

Daniel got down on his knees in front of the truck driver and tugged both boots off. "How 'bout my socks, too?" Cowboy Roy said. Peeling the damp, dirty socks off, the boy was nearly knocked down by the rotten odor that sprang up from the wrinkled purple feet and filled the cramped room. The smell reminded him of the sick bucket his mom sat by the couch whenever the old man was on a binge.

"It sure is hot in here, ain't it?" the boy said, as he stood up and stepped away.

"Yeah, Mom screwed all the damn winders shut the first year I went out on the road," Cowboy Roy said. "Poor old woman, she always got jittery when I was gone." Then he heaved himself up off the couch and stepped into the kitchen. "What we need is some cold beer."

The thought of any more alcohol combined with the smell of the trucker's feet made Daniel queasy. "Maybe later," he said. All his nerve endings felt exposed, the coating that covered them burned away by the speed. Even the light from the lamp hurt his eyes.

"Well, what about a shower?" the trucker yelled from the kitchen. Daniel could hear drawers sliding open, cupboards slamming shut. "That'd cool you off."

Walking into the bathroom, Daniel saw a shoot-em-up paperback floating in the commode, its pages swollen with water. An old road atlas lay on the filthy blue linoleum. He hesitated, then locked the hollow door and took his clothes off. Pulling back the feed sack that served as a shower curtain, he saw that the tub was caked in hard gray scum. He tore some pages from the atlas, and covered the trucker's slime with the endless highways of America. There wasn't any soap, but he rinsed off in the cold spray anyway, patted himself dry with a stiff, bloody towel that hung from a nail on the wall. Then he put his clothes back on and walked out to the living room.

Cowboy Roy was sitting on the couch, a can of beer in his hand. He was grinning wildly at Daniel, baring his brown teeth like a dog. Uncapping the pill bottle, he threw several more tablets in his mouth and chased them down with the beer. "Look what I found," he said, reaching down and lifting a long blonde wig delicately from a plastic bag on the floor.

"What the hell?" Daniel said, jumping back. He suddenly felt closed in, as if the room was a coffin, and the hair the trucker held in his hand the same as that which grew in the graves on the hill back home.

"Aw, come on," the truck driver said. "We're just fuckin' around."

"Whose is that?" the boy asked.

"It was my Mom's," Cowboy Roy explained. "But she don't need it no more. The cancer done ate a hole clean through her." He held the wig out to Daniel. "Go ahead, try it on."

Daniel took another step back. "No, I better not," he said.

"You was crying about not having no hair, wasn't you?" Cowboy Roy said. "I'm just tryin' to help you out is all."

"I don't know," the boy said. "Seems kinda weird."

"Son, your daddy caught you fuckin' a doll," Cowboy Roy said. "If that ain't weird, then nothing is."

Daniel ran his hand over his head. A cricket chirped from somewhere in the room. Glancing out the window, he saw the darkness settling over unfamiliar land. It amazed him to think that just that morning he'd slipped out of bed while his parents were still sleeping and now he was hundreds of miles from home. "Okay," he finally told the trucker.

"Now we're talking. Why walk around like that when you don't have to?" the fat man said, wiping the sweat from his bloated red face with the hairpiece. "Okay, just stand in front of that mirror and I'll help you put it on. I used to stick this thing on Mom all the time."

Daniel stepped over to the big oval mirror hanging from the paneled wall and shifted about nervously as Cowboy Roy set the musty-smelling wig on top of his head. "Hold still," he ordered the boy, working the elastic band of the hairpiece down over the boy's skull. "Got to make it fit right, don't we?" the trucker said, looking over Daniel's shoulder and grinning at him in the mirror. The boy could feel the man's belly pressing up against him.

Finally, the trucker said, "Not bad. What you think?"

The long wig cascaded down Daniel's scrawny back, a tangle of big blonde curls. "It's a little long, ain't it?" the boy said.

"Well, shoot, you just need a little trim," the trucker said. "Stay right there." Cowboy Roy hurried into the kitchen and came back out with a jagged filet knife. "I can't find no scissors, but this will do the job." He grabbed a length of the brittle hair in his stubby fingers. "Say about this much?" he asked the boy.

"Maybe I oughta do that," Daniel said.

"Just don't make no sudden moves," Cowboy Roy said.

"That's what my old man said."

"Oh, yeah, I forgot," the trucker said. "Hell, I ain't gonna hurt you. This damn thing cost thirty dollars."

"That's good."

The trucker started in, chewing his chapped lips as he hacked off pieces of his dead mother's fancy wig and let them flutter to the floor. After a few minutes, he stepped away and slid the knife into the back pocket of his coveralls. He reached behind him for a pint bottle sitting on the end table next to the couch, his eyes never leaving the boy. As he unscrewed the cap, he said, "What you say now, pardner?"

Daniel stared into the mirror. The hair draped from his head like a thick curtain. He kept turning from side to side, looking at himself from different angles. No longer did he see the scabs on his scalp, the bony triangle of face, the acne flaming across his skin like a brushfire. "It does make a difference," he finally said, turning away from the mirror, his voice barely a whisper.

"Goddamn if it don't," Cowboy Roy said. "Hell, I bet there ain't many dolls look so pretty." His face was flushed with heat, his body trembling. After steadying himself with a deep breath, he stepped closer and held out the bottle of whiskey. "C'mon, let's celebrate," he croaked.

Daniel tried to laugh, but that had always been too hard for him. He'd never had anything to celebrate, not once in his whole life. He took a small drink from the bottle, and as he handed it back, he felt the trucker's fat, sweaty hand touch his and linger there for a moment. And suddenly, Daniel knew that if he looked in the mirror again, he'd see the wig for what it really was. So instead, he closed his eyes.

I ran a cat over with my mail truck today. On purpose. It made me sick when I heard the thud, as if I'd stepped outside of myself and watched as I did such a terrible thing. I saw the fucker run out into the road and I didn't have time to think logically. I was only thinking about payback. Revenge.

CALVARY

Casey Taylor

Not revenge on the cat's owner, of course. I don't know whose cat that was. It was probably a stray. The cat didn't have a collar and looked like it hadn't been groomed in quite some time. My guess was that it was living off of mice and bugs, running around in the baseball fields at night and avoiding traffic during the day. That helped me get over killing the cat. At least I knew that no kids were going to cry because of what I did and nobody's parents were going to have to try and find a way to explain that things live and things die and that's why Boots was nothing but a smear on the road.

I jogged out of my truck and scraped the cat off of the road with an empty mail tray. It peeled off the road with a sick sound, like pulling a band-aid off of a weeks-old scab. The hairs pulled out gradually and the traces of pus clung to the wound. I gagged a bit and threw it in my truck next to a few packages I had left for Sycamore Street.

The truck was hot. I fucking hated delivering mail in the summer months. They didn't give us air conditioning in the trucks. Instead they had a small personal fan that didn't do shit except blow hot air around the truck. It didn't do much but make me sweat more than usual. I'd rather be cold as hell than sweating my balls off any day of the week.

I made deliveries for another half hour or so and my phone rang. It was Jim.

"Sulley's looking for you. Sounds pissed."

"What'd he say?" I asked. Probably a neighbor calling to complain about the dead cat. People were always calling the post office to complain about the dumbest shit.

"He didn't say anything. Just asked if I knew where you were delivering and I told him I wasn't sure."

"Whatever," I said.

"What'd you do?"

"I didn't do shit yet," I said. "Don't worry about it."

"You should change routes," he said. "I don't think this is good for you, man. I don't think you should deliver to that dude no more."

"I'm fine," I said. Jim was always worrying about something.

"You're gonna get yourself fired if you keep fucking with that dude."

"Some things are more important than a fucking job," I said. And I meant it. I didn't need the job at the post office. My integrity was on the line.

"Just watch yourself."

"We still getting drinks later?"

"Yeah."

I hung up the phone. Jim was always making me second-guess myself. He was a smart dude, way smarter than me. He always got a few steps ahead of the supervisors and they could never track down what he was doing. He'd miss scan points on his route so that they couldn't keep track of his time or deliberately leave mail behind so they'd think he was slammed and he'd need a few extra hours of double-time.

Maybe I shouldn't keep fucking with the guy at 1392 E. Buck Road. That's what I was thinking. Eddie was his name. Eddie was the guy who was banging my ex-girlfriend Susan. I'd seen her car parked outside of there during the day a few times and a couple more times at night when I'd swing by there on my way home from work.

I'd seen him a few times, always shirtless on his porch with a can of beer in his hand. The guy looked like a damn loser. I don't think he had a job, or, if he did, I don't know when the hell he went to work. He was always home, playing music in his garage and working on a shitty Firebird. I couldn't figure out what Susan was doing with a guy like that, but she stopped taking my calls a few months earlier so I couldn't even ask her for a reason.

She was a good girl, Susan. She was studying at night to get her R.N. and start making bank at the Chester County Hospital. She worked as a receptionist at a dentist's office when we were dating. I didn't know what the hell she was doing now. I figured she had to pick up a second job or something, because this Eddie asshole didn't do shit.

He was always sending out a lot of boxes. Like, every other day, four or five boxes outgoing. He was probably selling stuff on eBay to make rent and get beer money. Probably wasn't taking Susan out to the same restaurants that I used to on that kind of money. Even if I didn't look the part, I made a hell of a lot at the post office and could afford to get her whatever the hell she wanted. Worked that way for a few years and she didn't seem to mind.

I'd come home from work and on nights that she didn't have class we'd go out to some Italian joint (that was her favorite) and get pasta and wine and drinks and I'd never make her give me a cent. I'd tell her to save it and put it towards her classes and her R.N. Told her that I was good on money. She'd smile and thank me and kiss my lips when I put cash down on the check and got up to grab our coats. All I ever told her is I just wanted her to take care of me. Make me some lunch every now and again to take to work or rub my legs down when I was sore. I'd make sure she was good financially if she just loved me.

Then she just left. Started talking marriage and I told her I didn't think I was ready for something like that and she took her shit and left. Went back to her mother's house. It all happened really quickly. Brought up marriage on a Monday and was out of the apartment by Saturday. I thought maybe she was just looking for an excuse to bolt. Maybe the thought of being with a mailman sent her packing. I didn't think she'd really want to end up with a guy like me anyway.

Now she was fucking a dude named Eddie who sold shit off of eBay. And I was riding around with a squashed cat in the back of my truck.

I decided to save Eddie's place for last. I'd messed with his mail a little bit before, throwing around fragile packages or "forgetting" to leave notices about registered mail he needed to pick up at the post office. But, stuffing a dead cat into his mailbox was a horse of an entirely different color. Jim was right. I was going to get fired over that shit. I had to think it over a little more.

Every week we had to deliver marriage mail. Those stupid goddamn coupon booklets that old people used and everybody else threw away. They were annoying as all hell and all they did was break my fucking back. I always had a bunch of pieces left over at the end of my route because nobody wanted the stupid things. I usually threw them away. I figured I'd put a few of them to use and wrap the poor thing in it to cover it up in case anybody peered in.

I stopped down at the Wawa off West Chester Pike to cool off and grab an iced tea. The teenager at the counter with a spike through his nose gave me a weird look. I checked my shirt for cat blood and didn't find any. He was probably just being a dick.

When I went back outside, Sulley's fat ass was waiting for me in the parking lot. He leaned against the white Postal Service van, sweating heavily from his armpits. His waist and legs were putting a major test on the elasticity of his khakis.

"You got a minute Tommy?"

"Yeah," I said. "I'm pretty tight on time, though. I gotta get rolling in a few minutes."

"I got a call from somebody on your route," Sulley said. "Said you were fucking around with a dead cat or something?"

"What?" I said. "What the fuck are you talking about?"

"I'm just letting you know. Somebody called in a complaint and I had to come check it out. They said you peeled a dead cat off the road."

"I don't know what you're talking about."

"What are you playing with dead cats for? You must be seriously fucked up."

"I didn't touch a damn dead cat, Sulley," I said. I tried to act as offended as possible, which wasn't difficult because every time I thought about what I did it started to make me feel sick. "Are you nuts, man? Why would I be playing around with a dead cat?"

"Somebody said you were," Sulley said. "Look, it's crazy, but why the hell would somebody on your route call and lie about something like that?"

"I don't know. Maybe they don't feel like they get their mail on time."

"Maybe," Sulley said. "Still a weird ass thing to say, if you ask me."

"No doubt about that," I said. Sulley wasn't buying it. He kept looking around at my truck, as if I'd be stupid enough to leave an animal carcass laying around on my dash or some shit. I felt disrespected in a way that he really thought I was that stupid.

"Look," he said. "I don't know what to make out of any of this. All I know is, if I hear anything else about dead animals and your route, we're going to have a serious talk, okay?"

"Yeah," I said. "You got it."

Sulley waddled over to the driver's side of the van and got in, starting the car and blasting the air conditioning. It still boggled my mind that our supervisors, who don't do shit, got to ride around in vehicles with air conditioning while we sweat our asses off with dinky little fans.

I hopped back in my truck and started it up, ready to finish up with my deliveries. I had two more streets to finish before I got to Eddie's house.

The whole time I couldn't think about anything other than Susan. I thought about the way her hair smelled when she'd shower after getting home from class. I thought about her laugh and the way she'd cock her head all the way back when she found something really funny, like she was sitting in a dentist's chair ready to get her teeth cleaned. She'd leave me notes in my lunches sometimes. Nothing overly romantic, but simple reminders that she was thinking of me. *Hope you're having a good day. Love you.* That sort of thing.

I wished she'd answer my phone calls so I could just ask her what the hell went wrong. Why she wanted to get married so badly. From what I'd seen from my parents, marriage only fucked up good relationships. It made couples resent each other. I didn't want that shit. I wanted to love Susan regardless, keep enjoying our time together. Marriage would've only spoiled everything.

I'd also ask her what she's doing with Eddie from E. Buck Road. Was he really a better option than I was? The guy cleaned a shitty muscle car three times a week. He sold things on the internet. Or, maybe he was selling drugs. I don't really know, I guess. But, either way, he was too much of a loser to be with Susan. She was too smart for him. Too kind and loving. This asshole, with his shirtless Miller High Life sessions and 80s hair metal, had no business getting inside of my ex-girlfriend.

By the time I got to his mailbox, I was heated. I couldn't think. I threw his letters into his mailbox and said employment be damned. I meant what I'd told Jim on the phone earlier. This was more important than a job at the post office. Changing routes wouldn't accomplish anything. I'd still be thinking about it nonstop, knowing that this asshole was probably sleeping with Susan while I drove around in the heat delivering Bed Bath & Beyond coupons and *Us Weekly* magazines.

I wrapped the cat in the marriage mail I'd used to cover it and shoved it into the mailbox. It barely fit, so I had to really push it a few times to get it in there. I heard a couple of its bones snap as it slid back farther into the mailbox. The marriage mail was covered in blood.

I washed my hands with what was left in my water bottle and drove back to the post office. Sulley wasn't around. I clocked out and met Jim in the parking lot. He was smoking a Marlboro and he offered me one.

"Yeah, sure," I told him. I lit the cigarette and we walked to my car. We drove to Kildare's in silence. I flicked the radio to different stations and took long drags on my cigarette. Jim just stared out the window. He'd try to make conversation, but I didn't have much to say. I was tired.

I ordered a lager at the bar. Jim got a whiskey. We didn't smoke, because you weren't allowed to smoke inside in West Chester anymore. Times had changed.

"So what's your deal?" Jim asked.

"What do you mean?"

"You're quiet as all hell. I know you did something."

"Yeah."

"Well, what'd you do?"

I couldn't focus on his words. Instead I was thinking about the crunches coming from the cat's carcass as I shoved it into that bastard Eddie's mailbox. The way its dead eyes stared back at me from inside the marriage mail, begging me to shove it deeper to teach the prick a lesson.

"I didn't do shit," I said. "I mean, nothing out of the ordinary. I'm gonna get fired, though."

"Fired? You don't get fired over nothing, dude."

"Well, it wasn't exactly nothing, Jim. I mean, Sulley's just onto me. He knows some shit's up and I think I'm gonna get fired."

"What the fuck are you gonna do?"

"Nothing," I said.

I was like Jesus Christ. Or Martin Luther King, Jr. I was about to take a fall because of something I believed in. Maybe my quest wasn't quite as noble as theirs was. I didn't cure any Jews or get the government to let black people drink out of the same water fountain as white people. But, I did something that mattered. I kept my integrity intact. And if I had to lose my job over it, then so be it.

"Well, shit," Jim said. "I hope you're wrong."

"I'm not," I said. "I'm as good as gone."

"Maybe the union can bail you out."

He went on about Les, our union rep at the office, and how he'd saved a bunch of jobs in the past, but I stopped listening. I didn't care at that point.

I pictured the scene at 1392 E. Buck Road. Eddie emerging from his house without a shirt on and going to get his letters. He'd see the cat and drop his bottle of High Life, maybe jumping back into the road and shrieking like a little bitch. Susan would see him and make fun of him. Think less of him as a man. What kind of true man gets scared by a dead animal?

Or, maybe Susan would find the cat. She'd walk out to the mailbox, probably wearing one of his goddamn t-shirts or his sandals that were too big for her feet, and she'd find the cat and scream. Scream so loud that Eddie ran out of the house and tried to console her, but she didn't want to be near him. She wouldn't be able to look at his home the same way again, frightened that something like that could happen again. She'd go back to her mother's. Maybe she'd even return a few of my calls, telling me about everything that happened and asking if I knew who could've done something like that.

I'd have to start looking for a new job. Maybe I'd go back to school, get out of town for a few years. Studying something interesting, like history, and get a good job at a college doing research or something like that. Writing books. That'd be cool.

Or, maybe I'd just sell shit on the internet and get an old muscle car like Eddie. An old Camaro IROC or something. I'd drink big cans of Pabst while I washed it and hang out in my garage. I had baseball cards I could sell. That's the kind of shit people buy off eBay. Baseball cards and comic books. I had plenty of that stuff boxed up at my old man's house.

Then maybe she'd come back.

Contributors

Jennifer Bannan's collection of short stories, *Inventing Victor*, was published by the Carnegie Mellon University Press Series in Short Fiction in 2003. She has had stories published in *ACM, Radio Transcript Newspaper, Passages North, womenwriters.net*, and *Café Eighties*. She is a marketing consultant with Zer0 to 5ive. She lives in Pittsburgh, PA with her children Tova and Desmond. Bannan is at work on two novels.

Keith Banner is a writer and a social worker for people with disabilities. He lives in Cincinnati, Ohio and holds a BA in English from Indiana University and an MA in creative writing from Miami University (Oxford, Ohio). He teaches creative writing part-time at Miami University and has published two works of fiction, *The Life I Lead* (Alfred A. Knopf, 1999), a novel, and *The Smallest People Alive* (Carnegie Mellon University Press, 2004), a book of short stories. He has published numerous short stories and essays in magazines and journals, including *Other Voices, Washington Square, Kenyon Review*, and *Third Coast*. He received an O. Henry prize for his short story, "The Smallest People Alive," in 2000, and an Ohio Arts Council individual artist fellowship for his fiction in 2001.

Monica Bergers grew up in Nebraska and Arkansas. She received her MFA from the University of Iowa where she was a Glenn Schaefer fellow. An excerpt of her work has been published online in *Turbine*, Victoria University's literary journal. She is working on her first novel, which is set during the Dust Bowl in Nebraska.

Jane Bernstein is the author of five books, among them the memoirs *Bereft: A Sister's Story*, and *Rachel in the World*. Her awards include two National Endowment Fellowships, two Pennsylvania Council on the Arts Fellowships, and a 2004 Fulbright Fellowship spent in Israel, where she taught at Bar-Ilan University's Creative Writing Program. Her essays have been published in such places as *The New York Times Magazine, Ms., Prairie Schooner, Poets & Writers, Self*, and *Creative Nonfiction*, and her screenwork includes the screenplay for the Warner Brothers movie *Seven Minutes in Heaven*. Jane, a member of the Creative Writing department at Carnegie Mellon University, is working on a new novel, *The Face Tells the Secret*.

David Busis was born in Boston, MA and grew up in Pittsburgh, PA. A graduate of Yale University, he now attends the Iowa Writers' Workshop. He is working on a novel and a collection of short stories. He is twenty-five years old.

Marjorie Celona was born and raised in Victoria, British Columbia. She has degrees in writing from the University of Victoria ('06) and the Iowa Writers' Workshop ('09), where she was an Iowa Arts Fellow and recipient of the Ailene Barger Barnes Prize for Excellence in the Short Story. Her stories have been published in *The Best American Nonrequired Reading 2008, Glimmer Train, Crazyhorse, Indiana Review, THIS Magazine*, and *Best Canadian Stories* 2007 and 2010. In 2008, she won The Royal Bank of Canada's Bronwen Wallace Award for Emerging Writers and second place in *The Atlantic*'s student writing contest. She currently teaches fiction writing at the University of Iowa and the Iowa Young Writers' Studio.

Katie Chase's fiction has appeared or is forthcoming in *The Missouri Review, Prairie Schooner, Five Chapters,* and *Best American Short Stories*, and has been awarded a Pushcart Prize. A graduate of the Iowa Writers' Workshop, she has also received support from the MacDowell Colony, the Michener-Copernicus Society of America, and the Steinbeck Fellows Program at San José State University. She grew up outside of Detroit and currently lives in San Francisco.

Jason England was born and raised in New York City, where he split his youth between a welfare hotel for the homeless in Times Square and a housing project in Harlem. He has been a soda salesperson, camp counselor, parking lot attendant, waiter, bartender, civil rights activist, dean of college admissions, and an assistant adjunct professor. He graduated from Wesleyan University with high honors, and has won three awards for fiction. He received an MFA from the Iowa Writer's Workshop and is currently the Carl Djerassi Fiction Fellow at the Wisconsin Institute for Creative Writing.

Sherrie Flick is the author of the novel *Reconsidering Happiness* (2009) and *I Call This Flirting*, a chapbook of flash fiction (2004). Her work has appeared in the anthologies *Flash Fiction Forward* (Norton) and *New Sudden Fiction* (Norton). "Flash in a Pan," her craft essay exploring time in flash fiction, appears in *The Rose Metal Press Field Guide to Writing Flash Fiction* (2009). She is the recipient of a Pennsylvania Council on the Arts fellowship, a Heinz Endowments AEI grant, and has received artist residencies from the Ucross Foundation and Atlantic Center for the Arts. Co-founder and artistic director for the Gist Street Readings series, Flick lives in Pittsburgh where she teaches, edits, and writes.

Kevin A. González holds graduate degrees from the University of Wisconsin-Madison and the Iowa Writers' Workshop, where he was a Graduate Fellow. He has also received fellowships and awards from the Wisconsin Institute for Creative Writing, the James Michener Foundation and the Copernicus Society of America. His stories have appeared in *Playboy, Virginia Quarterly Review, The L Magazine*, and elsewhere, and have been anthologized in *Best American Nonrequired Reading 2007, Best New American Voices 2007,* and *Best New American Voices 2009*. His first book of poems, *Cultural Studies*, was published by Carnegie Mellon University Press in 2009. He lives in Madison, Wisconsin.

Diane Goodman is a writer and caterer/personal chef in Miami Beach. She is author of two collections of short stories, *The Genius of Hunger* and *The Plated Heart*, both published by Carnegie Mellon University Press. She has published articles and stories in national magazines. Her work often incorporates the waiters, chefs, cooks, and restaurant aficionados of her catering world.

Derek Green's fiction and journalism have appeared in many publications. His story collection *New World Order* was the first fiction title to be published by Autumn House Press. Set in various locations around the globe, the stories are interlinked by the presence of a dark, Halliburton-esque corporation, and take readers on a tour of the world as America's military-industrial complex reels into a new century. In addition to his work as a journalist, Green has worked as a consultant to multinational corporations on six continents. A skilled public speaker, he regularly conducts seminars in English and Spanish around the world. He lives in Connecticut with his wife and two sons.

Honorée Fanonne Jeffers has published stories in *Brilliant Corners: A Journal of Jazz and Literature, Callaloo, Indiana Review, The Kenyon Review, New England Review*, and *Story Quarterly*; a story of hers was cited as one of the "100 More Distinguished Stories of 2008" in *The Best American Short Stories 2009*. A poet as well, she has published three award-winning books, *The Gospel of Barbecue* (2000), *Outlandish Blues* (2003), and *Red Clay Suite* (2007). She has won awards and fellowships from the Rona Jaffe Foundation, the American Antiquarian Society, the MacDowell Colony, and the Bread Loaf Writers Conference. She teaches creative writing at the University of Oklahoma, where she is Associate Professor of English.

Samuel Ligon is the author of *Safe in Heaven Dead*, a novel. His story collection, *Drift and Swerve*, won the Autumn House Fiction Prize in 2008. His stories have appeared in *The Quarterly, Alaska Quarterly Review, Story-Quarterly, Post Road, New Orleans Review, Keyhole, Sleepingfish, Gulf Coast, Other Voices*, and elsewhere. He teaches at Eastern Washington University's Inland Northwest Center for Writers, and is the editor of *Willow Springs*. He lives in Spokane with his wife and two children.

William Lychack is the author of a novel, *The Wasp Eater*, and a collection of stories, *The Architect of Flowers*. His work has appeared in *The Best American Short Stories, The Pushcart Prize, The American Scholar, The Missouri Review, Ploughshares, The Southern Review*, and on public radio's "This American Life." His superhero power of choice would be teleportation.

Andrew Malan Milward's stories have been finalists for the National Magazine Award and have appeared in many places including *Zoetrope, The Southern Review, Conjunctions, Columbia*, and *Best New American Voices 2010*. He is a 2008 graduate of the Iowa Writers' Workshop and received the 2009 James McCreight Fiction Fellowship from the University of Wisconsin. He lives in San Francisco, where he is a Steinbeck Fiction Fellow at San Jose State University.

Dustin Parsons is an Assistant Professor of English at Fredonia State University. He is the Nonfiction Editor for *Mid-American Review*, and has stories in the *South Dakota Review, Blue Earth Review*, and *Southeast Review*. He has a poem in *The Portland Review* and *The Texas Review,* and book reviews in *Mid-American Review*, as well as *American Book Reviews* and *Orion*.

Matthew Pitt was born in St. Louis. He is a graduate of Hampshire College and NYU, where he was a New York Times fellow. His first book of short stories, *Attention Please Now*, won the Autumn House Press Fiction Prize. Other works have appeared or are forthcoming in *Oxford American, The Southern Review, Cincinnati Review, Colorado Review, New Letters*, and *Best New American Voices*. Stories of his were recently cited in *The Best American Short Stories, The Best American Nonrequired Reading*, and Pushcart Prize anthologies.

Donald Ray Pollock was born in 1954 and raised in Knockemstiff, Ohio. After dropping out of high school at seventeen, he worked in a paper mill for thirty-two years. He quit his job in 2005 to attend the MFA program at The Ohio State University. His first book, *Knockemstiff*, won the 2009 PEN/Robert Bingham Award and also the 2009 Devil's Kitchen Award from the University of Southern Illinois. He was awarded a grant from the Ohio Arts Council in the spring of 2010. He lives in Chillicothe, Ohio, just a few miles from where he grew up.

Casey Taylor graduated from Carnegie Mellon University in 2009 and currently lives and writes in Pittsburgh. He used to be a mailman, but now he works in advertising. This is his first publication.

Acknowledgments

Bannan, Jennifer, "Sexy Ida Makes a Vow," copyright 2010 by Jennifer Bannan. Reprinted by permission of the author.

Banner, Keith, "Winners Never Sleep!" copyright 2010 by Keith Banner. Reprinted by permission of the author.

Bergers, Monica, "Gangland," copyright 2010 by Monica Bergers. Reprinted by permission of the author.

Bernstein, Jane, "Knocked Out," copyright 2010 by Jane Bernstein. Reprinted by permission of the author.

Busis, David, "Coming About," copyright 2010 by David Busis. Reprinted by permission of the author.

Celona, Marjorie, "This is When I Love You the Most," copyright 2010, Marjorie Celona. "This is When I Love You the Most" was originally published in *Crazyhorse*, Issue Number 74.

Chase, Katie, "The Donor's Daughter, " copyright 2010 by Katie Chase. Reprinted by permission of the author.

England, Jason, "Communion," copyright 2010 by Jason England. Reprinted by permission of the author.

Flick, Sherrie, "Good Dog," copyright 2010 by Sherrie Flick. Reprinted by permission of the author.

González, Kevin, "Wake," copyright 2010 by Kevin Gonzalez. Reprinted by permission of the author.

Goodman, Diane, "Beloved Child," copyright 2010 by Diane Goodman. Reprinted by permission of the author.

Green, Derek, "Samba," published by Autumn House Press, copyright 2010. Reprinted by permission of the author and the publisher.

Jeffers, Honorée Fanonne, "All Them Crawfords." "All Them Crawfords," was first published in *VerbQuarterly: an Audioquarterly* Vol. 2/No. 1, 2006. Reprinted with thanks to the magazine.

The Autumn House Fiction Series

||||||||||||||||||||||||||

New World Order
Derek Green

Drift and Swerve • 2008
Samuel Ligon

Monongahela Dusk
John Hoerr

Attention Please Now • 2009
Matthew Pitt

• winner of the annual
Autumn House Fiction Prize

Design and Production

||||||||||||||||||||||||||

Cover and text design by
Kathy Boykowycz

Cover photocollage: "Walking
on Water," detail

Text and titles set in Myriad
Pro fonts, designed in 1991
by Robert Slimbach and Carol
Twombly

Printed by McNaughton-Gunn
on Natural Offset

FSC

Mixed Sources
Product group from well-managed
forests and other controlled sources

Cert no. SW-COC-002283
www.fsc.org
© 1996 Forest Stewardship Council